THIS
TIME

MARY SHARON
PLOWMAN

Goodfellow Press

This is a work of fiction. The events described are imaginary; the characters are entirely fictitious and are not intended to represent actual living persons.

 **A Goodfellow Press,** Inc. Publication
7710 196th Avenue N.E., Redmond, WA 98043-4710

Library of Congress Catalog Card Number 93-080294

Edited by Pamela R. Goodfellow
Cover and book design by Cameron Mason
Cover illustration by Debbie Hanley
Cover photography by Jeff Pruett
A special thanks to Nancy Deahl

Printed on recycled paper in the U.S.A.

*To the women of Camp Indianola, who encouraged me
to follow my writing dream. To my mentor and critique group,
who believed there was raw talent hidden beneath the surface.
And, to my family, who gave me the precious gift of time.
I could not have done this without you.
Thanks for believing in me.*

Every love story
fulfills a dream . . .

Prologue

The mountain road was headed for nowhere, and with it her plans for the summer youth retreat. What was she doing on this wild goose chase, anyway?

Caitlyn James impatiently ran her fingers through her bangs. She had been searching for over an hour, soon it would be dusk. Time to admit to the group, and to herself, that she had tried but failed.

Maybe the lodge went under financially, or maybe it burned to the ground. Either way, it was no longer in the Greater Seattle directory and she couldn't afford the ones that were. If the teens started planning now, held a few fund raisers, then by next year they could try again.

The pavement turned to gravel. Cait glanced in her rear view mirror for the third time. Not only was there no trace of Raging River Lodge, but there was no sign of civilized life at all. She nibbled on her bottom lip. How would she tell them Sunday morning?

Darn. She'd host the camp-out in her back yard if necessary. Anything would be better than disappointing the kids.

Popping open the glove box, she blindly scoured the inside. Where was that dog-eared advertisement? Her hand fumbled under the seat. If only she could talk to the owners, surely they could be persuaded to host the weekend. But without the brochure, and its map on the reverse side, her group didn't stand a chance.

She couldn't stop for directions. There hadn't been a soul for the last five miles. If someone did appear, how would she explain being lost way the heck out here, still dressed in her suit and heels? It would be obvious she was too obstinate to turn around. They might decide to shoot her, figuring the world was better off with one less lunatic. She shook her head to clear her thoughts.

The wooded hillside sloped sharply downward on her left, towards a ravine. She swallowed hard, a small lump forming in her throat. How would she find her way back after dark? The switchbacks were challenging enough in the filtered daylight, at night they'd be treacherous.

With renewed haste she rummaged through the clutter on her passenger seat, striking gold. Bingo!

Relief washed through her. Slowing, she flipped on the dome light to study the map, hoping to spot a landmark. Her heart pounded an unsteady rhythm in her ears. Only yards away stood a bare-chested woodsman.

His powerful stance against the backdrop of native Douglas fir commanded her full attention. His axe, held high over head, was ready for the next swing. Reflections of the late afternoon sun bounced off the steel blade, almost blinding her. Taut muscles rippled across his broad back as he swung the axe downward. It slammed with a heavy thud into the fallen tree. Timber creaking and groaning, he wrenched the blade free, then hoisted it again for a second whack.

She stopped the car, staring in fascination at the slim hips and sweat-coated arms stilled in motion. His dark hair and chiseled features were more sinfully devilish than handsome, totally unlike the polite, controllable men that she dated on occasion. The scent of freshly chopped timber drifted through the open window.

It wasn't until he turned his head towards her that she realized her mistake. As he lowered his axe, her breath stuck in her throat. He had caught her red-handed, staring like a lovesick doe!

His eyes raked hers boldly and she colored fiercely under his scrutiny. Time to make tracks, and fast. She floored the accelerator. In the mirror Cait saw him point the axe in her direction. He was shouting something unintelligible. She only snuck a quick peek. What was he so riled about?

Caitlyn knew the answer moments later when her car skidded across the loose gravel. She swerved sideways, her hips straining roughly against the lap belt. Gasping for air, she inhaled the pungent smell of burning rubber.

Tree branches cracked sharply against the windshield, shattering the glass. She flung an arm across her face for protection from the flying debris. The steering wheel, now unrestrained, spun out of control. The underside of her car smashed mercilessly against stumps and boulders.

A deep rut in the landscape jerked her violently forward. Screams of panic mixed with the sounds of crunching metal.

As she smashed through the six-foot fence, slamming her head against the wheel, she was conscious of one last thought. Was he worth it?

One

*J*ake Brandon filled his lungs with fresh mountain air before taking his first swing. What a glorious afternoon! This was the life that he'd been born for, blue cloudless skies, gentle forest breezes and peaceful soul-healing quiet. Thank God he was no longer tied to his desk job in Los Angeles.

With his foot, he rolled the fallen log so that it sat squarely on the ground. His priorities would be back in order soon. In fact, he would bet that before this piece was reduced to kindling, everything would be sorted out. When Victoria called at nine tonight, he'd be ready. Relieving his frustrations on the timber was far better, and more productive, than taking them out on her. A word-war with his ex-wife wasn't worth the breath it took.

He slowly ran callused hands over the long shaft of the axe, renewing his feel for the solid wood handle before lifting it high overhead. Pulling the blade downward, it sliced through the air and bit into the alder by his feet.

It felt good. If his other problems could be excised this easily, he'd chop enough wood to warm the entire town of Snoqualmie. As he prepared to strike again, an unfamiliar, rumbling sound caught his attention. He paused. A car up here on his private road? What the hell was going on?

Turning, he studied the driver. She was peering at him intently. Hadn't she ever seen anyone sweat before? The intrusion into his afternoon grated on his nerves. Maybe if he warned her she was trespassing, she would roll on by.

Curiosity glittered in her eyes. Her lips were open, but there wasn't a sound except for the soft hum of her motionless car. He flashed her his best 'Keep Out' glare, then nodded as she gunned the engine. His satisfaction was short-lived however. She was accelerating too fast for the curve up ahead. Hadn't she seen it?

He shouted, but it was too late. Not bothering to drop his axe, Jake leaped over the fence separating them in a single, smooth motion. Her Toyota swerved, then sped directly into the empty space, high above the ravine.

Reaching the road, he saw her car sail down the incline. It bounced over stumps and rocks before barrelling headlong into his fence. He slid down the steep bank. Her limp form slumped against the head rest.

Opening the car door, he carefully examined the bump above her brow, then ran trained hands down her slender frame. The details of his ski patrol first aid training came rushing to mind. So far, so good. He could move her without causing further injury.

Confident that there were no broken bones, his hands

paused in their searching mission, but his eyes did not. Jake took in the tailored cut of her business suit. Moving lower, he viewed the long legs enhanced by her hiked-up skirt. He forced himself to look away.

Kneeling beside her, he cautiously stroked her expressionless face. She was pale and cool to his touch, except for the flush high on her cheekbones. Small beads of moisture, liquid fear, pooled against the curve of her full upper lip. Jake called to her again, urging her with a low, insistent voice to wake up.

Her lashes, motionless until now against her smooth skin, fluttered slowly but did not open. She moved her lips, as if trying to respond, but managed only a whisper.

"Paul . . ." Her head rolled towards him, nestling against his palm.

"Paula?" Good, she was coming to! At least he knew her name now. He encouraged her to keep fighting. "Wake up, Paula. I need your help."

She snuggled deeper against his fingertips, wetting her lips before whispering once again, "Bunyan."

"Bunion?" He stopped mid-caress. Glancing down at the wood chips still clinging to his arms and chest, a grin slowly swept over his face. He quickly brushed the loose debris away, then leaned across to free her seat belt. It would be dark soon. He'd have to set a quick pace up the quarter-mile hill.

As he released the catch, his inner arm pressed against the silk blouse encasing her breast. She moved towards him again. He frowned. Would she be as trusting when she was awake?

Lifting her slowly into his arms, he steadied her against his chest to prevent excess rocking. He nudged her free arm upward, and it wrapped instinctively about his neck. He held her to him, feeling an instant protectiveness for the stranger who just crashed into his life. His earlier frustrations were long forgotten, replaced by anxious concern. He turned and headed up the trail for home.

■ ■ ■

Jake raced down the steps at the first ring of the doorbell. His long strides thundered across the gleaming hardwood floors. Drying his damp palms on his well-worn jeans, he wrenched open the door. The ponytailed visitor was quickly pulled inside.

"Slow down." Doctor Kelly McKay wrenched free and rubbed her shoulder. "I'm going to need this arm later."

"Thanks for coming. I owe you one." He looked beyond his neighbor to the chestnut quarter horse, Paprika, grazing on his lawn. He frowned. "However, if that mare of yours uses my yard as a privy, then the scale returns to zero."

"I beg to differ, you owe me three. One for each pair of feet I left sitting under the dinner table. Now, where's our patient?"

"Upstairs. Follow me." He turned and retraced his steps. Kelly had to sprint to catch up. "She tossed and turned when I first tucked her in. Now she's quiet. I doubt anything's broken. Think she'll be okay?"

"I'd like to see her first. That's my normal procedure, anyway." She tried to gentle the sarcasm in her voice. He sounded tense and his shoulders were set rigidly beneath the soft flannel work shirt. In the year-and-a-half that she'd known Jake, she'd never seen him so distressed. After all, he usually had no one to worry about but himself.

At the top of the oak staircase he proceeded down the left side of the U-shaped hallway. When he stopped abruptly to knock on the far door, she almost collided with him.

"Sorry," Kelly said.

He turned and scowled. "No answer. She's probably still out cold."

"Let's take a look." Kelly reached around him and turned the handle. Squeezing past, she crossed to the bed and set down her medical bag. Dr. McKay was all business.

It was apparent, from the pillows and blankets, that the patient hadn't been still for long. She slept, uncovered, one arm flung across her forehead. The other was outstretched as if she had been searching for something, or someone. Her injured brow was furrowed, even in sleep, and her discomfort pulled roughly at Jake's heart.

He was off-duty now; the expert was here. Still, he hung back by the doorjamb in case there was anything he could do, trying to shrug the tension from his shoulders. When Kelly swept back the patient's bangs, he saw the darkening lump for the first time.

"Where did you say you found her?"

It took a moment for the question to sink in, as Jake watched her probe the patient's scalp, neck and shoulder areas. He had examined her, too, before lifting her, but he could have overlooked something. Had his grip been steady enough during the climb home?

Clearing his throat, he tried to dislodged the lump that was building. "She skidded off the road at the first switchback, about five miles from the river bridge."

Kelly opened her emergency medical bag and pulled out a thermometer. From his voice it was obvious that he felt responsible for the accident. Despite his rough exterior, she knew that Jake was a sensitive, giving man. It showed every time her kids came over to borrow his canoe. He would spend hours with them, letting them fish off the dock and making them peanut butter sandwiches for lunch.

She tried lightening her tone. "Sounds like the same ravine that reached out and grabbed my daughter's bike last month."

He nodded.

"There's a dental bill I'd like to forget." She smiled, rummaging for a stethoscope.

Jake, tense and unable to help, joined her at the bedside. "I'm sure the repair bill for her car will be memorable, too. I had it towed to Andy's garage."

"Did you find a purse or briefcase before you had it taken away? We need to contact someone as soon as possible. There's probably a husband at home, worried sick." Kelly signalled for a moment's quiet, then checked their patient's pulse and blood pressure.

He used the break to scan for rings. None. Well, there might not be a husband, but surely there was someone. A lover. No, what was the word used these days? A significant other? A cohabitating partner? Whatever, it all sounded temporary to him. Just the way he liked it.

Kelly's brisk, affirmative nod, as she repacked her instruments, was good news. He allowed his jaw to loosen a notch or two. "There's a purse, and a pile of other stuff to go with it, downstairs. From the weight of it, I could pen her entire biography."

"That's an interesting comment. You've not allowed a woman, other than me, past your screen door before. Suddenly you feel an urge to write this young lady's memoirs?"

His only reply was an intense glare. She ignored it and continued to test her patient's arm and rib bones. "Yes, I'd say she's gotten to you, and she's not even awake yet. Must have been that long hike up the hill together that brought on this unusual closeness." Standing, Kelly examined her patient's lower limbs.

Her verbal missiles were landing, exploding, and taking their toll. "I didn't have a whole lot of choice in the matter, now did I, McKay? There's not enough traffic for hitchhiking!"

"That's the intriguing part. There's never any traffic this far up on Rattlesnake Ridge. I wonder why she turned off on your private road?"

Jake fell silent. He'd been wondering exactly the same thing. Elk Tracks Road had been closed to the general public for over a year, ever since the previous owner had foreclosed. Maybe she just missed the dead end sign.

All rational thought abruptly ended when Kelly raised one knee to check reflexes. He looked away, out of respect, but there was really no need. The feel of her endlessly long legs, cradled against his forearm, was already burned into his memory.

How much longer until things were back to normal? He paced to the window, drew the curtain and jerked the frame upward. It was too warm in this room to breathe. He'd better check the thermostat.

His attention was drawn back to Kelly, who was ransacking her medical bag. This time she retrieved a neon orange flashlight, then sat on the mattress's edge to examine the patient's eyes, ears and throat. Jake saw the engraved message, *We Love You, Mom,* on the wand as it zipped by.

Kelly's kids. How she did it all as a single mother, and still kept her wits, he'd never know. In her oversized T-shirt, print leggings and sneakers, Kelly looked more like a camp director than the primary resident doctor of the Snoqualmie Family Clinic.

Doc McKay was Jake's closest neighbor. Hers was the

only other home that fronted on Eagle's Nest Lake. When he first surveyed the acreage three years ago for a custom mountain home, Kelly's troop sat on the fence and watched his crew for most of the day. Jake remembered hoping that his new buyer wasn't banking on solitude. But he had them pegged wrong. As the construction phase wore on, he rarely encountered the McKays.

Sometimes he heard their laughter as they rode off on horseback. And when heading out with their day packs to hike the ridge, they would ask permission before taking a short cut through the edge of the property. They were always careful not to crowd his space. That had been the deciding factor when he bought the property for his own, last year.

Kelly's voice brought him back to the present. "I don't like the faint circles under her eyes, nor the fact that she hasn't come around yet. But all and all, it's not too serious. Her dilation and reflexes are good. There don't appear to be any broken bones. Lend me a hand for a second while I remove her jacket."

Following the doctor's no-jostling instructions to the letter, Jake carefully cradled, then lifted the unconscious woman several inches off the mattress. As Kelly efficiently disposed of the outer garment, he caught the faint scent of ginger. It reminded him of the wild ginger growing on the edge of the lower meadow above the river. He instinctively pulled her closer and drew a deep breath. She smelled good enough to eat.

Startled by his thoughts, he quickly exhaled and lowered her back down. My God, he was sniffing her as he would a cantaloupe in the supermarket! Abruptly he stood and strode towards the door. He needed fresh air. "Call me if you need anything."

"I'll need a robe for your overnight guest. Leave it

outside the door. Then start working on that biography. We need to contact someone ASAP."

Jake stopped and turned. "Hold it. What do you mean, overnight guest?"

"Listen up. Despite your aversion to company, she can't be jostled down these twisting mountain roads tonight. I'll know more when I'm finished here, but I think she should be fine by midday tomorrow."

Noting his stubborn stance, Kelly continued. "You didn't have any other plans for this bed tonight, did you?"

He glowered at her, then closed the door with a thud. Fine by morning, he muttered to himself. Fine for whom?

■ ■ ■

Jake looked at the mound cluttering his family room. Briefcase, gym bag, portable computer and, yes . . . a purse. The luggage tag on the laptop machine advertised "Property of OmniCorp" in big, bold letters.

He'd heard that name before. Most likely it was one of the dozen equipment suppliers that regularly called his partner, Nick Slater, to schedule a demonstration.

Nick's most recent crusade, a computerized design tool, was driving Jake right over the edge. Keyboards, processors and modems were the only words that could be heard around the Brandon and Slater offices any more. For several months Nick had been flashing one marketing folder after another under Jake's nose, for consideration. His patience ebbed from thin to none.

The two partners finally came to a tolerable agreement. He delegated all decisions regarding the new system to Nick. In exchange for peace and quiet, Jake agreed to give whatever system was selected a fair shake.

But there was one caveat. They had to resume getting real work done, too.

It was time to start on the task before him. Placing his Moosehead beer on the coffee table, he sat back against the sofa and emptied the contents of her purse.

"Good God!" His eyes assessed the to-do lists, sticky pad notes and phone messages as they swirled off the table and landed by his feet. He blinked in disbelief, then retrieved her wallet from the clutter.

"Caitlyn James. 36, Sammamish Hills, Issaquah." He should have guessed. Bedroom community for yuppy parents. Most likely there were 2.3 little James' somewhere, waiting for mom to get home and fix dinner. He and Caitlyn couldn't be more different. There was never anyone waiting here when he got home.

He skipped over the more personal details on the identification card and reached for the phone. When her answering machine kicked in he left only an abbreviated message. No reason to alarm someone unnecessarily. He'd explain the situation fully when he had all the facts. "This is Jake Brandon. It's Friday evening around seven. Please call as soon as you receive this." He left his number, then hung up.

Returning her ID card to the appropriate slot, he moved on to the plastic stream of photos. There they were, two kids. Teenaged daughters, nearly identical, too. Looking further, Jake noted the faded photograph of Caitlyn and her husband with giggling twin toddlers. She looked happy, tumbling on the lawn in front of an apartment complex. Her glowing radiance was the sort that was reserved only for newlyweds. Most newlyweds, he corrected. He couldn't remember Victoria smiling, unless she was circling an upper-crust cocktail party. Rubbing elbows with the right people was a key element in Tory's plan to rise quickly to the top of the real estate world.

Caitlyn's left hand was currently ringless. That might not be significant, but, then again, there were many divorce court casualties these days. Snapping the wallet shut, he returned it to her purse. It was none of his business. She wouldn't be around long enough for it to matter.

He opened her appointment book to search for another contact. Under today's date there was a note that someone named Brooke was scheduled to drive a 5:00 P.M. softball car pool. A quick scan of her address book produced only one match. He picked up the phone again and dialed. A young male voice answered on the first ring.

"Brooke Hastings, please." Jake held the receiver away as the young man bellowed for Mom. Fortunately, the boy only had to yell once.

A courteous but impatient voice answered the call. "This is Brooke."

"My name is Jake Brandon."

A deep sigh. "Whatever it is you're selling, I already have two, so make it fast. I'm barbecuing burgers."

"I'm calling in regards to Ms. Caitlyn James. Do you know her?"

"Yes, we work together. Who wants to know?"

"I do. Are her daughters with you?"

"Sorry, buddy. That information, and everything else, is confidential unless you plan to identify yourself. Are you with the FBI?"

Jake was taken aback. He tried turning the tables. "Is the FBI looking for her?"

"That's it. *Adios.* It's been fun."

"Wait." Jake rubbed his forehead, and rethought his

approach. Maybe he would get farther if he gave a little more and demanded a little less. "Ms. Hastings, your friend was in a car accident this afternoon. She's at my house at the moment, resting upstairs."

"Is she all right? Why isn't she at the hospital?"

"An ambulance would have trouble finding my place, even in daylight. The local doctor thought it was unnecessary. She's with her now. Ms. James needs to stay put until morning."

"Darn that stubborn woman! Probably out looking for that unlisted lodge again."

"What lodge?"

"The one she can't stop talking about. Let's see. The Rushing . . . no, Racing River Lodge. Something like that. No, Raging River. That's it."

Frost formed on the edges of Jake's words. "I know this area very well, Ms. Hastings. There is no such lodge operating in this part of the Cascades."

"What a shame. She had such high hopes."

He quickly changed subjects. "About her daughters; do you know where they might be?"

"Rose and Lynn are here, having dinner with my son Kyle and the rest of the softball team. I'll keep them overnight, no problem."

"Good. Is there anyone else that I should contact?"

"No significant others, if that's what you mean. Just a few insignificant ones, that I've arranged."

Jake felt a tinge of sympathy for the stranger upstairs. Maybe they did have something in common, after all.

Brooke continued. "I heard that groan. I usually don't interfere, but sometimes it's necessary."

"For her own good, I imagine?"

"Seven years is a long enough mourning period, don't

you think? Ever since Todd died . . ."

"Jake, our patient's waking up." Kelly stood above him on the open catwalk. Her voice drowned out Brooke's monologue. "Come up as soon as you can."

"I'll be right there." He stood.

"Right where?" The voice on the phone reminded him he was still holding the receiver.

"That was the doctor. Your friend is awake. I've got to run, so here's the plan. I'll drop Caitlyn off at her home around noon tomorrow. Her car will be in the shop for a while. If you can drive her girls home mid-afternoon, I'm sure she'd appreciate it."

"Fine. Anything I can do at present?"

"No, but if she feels up to working on Monday, she'll need a ride. Do you know anyone that could help out?"

"I do. In fact, I met Cait at OmniCorp."

"Great. I'll call again if there's any change. I've got to go, Kelly's calling."

"Kelly?"

"Kelly's the doctor. She's also my neighbor, that's why I brought Caitlyn directly here."

"Wait, one last thing. I didn't get your number."

He swiftly debated privacy versus common sense. After all, these were her kids. It wouldn't help shorten Caitlyn's stay if she were up all night worrying. His privacy lost. That was twice.

"I'll give you my phone number. Keep it confidential." Jake recited the digits as if he were revealing the combination to the Federal Treasury vault.

"Thank you. I'll try to stifle my urge to etch it on the Ladies' Room wall at the health club. And thank your wife for me, too. Not everyone would open her home to a perfect stranger."

"Forget it. And by the way, I'm not married." Jake set down the cordless phone next to his warm beer and turned to climb the steps.

Two hours, three women and one headache. So much for solitude.

Two

The buzz of voices from the hallway penetrated the hazy layer of darkness holding her captive. Blinking, Cait shielded her eyes from the overhead light, then instantly regretted her action. My God, how she ached! The last time she felt this bad was in high school, when she and Mary Claire polished off the altar wine instead of locking it in the fridge.

Brushing her bangs from her forehead, she felt a flash of pain. Memories came crashing to the surface. She struggled to sit up.

"My car. My . . . oh . . ."

"Whoa. Hold on a minute." The owner of the brisk but pleasant voice, crossed to the bedside and touched Cait's shoulder. "No sudden movements, okay? We'll do this slowly, together. By the way, I'm Kelly. Dr. Kelly McKay."

Cait slowly opened one eye, then the other. The doctor helped her to sit upright, propped against the pillows and headboard. After smoothing the lavender comforter, she sat down next to Cait. "How do you feel?"

Her voice was raspy and thick-tongued. "I feel lucky."

"You're a lot luckier than Jake's new fence is. The truth? It looks as if you're going to live." Kelly picked up the glass of water on the nightstand and placed it in Cait's hand. "Here, take a few small sips."

Jake. Jacob. Back home in Tulsa it was a friendly, biblical name. Too bad it was attached to such a fierce, serious man. Cait curled her fingers around the cool beverage. "Thank you. Things are still a little hazy, doctor."

"They may be for a while yet. Are you feeling pain anywhere?"

"No, not really. My forehead is tender, but that's about it. Can someone die from embarrassment?"

"Not on my nickle, they can't." Kelly reached for a flashlight then placed a hand under Cait's chin. "Open your eyes and look straight ahead. Good, just follow my light. Does it hurt when you move?"

"No. I just feel a bit drowsy. And stiff."

"You should be fine by morning. Your own doctor may want to check you over when you get back to town. I'll send a copy of my notes home with you tomorrow, including my phone number." Kelly snapped off the light, then gently prodded Cait's neck and shoulder area.

"Thank you for taking me in after all the trouble I've caused. I'm not usually so reckless."

A deep, masculine voice joined in from the hallway. "That's encouraging to know."

That voice! She'd recognize it anywhere. It was the same

one that had called to her earlier, encouraging her to wake up. Looking past the doctor's shoulder, she met the piercing eyes of the man in the doorway. He was huge, reminding her of the Douglas fir trees surrounding him at her first glimpse. His body, molded by hours working in the great outdoors, was every bit as memorable the second time around. Cait tried to speak, but the tightness in her throat choked off all sound.

"Get in here and stop baiting my patient. Caitlyn, say hello to Jake."

The last time her eyes locked with his she'd fled from temptation. Look where that decision landed her. She was in his house. In his bed? No, that wasn't possible. Surely this man wouldn't be caught dead sleeping in lilac and periwinkle print sheets. His wife, Dr. Kelly, must have selected this decor.

Jake entered the room, crossing to the foot of the bed. Relief that she was not only awake, but coherent, spread through him. The muscles in his upper shoulders began to unwind, but the thought that he might be partly to blame kept a sharp edge on his voice. "Good evening, Caitlyn."

Wariness crowded her eyes. He forced a smile, hoping to break the ice, and extended his hand. "I'm glad you decided to wake up and join us."

She accepted his handshake and returned his smile, but avoided meeting his eyes directly. They spoke volumes that she didn't want to hear. Not in front of his wife. "Thank you for taking me in. I'm very sorry about your fence. I'll reimburse you for everything."

He released her hand. She had long, smooth fingers with practical, unadorned nails. Not a glamour girl, perhaps, but certainly not the type who would enjoy the simple lifestyle shared by neighbors on Rattlesnake Ridge. No doubt she'd hate the isolation, too. Not that it mattered.

"Forget it. I can fix the fence. Save your money for the mechanic. Your car's in a lot worse shape than you are."

"I'm sure it is." The memory of hurtling down the slope was one she'd never forget. Nor would she forget the reason, or the wide callused hand that just touched hers. She cleared her throat and looked at Kelly.

"Now that it looks as if I'm going to live, I'd better get moving. May I use your phone to call for a loaner? Even a cab would do. I need to get home to my daughters . . ."

Jake interrupted, "They're fine. First let me apologize. I went through your purse, looking for someone to call. Brooke offered to keep your twins overnight."

"No. I couldn't ask that of her."

"I did, and she insisted. My guess is that Brooke's used to getting her own way."

One side of his mouth lifted. Even this half-smile was enough to soften his chiseled features. Cait sank back against the pillows. "You're right. She is."

Kelly closed her case and stood. She patted Jake's shoulder as if he'd just won the third grade spelling bee. "It's settled, then. Good job."

"Just following orders." He smiled knowingly at Kelly. Cait felt the warmth of a long-time friendship pass between them. Had she and Todd ever shared looks like that?

Kelly turned, commanding her attention. "Just forget about everything awaiting you down the mountain, and concentrate on getting well."

"But . . ."

"Jake didn't carry you all the way up here, just to have you turn around and leave. He's used to getting his own way, too, so save your breath."

She never doubted that, even for a moment.

Kelly continued. "You'll be staying put tonight. After a quick check in the morning, you can be on your way. Doctor's orders." Business concluded, she walked towards the door. "I have to run and check on the kids. If you jot down your doctor's phone number for me, I'll give him a call."

So Kelly and Jake had children, too. For some reason, knowing that made her relax further. She smiled warmly. "Again, thank you for everything."

"Remember, take it easy. Jake will be back shortly with a light dinner. If you need anything else, just yell down the stairs." Kelly used her elbow to nudge Jake towards the hallway. "You, come with me."

He raised his eyebrow at Kelly, then followed her out. Before closing the door, he looked back once again at his house guest. "Make yourself comfortable. There's a private bath behind that door."

This time she was able to meet his eyes. They were the majestic blue of distant mountains on a clear day. "Thank you, Mr. McKay."

Her softly spoken words stopped him. If he corrected her she might leap into her shoes and call a cab the minute he closed the door. It would be best if she got some rest first.

He gave her a reassuring smile. "No thanks necessary. And you heard the doctor; I'll be right back with supper."

■ ■ ■

When Jake met Kelly by the front door, she had just finished her list and was preparing to leave. "Here are tonight's instructions. It's very important that you wake her every three hours, check her pupils and take her temperature."

Jake glanced at the paper. She attached it to a clipboard, then handed it to him along with a manila file folder. He examined it as she continued. "I'd put her in the hospital if I could, but the ride back down this mountain isn't worth the risk. I'll come by first thing in the morning and check her, before you leave. Call me when you're both awake and dressed."

Jake looked up and scowled at the implied intimacy. "She's supposed to be getting some rest here tonight, doctor." He shook the clipboard at her. "How is she going to do that if I'm holding her hand and singing lullabies?"

"Was that on my list, too?" Kelly steadied his hand and gave the paper a second look. "Oops, it's not, but please feel free to do so, if she's having trouble sleeping."

He held his tongue. No use encouraging her.

Kelly opened the door and stepped out on the porch. "Remember, call me right away if you're unable to rouse her, or if her temperature rises above 101°."

His narrowed glare confirmed that he was paying attention.

"Oh, one more thing. Close that window upstairs. The night air can be downright frigid. If she catches a cold, you may have to keep her for a week."

He saw the edge of her mouth curl slightly before she held back her smile. They both knew that Cait would arrange for an airlift off the ridge, before agreeing to stay longer. "Does that mean no moonlight strolls together by the lake, either?"

"I wouldn't suggest it. She might get the urge to push you in."

"Very funny."

"Well, at least no long walks in the woods, dressed in your robe."

"I dropped by some pajamas instead." His bathrobe would overwhelm her small frame.

"Pajamas?" Kelly clutched dramatically at her heart. "You've just ruined my image of you!"

His eyes narrowed at her, but he continued. "I looked in her gym bag for a warm-up suit, first. All I could find was a lycra body suit and sports bra."

Kelly smiled. "Then convince her to stay in bed. From what I hear, you should have no trouble with that, Mr. McKay."

Before he had a chance to retaliate, Kelly mounted Paprika and rode away.

■ ■ ■

Jake gave the canned chicken noodle soup one last stir, then turned off the burner. He hoped that, with a few crackers, it would be enough. It was a bit late to grill steaks, and sandwiches sounded too cold. Well, tomorrow Caitlyn would be back in her own kitchen and his life would return to normal.

Once again, there'd be no one for him to worry about, except for himself. No one depending on him to fix dinner, to second-guess their likes and dislikes. Back to the way he liked it.

Well, back to the way he was used to, he amended. How many years had passed since someone really depended on him for anything? Sure, Nick and his staff relied on him, and his skiing buddies counted on him to round out their annual foursome to Crystal Mountain. But that was different, he acknowledged, as he searched the fridge for milk or juice. This situation, sharing his home, dinner, clothes, was personal. Very personal.

"I must have something healthy to drink, somewhere in this house." He moved aside the iced tea pitcher and assorted cans of cola and beer. "Maybe in the freezer."

As he strode down the hallway towards the garage he thought of his daughter, Jackie, now the wise old age of fifteen. She stopped being dependent on him somewhere between training wheels and training bras. His younger brothers, Patrick and Drew, outgrew their need for his protection years ago. He still saw Drew as often as he could manage a trip to Portland. But Patrick, well, it had been much too long.

Jake wrenched open the freezer door and shoved a few icy packages around. Frosty interior, just like his mother. She hadn't needed him, or anyone, for as long as he could remember. And that included the father Jake buried nearly twenty years ago. Her career had always taken precedence over the rest of the family's desire to put down roots. Ironic, now that he thought about it, that the first thing he'd done after his divorce was to pack his things.

Those days were over. He was here, firmly settled in, with every intention of staying until he was old and gray. Maybe Jackie would enjoy inheriting the place someday.

He reentered the house, frozen orange juice in hand, and heard the water running overhead. The last time the pipes vibrated like that was during Jackie's visit the previous summer. He never had overnight guests, in his own bedroom or otherwise, so that bathroom was virtually unused. He rarely had daytime guests either, except for Kelly or Nick. It wasn't that he didn't have the space, in fact the specifications for this structure included sleeping a small army. He just preferred it that way.

Staring at the ceiling, he tried to determine the exact source of noise behind the sheet-rock. Good thing he didn't use that subcontractor any more. He would have to insulate those pipes better before Jackie's annual visit, or it would drive him crazy.

Jake didn't hear the phone ring above the crunching and swirling of the frozen juice in the blender, until it was too late to catch it. He checked his watch. Victoria. She could wait. Tossing a banana on the tray, he surveyed the results. He could fix enough for two and share dinner with her, but the less contact between them, the better.

She'd be wary after he broke the news that Kelly didn't live here. Maybe he wouldn't tell her until later. Maybe not at all. No use making a big deal out of nothing. If she slept until morning, then what difference would it make anyway?

Damn, he almost forgot the instructions Kelly gave him. He turned and picked up the clipboard. It was going to be a long night.

■　■　■

"How could you possibly be worried about us? We have a full-fledged slumber party going on here!"

"I really appreciate your help, Brooke, especially on such short notice." Cait repositioned the pillow against the armrest of the couch and leaned against it. The room's sitting area was well-furnished, complete with telephone, portable TV and stereo. Too bad her anxiety was stopping her from enjoying the luxury. "How can I return the favor?"

"Don't worry, I'll think of something. How about you? That really gave me a scare when he called."

"I took a long, hot soak in the tub, and I'm feeling human again. My forehead's pretty tender, but the rest of my parts seem to be working fine." Cait adjusted the neckline of the borrowed pajama top and pulled the afghan over her legs. "All in all, I'm lucky and I know it."

"Is that an editorial comment about the accident, or about whose home you landed in?"

"What?" Cait straightened.

"What I mean, dear friend, is that you already told me you were daydreaming when you ran off the road, and that a lumberjack carried you home. I added in the sexy voice that I had the pleasure of experiencing first-hand, then just put the pieces together. He's quite a distraction, right?"

"Hardly. He's married. With kids."

"Kids? As in more than one?"

"Yes. I haven't seen them, but Kelly made it sound like there were several." Cait rested against the pillow again. "So forget the matchmaking this time. Your imagination is in overdrive."

"Who says?"

"I do. You're always trying to pair me with someone."

"No, I mean who says he's married? That the kids are his?"

"For goodness sakes, Brooke, I met his wife!"

"But . . ."

"Don't go dreaming up some marital riff that puts me in a prime position for husband-stealing, either." Her grip on the receiver tightened. "You should see the way she looks Jake right in the eye and makes him hop. If that's not until-death-do-us-part married, I don't know what is."

"He didn't sound to me like the type that took to hopping very well."

"Well, his glare could shrivel wallpaper, but he takes it just fine from Kelly."

"Are you through?"

Cait readjusted the afghan. "Yes."

"Then listen to me." Cait heard Brooke's voice shift to

her you're-about-to-be-grounded voice. "The man's definitely not married. His last name's Brandon. The doc's his neighbor. The kids must be hers, alone."

"What?"

"He told me himself. Why would he lie about that?"

"Well, I just thought . . ."

"Think again. You've got all night."

Cait glanced at her watch. Nine o'clock. She pulled back the curtain and looked out into the woods. A small light was shining at the far end of the deck below, then all was dark. The house was quite isolated, just like the gravel road earlier.

"Did he happen to mention if he lives here alone?"

"You watch too many movies. In real life, serial killers usually don't call to give out their name and address until afterwards." Brooke's laugh didn't relieve the uneasiness building in Cait.

"Be serious. Exactly what did he say?"

"We didn't have much time to discuss his personal life, not that he wanted to. You were too busy dying in his upstairs bedroom."

The bedroom. She looked around again. The flowered wallpaper and stenciled writing desk couldn't possibly belong to a man who wielded an axe. There must be another female involved, somewhere. "What else did he say about the doctor? They could be lovers, you know."

"That's a possibility, but she definitely lives next door. Jake puts a high value on his privacy. I had to sign over my next-born child in order to get this number."

"Why the good Samaritan act then?"

"Good question." Brooke's pondering tone matched Cait's own mood exactly. "That'll give you something to dream about."

A soft rap on the door interrupted their call. She sat

motionless on the edge of the bed, no time to think and no breath to speak. A second knock was accompanied by a deep voice announcing dinner. Jake was back.

■ ■ ■

The sound of a high-pitched voice engaged in a one-sided conversation could be heard emanating from the receiver. Cait sat motionless on the bed, holding the phone away from her ear, staring silently at him as he entered. From the look on her face, he might as well have been wielding the axe again, instead of a dinner tray.

He forgot that the answering machine was now in his guest room, farther away from his private work space. She must have picked it up when she heard Brooke's voice. His delay in telling her was backfiring. Taking a deep breath, he set down the tray and reached for the phone. She surrendered it without argument.

"Brooke? Jake here. Everything fine on your end?"

While listening, he watched Caitlyn draw back against the sofa cushions and tuck her feet beneath the afghan. It covered every square inch, except for her face.

"Kind of you to break the ice for me, Brooke. If you'll please excuse us, we're going to have dinner. Could Caitlyn call you later? Great. Goodnight."

He compressed the antenna and switched off the phone. Crossing to where he left the tray, he handed it to Cait. "Brooke said she'll be awake until eleven, but not to worry about calling back."

Smiling faintly, she reached for the tray. She was careful not to meet his eyes or to let her hands touch his. She tried not to blush, but the memory of her ogling him, then gunning her engine to escape, was still too fresh.

He stood motionless in front of her, hands in the back pockets of his jeans. He was very close. She stared down at her dinner, too shaken to eat.

"Hope you like soup and crackers. It's all I had that was fast."

"I do." Her voice broke as the words left her lips. She cleared her throat and tried again. Maybe, if she sounded agreeable, he would leave. "This will be fine, thank you."

She picked up one cracker and nibbled, trying not to look at him, or at the tempting eye-level view he presented. Darn. He didn't seem to be going anywhere.

He watched her bowed head and unsteady hand. He wanted to touch her, reassure her, to lift her chin until their eyes met. Instead, he took a step back. Pulling out the desk chair, he positioned it next to her, only inches from the couch. He straddled the seat and faced her. Now, they were eye-to-eye. Where should he begin? He cleared his throat.

"I'm sorry for any part that I had in your accident." That made her look up, and blink twice. She didn't look comforted yet, so he continued. "I shouldn't have yelled. It's one of several nasty habits I have." He cocked his head slightly to one side and lifted his eyebrow, asking for forgiveness.

He thought the entire episode was his fault? He couldn't. Maybe he was just trying to salvage her pride. Either way, his warmth and honesty was contagious. She returned it, meeting his gaze directly. "I understand your name's not McKay."

A grin softened his features. "No, it's not. Kelly's my neighbor. The name is Brandon. Jake Brandon."

"Please excuse my earlier error, Mr. Brandon."

"Call me Jake. After all, you're wearing my pajamas. It's too late to be formal." He extended his hand.

She accepted. His fingers were rough, but warm. So was the intensity of his smile. It spread slowly across his face, illuminating his eyes. The instant blue heat warmed her and invited her to laugh with him. She returned his smile easily.

"Again, my mistake. Not yours. When you awoke, Kelly was already here and firmly in charge. It's her nature, so I let her." He shrugged. "I didn't realize that it would peg me as a docile, hen-pecked husband."

"You?" She covered her mouth so she wouldn't spit cracker crumbs at her host. "I would never think that."

"Well then, believe this." He raised one hand, as if taking an oath. "There was no intention to mislead you. I wanted you to recoup without worry."

It wasn't worry that was causing adrenaline to race through her veins at this very moment. He was charming, attentive and heart-stoppingly handsome. A long-forgotten tingling quickly spread through her lower limbs. She reached for her spoon.

Dipping it into the bowl, she blew gently, then took a sip. The soothing chicken broth, albeit straight from the can, hit the spot.

She should leave, before becoming any more comfortable. Before taking further advantage of his generosity. She put down her spoon. "Since all I have is a headache and a few sore muscles, I'm sure it would be safe for me to go home."

"You're safe here." His voice was firm. "Except for the list Kelly left me for the graveyard shift tonight, you won't even know that I'm here."

The smile was gone from his face, but the sincerity wasn't. It enveloped each word. Her gaze was drawn to his like a magnet. As she watched, his eyes clouded over, his brow furrowed. "You'd rather risk your health than accept my word?"

Why did it matter? Most likely their paths would never cross again. She'd heard his earlier exchange with Kelly. He wanted her out. Now that she was offering to leave, he was balking, insisting. Her opinion of him must matter. She needed to let him know.

Cait picked up the banana, peeled back the ends and broke off a quarter. "I have no reason to be concerned about staying here alone with you. After all, Brooke has your name and number." She suppressed a grin as she took a small bite and chewed.

He relaxed, crossing his forearms on the back of the chair. He leaned forward and rested his chin against one wrist. "Do you know she actually threatened me?"

"The way she tells it, you threatened her."

"Maybe I did. Just a little."

Cait laughed. "I'm sure she deserved it. She loves to mother me."

Since they were trading secrets, she couldn't stop herself from asking what was foremost on her mind. She softened her voice, so that it wouldn't sound like the interrogation it really was. "Tell me more about Dr. Kelly. I hope my accident didn't ruin any plans that the two of you had tonight."

"We're good friends, that's all. You'd be at her place, except her bedrooms are full. Three kids. Space is not a problem here."

Cait felt a tinge of jealousy. Not because Kelly was Jake's friend, but because that kind of camaraderie was rare between a man and a woman. She wanted the same for herself. A true, deep friendship, the kind that she'd been hoping to have in her marriage. Instead, the closest she'd come had been with one of her husband's friends. Maybe someday, it would happen again.

She stopped that train of thought and sunk back against the pillow, carefully balancing the tray. Picking up another cracker, she offered one to Jake. He accepted.

"From my limited dealings with Brooke so far, she reminds me a lot of Kelly."

"Brooke and Kelly?" She laughed abruptly, causing cracker crumbs to slip down her throat the wrong way. She covered her mouth, suppressing a cough. Her voice was raspy. "The two couldn't be more different."

She coughed again, then reached for her juice. From the corner of her eye, she saw Jake move quickly, to stand behind her. He thumped her once, then twice, on the back. She held tightly onto the glass, and signaled with her free hand. She was fine. Luckily, so was her tray.

His hand, broad and warm, rested lightly between her shoulder blades. Too bad the fabric wasn't a little thicker. From his standing position, next to her pillow, his exceedingly male jeans were once again in close proximity to her line of vision. Cait averted her eyes.

"I'm okay. Really."

His hand stayed firmly in position, on her upper back.

"See? No more coughs." She took a quick sip of soup. "Mmm."

Jake stepped away. Half-standing, half-kneeling, he was still poised to spring. She was surprised, yet pleased too, at his overprotective response.

Not knowing what else to do, Cait continued to babble. She was lucky that she could breathe. "Let's see, Brooke and Kelly. Brooke is a full head shorter and has one of those wispy, over-the-ears, pixie cuts."

"The no-fuss type?"

"Definitely. And I know for a fact that she'd suck lettuce leaves for a week if she could wear lycra pants like Kelly's in public."

"Now I'm really looking forward to meeting her." His eyes gleamed with mischief. "I'm going to repeat your words, verbatim."

"You wouldn't! She'd be mortified and I'd be in deep trouble." Cait crushed the remaining crackers into her soup, emphasizing her point. She brushed her hands together, then reached for her napkin. "Later, when she recovered enough to show her face in public, she'd come after me. Maybe, after you."

"After me? Sounds interesting."

She leaned forward, confiding a deep dark secret. "She has ways of getting even that exceed the imagination."

"Is that right?" He leaned closer, too. "Try me. Mine is fairly vivid."

So was Cait's, and at that moment it was in overdrive. Their heads were very close together. Close enough to smell his fresh wood scent again. She must remember more than she originally thought, from their trip up the mountain. What were they talking about? Oh, yes. Revenge.

"Last winter I was innocently publicizing an upcoming overnight for my daughters' youth group, using photos from the previous year. One picture was of Brooke, a last-minute chaperone, sound asleep and snoring in her sleeping bag. It hung in the church hallway for several weeks before my daughter, Lynn, told her. Brooke was furious."

Cait tilted her head back to laugh, then quickly stopped. The ache brought on by the sudden movement caused her to cup the nape of her neck.

Jake moved quickly. "Careful. Let me help."

He stood behind the love seat, brushed her hand aside

and began a steady massage. "Continue. I hate cliff-hangers."

Continue? She could hardly breathe, with his hands softly stroking her neck. She forced herself to relax. "After a few weeks, I was convinced the incident had passed. Was I wrong. Brooke was just biding her time for the right moment, building suspense, until our office Christmas party."

"And then?" His solid touch was dissolving years of tension. She leaned forward, giving him better access.

"She coaxed the waitress to deliver a drink to our resident office Romeo, with a message saying I wanted to dance, preferably out on the moonlit terrace. I've had trouble with this individual before, persistently asking me out despite my refusals. Even if I'd consider mixing business with personal life, Geoff Martin wouldn't be on the list."

"Why not?"

"He's too full of himself, plus he makes me nervous. I've never seen him accept 'no' for an answer in the office setting, so I have no reason to believe he would after hours, either. Brooke couldn't have picked a better target. It took me the entire evening to shake him, while still leaving his ego intact."

"His ego?"

"Of course. I have to work with Geoff every day. He's the marketing representative for most of my major accounts. Since he can be rather revengeful himself, it's in my best interest to stay on his good side."

"And your date? What did he think?"

Cait went still for a moment before answering. "No date."

"Why not?"

Why all these questions from a supposedly private person? His strokes across her shoulders and down her spine were longer now. More powerful and extremely sensual. It was difficult to concentrate.

The question wasn't too personal, but it was very curious that he would ask. As a rule, Cait's life was an open book. In fact, when was the last time that a man cared enough to look beneath the surface?

"Why not?" He repeated his question, softer this time. His voice was rich, tempting and forbidden.

Why not, what? What the heck were they talking about anyway? His hands were just finishing their magic on her shoulders. He motioned with a slight pressure of his hand, signalling her to tilt her head. She bent towards the right, sweeping her hair away from her neckline.

Why not just stay like this forever, with his soothing fingers easing away all coherent thought? Why not . . . she pulled her thoughts back together. Oh, the Christmas party.

"For starters, I never mix business and pleasure. I also think that attending someone else's office party would be incredibly boring, unless you were involved in a serious, long-term relationship. Last, but not least, no one in my life falls into that latter category." Why did she offer that final tidbit?

She was instantly aware of the change in his touch, from massage to caress. Then his fingers went absolutely still, causing her heart to beat a wild pulse in her ears, in her throat, and lower.

Turning, she met his eyes. They were open and inquisitive. Searching for answers. Like hers.

She dropped her gaze to his lower lip. Full and sensual, and moving closer. His breath brushed lightly against her as he kissed her forehead, heating her skin. Once, twice, then he pulled away. Only an inch separated them. He was letting her decide.

Deep inside she always believed that there was someone out there, just for her. Someone who would touch each of her senses, one by one, causing them to explode. Was this the man? Should she take the risk, and find out? Her heart answered and she stretched the final distance.

As Cait turned, her bowl slid downward, jangling utensils along the way. Jake quickly leaned forward, over her shoulders, grabbing both the soup and the juice. The rest hit the floor with a thud.

In a way he was embracing her, but his palms were full of dishes. Not exactly the quick glimpse of heaven she'd seen. As he lifted his arms, she stared at the mess. She tried to help, one hand holding the afghan in place.

"I'll do that. Don't strain any further." He was now kneeling couch-side, reassembling the remains of dinner. The damage wasn't too bad, except to her dignity. She sat there helpless, watching him, the feel of his lips still heating her forehead.

"I'm sorry."

"Don't be. My instinct was good but the timing was bad."

Looking up, his smile slowly faded. His half-dressed overnight guest was only inches away. Her hands gripped the edge of the blanket. From worry? He specifically came up here to reassure her, then gave her something new to lose sleep over.

His wall of restraint slid back into place. He withdrew with the tray. "Get some rest."

"Jake?"

"I'll be in to check your temperature around midnight and again at four. Don't be alarmed when I wake you." He walked quickly towards the exit.

"But . . ."

"What I'm trying to say, however awkwardly, is that you're safe here." His nod was curt as he curled one hand around the knob, pulling the door wide open. "Goodnight." He left without a backwards glance.

Three

Jake looked back at the closed door and tried to clear his thoughts. What had come over him? Gripping the tray tightly, he pounded down the stairs. Each step put more distance between his failing self-control and the woman beneath the afghan. As he made his way to the kitchen, his boots rapped sharply against the bare wood.

"Kelly can take her list and . . ."

The jangling of the phone interrupted him. Setting the tray on the counter, he grabbed the cordless receiver from the wall unit. "Jake here."

"Am I catching you at a bad time?"

"It's always a bad time when you call, Victoria." He expelled a harsh breath. "Go ahead. We need to finish. Something about Jackie?"

"Well, at least you were listening for a change."

"Jackie's one of the few subjects where your opinions are worth my while."

The line went silent. He rubbed his eyes, then ran his fingers through his hair. Tonight's frustrations weren't his ex-wife's fault. Many of his other headaches were, but not this particular one. And listening was never one of his strengths, they both knew that. "Sorry. Rough evening."

"Earlier you were having a bad day."

"Believe me, things got worse." Jake walked to the fridge and reached for a beer, then changed his mind. Better to keep a clear head. He traded it for a cola, then shoved the door closed. Rounding the counter, he headed towards the table in the alcove where he'd been working.

He slammed the can down and pulled out a chair. "Let's start over. You've got my full attention." Settling back to listen, he popped the tab.

"Fine with me. I was just calling to let you know . . ."

"Dammit!" Soda flew everywhere. Whatever liquid didn't shoot straight upward, fizzed down the side of the can. His notes on the new Cougar Mountain construction site were drenched. He grabbed the nearest towel.

She waited until his cursing died down. "You told me you gave up drinking."

"Cola, Victoria. Get off my case." He sopped up what he could, trying not to smear his drawing. "I haven't had a really good reason to drink since I left Los Angeles."

Silence again. Good. He liked her best that way. He continued to blot his work papers.

"Maybe I should call back later. We never could make headway on any subject when your temper was short. If you're still a night owl, I could ring again at ten."

Her tone was more sympathetic than sarcastic. If he'd

stop being such a mule he could find out what was on her mind. It was probably important, since it involved Jackie. His peace of mind was already shot to smithereens, with no relief in sight. The midnight and four A.M. checkups still loomed before him.

"Later might be worse." He wiped the table one last time, then tossed the towel into the sink.

"Going out at this hour? You used to be such a home-body."

Sure he'd been a home-body, when his only option was accompanying her to business dinners. Shaking hands with big name property owners. Leaving their daughter with an MTV-watching, phone-gabbing baby sitter with a dozen earrings stacked up one earlobe.

"Not that it's any of your business, but no. Tonight, my troubles are right here with me." Moving the damaged paper aside to dry, he pulled out his chair to sit.

"No longer living alone? Well, congratulations. It's about time."

"Cut the crap. You don't want an update on my love life. What's this call really about?"

There was a long pause. "William and I have decided to get married."

"You want me to know where you're registered?"

"No."

"Want me to give away the bride?"

"Listen you pigheaded bully, it's about your daughter!"

Jake leaned back in his chair and shifted the receiver to his other hand. "Not taking the news well?"

"Exactly, but the problem's not my marrying William. The two of them get along together fine."

"What, then?"

"Our plan to relocate. Just the thought of living on

the East Coast has her upset."

"Moving is tough at any age, to any place. I should know." He reached for the half-empty can and took a long drink.

When she broke the silence, her voice was low and reflective. "You didn't have to leave, after the divorce. It's a huge city, after all. And we moved in different circles. We could have worked out some kind of holiday arrangement."

"Running into you had nothing to do with it." He shook his head. When he was young he always dreamed of having a friend, maybe two. Tough to do, as a kid on the move. In contrast, Victoria moved in 'circles.' Swarms of people, who usually wanted something. What had been his role in her life, besides window dressing at business functions?

"I left because what I was searching for in L.A. no longer existed. It just took me longer than most to figure that out."

"But you're all alone."

"I like it that way. I'm content here. It's my home. All mine, now and forever." He took a sip of his cola, swallowed and sighed. "Someday it might be Jackie's."

"But it's so secluded. Jackie filled me in after her last visit. I'm already worried about this summer."

"Don't be. She's my daughter, too." Jake set down the can, stood and thrust his hand into his back pocket. "Do you think I'd let something happen to her?"

"What if it did?"

"I have neighbors less than a mile away. A doctor, in fact."

She gave a small laugh. "The 'raven-haired beauty?' Jackie's words. Did this doctor have something to do with your decision to live out in the wilds?"

"Jackie must have ransacked your romance novel

collection again." He propped his foot against the chair seat then leaned forward, arm on knee. "I'll talk to her. Maybe I can help."

"I'd appreciate it."

"I'd do anything for her." His voice broke. This night was really taking its toll. He stood quickly, crossing to the kitchen window to look out at the darkness. His forest, where he'd come to start over. He cleared his throat. "There is something you can do for me, Tory."

"Sure. Name it." Her voice sounded wary.

"Make sure that this marriage is what you really want this time."

"Of course."

"Then fight like hell to keep it."

He heard her breath catch. Several moments passed before she spoke. "You surprise me."

"Amazing, isn't it, from someone who did neither?" His voice was all business, back in control. He walked over to the eating bar and chose the chair closest to the phone unit.

"Jake, sometime could we talk about what happened?"

"What's done is done. Except for losing Jackie, I have no regrets."

"But she spent all summer with you. And she calls every other week."

"It's not enough." Nothing could make up for the loss of a parent whether by choice, like divorce, or through death. And he'd lost both. His father to a stray bullet, his mother to his own stubbornness.

His brothers were able to accept their mother's decision, why couldn't he? Was it because, as the oldest, he felt he deserved an explanation? No, it was more than that. His own arrogance convinced him that he deserved some say in the decision process, too.

"What if she called each week, instead?"

He'd forgotten Victoria was still on the phone. How like him, to have dismissed her already. "What if she lived here, and you got a call each week?" He heard her sharp indrawn breath. "Think about that, Tory."

■ ■ ■

The hair dryer whined loudly in the background. Jake was trying to salvage his night's work. Having grown accustomed to the noise, he ignored it and grabbed a thermometer strip from the cardboard box. He placed it on the counter along with the flashlight, clipboard and glass of juice.

What a great invention. Too bad disposable thermometers weren't around when his daughter was little. All that wasted worrying about where it had last been.

He turned, then stopped. Caitlyn stood in the doorway, clad in the top half of his pajama set. It covered her to the best of its ability. Thank God she wasn't any taller.

His eyes traced her legs upward, from unpainted toenails to the hem of the oversized sleep shirt. Breaking away, he met her gaze. Her cheeks were flushed. He should be the one who was embarrassed, acting like a hormone-crazed teenager.

"What are you doing out of bed?"

She moved her lips in response, but he couldn't hear a thing over the loud humming.

"Just a minute." He crossed to the kitchen table. The dryer was propped upright by a hastily-formed stack of magazines, pointing directly at his smudged engineering drawing. He flipped the switch to off, then tested the paper. Satisfied, he began rolling it up without a backwards glance.

"I said, why are you down here?"

"I heard you moving about and saw the lights on."

"You should have stayed put. I was on my way up." He shoved the drawing back into its tube and stood it in the corner of the alcove.

"I hate for you to go to any more trouble." Cait glanced over to the tray he'd prepared. His gaze followed hers for a moment, then swung back and travelled down to her toes.

"Trouble is exactly what we'll have on our hands if Kelly finds out you were walking around barefoot."

"Is she here?"

Her voice sounded hopeful. He looked up, glaring at her. "Of course not."

"Well, my heels and hose seemed a little out of place. I had no other alternative." Her chin was defiantly up in the air.

"If you need something, ask. Here, put these on." Kicking off one slipper, then the other, he nudged them in her direction. They would be huge on her, but they'd do. She was silent as she stared at the offering. After a moment, he watched her step into them. His eyes began straying upward again.

"Take this, too." He shrugged out of his flannel robe and held it out to her. Maybe that would keep him from acting like a fool.

She reached for the garment. Her eyes glanced past it and were immediately riveted to his midsection. The bottom half of the pajama set. From the creases and wrinkles it was obvious that they had never before been worn. Now she knew why only the top had been in the plastic wrapper, still store-folded and pinned to perfection.

He was probably wearing them only for her benefit. Most likely he slept in . . . a lot less. Her cheeks flushed bright pink.

Two halves of a whole, cut from the same cloth. The intimacy was overwhelming, even in this spacious kitchen. She'd stay on one side of the eating bar, hopefully he'd stay on the other. Better yet, maybe she should just make a run for it.

"Put it on." His command forced her thoughts back to the present. She was instantly all thumbs. Slipping her arm through the sleeve, she tangled the belt about her shoulder.

He watched her flounder, then stepped forward. "No, like this."

Rethreading it through the loops, he overlapped the front to cover everything, throat, chin and mouth included. He cinched the belt, then stepped back and nodded. All but her ankles were blanketed. "Pick a seat. I need to take your temperature."

She watched as he crossed to where the tray sat near the sink. The robe was still warm from his body heat. It caressed her neck and shoulders. She wiggled her chin free so she could speak. "Thank you for letting me borrow your clothes. But taking my temperature is going too far."

He continued to approach, clipboard in hand, and pointed to a chair. "Be still. Doctor's orders."

She sat quickly, choosing the farthest stool. Glancing away, she avoided staring at the sprinkling of fine, crisp curls covering his chest. She looked past him towards the hall door, her escape route, and opened her mouth.

Cait noticed that he didn't move. Opening wider, she made an exaggerated sound. "Ahhh."

He stood silently before her for several moments longer, increasing her nervousness, before laying the thermometer strip across her forehead. Her gaze raised immediately to his. She retracted her tongue as color flooded her cheeks. The reading would never be accurate, like this. She shut her eyes to cover her embarrassment.

Jake stepped away. After a moment, he made a notation on Kelly's sheet. "Normal."

Her eyes opened. Amazing. She cleared her throat and started to climb down. "I'll go back up."

"Not yet." Picking up the small flashlight, he placed his hand under her chin. He tilted her head back gently. "Look at me."

As if she had a choice.

His fingers were rough as they lay lightly against her jaw line, lifting her line of vision to his. His eyes weren't nearly as dark as she'd thought. Clear and serene, with tiny laugh lines around the edges. Positive proof that he smiled on occasion.

He moved the light from one eye to the other. She was momentarily blinded. The thought that he could still see her made her uneasy. Could he also feel her pulse leaping? She flinched when the light was snapped off and dropped onto the tray.

He exhaled as if just completing an unpleasant task. She quickly climbed down. "I'll go. You can have the kitchen to yourself again."

He looked at her standing before him, ready to run although dwarfed by his robe and slippers. "No, wait."

Her presence threw him off guard, made him act defensively. What was he trying to protect against this woman, his privacy? He never entertained women in his home. Being dressed like the Bobsey twins made things even worse. It was too cozy. Familiar.

In less than twelve hours she'd be gone. He'd have his house back, and his clothes. He tried to visualize the quiet, relaxing atmosphere before her arrival, surrounded by his work and a little Cat Stevens on the stereo. For some reason, this time, being alone didn't cheer him up.

Cait was looking at him, questioning. She had obviously come down for something, a snack perhaps? His brisk attitude was driving her away without asking. He reached for the peace offering sitting on the tray. "I poured this just before you came down. How about a sandwich, too?"

"Too much trouble. Juice alone is fine."

"No trouble. I'm making one for myself." He stepped away and opened the fridge. Kneeling down, he retrieved the lettuce from the bottom drawer. "I have both turkey and ham, mustard and mayo. Name your favorites."

"Whichever is easier, they both sound good to me. Can I help?"

The flannel brushed against his spine. His jaw clenched. She was standing directly behind him. Glancing at her, he was once again thankful that the robe was full length. He swallowed. "Yes, but from the chair. I don't want you tripping." Another accident and Kelly might sentence her to a full week in his guest room.

He brought the sandwich fixings to the bar, then grabbed two dinner knives. Pulling out the stool to her right, he sat down and handed her the utensil. His chair swiveled, bumping his knee against hers.

She scooted further away. His broad chest, rippling with each stretching movement, was much too close. Food was the last thing on her mind. She reached unsteadily for the bread.

"If I touched a sore spot, I'm sorry."

How could he read her so easily? She scrambled for a response. It might sound prudish, but being direct was best in the long run. "Where I'm from, it's a house rule that everyone comes to the table fully dressed."

He stopped squeezing the mustard. His gaze held hers

silently for a moment. "I was referring to your knee."

Her cheeks turned from pink to flaming. Careful to look only at his eyes, she answered him. "My knee is fine." She grabbed the salad dressing.

"Are you sure? Maybe I should take a look."

"No." Her eyes widened. She readjusted the robe over her legs.

A smile curved his lips. He set down his knife and pushed his stool away from the counter. "Start us both a sandwich. Make mine ham. I'll be right back."

More clothes sounded like a very good idea to him, also. His own mood had certainly improved after covering her up. He should be flattered, but instead, felt like he was playing with fire. Disturbed was a good word for it.

Pulling open the coat closet, he glanced inside, then at his watch. Still a long night ahead. The more distance, and the more clothes, the better. He ran upstairs for reinforcements.

■ ■ ■

When Jake reappeared he was wearing a sweatshirt and pants. She noticed that he had also found a pair of wool socks to trade for his slippers. Cait was now warm and toasty, and infinitely more comfortable. She took a bite of her sandwich just as Jake asked another question. She waved at him to hold on.

"You keep doing that."

"Sorry."

She sipped her orange juice. "I've lived in Issaquah for the past seven years. The small town atmosphere suits me just fine."

"Small town nosiness, you mean."

"That, too. Privacy is impossible when you live in a sub-division. Especially with children. Most of what I say or do ends up in a homework essay or discussed at the bus stop. There's not an embarrassing moment left to hide."

"Isn't all that closeness suffocating?"

"Not to me." Another sip. "I love impromptu get-togethers."

"Parties?" Where had he heard this before? Visions of Victoria, primping for yet another dinner party, crowded his thoughts. In her line of work, looking good seemed just as important as performing well. He never could adjust to such blatant falseness. Felt that it rubbed off on him, just by being at her side.

"Not a party really, more like a softball game in the street, or a potluck barbecue. Sometimes, when life slows down, I invite my daughters' church group over for a movie night."

This was certainly different. "When do you have time for yourself?"

"A lot of what I do is for myself, too. Right now I'm planning a weekend getaway for them. A time to relax and rethink priorities." She set her glass on the counter. "That's what brought me to the mountains tonight. I was looking for the owner of Raging River Lodge."

Jake's double-take made her pulse beat faster. "Do you know him?" she asked.

He forced himself to stay calm. Leaning against the chair back, he linked his hands behind him. A long stretch further delayed his response. He wasn't sure what to say. Just hearing about her lifestyle wore him out. What would it be like to have all that noise and confusion loose on Rattlesnake Ridge?

There never had been a soft place in his heart for

do-gooders, even though the one sitting next to him certainly seemed sincere. They were usually head-in-the-cloud idealists with impossible visions for a better world. Sure, he had helped others a time or two, but, in general, life was what you made it. By and for yourself. It was better to set her straight from the start.

"Raging River was a short-lived commercial operation." He righted himself, resting his elbows on the counter. "Went out of business over a year ago due to financial problems. Rumor has it, the owner moved to the sun-belt to escape our liquid sunshine."

"And the property?"

"Currently a privately owned residence."

She let the news sink in. The lodge was no more. Her teens would take it hard. Maybe she'd wait until next Sunday to tell them. That would give her a week to think of an alternative.

When she spoke her voice was low, but not defeated. "I'll come up with something else, then."

"Another movie night?"

She shook her head slowly. "Not the same."

"Another place?"

"Too expensive. Raging River was the last on my list. It was a long shot, at best."

He silently watched her. Too bad there wasn't some other way for him to help. From a distance, though, something that didn't require their being together for long periods of time. One night of close proximity was more than enough for him.

She stiffened her shoulders, then raised her chin a few centimeters higher. He smiled. Her body language was easy to read. She had an idea and heaven help anyone who got in her way.

"My house will have to do."

"Your house?"

She nodded. "We'll pitch tents in the yard and hope for a cloudless night."

"Do you have the room?"

"A group of twelve will surely surpass the limits of my hot water heater, but we'll make do." She shrugged. "The house is small, but it's fine for the three of us."

He relaxed his grip on the glass, inquisition averted. With none of Victoria's sulking as to why he wasn't more supportive, nor his mother's insistence that he comply with her demands. Caitlyn's quick bounce back and undefeatable spirit intrigued him, despite his resolve to avoid involvement. His next question was out before he could stop himself. "Any plans for a fourth?"

"No more babies. I value my sleep too much to start over. And I don't play bridge." She smiled and took the last bite of her sandwich. The gleam in her eye told him that she hadn't misunderstood his question.

He spelled it out, attempting to sound casual. "I meant a husband."

She dabbed her lips with a napkin. "No one's on the horizon. Frankly, I'm enjoying my independence. I don't want to be tied down again."

He laughed. "'Tied down' is a man's term."

"It is not."

She certainly loved children, teenagers at least, so that wasn't it. What happened to bring that soulful look to her eyes? "Want to talk about it?"

"I married immediately after graduation. After the twins arrived, the cycle began." She picked up her glass and swirled the contents. "I would find us a decent apartment and myself an interesting, if not challenging, job. Like clockwork, as soon as we were settled, Todd would announce another relocation. Sometimes it wasn't worth unpacking."

"Unbelievable!"

"Don't laugh. I know it's not all that unusual, but to me it was very important. I wanted roots, a home to call my own." He touched her hand, stilling the glass before the contents spilled over the top. She looked up. He was grinning.

"I wasn't laughing, only referring to the fact that we just found something in common." He let his hand linger a moment longer, then released hers. Quickly standing, he walked to the fridge.

Her fingers still tingled from his warmth. His comment had taken her by surprise. Sure their lifestyles were different but important things, like compassion and integrity, ran deep within them both. Her being here in his kitchen tonight proved that.

She watched Jake pull a pitcher from the fridge. Maybe it was the lateness of the hour, but she wanted to know more. "You were married, too?"

He hesitated before giving her a curt nod. "A long time ago. But it wasn't Victoria that liked to move. No, she was quite content in our high-rise condo. It was my mother who had the wanderlust fever."

"So you escaped from the big city and fled to the woods." She smiled and accepted a refill. "You do like extremes."

"I like my privacy. Buying this house fulfilled a dream of mine. The construction firm that I started when I moved here from L.A. built the place. I know it's more than I need, but to me it symbolizes a fresh start."

She looked around the kitchen, noting the fine workmanship and attention to detail. The extra-wide counters allowed ample seating and work space. The pine cabinets were tall and deep. The double-paned garden window behind the stainless steel sink had decorative wrought-iron shelving, eliminating the need for curtains. All promoted the rustic appearance, but while still providing the comforts of a modern kitchen. "Amazing. Could I have a tour?"

"Maybe tomorrow, if you're feeling up to it." He set the pitcher back on the shelf and joined her again at the table. "So, if you hated moving about, why weren't you divorced?"

"How did you know? Oh, Brooke."

He nodded. "She said Todd died several years ago."

"What else did she say?"

"Not much, due to bad timing on your part. You chose that very minute to wake up."

"Lucky for me, or she would have bored you to tears with the entire, uneventful tale."

He leaned back, resting one ankle across his knee. "I'm listening now."

She looked at him, assessing his sincerity. Was he someone willing to listen without passing judgement or giving advice? Maybe, maybe not. She wanted to find out. "We had a fairly good marriage, or so I thought at the time. I didn't realize, until a year after his death, the magnitude of my frustrations."

"Too busy being Superwoman?"

"No, more like a martyr. After he died, I had a deep sense of guilt."

"Why guilt?"

"On the night of the crash, I was wishing his latest job offer would fall through." She drew a deep breath. "But not his plane. I know this sounds ridiculous, but I felt responsible."

They were both quiet for a moment, then Jake laid his hand on her forearm. When Cait finally broke the silence, the fire was back in her voice. "Thanks for not arguing the point with me. Most people did at the time. No one would simply listen to me. Finally, an old college friend of ours woke me up and helped to secure my job with OmniCorp."

"Sounds like you have a lot of regrets, a lot of living to make up for."

"Regrets? No. It's a waste of time to listen to what might have been. I make it a point to concentrate on the present." Smiling, she picked up her glass. "I could tell you all the wonderful details about my current job, home, kids and youth group, but you'd start snoozing. Who would carry you upstairs? Not me."

He looked at her for a moment longer, torn between wanting her to share more, but not wanting to get involved. He began stacking the plates. "Maybe you could give it to me in small doses then, but not while I'm driving you home. I'd hate to run off the road."

She laughed. He stood, taking the dishes to the sink. "I'll help you back upstairs, and finish these in the morning." Tossing down the towel, he helped steady her as they started up the steps together.

At her door, she turned and laid her hand on his forearm. "Thank you, for both the snack and for your company."

He looked down at her fingers gently resting against his arm. Her presence in his home tonight added an unexpected warmth and completeness. He drew back, turning his arm to catch her hand in his. "My pleasure. I haven't traded midnight stories with a friend for a long time."

"How long?"

He thought briefly of Victoria, then of the one-night

partners that followed for a brief period after his divorce. "I guess that depends on the definition of friend, Caitlyn. Maybe never."

He gave her hand a quick squeeze, then turned and walked briskly down the hall.

■ ■ ■

Rolling over, Cait stretched lazily before looking at her watch. "Ten o'clock!" She threw back the comforter and swung her legs over the edge, sitting up carefully.

Good, no dizziness. Looking down at her feet, she wiggled her toes, then smiled. She was still wearing his socks.

As she showered, memories of the previous night crowded in. A friend. She'd heard him use that word quite clearly. During their dinner, she'd sensed there was something more between them. Her presence disturbed him, beyond the intrusion on his solitude. He guarded both his words and actions, trying to reveal nothing of the tension underneath. But when his gaze locked on her bare legs below the pajama top, he was as easy to read as 'Dick and Jane.'

The fact that he found her attractive made her heart beat faster. It also caused her to do crazy Brooke-like things, such as her daring move last night at the bedroom door.

"Why didn't he kiss me?" She stopped toweling her hair to stare into the steam covered mirror, then draped the towel around her neck. "I gave him the perfect opening. Am I so out of practice that I misread the signs?"

It seemed like a lifetime ago since she had felt such a strong attraction to any man. The blood-pumping, finger-tingling sensations were scary. She and Todd had eased their way into a comfortable, predictable relationship over several years. Why would she want confusion, disruption, and possibly heartache in her life now when it was running so smoothly?

Not wanting an answer, she tried brushing it from her mind, along with the tangles from her damp hair. She used a great deal of force and frustration on both, but the question nagged on. She leaned forward and cleared a circular spot on the mirror with the edge of her towel. Stepping back, she looked at herself with new honesty.

"Because I feel alive again, after running on auto-pilot for too long. Brooke always said that it would happen again, if I was willing to take the chance." Bending from the waist, she wrapped her hair tightly into a turban. She took one last look at her reflection. "Maybe the right time has finally arrived."

She quickly slipped on yesterday's clothes. There was no way she could return home in his. His hastily scribbled note, however, attached to the worn jogging suit left outside her door, had touched her heart. Was it another proof of his generosity, or a warning not to come downstairs half-dressed?

Maybe a little of both, she thought, as she fingered the slip of paper, tracing her name. He might have an exterior as hard and brisk as the outdoors, but underneath he was a nurturer, like herself. "We're cut from the same cloth, Mr. Brandon. The only real difference is that I admit it."

Carefully folding the note, she slipped it into her pocket, then stepped into her heels. She made a final check on her appearance in the full length mirror by the dresser. There was a glow of excitement in her eyes that had been missing for much too long. Throwing herself into work and family had earned her satisfaction and self-esteem. Not for a minute did she regret all that she'd accomplished.

"Maybe it's time to take a risk again, time for something else." She quickly corrected herself. "Someone else, that is, if he can be convinced."

After checking her buttons and straightening her jacket, she opened the door. Jake's voice thundered from the kitchen below, but she couldn't quite make out the words. She listened for a minute. He was angry at someone, but there wasn't a second voice. Must be on the phone. She slipped off her heels so she wouldn't disturb him, or mark his hardwood floors.

From the balcony above the TV room she saw the sun streaming in the windows which framed the stone fireplace. The vaulted ceiling and forested view gave the room a majestic feeling, as if time could stand still. The room's furnishings looked comfortable and lived-in. She could almost imagine Jake resting his feet on the rustic coffee table.

There was one main difference between their two homes. His had no scattered shoes or forgotten textbooks laying about. Her pile of belongings in the far corner by the entryway was the only item out of place. He would certainly be shocked by the joyful confusion at her house.

She walked noiselessly down the steps. Jake's voice was softer. Patient, but also somewhat teasing. Cait crossed to her gym bag, hoping that her tennis shoes were still in there. They'd feel better than heels, even at the risk of being a fashion nightmare.

Kneeling, she unzipped the bag. It was hard not to overhear Jake's next words, coming from the kitchen.

"I love you, honey. It's fine by me if you want to move in."

Cait blinked twice. More company?

"Yes, I'm sure." He paused. "Leave everything to me."

What about his precious solitude, or was it only her he

wanted to get rid of? Perhaps he should have been more specific last night.

And what about his actions? If he was already committed to someone else, then he shouldn't be eyeing her. Or did she do all the drooling and panting last night? Parading around in his pajamas, inviting him to kiss her. She quickly covered her crimson cheeks.

His voice brought her back to the present. "Stop worrying, honey."

Leaping to her feet, she dashed up the stairs for her purse. He and his lover could both stop worrying. Caitlyn James would soon be history around here.

■　■　■

"Put your mother on." Jake waited only a moment before hearing Victoria's curt hello. "Well, I guess you heard."

"I did. I don't know what to say."

"She's fifteen, Tory. You've had her to yourself for years."

"But she's my life."

"Then where does William fit in?"

She drew a sharp breath before letting him have it. "That's a rude, thoughtless thing to say, as usual. She would never be in our way."

"Sorry." Why did he always blurt out the first thing that came to mind? His mouth had gotten him into trouble many times as a kid. Some habits died hard. He ran his fingers back through his hair. "Okay, let's both calm down and think this through."

"I've thought of nothing else all night, since she told me." She caught her breath, though it sounded to him more like a sob. "I think she's too young."

"At this age, kids are usually gone anyway, doing their own thing. It's time to start letting go."

"But so fast? School's out in less than two weeks."

"You and William are getting married at the end of summer. This will give you time to settle in together."

"Why run off now? In a few years, she'll be going to college. Maybe then."

Jake leaned against the door frame, his booted foot braced against the opposite side. He softened his voice. "Listen to me, Tory. Don't think of it as running away. You've done a wonderful job with her. Just think of this as my turn, before she's grown and gone for good."

The silence stretched on several minutes before Victoria spoke again. "This isn't some old college buddy coming up for a little carousing, Jacob. This is our daughter."

"I know that." He laughed at her use of his Christian name. It reminded him of his younger days, of constantly being in big-time trouble.

"She'll need a decent school. You can't let her grades slip."

"Yes."

"And not too much freedom."

"I'll tie her up every night."

"And respectable friends."

"I'll advertise."

He heard her sigh, giving in. "If you screw this up . . ."

"I won't." He stood and walked over towards the laundry room annex. Pulling open the door, he slowly ran his hand along the notches in the frame. He'd recreated them from a photo taken in their condo before he packed. The one from last summer was shoulder high to him. He'd be adding an update soon, despite Jackie's protests.

As he listened with one ear to Victoria's various

instructions, he picked up a fallen card and re-pinned it on the bulletin board above the washer. The cork was nearly covered with snapshots and memorabilia of his long-haired, freckled youngster growing up. He touched the yellowed paper containing finger painted stick figures, the home-made Father's Day notes with backward letters, and the school report entitled 'My Summer Vacation with Dad.' Crayons to computers. Booties to nylons.

He had missed so much.

Before attempting to interrupt her long dialogue, he swallowed hard to clear the lump from his throat. "I won't screw this up, Tory. I love her, too."

■ ■ ■

Jake watched Caitlyn sling her gym bag over the same shoulder already supporting her purse. He'd picked up that purse before. It was heavy. Had she forgotten about yesterday's accident so quickly? Next she reached for her computer. That was enough. He placed his hand over hers, stopping her from lifting it. "Where's the fire?"

"No fire. I'm just anxious to get home."

"Stay for breakfast, at least."

She'd rather settle for the last heel of bread in her refrigerator than enter his kitchen again. "I never eat breakfast." Her stomach gurgled, protesting her lie. She surrendered the laptop to him and placed her hand over her stomach. Not wanting to meet his doubting stare, she looked away.

"Fine. It's up to you. I've already eaten." He picked up her briefcase in his other hand, and headed out the door. She quickly followed.

Even as she played out her charade, Cait knew she was

being childish. After all, nothing happened last night between them to raise her hopes. Absolutely nothing, except maybe a tingling along her spine whenever he looked at her, or the racing of her heart when he stood close.

She straightened her shoulders. Time to stop sulking. So the sparks were one-sided. So someone else was moving in as soon as she moved out. It wasn't as if he invited her in the first place.

Time to smile and get the heck out of here, with her dignity intact. Forcing her voice to be calm and even, she spoke to his retreating back. "Please thank Kelly for me."

Between the mumbling and the cursing, the only word she could make out was 'furious.' Gravel crunched beneath his boot as he picked up the pace.

"Tell her I couldn't stay, I'm already behind schedule for the day. If I hadn't overslept . . ."

"Forget it. Since you'll be long gone, she'll have to settle for a strip off my hide." He flipped open the tailgate and stashed her bags, then slammed the door. Crossing his arms, he leaned against the bumper. If only she would look at him, maybe he could read the real motivation behind this farce.

She averted her eyes. He was right. There was definitely something behind the sudden departure, but he couldn't put a finger on it. Their final words to each other last night were about friendship, and how long it had been since . . . was that it?

Hell, he hadn't been talking about sex. If that was what she was so worried about, maybe he'd describe a few of his post-divorce one night stands. "Cait?"

"Yes?"

She looked up, but no farther than his top shirt button. As the seconds ticked away, she took a step back. Had he scared her that much? He'd given up trying to second guess the female race years ago. Why start again? "Never mind. I'll call Kelly before we leave. It'll only take a second."

He straightened and turned towards the house. Before taking a second step, he was knocked off balance by a bundle of fur nearly his size and half his weight. "Down, boy! Good God, what are they feeding you these days?"

He rolled to a sitting position and scratched the Newfoundland's head. In return, the dog playfully shoved his paw against Jake's chest. "Not now, Wolfgang. Go home."

The pooch gave his neighbor another nudge, then dropped a bright yellow football into his lap. The two sat eye-to-eye, neither about to budge. The rapid panting warned Jake that a slurp was about to follow. He picked up the ball and stood. "All right, but just this once."

One short 'woof' sealed their bargain.

Cait stepped forward to be introduced. "This is a dog? It looks more like a yak crossed with a Kodiak bear. You're lucky he let you up."

Jake turned and met her eyes. They were sparkling with laughter. "Meet Wolfgang, Kelly's pride and joy."

Kelly again. She should have guessed. The pooch was certainly at home here. Both he and his owner must be more frequent visitors than Jake had let on.

She watched for a moment as Jake tossed the toy back and forth in a teasing gesture. Not pleased, the animal growled in warning and lumbered over to sit on Jake's left boot. Jake responded with a few heel-toe movements. Wolfgang's hind side rode up and down, but he didn't budge from the shoe. Another game.

Cait knelt and extended her hand. "Here, boy, I'll play with you. The master has a call to make."

"Don't get too close, he's ferocious around strangers."

Cait looked up, unable to hold back a smile as her new friend rolled over for a tummy scratch. Jake just shook his head and returned her grin.

"Get up, you old phony. Go fetch." He drew back his arm and tossed the football down the driveway. It bounced twice, then rolled beneath a low lying bush. Wolfgang chased it, but then lost track of the target. Instead of searching under the rhododendrons, he trotted over to sniff near a roadside fir tree.

"Blasted dog. Kelly should have given him an IQ test before adopting him."

"I'll give him a hand while you finish up." Laughing, she followed the canine down the drive.

He called after her. "Be careful on those heels." She didn't pause or look back. "Don't pet him, for God's sake. He bites." A laugh was her only response.

Her reddish-gold hair swung back and forth across her shoulders, catching the morning light. He remembered how soft her bangs felt against his hand as he took her temperature. Good thing no one was taking his right now.

"Plenty of time for the dog, but not for breakfast. And obviously not for me." He kicked once at the gravel, then turned and headed back inside.

Cait knelt on the grass and reached under the bush. The ball was resting against a short wooden post. A sign. His house address? Maybe she'd take note of it in case she was ever in the mood to act foolishly again. She circled around towards the front and pushed back the overgrowth. The letters were faded but still readable in the bright daylight.

"No." Sitting back on her heels, she looked at the lodge in dismay. "It can't be."

But it was. After all this time, she'd found it. The Raging River Lodge.

Four

Rose threw open the front door and raced inside. "Mom, are you home yet?"

"Yes, honey. I'm upstairs. Be right down."

"Glad you're okay. Is the car a major wreck? How'd you get home?" By the time the younger twin reached the top of the steps, Cait was leaving her bedroom. She embraced her mother tightly. "We were up all night. Worried."

Looking beyond her over the balcony, Cait saw her other daughter standing in the entryway below. Lynn shook her head and rolled her eyes at Rose.

"No we weren't, you bee-brain. Not after hearing about the doctor." Lynn dropped the two overnight bags she was carrying. "You stayed up, all right, but you were watching movies. Remember?"

Brooke's video library was extensive, but most weren't suitable for sixteen-year-olds. Cait descended the stairs, giving Rose a questioning look. "Which ones did you see?"

"A love story, with a little shoot 'em up action to keep Kyle interested."

"Interested, and downstairs with you." Lynn grinned smugly at her sister.

"Well, it's his house." Rose stuck out her tongue, then faced her mom again. "Don't worry, it was PG-13. Brooke had the really good ones locked up."

"Thank heavens for small favors." Cait stepped off the landing and wrapped her free arm around her elder daughter. "I missed you, too. Thanks for keeping an eye on things. Especially on Brooke."

"Someone has to." Lynn winked, then her voice turned serious. "Glad you're all right. Promise you'll keep your eyes on the road from now on?"

"It's a deal." She pulled Lynn close and kissed the top of her head.

"Promises like that are made to be broken. You never know what might distract someone on a deserted mountain road." At the sound of Brooke's voice, Cait turned. Her friend lounged in the doorway, wearing faded stretch jeans, a sweatshirt advertising her age, and last night's mascara.

Cait peered closer, a smile curving the corners of her mouth. "What happened? You look worse than I feel."

Brooke gingerly stretched one leg, then the other. "You forgot to warn me about jogging with your little darlings. I may not walk for a week."

Cait signaled to her friend to follow, trying not to laugh. "Come on, I'll fix you some iced tea."

"With lots of caffeine, I hope."

"What other kind is there?" She laughed, then turned

towards her daughters. "Join us as soon as you unpack. I'll start lunch. Stinky softball clothes go straight in the washer, ditto muddy sneakers."

"Got it." Grabbing one duffel bag, Rose started for the stairs. "Dibs on the phone first!"

"Forget it." Lynn joined in the chase. "I carried your bag in from the car. I'm going first."

Cait smiled at their rivalry. It was music to her ears. She headed towards the kitchen, with Brooke following. After retrieving two glasses from the overhead cabinet, she set them on the counter, paused and sighed. "It's really good to be home."

"Quite an adventure, I'd say."

"What did you tell them about last night?"

"Not nearly enough." Brooke winked at her friend. "But it was all I knew."

"Stop smirking." She pressed one of the cups under the dispenser. Ice cubes clinked against the sides of the glass before sliding down. Retrieving the pitcher from the refrigerator, she poured two drinks and set one before Brooke.

"The suspense is killing me. Tell me about Jake Brandon."

"He's a very nice man and generous host."

"And?"

"That's all." Crossing to the sink, Cait opened the dishwasher and began loading the previous morning's breakfast dishes.

"Translate that to 'boring.'"

"Read it any way you want."

Brooke climbed off her stool and helped herself to a lemon in the fridge. Grabbing a paring knife, she stood near Cait and began slicing. "I didn't expect you back so early.

Does that mean you won't be seeing him again?"

"Not unless he starts shopping at the Issaquah grocery." She shut off the water and dried her hands. Her eyes didn't meet her friend's. "Since that's not likely, I guess this chapter's closed."

"Too bad." Brooke twisted one slice, then dropped it into her drink. She stirred slowly, then held the dish out to Cait. "I sensed a little chemistry between the two of you, from your voice."

Cait accepted one slice and hung it over the side of her glass. Her eyes watered. Certainly it was the citrus, not anything else. Blinking hard, she studied her tea silently.

The sassiness instantly disappeared from Brooke's voice. She covered Cait's hand with hers. "Do you want to tell me about it?"

Cait sighed, her shoulders slumping. "There's not much to tell. We enjoyed a nice hour or so of conversation. During that time he made it quite clear that he prefers being alone."

"So? Lots of men do. He'll come around."

She shook her head. "His definition of alone meant 'not me.' Just him and his live-in lover."

"Really?" Brooke's eyes widened. "Did she arrive during the night and find you tucked in down the hall, in your lacy camisole?"

"Brooke!"

"I remember that cute little number you wore yesterday. After all, we did aerobics together during lunch." Her grin turned sly. "I'm just assuming that you didn't sleep in the buff in a total stranger's home."

Cait quickly scanned the hallway, checking for two sets of teenage ears. The coast was clear. Stiffening her back, she defended herself in a loud whisper. "Of course not. He lent me his pajama top."

"My God, I'm starting menopause early." Brooke picked up the TV guide and quickly fanned herself. "He just stood there and peeled it off?"

"Why am I bothering to have this conversation with you?" Cait grabbed the magazine from Brooke, rolled it and threatened her with it. "Next time just dial 1-900-FANTASY. They have much better material than I do."

"I'm simply trying to shock you back into the land of the living." Recapturing the weapon, Brooke laid it flat against the counter. She set a cookbook on top. "You've led a sheltered, monk-like existence for the last seven years. This is the first time I've seen even a spark of hope. Let's make the most of it."

A moment passed in heavy silence, then Brooke spoke again. This time her voice was devoid of sarcasm. "I'm sorry. I'll try to keep it zipped while you explain."

"Thank you." Cait relaxed and drew a deep breath. She took the stool next to Brooke. "I'm sorry, too. You were right on, there was a flash of chemistry between us. Or so I thought." She picked up a pencil and began to sketch on the back of an old grocery list.

"Go on."

"This morning I overheard him on the phone, inviting someone to come live with him."

"Could have been his mother."

Cait raised her head. "His words were, "I love you, honey. Stay as long as you like.'"

Brooke nodded curtly. "Bingo. She's probably on her last legs."

"Be serious." Stepping down, Cait crossed to the sink and gazed out the garden window. "A man like Jake probably has a long list of candidates."

"Then why invite just one woman?" Brooke paused for a

moment, then joined her friend by the window. She placed her hand on Cait's shoulder. "I'm trying to be serious. It just doesn't seem to last very long."

"I need an aspirin."

"That I can help with." Brooke reached for her purse and scrounged for a moment. "I've never seen you like this before."

"I still have a slight headache. Doctor Kelly said it may recur for days."

"I meant over a man. He must be something."

"It doesn't matter." After swallowing two tablets, she gazed again at the backyard. Her tulips were past their prime and her rose bushes had not yet bloomed. A seasonal no-man's-land. It reflected her own mood exactly.

"Sure it matters." Brooke's voice was once again pumping excitement. "How about another foray into the mountains? Any chance of getting lost again?"

Cait leaned forward, forearms against the sink. "No more trips. I found the lodge."

"Great."

She silently shook her head.

Brooke frowned. "Not so great. Why not?"

"The lodge is closed. Jake lives there now."

"So? What a great opportunity."

"Forget it." She stepped around Brooke and began collecting spoons, glasses and napkins. "I told him I was looking for the lodge, and all about my grandiose plans. He either had momentary amnesia or he wasn't interested in helping."

"But . . ."

"No buts." She dropped the silverware into the sink. Metal clanged against metal. "He didn't offer and I'm not asking."

Rose appeared in the doorway. "Who didn't offer what, Mom?"

The two women were silent. Lynn stepped past her sister, into the kitchen. "With Brooke here, this is no doubt an R-rated conversation. They probably can't say." Grabbing a sack of carrots from the fridge, she joined her mother by the sink. "Am I right?"

Brooke leaned over, pushed Lynn's hair back from her forehead and looked into her eyes. "You say this child is only sixteen? I'd double check her birth certificate if she were mine."

Cait nodded, matching her friend's serious tone. "I already did. It says two more years, then college."

Brooke raised her gaze skyward. "Lord help the university. And fraternity row."

Lynn ignored them both and began peeling carrots.

"All right, we have a lot to do today, so let's have lunch and get to it." Cait called over to Rose, who was busy loading the washer. "Are you having soup or sandwich?"

"Soup. Anything fun planned for this afternoon?"

"No, just the usual. Errands, groceries."

"Forget it, Mom." Lynn turned, leaning against the sink. "You make the list, Rose and I will take care of the rest." She waved the peeler in emphasis. "The only place you're going today is to bed."

Brooke picked up one of the carrots and mimicked the movement. Her eyes sparkled. Cait's glare warned her not to comment.

Instead, Brooke puffed out her cheeks and expelled a loud breath. Keeping silent was not in her nature. Then she pushed away from the counter. "Since things seem to be under control here, I guess I'll scoot. Bye, girls." She leaned close to Lynn. "Let's do it again, soon."

Lynn echoed her sentiment, saluting with a half-munched veggie. "Soon."

Rose raised her head above the mound of laundry she was sorting. "Thanks, Aunt Brooke." As if on second thought, she added the next words quietly. "And tell Kyle thanks for me, too."

"I sure will. Anything to make my son blush." Brooke winked, then grabbed her keys. "And you, friend, have a quiet, restful day. I'm teaching on Monday, so I'll see you the day after. If you need anything, give me a call."

"I will." Cait smiled. "Thanks again. You're a life saver. I don't know what I'd do without you to back me up."

"Sure you do. You were thinking about doing it last night."

Cait glared another silent warning and walked her to the door.

When the girls were out of voice range, Brooke wrapped an arm about her shoulder. "Listen. I don't know what the story is, about the lodge and all, but this is the first time I've seen you interested in anyone at all. Remember, seven years is a long time to be alone."

"I'm not alone. My daughters and I . . ."

"Not the same. It won't all come back overnight, if you know what I mean. All that sharing, the give-and-take, the intimacy. Just take it easy, trust your instinct, and see where things lead."

"Things are leading nowhere."

"And don't jump to conclusions. If it's meant to be, something will happen. Even fate gets a little boost, now and then." Brooke glanced back towards the kitchen, where the twins were busy drawing up afternoon plans. She gave Cait a playful shake. "And as for plenty of bed rest, too bad you didn't stay at Jake's."

■ ■ ■

The window near the sitting room couch was open, letting in the fresh morning air. Except for the sparrow chirping outside, all was quiet. Serene. Just the way he liked it. Jake stripped the bottom sheet from the bed and tossed it onto the growing pile of laundry.

No doubt Caitlyn was busy teaching Sunday school, saving souls in her own small corner of the world. He, in contrast, had done a few things for himself. First, he finished chopping the log he started Friday. Next, he arranged Jackie's airline ticket. Non-refundable and soon, only two weeks from today. No reason to give Victoria time to have a change of heart.

Why did he always look for the worst in Tory? It wasn't that her ambition to be tops in her field was really all that unusual. His main objection was to the glitzy-ness of it all. That, plus the fact she expected him to participate. To be by her side, to play a role, just like an actor reciting lines.

At the end, he did the one thing he knew would boost her career. He left. No longer did she have to explain his behavior, or his absence. So if he'd done what was best for her advancement, why was he now feeling a tinge of guilt? Maybe because he did nothing to support her, while he could. Maybe because, by leaving her, he lost the chance to watch his daughter grow up.

He certainly didn't learn about marital unity and family cohesiveness from his own parents, based on the role model his mother proved to be. Where was she when Dad was beginning a new job on the West Coast, at her insistence? Headed north, with her kids as hostage. No, baggage was a better word.

What would have been her reason for deserting Dad?

She never offered an explanation. Not then and not once in the twenty-odd years since. He hadn't even seen his mother for the last fifteen years. Hadn't received a birthday card in ten, not since he sent the others back, unopened.

What a waste. His pride and determination had rejected her, perhaps in the same manner that she rejected his father. But even if his actions were based on loyalty to his father, she still deserved some degree of respect. She was still the person who had given him birth, who raised him to be the man he was today. And his determination, albeit learned if not inbred, had served him well.

He shook his head, wondering where all the guilt was coming from. Maybe it was Caitlyn's talk about family, church and self-giving. If they were so different, then why was he still thinking of her? Here he was fondling the sheets as if trying to bring her back. He scooped up the remaining bedding that he'd tossed to the floor earlier, and started down the steps.

The phone rang. Why was he paying extra for an unlisted number? He picked it up on the sixth ring.

"Jake, Nick here."

"This had better be important." He tucked the receiver under his chin and kept walking.

"Two quick reminders. You're filling in for me at tomorrow morning's Chamber breakfast. At the Roost."

"Wonderful. What's the other?" Jake entered the laundry room and dropped the basket on the floor.

"Come by the office afterwards before going out to the Cougar Mountain site."

"What for? That project's on a tight schedule." He stuffed the sheets in the washer with more force than necessary.

"For training. The workstations are in and the intro class is tomorrow."

"That's your ball game, remember? You don't need me."

"You promised to give this project a fair shake. How do you plan to do that if you can't operate the software?"

"If the rest of the design team likes it, then I'll browse the tutorial." Jake grabbed the box of detergent off the overhead shelf and began to measure. "Later."

"Give me just an hour or two, then. There's someone I'd like for you to meet."

"No can do." He slammed the washer lid down, then cranked the knob. Nick's voice continued on, but his words were drowned out.

"If this argument's important, you'd better speak up."

"I said, it'll give you a chance to meet our OmniCorp service representative."

"Why would I . . .wait." Jake stepped from the laundry room into the kitchen, and cupped a hand over his ear. "Did you say OmniCorp?"

"Hope that name rings a bell. I've been talking about them for the past two months."

If it didn't involve an architectural drawing or customer deadline, Jake typically didn't pay much attention. "What's our rep's name?"

"Brooke Hastings. She'll be at our office all day Monday, teaching class. I'd like for you to meet her."

Jake rubbed the back of his neck.

Taking his silence as agreement, Nick continued to press his point. "We'll be discussing Phase Two of the implementation during lunch. Can you join us?"

Jake ran his fingers back through his hair. This presented interesting possibilities. "I'll drop by after the council meeting. Can't promise for how long, though."

"Great."

"You owe me."

"Right. Add it to my tab."

Jake switched off the portable phone. He paused for a moment, listening to the sloshing and twirling in the room behind him, washing away memories of the weekend. Almost. Her fragrance might be gone, but the sound of her laughter still rang in his ears.

He glanced over to the counter where they sat Friday night, trading dreams and disappointments. Her presence still surrounded him, invading his privacy. Not a good sign.

An idea came quickly to mind. He was rarely impulsive, except when correcting building deficiencies. This time he made an exception. Grabbing a second cup of coffee, he headed up the stairs to the master suite. The boxes stacked neatly in the alcove caught his eye. That project had been put off long enough. No, he corrected himself, maybe just the perfect amount of time.

Before his thoughts had time to jell, he crossed to his desk and picked up the phone. The number he was looking for was on a torn scrap of paper by the lamp. He'd planned to toss it out, but hadn't. He swiftly punched the numbers in.

"Brooke? Jake Brandon here. It seems that our paths are about to cross again."

"No kidding. Says who?"

"My partner, Nick Slater. He just informed me we're having lunch together tomorrow."

"Nick?" Recognition warmed her voice. "Ahh, you're the elusive, or should I say reclusive, partner. Small world."

"And getting smaller. Look, I have a favor to ask."

"This makes number two, you know."

Did everybody keep track these days? Jake sighed. "Any

chance we could make lunch a foursome?"

Brooke paused a moment, then laughed lightly. "Oh, I think we can do better than that."

■ ■ ■

After signing the Chamber of Commerce register, Jake picked up the morning's agenda. He'd substituted for Nick before, so the routine was familiar. Only seven A.M. and already the banquet room was alive and buzzing with news of the latest local happenings. Several Issaquah business owners, milling near the coffee bar, glanced up as he entered the room.

One old-timer, sporting a blue ribbon beneath his badge, stepped forward. The gold lettering identified him as Emcee-of-the-Month. "Jake, isn't it?"

"Morning, Randall."

"Let's get you a name tag." The dignitary slapped him on the back. "Can't have you pretending that you're Nicholas all morning, can we?"

Jake followed him to the head table, stopping for several introductions along the way. After pinning on the required plastic label, he scanned the room. Smiles and handshakes were being exchanged in rapid fire by virtual strangers. Somehow the plastic tag seemed very appropriate.

By the time breakfast was announced, Jake had loosened his tie several times. He hated the thing. Was it that, or the thought of seeing Caitlyn again that was setting him on edge? She had run from him last weekend. He knew he wasn't mistaken about the chemistry between them; it just had to be mutual. So why? Enough with the guessing game, he'd had enough of that with his mother. He'd ask Caitlyn directly, as soon as the right moment presented itself.

Instead of joining Randall at one of the front rounds, Jake chose a seat near the door. Easier to make an escape this way, if the speaker droned on. Since several seats were empty, less small talk would be required.

When the waiter attempted to refill his coffee for the third time, Jake stopped him with a hand over his cup. Any more, and his remaining patience would disintegrate. "Grapefruit juice. Unsweetened if you have it."

"Is it safe to sit here, Jacob? Sounds like your disposition is already running a bit sour this morning."

For a split second, he refused to turn his head. This could only be one person, one he'd been avoiding for years. Had his thoughts conjured her up? He wrenched around and met the guarded eyes. They were the same piercing blue as his. "Hello, Mother."

She pulled out the chair beside him. "Surprised?"

"Yes, and not pleasantly." His voice snapped at her. "What are you doing here?"

"I'm one of the regulars. Nick apprised me of your business success at last month's meeting. I must confess that my curiosity got the best of me when I saw your company listed on the roster." She picked up her iced water and sipped. The cubes rattled slightly.

"I've lived on the East Side for over three years."

"Not so you'd be close by for the holidays."

Ignoring her baiting tone, he accepted the juice glass from the waiter and took a deep gulp.

"Strange that you would return here, Jacob. I thought you hated Seattle. Couldn't wait to escape to L.A."

"You never could read me correctly, or didn't care to." He shook his head slowly. "No, I only hated the reason I was here."

"But now you're back. Why?"

"This place is perfect for the type of work I do." He sliced into one of his unadorned pancakes, then stabbed a section with his fork. It was too late for margarine. It was too late for many things. "I try not to think about the rest."

"Well, I'm glad you've found at least one thing in life that gives you joy. Architecture."

He winced. "You've dismissed Jackie as easily as you did me?"

"I never . . ."

"Well, maybe not physically, but you certainly ignored my feelings. Drew's, Patrick's." He slammed down his forkful of untouched food. "Not to mention Dad's, of course."

"If only you knew."

"Well, I don't, do I? You refused to discuss it."

"You never were one to listen, even as a boy. You gathered your own facts and drew your own conclusions."

"You never offered even one explanation."

"Would you have listened to one? Would you, even now?"

"No explanation necessary, Mother." Scooting his chair away from the table, he stood and threw down his napkin. "Unlike me, you were always easy to read."

"And you were always extremely judgmental. Righteous."

Jake stood silently, too angry to speak and too frozen in place to walk away. Here was his chance. What if he did listen, at least for a while?

"Is there a problem, sir?" The waiter appeared by his side, trying to minimize the disruption to the other diners. "I'd be happy to rewarm your breakfast."

"Don't bother. I've lost my appetite."

■ ■ ■

Cait walked slowly down the center aisle, carefully avoiding the tangle of extension cords. The formica tables stood three rows deep on each side. Each contained a personal computer. The machines softly hummed and beeped as they progressed through their start-up procedure. She moved among the handful of students already seated, distributing quick-reference cards.

The day already seemed endless, and it was only eight A.M. She and Nick had been busy since dawn, converting the BASC conference room into a makeshift training center. While they connected the machines, Nick filled her in on each person's level of experience. They'd challenge her from both ends of the spectrum today.

The employees ranged from university students to retired homemakers. Nick would bring the count to five. If his partner joined them she'd have an even half dozen. He was expected to arrive before the first break.

Cait flexed her neck and shoulder muscles. Too much, too fast. Hopefully the aspirin would kick in soon. Normally she arranged the equipment the night before, but today was anything but normal. Live demonstrations were always somewhat risky, this one more than most without her usual advanced planning.

Unfortunately for Cait, Brooke had a seat-of-the-pants approach, leaving everything to the last minute. Well, it wasn't Brooke's fault that her mother fell ill overnight. She owed her friend at least this much.

Cait flipped open her notebook and scribbled a few revisions to her opening comments. Taking a sip of coffee, she quickly reviewed the morning's agenda. A young hot-shot engineer, sipping espresso in the back row, caught her attention. He might prove to be a handful. She quickly pulled a set of challenge questions from her briefcase and tucked them beneath the original stack of materials. Those should help balance the scale.

Wanting to stay on schedule, she decided to begin. "Good morning, class. My name is Caitlyn James. Brooke sends her apologies. She's handling an emergency this morning. Promised to be here for the afternoon session, though.

"First let's look at the basic operation of the system. Place your floppy in the upper drive and push gently until it snaps into place."

"Excuse me, Ms. James, but my disk hits a brick wall when I put it in that little slot. I normally use the bigger one on the bottom. Maybe I'll try the lower one, just in case." The words trailed off as the older woman in a rayon-flowered dress, ducked beneath the table. Her right hand reappeared briefly as she fumbled along the tabletop for her bifocals.

Cait glanced at the cardboard name plaque on top of the machine. Margaret Sullivan. Administrator-extraordinaire, according to Nick. Could type 100 words a minute, when her computer was plugged in. With five children and a high school equivalency certificate, she was lucky to have this job. Cait was looking forward to meeting Nick's kindhearted partner who had taken a chance on Margaret. They had something in common.

"I'm afraid that won't work at all, Margaret." Cait joined her under the table and reached for the diskette. "Make sure the label is face up and pointing towards the back. Then slip it in, just like this." The soft click proved her point.

Rising to her feet, Cait glanced at the french-braided brunette across the aisle. Her menu was displayed perfectly.

Since her eyes contained empathy instead of criticism, Cait enlisted her help. "Would you mind assisting Margaret while I see why the screen in the back row is flashing?"

"Sure." The two women huddled together.

Cait's composure was a result of her last two years of teaching for OmniCorp. Her key to success was a combination of simple explanations and face-saving solutions. Raising twins required many of the same skills, plus infinite flexibility and patience. She was ready for anything, as long as it involved computers or teenagers. The back row contained the equivalent of both.

She crossed the room silently and stood behind the young engineering intern. Madonna was being painted on his screen in twenty lovingly accurate flesh tone colors. He didn't sense her presence until it was too late, then blushed as he tried to clear the screen. It kept on painting. She reached over his shoulder and pressed the delete key.

"Try to stay with us, please." Cait called his laughing co-workers back to attention. "Turn to page three. Follow along as I demonstrate."

She returned to the front of the room and pulled out a chair in front of the master PC. The mouse moved and clicked in rhythmic sequence across the screen as she explained each function. The image was projected behind her onto the far wall. "Now it's your turn to try."

Muffled snickers sounded again from the back of the room. Without missing a beat, Cait strolled over and bopped Hot-shot on the head with a roll of printout. Nick appeared in the doorway in time to observe the exchange.

"Sorry for the delay. How are things going?"

"With a little patience on everyone's part, we'll be into our first lab session soon."

"Great, then I'm just in time." The casual easiness of the

early morning hours was gone. Nick's eyes were locked on the young man. "Join me up front."

"Yes, sir."

As the intern scrambled to collect his things, Nick leaned close to whisper to Cait. "Another new hire. My partner saw a little of himself in this young man."

Cait suppressed her smile as Nick led the way to the front row. Now she was really looking forward to meeting Nick's partner. What an odd match they must be, this rough-around-the-edges construction boss and Mr. Softheart.

■ ■ ■

Jake pushed open the glass door bearing the name Brandon and Slater Construction. He scowled at the foot-high advertisement. Hopefully Brooke told Cait to enter via the parking garage. If she came through the lobby, his surprise would be blown. And, most likely, Ms. James would be long gone.

He rifled through his mail, sorting the urgent from the junk. Why was he delaying the inevitable? After this morning's breakfast, he should be ready to confront any adversary. His jaw tightened and he tossed down the letter, then drew a deep breath. The sooner the better.

The sound of her voice, hauntingly familiar, guided him towards the classroom. It varied from soothing to animated, making each student feel important. He had felt the same, while sipping juice with her in his kitchen. As if she was there just for him.

His footsteps hammered rapidly against the tile. He forced himself to slow down. What had brought about her abrupt change Saturday morning? Their ride back to town passed in uneasy silence, broken only by single-word answers. He had checked himself in the rear view mirror twice, thinking he had grown fangs and fur overnight. His gut reaction was to ignore it. Ignore her. Write the entire episode off like free tickets to a bad movie. But he couldn't. Maybe after he knew the answer, putting it behind him would be easier.

Luckily there was a good excuse for his being here today. He was neutral about Nick's selection of this software, but Caitlyn didn't know that. As he watched her from the darkened doorway, he reconfirmed his initial suspicion. He wasn't at all neutral about the software's support staff.

Cait's tapestry vest and crisply tailored blouse topped a slim gabardine skirt. Her hair was pulled back into a severe knot. Quite a change from her bedraggled appearance in his guest bed, Friday night.

He watched as she moved about the room with grace and precision, her long legs deftly sidestepping the wires. What if she fell? His pulse increased a notch. When she turned back toward the podium he stepped into the classroom, taking the empty seat in the last row. She knocked him off kilter. After years of enjoying his solitude, he was now preoccupied with thoughts of her sitting perched on his kitchen stool, wrapped in his robe. She had filled his big empty house with life, if only for a few hours. He wasn't ready to let that feeling go, yet.

"Will someone please turn off the front spotlights?" Busy fiddling with the overhead projector, she didn't look up. Jake reached back and flipped the switch, happy to oblige.

"Thanks. The last thing we'll look at before the next lab session is how to capture and magnify a single, three-dimensional image. This feature will be useful when doing up-close structural analysis."

Taking advantage of the darkness, Jake voiced his approval of the assignment. "Very useful, Ms. James. How close can one actually get?"

Her breath caught in her throat. It couldn't be. It was bad enough that his voice pierced her dreams at night. Did her subconscious have to seek him during the daylight hours, too?

The projector didn't shed enough light for her to distinguish who was sitting in Hot-shot's vacated seat. Nick's tenderhearted partner couldn't be the same man who refused to acknowledge her pursuit of the lodge, her dream for her youth group.

Her shaking fingers searched for the remote control. She forced herself to focus on the first slide. It seemed to be written in Swahili.

Nick's voice bought Cait a little time to think. "You're late, Jake, so pipe down. We'll bring you up to speed during the break."

"My apologies. I was detained at the auto body shop on my way in, checking on something for a friend. Please continue, Ms. James."

One and the same. Cait gripped the pointer, her nails biting into her palm. Someone owed her an explanation. She knew just which persistent matchmaker to start with. Keeping her voice steady, she recited the keystrokes needed for the first example. Thank goodness she could do so by rote. Soon the slides were flashing by, despite her finger sliding off the control button. As she revealed the mysteries of computing to her students, her mind worked on another mystery, the one who was watching her every move. Should she be flattered or furious? She needed time to compose herself and figure out a dignified escape.

Unfortunately, Lesson One was only twenty frames long.

■ ■ ■

She called for a break. When the aisle cleared, Jake moved to the front of the classroom. He was in no hurry, this time she couldn't run. That would mean breaking her commitment to BASC and to OmniCorp. Somehow he knew that was not in her character.

No, she'd stay. Maybe after she calmed down he could get her to explain what happened between them. The way he figured it, they had all afternoon.

Nick rose to make the introductions. "Cait, meet my partner Jake Brandon. Jake, Caitlyn James."

"How do you do?" She nodded stiffly, then looked away, searching for her purse to avoid his handshake. A fast exit was just what she needed, until her thoughts could be pulled together. Her heart pounded in her ears.

Jake almost laughed at her formality, but caught himself in time. After all, he had all night to prepare for this. He shouldn't gloat at her confusion. His answer was equally formal. "Pleased to meet you."

Nick raised his eyebrows at him, then quickly cleared his throat. "Cait is substituting this morning for our regular account rep, Brooke Hastings."

"Brooke. The name's familiar." Jake tapped his jaw for a moment, then extended his hand. "Welcome to Brandon and Slater Construction, Ms. James."

Cait let his carefully chosen words sink in, then stared at him in amazement. She never asked what the acronym stood for. Around the OmniCorp offices, Brooke pronounced it 'bask'.

"Ms. James stepped in on very short notice." Nick hurried his explanation. "Luckily for us, Brooke remembered that Cait taught this very same class recently."

Jake's mouth curved slightly upward at one corner. Amusement sparkled in his eyes as he seconded Nick's statement. "Very lucky indeed."

Cait smelled a rat. Two rats, in fact. On one hand she was flattered that he'd taken the time to set this up. It must have been him. If Brooke had recognized his name, she certainly would have spilled the beans. No, the switch must have been his idea. But why?

He could have called her. Perhaps invited her out to lunch. All the last-minute scurrying could have been avoided. No, wait. He had a house guest arriving. Someone who had the right to keep track of his whereabouts. Was this entire sham just a cover-up of some sort? The very idea made her angry enough to . . . what? She'd figure that out later, after class, when she was far enough away to think straight.

Loosening her clenched fist, she steadied her voice. "Thank you, Mr. Brandon. Believe me, being here with you this morning was really the very last thing I expected."

"I'm sure it was." Jake bit back a smile. "Personally, I try to be prepared for just about anything. You never know when you'll hit an unexpected turn in the road."

Cait gripped her handbag tighter and motioned to be let through. "If you'll both please excuse me? This is only a ten minute break."

Jake remained firmly in place, not yet ready to be dismissed. "I understand that you're teaching until noon?"

"Yes."

"Good. I could use some individual help, troubleshooting, after lunch. My workstation hasn't printed a single drawing since it arrived." He shrugged his shoulders, signaling technical futility.

She gritted her teeth and refrained from telling him what

he could do with his hard drive. If he looked any more innocent she would offer to buff his halo. "Mr. Brandon, I recommend that you ask Brooke to examine it after class. She's much more experienced with configurations such as yours."

The inflection of her voice made it sound like a four letter word. Jake bit his lower lip, trying to restrain an outright laugh. She gave as good as she got. Instead he furrowed his brow and regretfully shook his head. "Can't wait. Need it this afternoon."

"Maybe you could use another."

"They're all in the classroom." He snapped his fingers. "I've got an idea. I'll accompany you back to your office. You could set me up with a loaner, help me get started." He glanced over at Nick. "Wasn't that part of our service agreement?"

The eloquent skunk. No way was she spending one more minute with him than absolutely necessary.

Nick broke in, thumping Jake on the back. "Great idea. Cait's car is in the shop. I offered to run her back after lunch. But if you're already headed that direction, I'll use the time on something else. We'll reschedule lunch." Nick turned to go.

"Wait." Talk about disaster. All afternoon together? If the malfunction were small she would be delayed only a short while. If it were serious she'd recommend the unit be sent back. Her voice was all business. "Maybe it would be easier after all, if I just stayed a bit longer and looked at your machine. What is the exact nature of the problem?"

"No picture on the monitor."

Maybe something as simple as a loose wire? "It could be . . . "

"A dozen different things, Ms. James. Thank you for your promise to help." Jake took her hand and covered it with both of his, publicly sealing their agreement.

She glanced at Nick, he was also smiling. Why did she suddenly feel that, instead of escaping she had just walked into a finely crafted trap?

Jake released her hand and stepped aside so she could pass. They walked shoulder to shoulder towards the back of the room, Nick trailing behind. "We'll discuss the specifics later, Ms. James. See you at twelve-thirty." He turned to leave.

She stared at his retreating shoulders. Gone the rest of the morning? While she was still here, with free time on her hands if she worked through lunch? Nodding to Nick, she smiled and headed in the opposite direction. Who had the last laugh now?

■ ■ ■

As soon as they broke for lunch, Cait quickly gathered her things. She was going to search for the alleged non-working computer. On her way out she spied two orthopedic shoes sticking out into the aisle way. Margaret was under the table again. "Can I give you a hand?"

"I'm looking for the switch." Margaret's remaining words were muffled against the humming power unit.

"Here it is." With the toe of her pump Cait flipped off the power strip.

Margaret crawled out and stared for a moment, pushing her glasses back in place. "Oh, back there. Clever. Thanks, you're a life saver."

Cait extended her arm to help the administrator up. "Now you can give me a hand." Glancing swiftly around to make sure they were alone, Cait plunged ahead. "Do you know where I can find Mr. Brandon's machine? He told me it wasn't working properly."

"Talk about another savior." Margaret's sigh emphasized her obvious admiration. "He took a chance on me, when no one else would. Did I tell you . . ."

Cait interrupted her litany. "The directions, please?"

"Oh, of course. His office is the third door on the left. He seldom uses it, so go right in."

"He won't mind?"

"Heavens no. It's like a morgue in there. Always out in the field somewhere, or working at home. That dear boy works too hard, if you ask me." Margaret patted Cait's shoulder, dismissing her concern.

Cait hurried off. Once she was safely facing the other direction, she rolled her eyes at the mere thought of dear Saint Jacob.

■ ■ ■

There was no response to her knock. She tested the handle, then opened the office door. Stepping inside she took a deep breath. Instead of smelling the fresh air and wood smoke scent that surrounded Jake this weekend, the room reeked of furniture polish. Peeking out, she double-checked the name plate by the door. This was definitely the right one.

His office was sparsely furnished. Other than the professional licenses hanging on the far wall, there were no embellishments. She expected pictures, coffee cups, or least a few loose paper clips laying about. But, instead, his rich mahogany desk top was clean enough to perform surgery. Jake didn't work here very often, if at all.

So he'd made a special trip, just to see her? She was flattered. It was obvious he was a very busy man. Not only was Brandon and Slater a relatively new firm, but their business base was quickly increasing, according to Brooke. Thus the need for Omni's new design tool.

Cait spun around, just realizing what was missing from the scene. Anger seared through her. No matter what else she expected to find in his office, she figured there would be at least a computer terminal. Broken or otherwise.

"A hoax." She glanced under the desk. Not even one wire. Why such an elaborate excuse, and one so easy to figure out?

She hurried back to the training room, grabbed her briefcase and packed her things. She stepped into the hall, looked both ways, then glanced at her watch. She didn't want to risk running into Jake. Hopefully Brooke would arrive soon.

She approached the reception area and passed by his office quickly, then Nick's. Brooke's voice rang out from behind his partner's door, followed by burst of laughter.

"Is everyone in on this little joke but me?" Justifiably angry, Cait briskly flipped through the yellow pages. She desperately needed a cab.

Margaret took a lobby seat opposite her. Once her sandwich, apple and thermos were set out, she tucked her napkin beneath her chin. "Mind if I join you?"

Margaret didn't wait for a response before she rambled on. "I can't tell you how much I enjoyed your morning session. I only hope that this afternoon will be as easy to follow. You really have a way with words."

"Thank you." She quickly dialed the phone on the corner end table and made the arrangements.

Margaret continued to munch, then took a sip of coffee. "Did you find what you were looking for? Too bad Mr. Brandon didn't stick around a little longer. He would have been happy to help out. It's just like him, you see, doing something nice for someone else. It certainly made my day to see his smiling face again."

Cait blinked twice as she watched Margaret wave the peanut butter sandwich in the air. Nice wasn't the word she'd use to describe his surprise visit. She opened her portfolio and grabbed a slip of paper and a pencil.

As her companion continued to extol Jake's virtues, Cait wrote Brooke a nast-o-gram, then handed it to Margaret. "Would you please give this to Ms. Hastings when you see her?"

Margaret accepted the folded paper and slipped it beneath her thermos. She smiled and shook her head. "That Brooke, don't you just love her, too? Always wearing the latest fashion, right out of the Spiegel catalog, if I was to guess."

She lowered her voice and leaned closer to Cait. "Not everyone can wear off-white hose in public, you know." Margaret glanced down at her support stockings. "Why, if my calves were just a bit thinner, I'd join her." She sighed.

"Have her call me at the office, as soon as she has a chance."

"Sure, but . . ."

Cait stood and picked up her handbag. She stepped around the coffee table. "I'd better wait for my taxi near the front. Thanks for the company."

"Well, if you must." Margaret waved. "I enjoyed it, too. Bye."

When Cait reached the door it swung inward. Drawing back, she lifted her chin defiantly at the man blocking her path.

"Going somewhere?"

"Yes, my taxi's almost here. Please excuse me." She

stepped sideways, hoping to pass him.

"Don't we have an afternoon appointment?"

She looked at Jake in disbelief. His poker face required more audacity than even she thought he possessed. "Funny thing about that workstation. You have no PC. And every other computer in this building seems to be working fine."

"But . . ."

"I'm leaving." Securing her purse strap once again, she tried to step around him. The door to Nick's office opened behind her. Brooke's voice rang through the lobby. Caitlyn glared at her soon-to-be-ex friend.

"Hi." Brook shifted her case uneasily from one hand to the other. "Good to see you."

Cait was too angry to speak. Her nod was stiff.

Brooke continued, "Thanks for filling in for me."

"I wouldn't want your mother's cough to turn into pneumonia. Maybe I should send her a card."

Brooke blushed. Nick, not understanding where the friction was coming from, hurried to make the introductions. "Jake, have you met . . ."

"No, but we've spoken on the phone." Jake extended his hand. "Glad to finally meet you, face-to-face."

If Nick wasn't there Cait would have stopped the farce immediately. But there was no way she would risk her professional image on account of these two co-conspirators. Tightening her grip on her briefcase, she reached for the door. "I have to run. Brooke, call me later."

"What about your promise to examine my workstation?"

"What?" Brooke glanced from her friend to Jake. "But your machine . . ."

Cait cut in. She'd had enough help for one day. This she could handle herself. "I did agree to help. However, as I just pointed out, every terminal in this building is in perfect working order. Now, if you'll please excuse me."

Brooke's voice was low but poignant as she swung her gaze to Cait. "Jake has a remote."

"What?"

"His computer. It's not here."

Cait looked sharply at Jake.

"Sorry for the confusion." A smile slowly lifted the corners of his mouth. "I must have forgotten to mention that my primary office is at home."

He opened the door and stood aside. "After you."

Five

Caitlyn squared her shoulders and preceded Jake into the entryway. It was unbelievable that she was here at all, let alone so soon. She took a moment to survey the interior of the lodge from her new perspective.

The tall, vaulted ceilings and oversized recreation room were perfect for ping-pong on a rainy camp day. The rustic pine table and long bench seats in the dining hall could easily accommodate a dozen-and-a-half teenagers. Visions of disheveled campers, passing institution-sized serving platters down the length of the table, raced through her mind. She tightened her grip on her tool kit.

"Which way?" Her voice was sharper than intended. Hopefully her good humor would return after she repaired his workstation, and left the lodge for good.

"Follow me." Jake edged by. He walked down the hall and into the kitchen. Cait followed. The late afternoon sun was shining through the windows behind the breakfast nook.

She tried to refrain from looking at the bar stools pushed beneath the tiled counter, where they had shared their late night snack. It was too disturbing. Instead she scanned the cabinets. One was ajar, revealing row after row of perfectly stacked dinner plates. Enough for an army. The clues were so obvious, how had she missed them?

Setting her case down, Cait shoved her hands into her suit pocket. "Interesting. I don't know many customers who store their computers in the kitchen. Where's it hiding?"

"Upstairs." He opened the refrigerator and began rummaging. "I thought I'd fix us a drink first."

"Forget it." She took a step forward, fists on hips. "This is strictly business. If you think for a minute that I'm interested in shenanigans . . ."

Cait stopped short as Jake emerged with a tall pitcher. The amber liquid, complete with floating tea bags, was visible through the clear plastic. His eyes narrowed as he stared at her. A crimson flush stained her cheeks. "I thought . . ."

"You thought wrong." His gaze continued to hold hers. "Again."

Turning away, he grabbed two glasses and filled them with ice. "There's still some juice left, if you'd prefer. From the other night."

She didn't need to be reminded. The intimacy of sharing their hopes and dreams, while wearing two halves of one pajama set, still caused her pulse to race at unguarded moments. She forced her voice to remain steady. "Iced tea is fine. The colder, the better."

Did it sound as if she were requesting a cold shower? Backing away rather than causing further embarrassment to herself, Cait grabbed the tool kit. "If you'll point me in the right direction, I'll get started."

"Up the stairs. Right instead of the usual left. First door."

The 'usual left.' As if living here in his guest room was becoming a habit. She started forward, but halfway down the hall she stopped.

She had misjudged him, twice. First, she accused him of fabricating the entire computer problem, just to delay her. Then the confusion over the drinks. She owed him an apology.

Retracing her steps, she found him staring at the doorway. Straightening her shoulders she plunged ahead. "I doubted your story, and your intentions. I'm sorry. It just seemed . . ."

"Save it." His jaw was set in a hard line. "Go on up. I'll follow with the drinks in a minute."

Cait nodded, then quickly left the room.

■   ■   ■

Crossing his arms, Jake leaned back against the counter. He was a worse bastard than even he thought possible. Her instincts were right, just a bit off target.

All he wanted was a few more hours together, to find out why she ran off so abruptly the other morning. He also wanted . . . what? Couldn't quite put a name to it. Just a longing to know more about her, to spend more time with her. To see where things might lead.

He squeezed his temples, trying to sort things out. This place, his sanctuary, was now a rat's nest of confusion. He looked up at the ceiling. His ruse would be revealed by now. Time to face the music.

■ ■ ■

Cait opened the door he'd indicated. She stopped, taking a deep breath. She knew that it was the master suite, but it was so overwhelmingly masculine. And inviting. A refuge from the outside world.

The furnishings were a subtle blend of cobalt blue, heather grey and warm oak. The room's centerpiece, a king-sized bed with a floor-to-ceiling bookcase built in to the headboard, drew her gaze. The right hand shelves were filled with a variety of hardback novels, both current and classic. The left side was empty.

Forcing her eyes away, she noted the stone fireplace with a dozen odd-sized pictures gracing the mantle. She left the door ajar and walked around the reclining chair to take a closer peek. The snapshots were of vacant ski slopes, all except for one. The exception was of a woman, the wind blowing her dark wavy hair as she raced through moguls. Her form and grace were exceptional. His lover?

She raised her chin and turned. Time for the task that she'd been brought here to do. To her right was an alcove filled with boxes. They were still sealed with strapping tape, bearing the dealer's name. OmniCorp.

She set her tool kit on the floor and walked over to his desk. His machine didn't work? It'd never been out of the box.

Her hands balled into tight fists. He'd tricked her, let her believe . . . no wait. Stop imagining the worst. There must be a reason. She drew a deep breath and tried to imagine some other possibility.

She ran her nail slowly along her bottom lip. Maybe he didn't know the first thing about computers and was too embarrassed to say so. What if he were desperate and had no one to ask? No one he could trust, except for her. His 'friend.'

That word was like a bitter pill, but Cait swallowed it anyway. She wouldn't betray his trust. It was her own silly fantasy that she might have become more. She removed her suit jacket then pushed up her sleeves.

It was time to get to work.

■ ■ ■

Jake paused in the doorway. He had expected Cait to come barrelling down the steps, demanding to be taken home. Instead she was prone, halfway under his desk. Her shoes were kicked off and her blazer was tossed carelessly on his bed. The boxes were sliced open and manuals were strewn about.

He cleared his throat. "I'd like to explain."

"No need."

Her voice was muffled, but pleasant. Not at all what he'd been expecting.

"Do you have a flashlight? I'm looking for the nearest outlet. The lighting is poor under here."

"Sure." He grabbed the emergency light from his nightstand, then crossed the room. The slit of her long, slim skirt would soon reveal more than just leg. What had he started, with this scheme?

"Come out from under there. I don't want you hitting your head again." He knelt beside her and peered under the desk. "Let me do that."

She wiggled free, turned over and sat up. She smacked

the palms of her hands against each other. "You don't have enough outlets. We're going to need a power strip." Cait pulled herself to her feet. "I'm not sure what box that's packed in. Let's unload the equipment first, so I can see exactly what pieces we've got here."

"Fine." Where was the bristling anger that he expected? He watched her curiously as they worked side by side. As Jake lifted, she checked for packing slips and tossed boxes out of the way. He kept waiting for the inevitable questions, but they never came. He couldn't figure out why she had accepted this situation without argument.

They cleared the top of his desk and placed the workstation into position. Jake crawled under the desk to plug in the strip. "Ready." He backed out, but remained seated on the floor. She was standing too close for him to move. His face was halfway between waist and skirt hem level.

"I'll turn it on." She leaned over the desk.

He swallowed hard and simply nodded. She was referring to the computer, because he was already purring. He stared at the softly textured gabardine, inches from his face, wondering how much closer she would move before he reached out and grabbed her. He placed both palms flat on the floor.

"It looks good. You have the right amount of memory."

Boy, did he. And he was remembering the sight of her long, bare legs right before he covered them up with his robe.

She looked down, then knelt beside him. He wanted to close his eyes, but didn't.

"Jake?"

He cleared his throat. "Yeah?"

"The system's quite simple to use. Come on up. I'll take you through the basic steps."

Right. Ignoring her outreached palm, he grabbed the edge of the desk and stood. Better to keep all his appendages, hands included, to himself.

"Sit here." She was motioning to the single swivel chair. If he took it, she would be standing behind him for the lesson. At least her legs would be out of view. "Fine."

"I have a spare tutorial in my briefcase. We can run through it together."

He cleared his throat. "Your case is still in the truck. I'll go get it." This was the break that he needed. The fresh air would do him good.

His pager beeped, interrupting his escape. Unclipping it from his belt, he frowned at the number it displayed. "My foreman for the Cougar Mountain home."

"You take care of business. I'll be right back." He watched silently as she slipped her jacket on.

He nodded and tossed her the keys. This worked, too. A few moments alone would do him a world of good. Sitting at the desk he drew a deep, relaxing breath, then dialed. He listened closely to the problems with their concrete contractor, trying to drive Cait from his mind.

While he listened, he idly slipped the diagnostics diskette into the appropriate slot. He was midway through configuring the machine when Cait arrived back upstairs.

■ ■ ■

Not wanting to interrupt his call, Cait waited by the doorway, watching as he clicked from screen to screen. He selected options and interpreted computer jargon like a highly trained technician. When the call to the foreman ended he set down the phone and resumed typing.

He didn't need her help. What was really going on?

Cait's voice faltered as she spoke from the hallway. "Why am I here?"

Jake's hands stilled at the keyboard. Funny she should ask him that now. Surely the unopened boxes spelled out his intention. He wanted her here, with him.

Slowly he met her eyes, not sure how to begin. "It was the only way."

"To do what?"

Pushing back his chair, he stood. "To spend more time with you, where you couldn't run off." Jake walked towards the door. Cait put down her briefcase and brushed both hands against her skirt.

"Run off? What about your blasted privacy?"

He continued towards her. "Ever since Friday night I've pictured you here. Warming my kitchen and brightening my home. I thought that you'd refuse, if I asked outright."

He stood before her, almost toe-to-toe. Her wild ginger scent jogged his memory, making him want to pull her close. Looking down into her eyes, he saw that she was wary of him. No wonder. He was stalking her as if she were tonight's main course. Taking a step back, he rested one shoulder against the doorjamb.

She exhaled the breath she'd been holding. "You hated my being here."

"No."

"I invaded your sanctuary. You snarled and snapped whenever I came into sight."

He reached out and let his free hand trail down her arm. When he reached her fingertips he captured them and drew them to his lips. His breath was warm as it whispered against her skin. "There's never been another woman here. It disturbed me more than I wanted to admit. After you left the house was too quiet."

She pulled her hand back. "I wanted to be gone before your live-in lover arrived."

"My what?"

"You heard me. Or should I say, I heard you?" She stepped past him and began collecting her instruments. "I couldn't help but overhear. Who you choose to have living here is none of my business."

Pausing for a moment, he recalled bits of the early morning conversation. He forced back a smile. "Actually, you're right. There is someone moving in."

"The love of your life, if I remember correctly. The one you invited to stay forever." She hastily threw screwdrivers and pliers into her tool kit. Kicking one box aside, she reached for her spare cable.

Jake crossed to the mantle and picked up the photograph of the solo skier. "This is the young lady. She'll be here in a couple of weeks."

"What did you have in mind for me, then? To fill in for a while?" Shoving the chair into the desk, she reached beyond it for her purse.

Jake moved closer, trapping her in the office alcove. He held the picture out for her examination. She refused to take it, lifting her chin. "I'm in a hurry."

"I drove." He tapped the frame, calling it to her attention again. "Her name is Jackie."

"How nice."

"Jackie Brandon."

Her gaze dropped to the photo, then raised to meet his. "Wife?"

He silently shook his head.

A small glimmer of hope shot through her. "Sister?"

"Daughter. Named after me." He grinned. "As close as I could get, given she's a girl."

With his free hand, he pulled out his wallet and flipped it open. "Here's a close up, taken in the ninth grade." He held the two side-by-side. "Her mother is remarrying and moving east. I agreed to let her live with me, despite my reservations."

She swallowed. "Your privacy?"

"Hell, no." He flipped the wallet closed and stuffed it back into his pocket. He stared at the picture frame. "It's a huge responsibility, being a custodial parent. My child-rearing skills are rusty."

"Better take another look. She's no child."

"Just turned fifteen."

Cait softened towards him. He had a lot to learn. "Instead of being her baby sitter, you'll be educational counselor, moral leader, and love-life advisor. All rolled into one."

His eyes widened. "She's too young to be dating!"

"Think again." Cait laughed. "My girls are sixteen and have been going out with boys, in group situations, for more than a year."

"I still think I'm safe. No boys around here, anyway." Setting the photo down, he ran his fingers through his hair and began to pace. "In fact, there's no one around here at all, except for Kelly's kids. In the past, summers have been lonely for Jackie. She'll have to wait until school starts to meet a few people her own age."

Cait's eyes sparkled with an idea. "It doesn't have to be that way. She could join my daughters' youth group."

He shook his head. "Would never work. My only interest in churches is maybe to build one someday."

"That doesn't matter. Your daughter could still participate and make lots of new friends. We'd be happy to include her." She paused for a second. "Our next big activity is the upcoming camp-out."

He stopped pacing and looked quickly over at Cait. "The one at your house?"

"Somewhere." She smiled slightly.

He furrowed his brow and slowly walked towards her, one hand stuffed into his back pocket. "Look, I left a few details out the other night when you asked about the lodge."

"I know. I saw the sign."

It was his turn to be surprised. "You didn't say a word."

"No need. You made your position quite clear. No trespassing."

She hadn't thrown the omission in his face. How refreshing to find a woman that wasn't a whiner, like Victoria, or revengeful like his mother. He cupped her chin in his hand and studied her.

Her skin was warm and smooth against his thumb. He drew it across her lower lip. Their eyes met and held. "More worried about footprints across my heart, than across my floors."

His breath caressed her face as he lowered his head. "Is it too late for me to reconsider?" he asked.

"Or for me?"

"Never too late." He smiled, then eliminated the gap between them.

His mouth tenderly brushed hers, promising much but demanding nothing. So different from his commanding personality and hard, rugged appearance. Just perfect. She let herself be drawn into the sensation.

Much too soon, the kiss ended and her eyes met his again. Was he giving her room to think, and the freedom to pull away? To call a halt to this before any more passion grew between them?

As she took her time deciding, his lips gently tasted hers

again, kissing each corner before returning to the center. Yes, he was definitely asking, rather than making a statement.

She answered by leaning into him.

His arms tightened. He deepened the kiss, parting her lips and letting his tongue taste hers for the first time. It had been ages since he had wanted to really let go. To let someone into his life. To share both the good and the bad. Now here she was in his bedroom, heating his blood and making his heart pound.

He felt her heart respond, beating a furious rhythm against his chest as he held her close. She snuggled her length full against him, her body fitting perfectly to his.

It felt right, but it had been a long time since he'd been with a woman. The same for Cait, judging from her comments. It wouldn't be fair to let this progress too quickly.

He drew back, cupping her chin once again. She loosened her grip and let her hands rest lightly against his shoulders. He raised her chin and met her eyes, then smiled. "It's a deal, on one condition."

Her voice faltered. A shiver of dread passed down her spine. "What condition?" Was this how men negotiated these days? The way she felt at this very moment he could probably ask, and receive, anything.

"You'll need to advise me. I don't know a blasted thing about dealing with a 1990's teenager." He smiled and rested his forehead against hers.

"Of course."

"Great. Then you've got yourself a lodge. And I've got my very own 'Dear Abby.'" He gave her a quick kiss on the tip of her nose, then released her. "Let's get you home."

She shook her head in amazement as Jake picked up her briefcase and tool kit, then motioned toward the door. A few moments ago, as she clung to him and merged her breath with his, he held the afternoon's destiny in his hands. And his choice? He was taking her home.

His actions told her that he wanted more than just one afternoon together. He turned, reaching out to her. She smiled and interlaced her fingers with his.

■ ■ ■

"You're actually going to do it? What about his live-in lover?"

"Shh!" Cait scanned the hallway for eavesdroppers. "The office will think I'm planning an orgy, or worse."

Brooke leaned closer, raising her eyebrows in mock horror. "Give me a clue. What could be worse?"

"Get in here." Cait linked her arm with her friend's, ducked into her office, then shut the door. It was barely closed before Brooke started in again.

"I just can't believe you're going through with it, that's all." She gave Cait's shoulders a quick shake. "Just think. A fresh beginning."

"Stop, will you?" Cait stepped away and crossed to her desk. Picking up a stack of letters from her in-basket, she sorted through them. She paused when she saw an interoffice memo, signed by Geoff Martin.

"Look at this. Says he'll be gone to the Portland office for a few days for a corporate meeting. Geoff gone. Now, that's the first bit of good news I've heard for a while." Cait looked up and glanced over at her friend. "Other than your mother's swift recovery, that is."

Brooke smiled sweetly at the reference, then read the letter Cait was holding. "Actually, I've heard that several of the top Sales Representatives from each office will be attending. Something big is in the works. Rumor mill has it that a restructuring is being considered. New positions, new opportunities. This could be your chance."

"I doubt it." Cait reached for the letter and scanned it again. There was a time, when first starting out at OmniCorp, that she'd dreamed of progressing quickly up the corporate ladder. It was tied to her desire to provide a secure future for her girls. But lately she closely protected any free time she had, in order to be involved in their lives. She wanted to provide opportunities for them they otherwise wouldn't have. Her taking on the youth group was just one example. She was no longer sure she'd be willing to trade her free evenings for business any longer. Fortunately her career, and her standing with OmniCorp, had never been tied to a decision like that.

"Not that I wouldn't be pleased to be asked, but I haven't exactly seen my name on any invitation list." She shoved the memo back into the stack. "One less thing to worry about, from my viewpoint."

"But no one's better qualified. If it weren't for you Martin would be selling used cars instead of computer systems."

"Tell him that, would you? It will make his day."

"For right now why don't you just brighten mine a bit. Tell me more about you, Jake, and his offering you the secluded mountain home."

Cait tried to keep her tone calm. "I'm just borrowing the lodge for one weekend, not signing a pre-nuptial agreement."

"I know, I know." Brooke edged closer, unable to stop smiling. "But the last time I saw you with him, you were ready to spit fire. At both of us."

"You, my close-but-not-so-trusted friend, deserved it."

Cait looked up from the mail. "I still can't believe you set me up like that."

"He was the one who called with the arrangements. Not the other way around." Brooke placed a hand over her heart and started a quick tap-tap-tap. "That should say something. I know it does to me."

Cait turned away and switched on her terminal. She watched as the memory count spiraled upward, faster than her eyes could track. Her pulse raced exactly the same way yesterday afternoon, when Jake pulled her into his arms. Sitting down, she swiveled her chair absently back and forth.

"Hello." Brooke waved a hand in front of Cait's face. "Are you still with me?"

"Unfortunately, yes." Cait halted the chair, tossing the correspondence onto her desk. She tried clearing her voice of all emotion. Pure business. "Actually, Jake and I are just being practical. He's looking for nice, relatively-safe friends for his daughter, I need a cheap alternative for the upcoming camp-out. That's called a 'win-win' situation, my friend."

"I know what it's called, a smoke screen." Brooke sat on the edge of the desk, rotating Cait's chair with one foot until they were face-to-face. "Rewind about thirty seconds worth. Did you say his daughter?"

She nodded. "Jackie's moving here permanently. She arrives a week from Friday."

"But why?"

"Jake's taking over custody. Her mother's remarrying and moving east."

Brooke crossed her arms. "Let's hope it's to the Far East. Your chances will be much better."

"Stop." She raised her voice several notches louder, hoping to get her point across. "Get this straight. Two nights at his place. That's all I'm interested in, then I'll be gone."

A quick knock on the door broke off their discussion. Geoff turned the handle and poked his head in the doorway. He gave the two women a lazy grin.

Brooke sighed. "I thought I told you to stay on your own side of the building, Martin? Don't they have enough for you to do in marketing these days?"

"Ladies, I feel obligated to inform you that you're standing beneath the central air-conditioning duct." He pointed towards the ceiling and winked.

Brooke and Cait looked quickly upward, then at each other. Cait covered her shocked expression with both hands.

"As much as I enjoyed hearing about Cait's new love 'em and leave 'em two-night stand policy, I'd much prefer to discuss it in private." He winked and let his gaze move slowly down her slender frame. "When can you squeeze me in? Hopefully before my trip. If you do, maybe I can put in a good word for you while I'm there."

Cait clenched her fists. "Of all the unprofessional comments."

"Now, now. I didn't start this. And as proof of what a gentleman I am, I'm willing to move this entire conversation to after-hours." He feigned a half-smile, his eyes remaining zeroed in on Cait. "We do have several customer files we need to review sometime. Tonight's as good as any, for me. What do you say?"

Laying a hand on her friend's shoulder, Brooke stopped Cait from rising. "Ignore him. He's all talk."

"I know, but it's insulting." As Geoff's latest target, Cait had to deal with him on a day-to-day basis. She was the prime technical support for his accounts. There would be no easy escape until the next unsuspecting female captured his attention. Cait mentally adjusted her lunch hour schedule, swearing to buy a pocket recorder that very day. She need only lay the dictaphone on her desk, and point to the record button. The impending threat would cool his approach.

Brooke continued to pat her shoulder. "Come on. He's not worth it."

"Oh, I beg to differ. Cait, I could definitely make it worth your time."

"Okay, so I was wrong." Brooke withdrew her grip on Cait's shoulder. "Get him."

"Do you want to throw something, or should I?"

"Let's both do the honors."

"Is this heavy enough?" Cait selected a system reference manual from the bookcase.

"Might be." Brooke shrugged. "Let's give it a try."

"I'm leaving, I'm leaving." Geoff closed the door, then reopened it just a crack. "But remember, the offer stands. I don't leave until Wednesday."

The document sailed across the room, hit the wood, then thumped to the floor. The echo of laughter followed him down the hall.

■   ■   ■

The church's ground floor classroom echoed with excited teenage voices. Cait endured the noise with a smile, opening the windows wide. Standing back, she breathed in the warm evening air. Almost summer, let them celebrate. After all, good news like this wasn't announced every day.

"All right, time to listen up." Cait rapped her knuckles against the white board. "Now that the retreat is a 'go,' we have a lot of planning to do. Let's get to it. There's only one month left."

Chairs scraped against the linoleum as everyone took a seat.

"We'll be staying at the Raging River Lodge. It's near the town of Snoqualmie, in the Cascades."

"Cool!"

"Is there a rope swing?"

"Can we stay for a full week?"

"I don't know the details yet, but I'll try to bring a few photos to our next meeting. There'll definitely be canoeing and, of course, our traditional campfire. And no, we're not staying longer than the weekend."

"Can we run the Iron Man contest, like last year?"

"Yeah, can we Mom?"

"Without a doubt. That's one of my favorites too, Rose." Cait picked up her clipboard containing the original sign-up sheet. "There are two large dorm rooms with four bunks apiece."

She paused, expecting the several hands that shot up, Lynn's included. It was the dreaded fear of all teenagers, and she put their anxieties immediately to rest. "Yes, there are plenty of showers and electrical outlets."

She smiled and walked around to the front of the varnished table. Leaning against it, she rested one foot on a front row chair. Her pencil tapped out each name as she re-counted the list. "We already have seven young ladies and five young men registered."

"You mean 'boys.'" Someone smacked a notebook against another's shoulder. Giggles and hoots of laughter followed. Cait stood and placed herself between the two culprits, hands on her hips. "Pipe down, and show a little more respect to each other, please."

"Yes, Ma'am." The words resounded in duplicate.

"That's better. Any more antics and you'll both be on permanent KP duty. Together." She nodded for emphasis, then retook her spot against the table. "The owner's daughter, Jackie Brandon, will be joining us. Anyone else wanting to bring friends, get me their names soon. I'd like to keep the numbers to fifteen or less, or else we'll need more chaperones."

Boos and hisses rang through the crowd. Cait just smiled, expecting that, too. "Those are the district rules, you know. Take these permission slips home tonight and return them next Sunday night."

As the stack of paper made the rounds, she began writing on the board. "Here are the committees. Meal planning, workshops, contest prizes, and entertainment. Sign up for one or two, but remember, not everyone can be on entertainment." Cait stepped back. There was a mad rush for the markers.

"Ms. James!"

She turned towards the door. One of the church elders stood there, quilting block clenched in her hand. Seeing the outraged expression on Pamela Sydow's face, she hurried over. If this widow were planning to have a coronary tonight, Cait didn't want to fuel the fire. "Yes?"

The crimson red lips puckered before delivering their assessment of her senior high meeting. "You seem to have forgotten that the Ladies' Quilting Circle is meeting upstairs tonight." Her foot tapped an impatient rhythm.

Cait gave Pamela an apologetic smile. "Sorry if we've disturbed you." She flinched as a chair behind her fell over.

Turning, she saw ten instantly contrite faces staring back. Rose apologized for the entire group. Pamela nodded and the teens scurried to take their seats. Cait took the widow by the elbow and ushered her out the door, closing it behind her.

"As I was saying, Mrs. Sydow, the noise is certainly unintentional. The extra energy is coming from the good news I told the group tonight."

"What good news, may I ask?"

Not the Second Coming, Cait thought, but she might as well relay the information, anyway. "This year we won't have to hold our camp-out on the church grounds. I found an honest-to-goodness mountain lodge for us to use."

Mrs. Sydow's eyes narrowed with skepticism. "Is this how you spend your mission money?"

"Oh, no. The lodge is being donated."

Pamela's eyes were now just slits, amid a sea of disapproval lines. Cait hurried to put one hand behind her back, crossing her fingers, before offering further defense. "Donated by an upstanding member of the business community."

Well, Jake was standing, the last time she saw him.

"I'm not sure this will be approved."

"I've already run this entire idea by Council Chair, Audra Stockton. I'll be submitting all of the appropriate paperwork to the Council of Youth Activities, so everything will be in proper order. As usual, the council will do its own independent, and complete, background check."

Mrs. Sydow was still perturbed. Caitlyn smiled sweetly. "Certainly you agree that the CYA will do a thorough job?"

"This will never go through." The older woman shook her head. "You're young. You'll learn. After you've been here longer."

"At least I'm trying. You don't see any other parents in here, do you?" Cait stopped and marshaled as much warmth as she could. Her tone softened. "As you may recall from your own child-rearing days, this is a tough age to keep interested."

"Well, there's no point in providing the wrong things for them to be interested in, either." One eyebrow lifted.

"Unnecessary temptations."

"Maybe you'd like to be one of our chaperones? I could certainly use an extra hand, and you could see for yourself.

"Me? Traipsing around in the mountains? Not likely." Pamela waved her quilting square at Cait. "We'll talk again. I have friends on the council, you know."

Six

"How was your flight?" Jake slung the carry-on bag over his shoulder. He slipped his other arm around his daughter and steered her towards baggage claim.

"Super. It's great to be here." Jackie pressed closer to her dad's side. "The last few nights were awful."

"Hard to say goodbye to sunny L.A.?"

"Heck, no. Who wants skin cancer anyway?"

He traced her sunburned cheeks then tweaked her peeling nose. "Obviously, you do." The bag began to slip. He resettled it.

"Oh, that. So I overdid my one last outing to the beach." She scrunched her face, trying to get a peek at the damage, then shrugged. "Actually it was Mom who was driving me nuts, checking my suitcases over and over. And you should have seen her at the airport. She was a nervous wreck. It seemed like forever until they called my row number."

"I thought the airlines let kids board first."

"Dad!"

Jake watched her eyes widen as she drew back. Her movement caught him off guard and the shoulder bag slipped again. Jake looked at her, perplexed. "What?"

"I'm fifteen. Not a kid."

"Of course not." Re-hoisting the tote, he secured his arm around her again. "You and I know that, but couldn't you have kept it a secret until you were on board?" Leaning close, he lowered his voice. "The early boarders get the pillows."

He hugged her to him and she flashed him a smile. That was a close one. He might not be able to think of a come-back next time. He'd better get the knack of this, fast.

The traffic was unusually light for a Friday night at SeaTac airport. Jackie's suitcases were some of the first on the carousel. He retrieved them. Within minutes they were on the freeway, headed north.

As he drove she filled the time with non-stop conversation. It was as if she'd left Seattle only yesterday, instead of nine months earlier. Jake couldn't help notice the obvious physical differences. Braces off, Jackie smiled and laughed as she related story after story without the self-consciousness of the previous summer. Her bangs, now fully grown out, were pulled back off her face with a large metallic clip. Last year he had the feeling she was trying to hide beneath them.

He glanced at her and caught her staring. Was her tongue getting tired or had she asked a question? "Earth to Dad. Come in, please."

"What?" He'd better stop reminiscing and pay closer attention.

"I said, you haven't asked me anything about William yet."

Like what? Jake thought. His ex-wife's fiancé was financially secure, a respectable banker several years her senior. Someone who not only would enjoy escorting Tory to business dinners, but also would gain professional benefit from doing so. Jake remembered feeling smug when he first saw Jackie's photograph of her mother with her gray-haired companion.

What was his daughter really asking? He turned to study her. She was looking away from him, out the window. A light bulb went on in his mind. He was slow and inexperienced, but better late than never.

"From what I've heard, William's an all-right guy. He's provided the security and stability that your mom wanted and that you needed." He saw her spine stiffen and quickly amended his statement. "Needed when you were younger, of course." She hunched forward again and snapped her gum.

Pure luck. He decided to turn the tables. "What do you think of him? Is he fun to be with?"

"Well . . ."

It was amazing how just four characters could be stretched into so many syllables. He waited.

"He's not like you."

"I hope not."

"He's kinda boring. Takes me to museums instead of ball games. Reads *Business Week* instead of *Sports Illustrated.* Stuff like that." She knitted her eyebrows as if suddenly suspicious. "Do you know he's never eaten at McDonald's or worn shorts? I wonder what he's hiding." She tapped her finger against her lower lip.

Jake laughed. "No wonder your mother loves him. He sounds just like her."

Jackie flopped back against the seat and crossed her arms. When she spoke next her voice was soft. "But she used to love you. At least that's what she said."

She did? His smile instantly disappeared; he was thankful it was dark. Nice that Tory remembered, after the heartbreak of their divorce. In the beginning there was enough love between them to warm an entire room, not to mention sizzle the sheets. But that was years ago. Since then there had been many mistakes on both sides.

He shifted uncomfortably in his seat. Things were changing, all around him. Recently he and Victoria had been able to set aside their bitterness. They tried to be civil, if not downright amicable, for Jackie's sake. The animosity was gone. It took two to make, or break, any marriage. He drew a deep breath. How could he explain it without pointing out Tory's blind ambition or his failure, no, his refusal to meet her expectations? At times guilt at not trying harder nagged at him, just as she used to do in living color. "People change, honey. In your mom's and my case we married young, then grew apart. Became interested in different things."

"Couldn't you have stayed in love forever, instead of moving away?" Her voice caught and she paused before finishing. He barely heard her last words. "Instead of leaving me behind."

He reached out in the darkness and covered her hand with his. This was a difficult conversation, especially while driving. He could wait until they reached home, but it would be a painful thirty minutes. For both of them.

Squeezing her hand, he answered the best he could. "Leaving you with your mom was the worst part. But I focused on what was the best for you, not for me. Growing up in a household with fighting parents, as I did, would have been a nightmare. Trust me."

"Grandma and grandpa?"

He nodded. "I moved here to figure out a few things in my life."

Turning, he caught the glimmer of tears sparkling in her eyes. He lightened his voice. "Listen, you're my only girl, aren't you? I love you with all my heart. And now we're going to live together for, oh, let's say the next twenty years or so. Until you're old enough to start dating and possibly get married yourself."

"Possibly?"

He nodded. "Only if I approve."

She wiped at her eyes and looked at him in surprise. "Did I hear you right? Twenty years? You've got to be kidding!"

"Okay, maybe fifteen."

"Get real. I'll be over the hill by then." She withdrew her hand playfully and punched his shoulder. "Like you, Dad."

"Guess you'll have to help me along, then." He was relieved to see her smiling again.

They rode silently together. When he signalled to exit, he looked out over the thickly forested mountains, bathed in moonlight. This was his home. It felt good to know he was going to share it with someone he loved. Why had he been so reluctant before to give up his freedom? At the moment he didn't view it that way at all.

"Then what?"

Glancing sideways he took in her expression. This habit of hers, starting a conversation out of thin air, caught him off-guard again. "I need a hint, darling. What are we talking about now?"

"Those things you wanted to figure out when you moved here. After you find all the answers, then what are you going to do?"

Good question, one he had personally avoided for years. "I don't know yet. I'm still working on it."

"Will you get remarried, like mom?"

He downshifted too soon and the vehicle lurched. In a rush to cover his mistake, he switched on the wipers instead of the turn signal. Hopefully Jackie was considering a law degree in her future. She'd be good at cross-examination.

"Someday, maybe."

"Any girlfriends?"

"Is that your business, young lady?"

"It would be, if she wanted us to move." Her voice broke. "Maybe she'd just want you to move, and for me to get lost."

Jake watched his daughter across the darkened car. The evenly spaced lampposts created a strobe light effect on Jackie's worried face. He reached for her, this time catching her shoulder instead of her hand. "I moved often enough as a kid to last my entire life. From here on out, I'm staying put."

She leaned into him, across the console, looking up from beneath her lashes. "Did you hate it?"

He nodded. Rarely had he considered spilling his guts to another person. Now he wanted to. Funny, Cait invoked in him exactly the same feeling. Was he mellowing in his old age? And why now, after all this time?

"Here's the deal. Some evening, when our fishing poles are in the water and there's a full moon on a cloudless night, I'll tell you all about it over hot cocoa. Sound good?"

"Yeah." She smiled. He had remembered that was one of her favorite activities from last summer.

"This house will withstand time itself." Jake drew her closer. "It's yours and mine together, for as long as you want to stay. I'm not going anywhere."

Driving down the last stretch of road, he rested his cheek against the thick, wavy hair that was so like his own. "And if any front-running marriage candidates come along, they'll have to feel the same way, too."

■ ■ ■

Jake unlocked the front door and pushed it wide. Jackie raced inside.

"I can't believe I'm really here." She twirled around, arms extended. Her smile was radiant.

"Believe it, darlin', and move aside. Your suitcases must be filled with bricks."

She ignored him and darted across the recreation room. Standing before the sliding glass doors, she exhaled deeply. "Exactly how I remembered it."

Jake looked about the room and gritted his teeth, thinking about the unpacked boxes still in his attic. He spent so little effort making it a home. That was about to change.

Setting her bags down, he joined her by the patio entrance. "A few additions. A new fence on the west side. Plus I've restocked the lake."

"Trout?"

He nodded. "And now for a surprise." He unlatched the door and they stepped onto the deck. He pointed to the far corner. "Tell me what you think."

She spied the sunken hot tub immediately. Spinning on her heels, she wrapped him in a quick bear hug. "Wow! It'll be really great after a long hike or day of paddling." She drew back. "Can we put a TV out here? Maybe a phone?"

"No, and no." He patted the top of her head. "We could throw a few steaks on the grill, though, then hop in. What do you say?"

"Great." She darted off to lift the covering and test the water.

Jake called after her. "It was just installed Monday. I've been wanting to try it out myself."

"You're kidding. That was ages ago." She shook her head slowly. "Unbelievable. We'll start work on your priorities, right away, after I find my swimsuit. Race you up?"

He laughed. "You go ahead, I'll start the coals."

"But who'll carry up those heavy bags?" She tilted her head towards the entryway.

"Whoever packed them. Not this old man."

"No way!"

"Way." He'd heard that on some show recently, before he flipped the channel. Jackie laughed and ran off.

He drew a deep breath and listened to the silence, broken only by the sound of croaking frogs. It was destined to be a very high-energy summer. He glanced across before his gaze settled on the smooth, moonlit lake. His head already hurt from keeping up with her endless conversation and tireless movements. Nonetheless, he enjoyed it. It felt right.

As he reentered the house he saw that two of the cases were gone. A smile curved his lips. Say one thing, do another. Something else to get used to. Grabbing the remaining bag, he climbed the steps. She was sprawled across her bed reading a teen magazine. He stopped in his tracks.

It had been a while since he'd been in this room. He could still envision Cait lying beneath the comforter, unconscious, her hair spread across the pillow. The agonizing minutes that seemed like hours, before Kelly arrived.

Caitlyn. The first of two small hurricanes that suddenly blew into his life. But, unlike Jackie's turbulent arrival, there was an underlying peacefulness whenever Cait was near. Despite the fireworks when she was in his arms.

"Am I in the wrong room or something? You're looking at me really weird, Dad."

"No. Just wondering if I'm going to be testing out the new hot tub alone."

"Sorry. I forgot." She closed the magazine and hopped off the bed.

Jake set her suitcase on the loveseat and quickly collected his thoughts. Cait was visiting tomorrow with her girls, to help ready the lodge for their camp-out. He'd have to break the news to Jackie soon. Over dinner. Somehow.

■ ■ ■

The stars were out in full, glittering splendor by the time they slipped into the hot tub, a special treat for someone who had spent most of her life in L.A. When the charcoal was ready Jackie set the table, while chatting constantly. Jake grilled the steaks in silence, practicing his listening skills. Tory was right, he wasn't very good at this. But he could always learn.

When Jackie ran inside to retrieve a hooded sweatshirt, Jake's mind wandered back to the subject of tomorrow's guests. Maybe, if the subject were introduced in a low-key way, Jackie wouldn't worry. Wouldn't misinterpret the situation.

He couldn't just blurt out that he'd met a woman with

unforgettable legs, whose scent of wild ginger made his pulse race. Waiting for the perfect opening put him on edge.

Jackie reappeared and picked up the conversation exactly where she left off, which was in mid-sentence. He smiled as patiently as he could, letting his eyes roam from his wrist watch to her then back again. Any minute now she'd take a breath. He flipped the steaks, waiting, losing track of the time. By the time his attention returned, dinner was char-broiled. He liked medium rare.

■ ■ ■

During dinner Jake tried bringing up the subject several times but his daughter was always quicker. Was she starved for someone to listen to her stories? Had Victoria felt the same way? Jackie rambled from one anecdote to another. Behind each were her hopes and disappointments. Maybe allowing her to live in Tory's high-rise condo year after year, without even trying to gain custody, wasn't the smartest of decisions. Jackie had been lonely, maybe more than he'd been. He paused. Boy, that sounded good in the past tense.

Setting down his fork, he patiently leaned back in his folding chair. Occasionally he encouraged her with an 'Oh, really?' but most of the time she required no prodding. This need of hers would hopefully fade. Meanwhile he was happy to give her free conversational rein.

After the dishes were washed, they slid again into the steaming, swirling hot tub. Jake closed his eyes as Jackie retold a horseback riding story from last summer. He recognized her pattern now. First a long narrative followed by a series of rapid fire questions. He tried to be ready for each interrogation, so she wouldn't catch him off-guard again.

"Does Dr. Kelly still live next door?"

So predictable. "Of course. She asked about you just a few days ago. Said she'll drop by sometime this weekend."

This weekend. Saturday morning was less than twelve hours away. He couldn't put the subject off any longer. Drawing a deep breath, he plunged ahead. "Tomorrow . . ."

"Think you'll ever marry her?"

He stared, speechless. This one he wasn't ready for. "Marry Kelly? She's just a friend."

She peered at him openly, wanting more.

"I've never thought about it."

"Then start thinking, Dad. She's drop dead gorgeous, and likes a lot of the same things you do."

He sat up straight. "Like what?"

"Like living in the middle of nowhere."

He looked around, blinking twice. "That's not enough to build a marriage on."

"Yeah, but if she hated this place it wouldn't work either. Case in point. You, mom and the condo." She wagged her finger. "My vote is that you do marry her, then we could stay here forever." Her smile told him that in her mind, it was all settled.

He stared at her. During the ride home, just an hour or so earlier, she was worried that he might remarry. Now she had the bride picked out. Kelly was a known quantity; did that make her more palatable to Jackie? Marry Kelly, stay put. What would her response be when she met Caitlyn in the morning?

Jackie was still watching him. Her expression was patient, as if she had just finished explaining why the sky was blue. "There's a lot more to consider than where to live. I'm not ready to . . ."

"In the car you said you were thinking about it." She

sank down into the tub, letting the bubbles tickle her chin. "You're not getting any younger, you know."

He suppressed the urge to dunk her. Instead, he sat up straight and turned the tables on her. "I said there were no front-running candidates."

"Well, check the grays in the mirror, Dad, then crank up the momentum a notch or two. Okay?"

This was the opening he'd been waiting for. "Since you are insisting, you'll be happy to hear that there's a woman coming over in the morning. She's volunteered to help me get the lodge ready. We had nothing scheduled for tomorrow, so I took her up on her offer."

"Wait. Who? Tomorrow? And what do you mean, ready?"

Jake could tell from his daughter's expression that he had her full attention. That plus the fact she nearly shot straight out of the tub. There was no need to rush. He sank back against the edge and nodded. "One question at a time."

"All right. Get the lodge ready for what?"

"Her teenage daughters belong to a youth group at their church. In fact Caitlyn, Ms. James, runs it. I'm lending them the lodge for their summer retreat."

"She has teenagers?" Her eyes widened. "Must be ancient. And did you say 'church group?' Excuse me. I've never attended church in my entire life."

"Maybe it's time you did."

"But Dad, we didn't have company even once last summer, other than Kelly." She stood in the bubbling water, hands on her hips. "You hate company."

His expression was teasingly smug. He sank further into the tub. "Maybe you're right about time passing me by. Tell you what. I'll ask her if she likes the place or not. If she does, maybe I'll consider marrying her." He glanced her way.

"That was the most important factor, wasn't it?"

"No. And how could you lend our home to a group of strangers? Mom constantly filled the condo with people I didn't know. Sometimes they brought their kids over. So I wouldn't feel left out, I guess. Made me entertain them all day while the adults did their own thing."

Jake watched her, feeling guilt sweep over him again. She'd been alone for too long, just like him. Didn't Victoria realize that crowds of people could make someone feel even more like an outsider? Maybe together they could pull out of this. "I won't leave you alone to entertain them. It will be more like a family event, with all of us involved. I must confess, though, I am hoping that you and Caitlyn's girls hit it off. You'll need some friends to do things with while you're living here, or you'll be stuck with just an old fogey for company."

He reached for her hand beneath the swirling bubbles, and held it tight. "I'd never force someone on you. Never leave you alone with people you didn't know."

"Then you won't invite them over, unless I say it's okay?"

He gave her hand a squeeze. "No, I didn't say that. Just that I wouldn't desert you. After all, I'm not getting any younger, remember? Time to get a list of lodge-loving candidates together." He closed his eyes. Although his tone was teasing, he refrained from smiling. Her mistrust of strangers had to be taken seriously. "Look on the bright side. There's a lot to do to get ready for this camp-out."

"That's the bright side?"

"It sure is." He peeked out from beneath one eyelid. "My guess is that Caitlyn will have to visit fairly often. By the time we're through, she'll probably love the place as much as we do."

Jackie stared at him. The questions racing through her

mind were almost tangibly visible. She opened her mouth, but couldn't articulate a single one.

He closed his eyes again. This time he didn't hold back his smile. For the first time since her arrival, his daughter was speechless.

■ ■ ■

"Hi, Mom. Did I wake you?"

"Of course not. I was waiting up. How was the flight?"

"Fine." Jackie crossed to the bed and rummaged through her makeup case, finding her lipstick tote. "Dad made me call. Thought you might be worried or something."

"Well, I'm glad at least one of you thought of it."

"You could have called here, you know. The phone works both ways." Jackie snapped her gum, then flipped open the small mirror. She quickly applied a single coat of Passionate Pink.

"Watch your tone with me, young lady. Parents have a right to be worried."

Jackie frowned and examined her face in the mirror. Deepening her scowl, she silently mouthed her mother's last words, mimicking her usual expression.

Victoria broke the silence, her voice sounding softer. "I didn't want to interrupt the reunion with your father. He's been looking forward to this for a long time."

"Oh yeah?" Her tone turned sharp. "Then why are we having company tomorrow, on my first day here? Huh? Explain that."

"I don't know. You'll have to ask your father."

"He has a name you know. Jake. Don't want to say it anymore, do you? Afraid that you'll mix up the names, maybe late at night?" She shoved the lipstick case into her makeup bag and pulled out a brush. Her voice rose a notch as she yanked it through her hair. "I'll say it for you. Jake, Jake, Jake."

"Jackie!"

"Yeah?" She braced at the sound of her mother's indrawn breath.

"Did something already happen at your dad's, I mean at Jake's, to upset you?" There was a long hesitation on both ends of the line. "Honey, I can't help if I don't know what it is."

She shrugged and drew the brush slowly through her hair. "It's just that Dad's interested in women now. I wasn't expecting that."

Victoria cleared her throat. "Jackie, your father has always liked women."

"No, I mean really interested. It's kind of different."

"Are you saying women, as in several?"

"Not sure yet, but he did say that he was making a list." Cradling the receiver between chin and shoulder, she pulled her hair back into a ponytail. "Maybe he'll let me see it so I can add my own comments."

"Tell me, honey, are any of these women living at the lodge?"

"Nah. If they are, he's got them pretty well hidden." Hearing her mother's loud exhale, she added more fuel to the fire. "I'll meet the first one tomorrow, I guess. Some woman, with teenagers, is coming over. Imagine. She must be old." Jackie rolled her eyes.

"Same age as your father, give or take a few years."

"I know, but . . ."

"Actually, that was very thoughtful of him. I was worried that there would be no one your age around to do things with."

"I guess." Jackie was about to zip her bag shut when an item, wrapped in pink plastic, caught her eye. She frowned. "Uh, Mom?"

"You can tell me anything, dear. Something else about this woman worrying you?"

"No. Different subject. What if I need something at the store?" Jackie chewed her bottom lip for a moment. "You know, something personal. There aren't any stores up here. I won't drive for a year."

"If there's anything you need, ask your father."

Jackie's eyes widened. "No way."

"Jake knows all about personal things."

"I mean, really personal."

"Jake knows all about feminine care products, honey." Victoria chuckled slightly. "We used to share the grocery shopping. He's well trained."

"Get real. Ask Dad? It'd be too embarrassing."

"Write down 'tampons' on the grocery list. I promise you he won't ask. Won't even mention it. Your supplies will just appear on the dresser the next day."

"Well, if you're sure. Maybe you could mail me what I need."

"For the next year? That's not very practical. Do you want me to talk to him for you?"

"No way. That would be worse. He'd think I couldn't handle it." Jackie grabbed her toothbrush and paste, then zipped her case shut. She stood and sighed. "Better go. Love you, Mom."

"Love you, too. And listen, if you ever feel that this decision isn't working out for whatever reason, just say the word. I'll send you a ticket."

"I'll be okay. I really do like it here. It's cool." Jackie crossed to the desk. She ran her hand along the top of the portable TV. Next to it was a stack of teen magazines that her father had purchased just for her. "Dad's pretty cool, too. I think you'd like him now. If you saw him again, that is."

"I've always liked your father. That wasn't the reason we went our separate ways."

"I know. He told me."

"He did?"

"Yeah. Said he learned a few things by moving up here and is still figuring out some others." Jackie threw her gum into the waste can. "Maybe I can help."

"I'm sure you will, honey." Victoria drew a deep breath. "In fact, maybe you already have."

■ ■ ■

Opening the double doors, Jake crossed to the deck rail. Below, on the back lawn, Jackie, Rose and Lynn were covering the old army-green bunk beds with a fresh coat of enamel. So far, so good.

This morning's rendezvous with Caitlyn at the North Bend hardware started off with stilted introductions and a few awkward glances. He tried to act casually, as if selecting paint with a friend was an everyday occurrence in his life. That had been Cait's idea, to play things low-key. The less fanfare the better, when introducing new concepts to teenagers, usually produced success.

As expected, it worked. Soon the three girls formed a united front and did what teens did best, advise their parents on what was cool and what was not.

He shielded his eyes from the glare bouncing off the newly painted bunks. Metallic blue wasn't his idea of an appropriate color, but he'd been out-voted. His selection, tortoise-shell brown, was dismissed with a short burst of laughter from Cait's twins and a sympathetic look of dismay from Jackie. Cait soothed his ego with a smile and a pat on the shoulder. As he paid the bill, she reminded him that the beds could be repainted, after Jackie left for college.

Jackie. The past year had made such a difference. On the verge of being fully grown, she was now a melting pot of anxiety, wonderment and hormones. At first she was worried that he might consider marrying someday, like Victoria was. An hour or so later, she had him paired with Kelly, just so he would never move off Rattlesnake Ridge. As soon as he mentioned a woman's name himself, she was dead-set against him tying the knot ever again. Especially an unknown quantity, Caitlyn James. Too bad Jackie's first night had ended in a sulk.

As he watched her, painting and gabbing with Caitlyn's daughters, her laughter seemed to indicate that the entire day's outing was her idea. Would he ever become used to her constant flip-flops?

Cait's girls seemed to take the news about him a little better, but he still needed to be on guard. There were three pairs of eyes watching his and Caitlyn's every step, evaluating their every exchange. For a while their personal relationship could go nowhere. That wasn't all bad, really. The breathing room might allow him extra time to figure a few things out.

He called to the trio below. "How's it going? Ready for the second set of bunks, yet?"

Jackie peered out from behind one, waving a dripping wet brush. "Hey, don't they look great?"

"Yes, but I'll have to start wearing sunglasses indoors."

"Very funny." Jackie made a face.

Rose joined her, grinning from ear-to-ear. "You'll get used to them, Mr. Brandon."

"If I don't, I can always shut the bunk room door. You're the ones who'll suffer."

"Why us?"

Lynn set her brush on the paint can lid. "Because, sis, that's where we'll be sleeping next month with the youth group. Right?" She stood poised, one hand on her hip, and squinted at him.

Jake nodded. He had the distinct feeling that Cait's elder took great pride in being right. Constantly.

Jackie's brush soon joined Lynn's. "Ready for inspection, Dad. What do you think?"

He took the steps two at a time and joined them on the lawn. His expression was serious as he circled their respective works of art, gazing in wordless appreciation. The strokes were smooth, and the previous shade was completely covered. But what impressed him most was that they had stuck with it. That, plus the fact there was more paint on the beds than on their clothes.

Just last year Jackie would have wandered off, bored after ten minutes. Seeking play time. She had grown up, without him. The thought consumed him, until his daughter broke in.

"Dad? Is there something wrong?"

"No. The beds are fine." He saw her shoulders sag. Looking past her, he saw two other expectant faces. Oops. Not enough enthusiasm. He recovered quickly.

"Actually the bunks are great. I was just thinking that it was a shame we're wasting a sunny day working so hard." He studied the newly painted rails again, as if to confirm his approval, then nodded. "Yes, I believe one coat will be enough. How about if we hold off on the others until tomorrow, and get out the canoes instead?"

"Really?" Rose looked at him tentatively.

He gave her a warm smile. "Of course."

"All right!" In a scurry of excitement, Jackie began collecting brushes. "We'll have this stuff spotless in a flash." Rose followed her lead.

Lynn tapped Jake on the shoulder. "Mr. Brandon, don't you think we should finish the second set? After all, Mom talked you into this camp-out. We need to do all we can to help get ready."

"First of all, call me Jake. Mr. Brandon makes me feel ancient." He grinned. "You know, over forty."

She didn't smile. Maybe she thought he was. This one was a tough cookie. He'd have to play his cards a little differently to win her to his side. "Second, Caitlyn didn't twist my arm. I practically volunteered. Jackie's having a ball. That's what is important to me."

"She's fun." Lynn's glance shot to her new friend, then back to Jake. She met his eyes without so much as a flinch. "Sound's like she's had kind of a tough life."

"She has. But that's going to change." Jake looked skyward, shielding his eyes. "The day won't be any more perfect than it is right now. The rest of the items on your mom's list can wait until tomorrow. Let's wrap this up."

She frowned. Her voice sounded suspicious. "Mom didn't mention anything about coming back tomorrow."

"That's because she doesn't know about it yet." He glanced at the lodge. "Leave that part to me."

"We're done." Rose joined her sister, wiping her hands dry on the seat of her shorts. "Can we go in and change?"

"How clean are those brushes?" Jake surveyed the newly created mud puddle and the swatch of painted grass where the stir sticks were scattered. The hose was still running.

"Clean enough?" Rose's voice was hopeful.

"I'll help them finish. You work on Mom." Lynn linked

arms with her sister and led her off.

Jake made his way to the kitchen. Cait was busy putting away the last of the dry goods that she'd brought from town. Crossing his arms, he stood by the door and watched as she double-checked their supplies on the top shelf.

She had one foot on the last rung of the barstool and a knee resting on the counter. Her pencil flew across the page, marking items off on her clipboarded list. The faded denim jeans hugged her in all the right places.

His eyes travelled upward, admiring the gentle curve of her waist. The tail of her jade-green T-shirt was no longer tucked in, providing a tantalizing view each time she reached for the top shelf. He shifted at the sudden tightening of his jeans. Their daughters could join them any minute. He had to put his mind on something else. "I gave the girls time off for good behavior. We're going canoeing."

"How can we? There are a zillion things still to do."

"Easy. We just quit." He reached for her note pad and set it down on the counter.

"But they haven't start painting the beds in the north bunk room yet."

"Time enough tomorrow."

"Tomorrow?"

He nodded. "By staying overnight you can avoid making the long drive twice."

From her position on the counter top her bust line was even with his chin. He kept his eyes firmly locked with hers, not letting his gaze drop those critical few inches. It was extremely difficult, though. Not only did he want to look, but a few other ideas quickly sprang to mind.

With a hand on each side of her waist, he swung her down to the floor. That was better. Safer. They stood toe-to-toe for a moment in silence, his eyes flashing a message that needed no translation.

An instant wave of heat washed over her. Cait knew she should step away, but her feet refused to obey. Instead, she attempted to speak. Her voice faltered once before the words came out. "Stay the night?"

He smiled and slowly nodded. His firm touch beneath the errant shirttail seared her exposed skin. She cleared her throat. All she could manage were single syllable words. "Here?"

"No, not here."

Her burst of relief was intermixed with traces of disappointment.

"This linoleum would be too uncomfortable. The girls can stay in the wing with the unpainted bunks. You can join me upstairs."

Her eyes immediately widened. She tried to step back but his grip held her in place.

He placed a finger over her lips stopping any objection, then slowly traced their shape. "Jackie's room will be free. You can stay there."

Her cheeks burned red. She couldn't respond. He re-settled his hand at her waist. Leaning forward, he touched his forehead to hers.

Their lashes were close enough to interlace, if either dared to blink. She breathed in sharply as his fingers drew lazy circles near her belt. She waited, but he moved no further upward.

More disappointment. But why? Certainly she didn't want him to continue, not right here. As her mind raced to answer the question, Cait's gaze dropped to his slightly parted mouth, only inches away.

He brushed his lips gently against one cheek, then the other. His breath whispered a path across her face. Kissing the tip of her nose, he murmured against her lips. "Please stay."

She started to offer her mouth to his when the back door slid open. A trio of high energy voices quickly followed.

"We're ready!"

"Mom, we didn't bring our suits. Jackie said we could try hers on."

"Speak for yourself. I brought mine." Lynn said. "Jackie, where do you think the parents are?"

Jake placed a quick kiss on her forehead, then tucked in her shirt. Cait stood there frozen.

"I can keep them at bay for a few moments, that's all I can promise."

Unable to speak, Cait just stared at the kitchen door, willing it to stay closed.

"Look behind you." Palms on her shoulders, he gently turned her towards the laundry room. "An escape hatch. Head in that direction, then out through the garage for some fresh air. I'll reroute our daughters."

Glancing back, she nodded. He kissed her again, quick but tender, then left the kitchen issuing orders. "Jackie packed enough gear for an army. She can certainly spare a suit or two." He closed the door firmly behind him. Cait could hear his retreating voice. "Let's show Lynn and Rose where your room is, okay?"

"Follow me."

"I think that old tennis shoes would be better than those leather sandals, girls. Jackie, search through your shoe collection and see what you can find." His voice drifted off. Cait listened to the thunder of their footsteps as they raced up the wooden staircase.

Even four pair of feet couldn't equal the pounding of her heart.

Seven

The rusty hinges groaned as Rose pushed the door inward. She peered in cautiously. The boat house smelled of cobwebs and creatures. Small, multi-legged creatures in fact, with furry bellies. She winced, then called out to Lynn and Jackie who were taking their own sweet time strolling down the trail.

"Hey, you guys. Step on it. This place makes my skin crawl."

They jogged the remaining distance, then stood on either side of her. Rose's grip on the door frame tightened as she spoke. "Do you think there are any spiders in there?"

"Don't be ridiculous." Her sister poked her head in and quickly surveyed the musty, damp interior. "Of course, there are. Big ones, too."

Rose jumped back and heard Jackie laugh. She folded her arms across her chest and rubbed her bare shoulders. "I'll bet that there are snakes, too."

"Not likely." Jackie rolled her eyes. "This place is only called Rattlesnake Ridge because of the way the mountains twist and curve. You can see it from the air. Better yet, on a map."

"How do you know?"

"That's what Dad said, and he only speaks the truth."

"Please." Lynn made an exaggerated face, then wandered back up the trail the way they came. Rose followed, urging Jackie to come along.

"What did she mean by that crack?"

Rose shook her head. "Ignore her when she's like this. It always works for me."

"I'll try, but I think we should get Dad." Jackie glanced towards the house. "I thought he'd be down here already."

Rose's gaze followed hers. "Me too."

Lynn called over her shoulder. "Let's find a place to sit. They may be awhile."

Annoyed acceptance tinged her sister's voice. Rose pointed to a log. "We can wait here."

"Dad said they'd be right along," Jackie pointed out. "Don't get too comfy."

Lynn's eyes widened, in mock exaggeration. "And you believed him?"

"Cool it, you two," Rose warned. Sometimes her sister could be vicious, especially when it came to verbal warfare. She brushed the loose bark away from the fallen tree, clearing a seat for three, then wiped her palms against the long shirttail. She had borrowed the cover-up from Jackie, to wear over her swim suit.

However, Jackie was not about to drop the subject.

"What are you trying to say, anyway? Just spit it out." She put her hands on her hips and scowled at Lynn.

"You saw the way he was looking at my mom earlier, didn't you?"

Jackie gazed at her with a blank expression. Lynn shrugged. "I figure, if we give them a few minutes alone, then maybe we'll have their attention for the rest of the afternoon."

Jackie's voice sounded full of conviction. "My dad's not interested in your mom."

"Don't get your dander up. Take a seat." Lynn patted the spot next to her.

The ongoing argument was making Rose tense. She never liked it when her sister played one side against another. So what if Mom was interested in Jackie's dad? He seemed like a nice enough guy. And it wasn't as if there were a long line breaking down their door to get in. "Let's stop worrying, okay? Besides, I kind of like the idea of Mom dating someone."

"Yeah, she'll do okay." Lynn nodded. "Mom can take care of herself."

"What do you mean by that? My dad can't?" Jackie snapped her gum.

"Mom's got a Teflon coating when it comes to men," said Lynn. "She can handle whatever move Jake throws at her."

"So Dad's the one doing all the chasing? No way." Jackie braced her foot against the tree and glared down at Lynn. Rose winced, knowing the discussion was still heating up, not dissolving. She stepped in between the two.

"Let's not argue about it."

"Well, Dad wouldn't get involved again. Not after all this time."

Rose put a hand on the other girl's shoulder and led her to an empty spot on the log. She chose a place for herself in the middle.

"Oh, right." Lynn was determined to keep the argument alive.

"Of course I'm right. Especially not with a Sunday school teacher."

Lynn's chin rose a few inches. "Youth counselor."

"Whatever."

"Well, watch what you say."

Rose signalled 'time out' to her sister to silence her, then redirected the conversation. "Mom's pretty 'with it', compared to most. You should have seen her when the blue-haired raisins started to object to this co-ed camping trip."

"What did she do?"

"She could have told them off, but that would have gotten us nowhere. Instead, she sweet-talked the lead whiner, hoping to stall her for a while until the next council meeting. The chairwoman is on our side. That really helps."

Lynn leaned forward and nodded, as if in confirmation.

Jackie nibbled at her lower lip for a moment. "It would be weird if Dad got married again. It'd take some getting used to."

"Not marriage. Mom's too set in her ways." Lynn stood and tilted her head towards the lodge. "What I saw going on was lust, pure and simple."

Rose scowled. "I suspected something was up, maybe even hoped a bit. But I certainly didn't see anything. You're saying you did?"

"Yeah, I did."

Rose's expression was incredulous. "What exactly did you see?"

"Hot and heavy looks. You know, in the paint store this morning," Lynn said.

"Well, if that's all . . ." Rose shrugged.

"No way!" Jackie's tone was defensive.

Lynn held up two hands, as if signalling defeat. "You two keep your heads in the sand if you want. Fine. But don't count on me keeping a straight face if Mom arrives with her shirt buttoned wrong."

Rose's expression was horror-struck.

"Shh." Jackie said. "Here they come now."

After giving her sister a stern look, Rose ran up the trail to meet their parents. "Hi! What took you so long?" She stepped to the side. She wanted Lynn to not only hear the answer, but to see the adults' innocent expressions. If there were any.

"Sorry for the delay." Jake smiled. "Your mom was getting dressed."

"Exactly." Cait nodded. "It took longer than I thought it would."

From her position by the log Jackie simply stared at the two adults. Rose's mouth hung open. Lynn checked her nail polish.

Jake studied their expressions. "Is there something going on here that we should know about?"

Lynn stood and came forward to join her sister, giving her a slight nudge aside. "Nothing. Absolutely nothing."

■ ■ ■

The girls selected life preservers. Jake chose a kneeling cushion for himself and Caitlyn. The paddles were the one-size-fits-all variety, so he handed them out randomly. They quickly hosed down the two canoes, then headed for the water's edge. Based on the moaning and grumbling from the girls up ahead as they carried their own boat, Jake was glad that the dock was only a short distance away.

Lynn slid her end of the boat into the water while Rose tied the bowline to the pier. Jackie turned to look at her father, hands on hips. "I've got an idea. Lynn and Rose can take this one. You and I can take the other."

"Great idea!" Rose responded on cue. "Mom, climb in back. I don't mind sitting in the middle."

"Hold it. I had other arrangements in mind." Jake set down the second canoe and stepped onto the dock, adjusting his sunglasses. "I want to show Cait several sites around the shoreline. We're going to do some serious paddling, so we'll ride together."

"But so are we."

"Yeah, I love to paddle. The farther the better." Rose joined Jackie on the platform. Both heads bobbed in agreement.

"I know you better than that, Jackie." Jake refused to allow the switch. "The three of you will float out to the center and bake in the sun. Forget it."

His daughter stared at him. "No, we won't."

He wrapped an arm about her. "That was your first priority every sunny day last summer, no matter what the temperature was." He tapped her baseball cap. "And, judging from your California tan, I don't believe you've changed that much."

"But . . ."

"It's settled." Jake knelt and steadied the lead boat. "In you go."

Jackie tightened her vest, then stepped down into the center. The glare she shot his way told him what she thought about his idea. The twins followed in silence. Jake untied and re-coiled the line, then gave them a quick shove. "Be careful. The water is still chilly this early on."

"Right." Jackie tone sounded full of hurt and betrayal.

Lynn saluted him as they floated off. "You be careful, too."

Rose paddled while Lynn steered. Jackie was too busy pouting to help. Jake watched as they moved away from the dock. The girls were actually circling, although they appeared to be working hard. Their boat never strayed beyond eyesight.

Jake walked back to where Caitlyn stood next to the second canoe. She was wearing jeans, not wanting to burn the tops of her legs. That was the reason she gave him, anyway. He thought her decision might be more related to the earlier kitchen incident than to being fair-skinned. But, based on his reaction to her in shorts, he endorsed her choice.

The sun was behind her, catching and magnifying the golden lights in her hair. Her frown matched his mood. He sighed as he reached her and glanced back at their daughters. "Well, you're the expert. What was all that about?"

Cait leaned forward to peer around him. She waved to the girls. "Smile and wave."

He followed her example. "Why?"

"Because I don't have a clue what it is we've done to arouse their suspicions, but they're definitely worried about us."

"Us? And I thought we were being careful." He shook his head. "Here, grab the other end of this boat and we'll get moving." Together they lifted it over their heads and walked towards the dock. "They were nowhere near the kitchen. Wonder what made them suspicious?"

"They didn't actually see anything, but Lynn's a sharp

one. I never could hide anything from her," said Cait.

Jake turned his head and spoke over his shoulder. "What about Rose?"

"Lynn most likely filled her head with ideas, Jackie's too, while they were waiting for us to appear."

"Ideas." His frown deepened. They swung the boat down onto the wooden planks. He turned to face her. "What kind of ideas? They're only . . ."

"Don't say it. Some kids their age have children of their own." She picked up the seat cushions and tossed them into the canoe. "Shall we go?"

Jake stared at her, disbelieving. Her smile was meant to be reassuring but instead was causing him turmoil within. How could he pursue any kind of relationship with her if he not only had to watch out for inquisitive eyes, but also for over-imaginative minds?

He stepped into the boat and turned to steady it as Cait joined him. Soon they were paddling through lily pads near the north shore.

"How far does your property go? Over to that fence?"

"Yes. If you were to follow those split rails about a quarter mile, it would take you down to the access road. Where we first met."

She turned and glanced at him. Jake smiled. He enjoyed watching her blush.

How could she ever forget that road, or the reason she landed in his ditch? Facing the front again, she dipped her paddle into the water and said nothing.

She heard his slight chuckle before he changed subjects. "See the row of alders just past the meadow? Beyond that is Kelly's land. The property line continues dead straight through the center of the lake, splitting it in half near the dock ahead. The yellow rowboat is hers."

Staring off into the distance, Cait spoke without thinking. "How convenient."

"What?"

"I said how convenient that you both have your own boats, so near the water and all." Did she really say that? Out loud? Soon he'd think that heat stroke had melted her brain. She continued to look ahead, trying to keep a straight face.

"What?"

She had to say something. "I mean, how convenient it is that your next door neighbor is a doctor, in case of an emergency." Her face and neck turned bright red.

His laugh was clear proof that she'd dug herself in deeper. "Yes, very convenient."

She quickly resumed paddling. Her first stroke was shallow and wide. Water sprayed backwards, covering Jake from head to toe. She turned abruptly, rocking the boat. "Oh, I'm sorry."

"Cait?"

"Really. It won't happen again." She swiveled forward.

"Caitlyn, turn around." His voice was low and even.

"I'm fine." She executed several fast, perfect strokes before drenching him again.

"Put down your weapon and talk to me."

Debating what to do next, she heard the wooden clunk of his paddle being stowed beneath the seat. The boat rocked as he moved towards her. She reluctantly turned.

He had removed his dripping wet shirt and used it to wipe away most of the spray from his face. It was still wadded in his hand. As the seconds ticked away, Cait tried looking anywhere except at his chest. Dark, glistening curls spanned its width before narrowing and disappearing beneath the waistline of his cutoffs. She didn't have the sense to stop there. Her gaze continued downward, noting the white-worn denim near his zipper and across his raised thigh. The fabric hugged him like a second skin, concealing nothing. She parted her lips and drew a deep breath. It wasn't the fresh mountain air on her mind.

"Come here."

His hand on her arm broke the spell. She raised her eyes to meet his. With only a single thwart separating them, she could easily lean into his embrace. Here in broad daylight for everyone to see. Including their daughters.

She jerked away from his touch.

He tilted his head. "Shhh. Be still for a moment."

While they were occupied the canoe had drifted towards the dock. It was now bumping against it. "Jake, no. Not here." Cait scanned the horizon for the girls' canoe.

"Wait. I hear something," Jake said frowning. "We've got to get back."

Her paddle thumped against the aluminum as she tried unsuccessfully to free it.

Jake scooted quickly into his seat. "Damn. Move it. Fast!" He grabbed his paddle and used it to shove abruptly away from the pilings.

"I am moving. I'm just having a little trouble."

"Hurry, Cait." His strong, even strokes sliced through the water, but alone they weren't enough. "We're not going to make it!"

"What are you talking about? We're already in a peck of trouble. A few more moments won't make it any worse." The thrashing of nearby bushes near the dock caught her attention. She heard a low growl.

Adrenalin shot down her spine. "What is it? A bear?"

"Worse!"

"What could be worse?"

"Wolfie! Stroke, Cait!"

"I am, I am. What's a Woofie?"

His answer was unnecessary. At that moment a hundred pounds plus of black fur emerged from the bush, lumbered down the dock and leapt airborne towards them. Wolfgang's front paws caught the gunnels and dumped them both into the icy water.

Cait was the first to surface, spewing water. She had time to cough once and grab the cushion, before going back under. When able to breathe again she found herself beneath the capsized boat. Jake was only inches away, holding onto the center bar with one hand, her arm with the other.

"What are you doing?" She coughed again. "Trying to finish the job?"

He slid one hand up her goose-fleshed arm which was firmly hugging the flotation seat. His smile surprised her. "I finally have you alone."

"This is ridiculous. I'm freezing."

He swept back her wet hair, then leaned forward to brush his mouth against hers. "Here, let me help."

His breath was hot against her lips, a stark contrast to the chilling water. "The girls. They'll be worried."

"About us or Wolfgang?" He kissed her again, softly.

At the sound of his name, the Newfoundland barked and scratched at the aluminum with his paws. Cait drew back, cocking one brow. "That's another thing. The ferocious, woman-eating dog that you warned me about the other day is named 'Woofie'?"

"Wolfie. And maybe I exaggerated a bit." He grinned. "That mongrel can swim, so don't even think about saving his miserable life. Come closer."

Wolfie chose that moment to appear beneath the canoe and greet them with a playful bark. It echoed off the aluminum sides, creating a deafening noise. Jake dunked him, only to have the dog resurface immediately and pant for more.

Jake tugged again at Cait's arm. "Come on, let me share your cushion."

"Get your own. I'm sharing mine with Woofie." She smiled, treading water faster, nudging his own seat towards him. "Don't drown us both."

"What a way to go." He encircled Caitlyn and her pillow with his free arm. "Hold onto the rail. Or, better, hold on to me."

He caught her lips full against his. No longer caring about the water temperature, she opened to him. His tongue traced the changing contours, then retreated. She returned the intimacy.

Wolfie barked again and Cait broke away from the kiss. The side of the canoe was raised. Above them were the blazing afternoon sun and three pair of inquiring eyes.

■ ■ ■

The credits from the video rolled across the screen. Jake reclined against the light denim sofa, one ankle crossed over his knee. As he studied the TV guide, Cait memorized his profile unobserved.

His lashes were incredible, sinfully long for a man. She watched him blink, then closed her eyes, imagining how soft they would feel fluttering against her neck, her collarbone, and lower. Her body was still vibrating from earlier. Good thing they were interrupted when they were. As it turned out, the girls seemed readily to accept Jake's rendition of why they were under the boat, and his daring rescue of her. If Woofie hadn't barked out his warning of the girls' approach there would have been a lot more explanation needed.

A sharp burst of laughter broke through her thoughts. Their daughters were busily gabbing away in the bunk room, behind closed doors. She'd tried joining them more than once, but they had asked for some private time to talk. That exiled her to the living room.

No big secret what tonight's conversation was.

She snuggled deeper against the cushions, hugging the small throw pillow closer to her. Her breasts, hidden under folds of borrowed fleece, were sensitive to the pressure. She wanted to continue what they had started earlier, but knew they couldn't. Opening her eyes she glanced at Jake, only an arm's length away.

He must have felt her gaze shift towards him. Without looking up he broke the silence. "What are you in the mood for tonight?"

Her expression widened in surprise. What she was interested in wouldn't be found in the television section. Surely the afternoon had affected him the same way? It must have. He was keeping his distance for their daughters' sake, and so should she.

She sighed and ran her fingers up and down the worn sleeves of the sweatshirt. He might have to expand his wardrobe if she became a regular visitor. She mimicked his deadpan voice, trying to play along with the game. "Whatever sounds good to you is fine by me."

He mumbled an acceptance of the huge responsibility and turned back to the previous page. She stared at him, amazed. He was coping much better than she.

The click of her button-fly jeans tumbling against the sides of his dryer caught her attention. Earlier, when she had removed the bundle from the washer, an unexpected blush covered her cheeks. Such a domestic, and yes, intimate sight. Pant legs twisted together, cotton briefs and french-cut panties intertwined. Getting hotter and hotter with each revolution. The sound permeated the room in a way that even soft music and dim lights couldn't rival.

Her choice was simple. Since the girls had banned her from the bunk room, she could either wait up a little longer, or follow his earlier suggestion to sleep in Jackie's room. Upstairs, next to his.

He exhaled deeply, stretching his long rugged frame against the couch, arms and paper extended overhead. Over ninety inches of masculinity from tips to toes. She stared, mesmerized. Suddenly he moved, tossing the TV pages squarely into her lap. "I give up. Put on whatever you like."

She paused, thinking; how about an incredibly sexy nightie and your robe? With every movement the brushed flannel will caress my skin, heightening the anticipated pleasure. The lace bodice, tied with delicate satin ribbons . . .

His eyes narrowed, she swallowed hard. Quickly picking up the guide she scanned the lineup. The letters blurred and ran together. Words wouldn't come. "How about a Gilligan rerun?" Her voice faltered.

Jake focused his attention on her face. There was a faint blush on her cheeks and her breathing was uneven. She was not interested in television. Here he was, trying his damndest to forget about this afternoon, and she was busy fantasizing a new ending. A smile slowly curved his lips.

The bunk room door was still firmly closed. Their eyes met and held over the printed page. Grabbing the paper, he tossed it aside. "Let's go for a walk."

It was her turn to glance at the dormer. Her voice dropped to a near-whisper. "Do you think we should?"

He raised one brow and held back a laugh. "I think we'd better. Don't you?" He reached for her hand as he stood and drew her to her feet.

"Wait!" A warm throbbing began in her stomach as his arms encircled her. It moved downward, heating her thighs and threatening to buckle her knees. She wanted to be crushed against him, to be kissed senseless. But now he was motionless. Second thoughts?

"I'm waiting." He lifted her chin and kissed the tip of her nose. "You asked me to."

She needed to decide, but what decision was she making, exactly? Neither was ready to commit. How big was the first step these days? Brooke would blame Cait's naivety on lack of practice. But, whether experienced at the singles game or not, this time was different. Jake was unique, and definitely unpredictable. Her hands clenched into small fists against his chest. There was no way to know, but to ask.

Drawing a deep breath, she began, her voice almost inaudible, "If we go outside, well, what exactly do you have in mind? For us?" She flushed deep crimson. For us? No, for the dog! She was babbling like a schoolgirl. Biting her tongue to stop it from flapping further, she waited for his reply.

A smile tugged at the corner of his mouth. His hand slowly trailed along her jaw line, then finger-combed the soft strands above her temple. Her pulse beat a rapid tempo against his touch. Was she nervous? Well, so was he. "No more than you're comfortable with."

He drew one of her hands away from his chest, uncurled it and placed it around his neck. Pulling her closer, he kissed her forehead then leaned his own against it. His voice was rich and steady. "You can trust me on that."

Heat shot through her again. Instead of scaring her, though, it surrounded her like a security blanket. She did trust him. And she wanted him. Badly. Wanted to be a woman again, instead of just somebody's mother.

"I do." She lifted her head and signaled towards the door. "Let's go."

■ ■ ■

They followed the path towards the lake. The full moon slipped in and out behind the tall Douglas firs, lighting their way. The night air was unusually warm for June. Except for the deep-bellied croaking of the frogs, all was silent.

The boat shed hid the dock from view of the house. Cait turned to Jake expectantly. Instead of taking her in his arms, though, he motioned for her to sit. He slipped off the tennis shoes that she'd borrowed from Jackie, then his own. She pushed up the banded legs on the sweat pants she was wearing. He folded over the cuffs of his jeans. Together they trailed their toes in the cool water.

Since his divorce, his own personal space had been off limits to any and all women. Less complicated that way, less involved. No memories to linger on afterward. Now things were changing fast, on too many fronts. What worried him most was that it felt so right.

He glanced at the woman sitting next to him. She stared off into the night, chewing nervously on her bottom lip. Her hand gripped the dock between them. He knew he wasn't the only one taking a risk here tonight. He covered her hand with his. "When I was a boy, I used to dream of a place like this."

"A home in the mountains?"

Shaking his head, he watched the ripples from their foot movements slowly circle outward. "No. A place of permanence. Anywhere. Any one single place would have been fine with me."

"Did your father share your mom's wanderlust fever?"

He shook his head slowly.

"Then why did he agree to uproot the family so often?"

"Dad agree?" His laugh was abrupt. "Not a chance."

"Then why?"

"Not tonight. Let's just say it's important to me that Jackie has the choice I never had, of where to call home."

Cait smiled. "She loves being here with you. It shines in her eyes every time she looks your way."

"Think so?"

"Why else would she watch me, watch us, with such skepticism?"

"Trying to figure out where you fit in." Turning, he cupped her chin and rubbed his thumb over the smooth skin of her lower lip. When he reached the corner his touch lingered. "Just as I am."

Cait wet her lips nervously. He retraced the dampened area, then raised his thumb to his own mouth, tasting her. Her breath caught in her throat.

She didn't know which of them moved first, and didn't care. They were finally together. Their kiss was a leisurely consummation, without the urgency of the earlier moment. Just two mouths gently brushing against one another. A learning of textures, a sharing of tastes.

He guided her down to the weather-worn planks of the dock, then lay beside her. The boards were rough and uneven. Grabbing a life jacket from the rail above, he tucked it beneath her head as a cushion. "How's that?"

It was hard to speak, but she forced out a single word. "Fine."

"Then, how's this?" He gave her neck a small bite right

above the ribbing of the sweatshirt, then soothed it with his tongue. A small groan escaped her.

"Sounds like another 'fine'. And this?" he said gruffly.

His tongue, trailing slowly along the edge of the neckline, drove away all remaining, rational thought. "Yes."

Dropping his hand to the lower edge of the sweatshirt, he gently stroked her skin above the waistline of the pants. She stilled. Her jeans were still tumbling in the dryer, along with her other clothes. There was nothing beneath the borrowed fleece, top nor bottom. It would take so little effort to lie naked with him beneath the full moon.

His hand moved slowly upward until it rested just below the rise of her breast. She curled her arms tighter about his neck, bringing him closer. He still felt miles away. "Touch me." She didn't realize that she voiced her need aloud until he chuckled slightly.

"Yes, ma'am. I was just getting around to that."

He covered and stroked her nipple. A shiver raced through her, and she began to tremble. His mouth captured the sound of her pleasure. Reaching between them, she began unfastening his flannel shirt. Faltering on the second button, he released her to help with the task.

She pulled the shirttail free from his jeans and ran her hands over his smooth, taut muscles. He pushed her sweatshirt higher, they now met flesh to flesh. Adrenaline raced through her, stopping to pool in the pit of her stomach. Her blood pounded. So tempting, so enticing. And all within her reach.

She arched against him, hoping to relieve the tension but her action had the opposite effect. His manhood throbbed harder against the thin cotton covering her thigh. As he rolled on top, she instinctively moved one leg aside. He was cradled against her heat, with only a mere bit of fabric between them.

Lifting his head, he met her eyes. His voice was smoky with passion. "This is not good. Not safe."

Her voice was unsteady. "I disagree. This is very good."

A laugh rumbled in his chest as he nipped at her bottom lip. She opened her mouth, welcoming him. Soon the thrusting of their tongues mimicked the other joining they both craved.

Her rocking was slight but steady now, his body answered hers in turn. His groan of anticipation vibrated between them. She savored the feeling of togetherness, of oneness, as though their bodies were communicating with one another on a new plane of understanding. Was she losing control, or gaining it? Emotions, suppressed for too long, rushed to be free at last.

Tracing and memorizing the sculpted muscles of his shoulder blades, she ran her thumb down his spine towards his waistband. She was rewarded with a small sound of pleasure. Of encouragement. When her fingertips reached his belt she hesitated. Jake raised his head. She answered his unspoken question with her eyes.

His movements stopped. If the time came for him and Caitlyn to go their separate ways, memories would linger behind. Images of their time together on this dock would last for as long as he lived here.

Why were they in such a hurry anyway? There were so many good things between them, why risk it all, satisfying a few runaway hormones? In time they could figure out where their relationship was headed. With time.

Rolling to the side, he sat up.

"What is it?"

He looked down at her. Her eyes were still sleepy with passion, but a slight frown creased her brow. She extended her hand. "Jake?"

As he stared at her outreached palm, then back at her, a resigned expression covered his face. Cait stood and quickly straightened her top. She turned to leave.

"Just a minute." He captured her hand in his. "Let me explain . . ."

"No." She tried to pull away. "Forget it."

"But I want to. Please." He stood and pulled her back into his arms, gently stroking her hair. "There's nothing I want more, right now, than to make love to you."

She buried her face against his bare chest, wishing she could stop the 'however' part. He whispered softly against the crown of her head.

"It's too soon for us. I couldn't bear for you to regret this later. Or for me." He lifted her chin. "We have things to work out. Maybe I do, even more so than you. When the right time comes, we'll both know it. Until then let's take it slowly."

He was right, darn him, no matter how she yearned for his touch. Knowing that didn't make her like it any better. As he held her close once more, she felt his lower body still answering hers. She closed her eyes, enjoying the feel of his arms and the roughness of his chest while she could. The thought that not only she would toss and turn tonight brought a slight curve to her lips.

"Will you dream of me, Caitlyn?"

"No." Her eyes sparkled.

"Then dream of us."

Smiling, she lifted a single brow in mock seriousness. "Women have names for men like you."

He nipped her earlobe, then wrapped his arm about her shoulder. Silently they followed the path back to the lodge.

. . .

"Pass the cornflakes?" Jackie asked.

Rose picked up the cereal box, but held it out of reach. "Only if you pass the strawberries."

"Deal." Jackie returned the serving spoon to the dish. The two girls traded.

Standing in the doorway, Lynn sighed. Jackie and her sister were busy filling their bowls to overflowing, without a worry between them. She, on the other hand, had tossed and turned all night, wondering what the next day would bring. More kissy-face? Behind the boat house next time? Lynn wasn't fooled. Jake wasn't like other men; this time Mom was definitely interested.

They both knew that when Mom set her mind to something she usually got it. That held true at church and at PTA meetings. At work, too, if Lynn could believe Brooke. No reason that it wouldn't hold true when it came to love. No, if Rose didn't watch out she could end up as big sister to not only to Jackie, but to a newborn with a hyphenated last name.

Lynn glared at her sister, laughing over her breakfast, still dressed in Jackie's bathrobe. In contrast, she was wearing shorts and sneakers, just back from a brisk run. This morning she had done her normal four miles, but on gravel mountain roads instead of the track. She had done them alone.

Mom usually joined her, but today she chose to hide under the covers. Frankly, Mom looked terrible when she peeked in on her. So did Jake. He was standing by the counter, staring into his coffee cup. Parents. Maybe someone should put an age limit on falling in love. Lynn shook her head, disposed of her jacket on the nearest chair, then crossed the kitchen to get a juice glass.

Jake took another gulp of caffeine, hoping it would help. He spent a good portion of last night tossing and turning, and now faced a long day ahead. There was bound to be awkwardness with Cait, and questions from the girls.

Here came Round One. He glanced at Lynn over the rim of his cup. Too bad he had to deal with her first. He would have preferred warming up with an easier opponent.

She stopped in front of him. "Stay up too late? Must have been a great movie."

What movie? Oh, yeah. The one that ended around eleven. He should have used it as a guidepost to say goodnight. Mumbling a noncommittal response, he took another drink of the dark brew.

"Yes, must have been great. Mom didn't get to bed till way past midnight."

Jake looked at the teenage interrogator. Where was Cait, anyway? She should be answering these potentially incriminating questions, not him. She was the expert.

Was it all right to tell kids this age to go away and let them imagine things for themselves? Or did you tell them the R-rated truth? He wished he knew. He forced his voice to sound natural. "We went for a walk."

"Outside?"

Where else? Around the rec room? He swallowed his sarcasm and tried to stay middle-of-the-road. "We didn't want our talking to keep you awake." He smiled. Hey, he was doing great.

He crossed the kitchen, pulled out his chair and re-joined the others. He snapped the newspaper back into place and resumed reading. Consuming the Sunday paper was something he usually did in peace, from front to back. That was weeks ago, B.C. Before Caitlyn. Now he had trouble concentrating on anything.

He turned the page. A sharp rap on the kitchen door interrupted his five non-stop minutes of calm. Jackie jumped up to answer it.

"Kelly!" She gave the doctor a hug. "Great to see you again. Just in time for coffee."

"Did your dad have his yet?"

Jackie tilted her head towards the table. "He's working on it."

"Then I'm not coming in." They both laughed.

Jake set his mug down with a thump. Great, more company. More sarcastic company. "Get in here. One more body won't make any difference."

Kelly entered the kitchen, grinning but silent. She turned to Jackie and held her away at arm's-length. "Your dad might not have changed any, but look at you. My how you've grown." She winked.

"Yeah. Your exercises really worked." Jackie smoothed her robe, emphasizing her newly developed figure. She looked up and returned Kelly's smile. "I can't thank you enough."

"Hey, what's a doctor for?"

Jake pressed one hand against his temple. The pounding continued. So did the lighthearted chatter surrounding him.

Jackie pointed to their guests at the table. "Kelly, meet Lynn and Rose."

"Hi." Kelly waved from across the eating bar, then opened a cabinet. She selected her usual mug.

"Hi to you, too." Rose waved back.

"Mom mentioned you," Lynn said cheerfully. "You're the doctor who lives next door."

"That's right."

Jake lowered his paper and stared at Lynn. It wasn't like her to be so cheerful. She was practically smiling. Something must be up. Lynn's mind must be working overtime again. He'd better warn Kelly.

Jake released the newspaper, stood and crossed to where the doctor waited by the coffee pot. He lowered his voice to a near-whisper. "They're Caitlyn's daughters."

"Your accident victim?" She leaned closer. "Silly me. I thought she went home weeks ago."

Jake set his mug down hard on the counter, glaring at Kelly. "Could I see you outside for a minute?"

"Of course."

He slammed the door behind them.

■ ■ ■

Rose glanced at Jackie, raising her eyebrow as Kelly and Jake departed. "Is she your dad's girlfriend?"

"Heck, no. At least he said she wasn't."

"That would complicate things, wouldn't it?"

"Yeah."

Lynn scowled at the closed door. Visions of her mom crawling out of bed, the classic 'before' picture, ran through her mind. What a contrast. Not that she was too hot about the idea of Mom and Jake together, but if Mom was interested, she deserved at least a fighting chance. After all, it was her life.

Yes, it would be best if she stayed out of sight until after her hair was fixed. Lynn stood. "I'd better warn Mom."

"Good idea, sis."

Jackie tapped her finger against her cheekbone. "Kelly's been friends with Dad ever since he moved here. Nothing's happened between them, so it probably won't. I was kinda hoping it would when I first arrived." She shrugged. "But of course now things are different."

Lynn picked up her jacket and walked toward the door to the entryway. "I overheard Mom talking to Aunt Brooke about the doctor. It was a few weeks ago, right after the accident. She has an unfair advantage, you know, being single and living so close by."

"Yeah, bummer." Rose tapped her spoon absently against her bowl, remembering Kelly's slim leggings. Mom would probably reappear in those oversized sweats from last night. "Big bummer."

"Dad said there were a lots of things to consider when picking a wife. Not just where she lived."

"That's good," Rose said.

"What I do know is that your mom's name is on the list."

"The list? Excuse me?"

Jackie nodded. "That's what he said."

"Really big bummer." Rose rolled her eyes.

"Let's not panic." Lynn was all business. "Mom's got to be in the running. Just yesterday your dad was kissing her. That must mean something."

Jackie frowned, slowly nodding in agreement. "But I'm afraid to say what."

■   ■   ■

Outside, Jake took Kelly's arm and stepped away from the house. "Big ears, you know."

"Hey, neighbor, all kidding aside, if you and Cait have hit it off, I say that's great. I'm just surprised. Happened kind of fast, don't you think?"

"Yes. You're no more surprised than I am." He shoved

his hands in his pockets and began to pace. "In fact, most of the time I'm just plain confused."

"Confused can be good. So what's the problem? "

"You sound like my daughter. I don't understand what she's saying half the time. Makes me feel ancient." He stopped and stared at Kelly blankly. "What do you mean, confused can be good?"

"It means that if romance was simple, it would be too boring to bother with." She returned his gaze. "So what part's confusing you, old man?"

He held his tongue in check; he needed her advice. "She's a people-person, I'm a loner. She's business suits and briefcases, I'm faded jeans and hard hats. What do we have in common?"

She opened her mouth to speak, but he held up his hand. "I'll answer that. Nothing. So why can't I get her out of my mind?"

Kelly stood silently as he paced. He took several revolutions, eventually stopping in front of her. "Well?"

"Oh, now is this going to be a two-sided conversation? You were doing quite well on your own."

He stared at her and counted to three. It didn't help, so he tried ten. Better. "Go ahead. I'm listening."

"All right, then. I can see a few things in common right off the bat. You both have teenage daughters, who obviously get along pretty well. Am I right?"

"Yes."

"That's a good start. Kids can easily blow a relationship. Next, you say she's a bleeding-heart type. Well, what about that woman you took on at the office last summer? I was over here the evening your partner tried to talk you out of it, remember?"

"Margaret proved her worth."

"I'm sure your hot-shot summer intern has, too, but that's not the point. Who else would have given either of them the chance?"

"But . . ."

"I'm not quite through. What about this past fall, when part of the roof blew off the elementary school? Who re-routed a team of carpenters and a truckload of materials to fix it? I know, I know. It was probably just a tax write-off, correct? That's why you personally spent three non-stop days in the frigid cold, supervising."

He scuffed his boot at a mound of grass. Kelly stepped forward and put her hand on his arm. "Don't let your narrow vision of yourself get in the way. You have a lot to offer."

"But I hate change. I'm content just the way things are." He looked back at the lodge. "Or should I say, the way things were."

"Then don't change too much. And certainly not too fast. Let things ride for a while."

He exhaled loudly.

"She's not going anywhere, right?" He shook his head. "Then give it time. The right woman will see through your tough-as-nails exterior, and chisel out a space for herself in your heart. I guarantee it."

Eight

ait pulled the Toyota into her assigned spot. It was the first Monday morning she'd looked forward to for a long time. Really looked forward to. Anything to be away from Lynn's intense questioning and Rose's lovesick eyes. She didn't know what to say yet, it was all too new, too fragile. Like freshly mixed gelatin, the shape of their relationship was still forming. It took time to set.

She went directly to her office, hoping to hide. She didn't want to run into anyone yet, especially not Brooke. Her voice mail reported eleven new messages. Was at least one from Jake? She played them through, fast forwarding each greeting as soon as she recognized the speaker. She could always rewind them later, when her mind was on the task.

Her heart stopped on number ten. It was him.

"I hate these blasted machines." His voice was gruff, not the warm, teasing sound she wanted to hear. Was he feeling as awkward as she was?

"I'll be out on site all morning. Page me." A long pause followed as he cleared his throat. "I'd like to meet for lunch, if you can get away. Here's the number." She quickly grabbed a pencil.

Lunch. Just the two of them. No teenagers running interference or taking notes. Would he want to talk about what happened Saturday night? Or should she say, what almost happened? Her heart pounded. There wasn't a chance to discuss much of anything on Sunday. The painting of the bunk beds in the south dormer was completed quickly. They worked side-by-side with their daughters, without a personal word or private glance passing between them. It was as if they didn't want to risk being alone with each other, or to examine things too closely.

Now he wanted to have lunch.

There was a sharp rap on the office door. It swung inward before Cait could find her voice.

"Oh, sorry. I didn't realize you were in. You normally don't close your door. Here are my notes on the . . ." Brooke paused. After a moment of silence Cait raised her eyes to meet her friend's.

Brooke moved closer to the desk. "Hey, what's wrong?"

"Nothing. Don't be silly." Cait's voice was unnaturally bright. She cleared her throat and wiped her palms together before reaching for the file. She immediately opened it and began staring at the pages, pretending to be absorbed.

"Don't give me that 'it's nothing' bit. I'm not buying it." Brooke circled the desk and grabbed the back of Cait's seat. She swiveled the chair so they were facing each other, then sat on the edge of the desk. "Must be Mr. Mountain Man. How did the lodge preparations go on Saturday?"

"Fine." That word instantly called back memories of the dock. Of other 'fine' things.

"I called early on Sunday. You must have been still at church. By afternoon, I decided I was being nosy and backed off. Figured you'd call if you needed someone to talk to." Brooke glanced down at Cait's clenched hands. "Do you?"

The question brought her thoughts back to the present. "Do I what?"

"Need to talk? I can lend you a sympathetic ear."

"I do." Cait sighed. "But I'm not up for a repeat of the other day."

Brooke folded her arms across her chest. "You mean where you try to talk, and I constantly interrupt with bad advice?"

Cait nodded.

"All right, mum's the word. You've got the floor."

Cait twisted her chair a quarter-turn, so that she was facing the window. She stared out at the morning line-up by the espresso truck. "We skipped church. Didn't arrive home until late last night."

The room remained silent. Glancing back, Cait took in Brooke's raised eyebrows, but her friend didn't utter a sound. "We stayed over." She continued. Brooke bit her bottom lip. "I know you're ready to explode." Cait gave her a half smile. "Go ahead, say something."

"You're kidding!" Brooke stood and grabbed a conference chair. Soon she was seated at Cait's side, leaning forward as if for more information. "With the kids there and all?"

"It wasn't like that. We needed the extra time to finish."

"Really? Finish what?"

"Painting." She took in Brooke's smile; it was closer to a smirk. "That's the truth. The lodge is huge. The girls and I shared one of the downstairs bunk rooms with his daughter, Jackie. Jake slept upstairs."

"Very prudent of him."

Cait sighed. "He thought so, too."

"But you didn't. Interesting." Brooke tapped her finger against the chair arm. Cait's eyes shot her a warning, not to pursue the subject further. Brooke leaned back and crossed one leg over the other. "So, when are you seeing him again?"

"I don't know." That was also the honest-to-God truth, since she hadn't confirmed lunch yet. But it was only a matter of time.

"Well, he'll either hold out until Friday night, or invent an excuse to see you sooner."

"Why Friday?"

"OmniCorp's tenth anniversary party. You remember. Dining and dancing with the execs? Rumor has it that Mr. Anderson might be coming up from Portland to announce that new restructuring we were talking about."

Bill Anderson. Just the thought of her mentor and long-time friend brought a twist of a smile to her face. He'd been there through some very difficult times, from her early married years onward. After Todd's death, Bill had been the one to arrange the interview for her at OmniCorp. Too bad that, after she'd hired on, they were forced to keep a respectable, professional distance. She'd love to have him over to see her daughters, while he was in town. Chances were good that his wife, Carol, and their three children would accompany him, if he chose to drive instead of fly.

"Hello?" Brooke waved her hand in front of Cait's face. "Come back to earth. Are you day-dreaming about a possible promotion, or the for-certain candlelight dinner with Jake?"

Cait stared at her blankly.

"You've invited him to go with you, haven't you?"

"Go where?"

"To the gala. For those of us leading ordinary lives it's the biggest event all year. I know it doesn't stack up very well against getting lost on mountain roads."

Cait sat upright and lifted her chin. "I don't know if BASC accepted their invitation or not. They're your customers, not mine."

"Don't be ridiculous. If Jake goes it should be as your date."

"It wouldn't be right to mix business with . . . non-business."

"Pleasure, you mean." Brooke filled in the word Cait carefully avoided. "And you wouldn't be, anyway. As you just pointed out, friend, he's my customer not yours."

"But I can't." Cait shook her head. "I just can't. He avoids his own office gatherings. Why would he want to attend ours?"

"To be with you. Now, no buts. Either you invite him or I will." Brooke stood and wheeled the chair back to its original location by the conference table. "After all, I don't have a date for the gala yet, either. He'd be perfect."

Cait stood, slamming the folder down. "But how would that look?"

"I think he'd look great." She smiled as she paused in the doorway, one hand on the knob, one on the frame. "As for the other, you know I don't give a hoot about propriety. Who would blame me, anyway, with such a gorgeous man in tow? I'll give you until tomorrow to make up your mind. After that I'll consider him free game. And, by the way, if anyone's promoted, I hope it's you. See ya!"

Cait placed both palms against the desk top, thoughts racing and jumbling in her head. Jake already knew, or would know soon, about the party. He'd wonder why she hadn't invited him herself. There was no reason she shouldn't, except that the very thought of seeing him again made her want to revive the nail biting habit she'd given up thirty years ago.

She paused. This was ridiculous. Of course she'd invite him. Jake would probably turn her down anyway. And, if he did accept, the office staff would have the chance to meet one of their newest customers.

Baloney. Time to stop rationalizing, to be honest with herself.

She wanted to be with him, that was the bottom line. But she wasn't ready yet, not until she could put the dock incident behind her and look at him without panting. He'd asked her for some breathing room, and she wanted the same. Well, in her mind, she did. Her heart just hadn't received the message yet to slow down.

Lunch today was definitely out. She was still overwhelmed. In time her wits and common sense would return. She could survive a phone call, though. And his 'no' regarding the business dinner would be easier to handle if they weren't face-to-face.

She tossed the folder aside, uncovering the note pad which contained his pager number.

■ ■ ■

Jake unrolled the blueprint. A flash of metallic paint, still beneath his thumbnail, caught his attention. He slowly shook his head. He thought he'd gotten it all off last night.

Caitlyn's phone call certainly had been a disappointment. No time in her schedule for lunch with him. After their closeness on Saturday night he'd been envisioning a little quiet, secluded time together. Time to rehash what almost happened and to explore what was still to come. He'd been so certain that she'd say yes that he'd already made reservations at Jay Berry's. That was about as romantic a getaway as he could think of, without leaving Issaquah.

Instead she'd invited him to a painting party downtown. Just her and twenty of her favorite teenagers. Not exactly the same. But still, seeing her under any circumstance was better than not at all.

She'd also mentioned the OmniCorp dinner party on Friday night. Now that sounded a little more like it. Last weekend's hesitation was gone. Memories of her silky skin close to his almost made his palms sweat. Hell, he could barely separate their laundry the next morning without his hands shaking. Time to move their relationship forward into a physical one. And from there, who could tell? Maybe it was time to settle down, let someone else permanently into his life.

Sure, the risks were still there, but he'd face them one by one. Even tolerating a business dinner didn't seem too heavy a price to pay for time alone afterwards. At this point he'd agree to attend church, if he thought he'd have a few minutes alone with Caitlyn.

He glanced down at the blueprint again. Nothing but hieroglyphics. His mind and his heart weren't in this today.

A knock on the door saved him. "Jake?"

"Yeah, I'm here. Come on in."

Nick entered the office. "Ready for the inspection?"

He nodded, stuffing his hands into his back pockets. "Just reviewing a few final notes."

Nick scowled at the drawing, then rotated it. He read the name along the side of page one. "I hate to be the one to break the bad news, but our walk-through is scheduled for the house on Tiger mountain. This one's on Cougar mountain. It's still under construction, remember?"

Jake looked up, a blank expression on his face. How could he have gotten the two confused?

"Got your felines mixed up, buddy." Nick grinned. "Something else on your mind?"

Jake swore, then pressed the intercom button. "Margaret, could you run off a second set of papers for me?"

"Sure, Mr. Brandon. I'd love to. My time is your time. Whatever you say. When do you need it?"

"Today, please. The diskette's in my office. Thanks." Jake grabbed his briefcase and slammed it down on the desk. Popping the lock, he pulled out the computer disk that he'd just put away.

Nick glanced at the floppy and raised an eyebrow. "From your machine at home?"

Jake nodded. "It's more current than the central directory file here. I added markups after our last meeting."

"That must mean that the system's working fine for you."

"So far."

"No problem getting started?"

Jake set his jaw. He knew what was coming.

"Was it the reference guide, or did you get a little off-site tutoring?"

Jake's eyes bore into Nick's for several tense seconds. Nick's smile had plenty of time to fade. "We've been at this, together, for a long time." Jake came around the desk, his voice low. "If you want to continue this partnership past today, then . . ."

"Whoa. Hold your horses." Nick raised both hands. "You've never objected to teasing before. How was I to know? She must be . . . let's say, a little out of the ordinary."

"Don't say a thing."

"You've got it." He crossed his fingers. "My word."

Jake nodded once.

Nick's expression brightened again. "Say, if that's how it is, maybe you'd like to attend the OmniCorp dinner? It's this Friday night." Lowering his hands, he patted his shirt pocket, coming up empty. He shrugged. "Sorry, the tickets must be in my office. I'll get back with you on the details."

"No need." Jake reached over and snapped his case shut.

"Might be fun." The playful tone was back. "Think it over."

"Already did. I've agreed to go."

Nick stopped short and blinked in surprise. "You're kidding? You, in a suit, with no funeral to attend?"

Jake swung around, glaring at him.

"Mr. Brandon?" A soft knock caused both men to look towards the half-open door. Margaret poked her head in. Her smile looked overly apologetic. "Am I interrupting?"

"No problem. Here's the file."

"Great. I'll get started right away. Never know when that printer might decide to jam. This one never has, but in my sister's office, they have an entire wall of them. And do you think one would work when you need it to? Never." Margaret's tongue made a clucking sound as she crossed the room.

"Here, let me help." Jake picked up the diskette and headed for the door.

She followed. "Why, there's no need for that."

"I insist." Jake frowned. Did he really just offer to stay by Margaret's side for the fifteen minutes that the drawing would take to print? Incredible. He shook his head. But anything was better than trying to answer Nick's questions. Even listening to Margaret's updates on every niece and nephew born since the floating bridge was built would be better than withstanding any more of his partner's interrogation.

■ ■ ■

Jake yanked open the hall closet and grabbed his jacket. The sun might be shining at present, but by the time they got back home it would be pitch dark. Especially if he and Cait were able to slip out for a cup of coffee alone, after painting. He scowled. Probably shouldn't get his hopes up. After all, it was the middle of the week. It would be late by the time Cait returned all of her Sunday-schoolers home. Lynn worked most weekday mornings during the summer and, even if she didn't, Caitlyn certainly did.

He personally could benefit from a little extra sleep, too. He'd been a bigger grump than usual; argumentative and impatient. All of the attributes that Victoria used to label him with, and that he'd denied. Funny that now he could see them for himself. The sound of Jackie's footsteps on the staircase caught his attention.

"You'll need a jacket. How about this one?" His voice faded as he stopped to stare. Where did Jackie think she was going, anyway? Downtown, to walk the streets?

"What's wrong, Dad?"

"You're what's wrong." He pointed to the oversized tank top she was wearing, and to the bra straps it didn't hide. "You'll have to change into something else."

She glanced at the inch-wide flowered band covering one shoulder. "Why?"

Jake's tone became sharper. "Because we don't go outside with our underwear showing."

Her laugh was short. "Get real, Dad. We don't, because only one of us wears a sports bra." She grinned, as if that fact had escaped his attention and it was her duty to enlighten him.

"Jackie, I said change." He tried to keep his voice calm as he shrugged one arm into his jacket. "And be quick about it. You've already made us late."

She put her hands on her hips. "But Mom . . ."

"You're mother's not here. And if she were, you'd still have to change."

"But why? Ask anyone. This look is really in. Why should I be punished just because you choose to be a fashion nightmare?"

Jake clenched his jaw. "One more argument and we're not going."

"Fine. You're the one who wanted to tag along anyway, and ruin everything for me." Jackie stomped off towards the steps. "Just so you could chase after the leader, and embarrass me."

"I'm not tagging along to embarrass you. I was asked to help."

"Oh, right." She climbed two steps, then turned on the third. "Lynn's mom walks on water, or haven't you heard? She's never needed help with anything, from anyone, her entire life."

"That's not true." Jake crossed to the stairs. Jackie moved further up.

"Take her side, why don't you. What about me? Did you let me move in so you'd have someone to push around, or just someone to ignore? Is this how you treated Mom?"

"Jackie!" His face was red with anger. It was as if a blow

slammed into his gut. He couldn't speak.

"Never mind. I can guess the answer." She turned and ran up the remaining steps, then slammed her door.

Jake flinched, then leaned against the rail. His pulse pounded as if he'd just run several miles. Where had all that anger come from? As her father he had the right to censure her outfit, to question any and all behavior. If he didn't, he wouldn't be doing his job as a parent. How their conversation degenerated so far, so fast, was beyond him.

Tag along to embarrass her? He wanted to spend time together and thought Jackie would feel the same. That was called quality time, right? Maybe it didn't count if she suspected an ulterior motive. Maybe he needed to be clearer in his own mind just for whom he was doing this, and why.

The way in which their simple, one-topic disagreement went off-target, blossoming into a full gun barrel attack, was reminiscent of his later arguments with Victoria. Maybe Jackie had overheard more that he'd thought, at her young age. Time to own up to part of the blame, both then and now. He'd meant to sound disapproving of Jackie's outfit only, not of Jackie herself. Maybe Caitlyn could give him some advice on handling confrontations a little better.

He glanced up the staircase. He'd apologize, no question about it, then they'd begin again. There was so much he was sorry for these days. Maybe, by letting some of it out, part of the guilt might go away. He could only hope. Either way, Jackie needed to know that no matter who else was in his life, in his heart, there was always ample room for her.

■ ■ ■

The dingy tan paint covering the inside walls of the women's shelter in downtown Seattle was quickly disappearing under the new coat of Angel Bright White. It was undergoing a brilliant renewal. She could see it on the faces of the current residents as they prepared lemonade in the kitchen. A small bit of sunshine sneaking into their troubled lives. The same sunshine was touching her life today.

Cait smiled as she passed two of her teens in the hall. Despite their smudged cheeks and questionably clean hands, she gave one a hug. They were good kids, and this was quite a commitment. Not everyone would spend free time doing something for others. But then, her youth group wasn't like most. When they had a purpose in mind, and were promised some fun at the end, they could be very dedicated. Cait smiled, savoring a tiny bit of the credit for their enthusiasm. After all, the post-painting, hot fudge sundae party aboard the Vashon ferry sunset-run was her idea.

She wandered down the hallway towards the community room. Jake was crouched down, wiping paint spots off the floor. Rap tunes radiated from the boom box in the corner. It was no wonder he didn't hear her approach.

It was amazing that he not only offered to drive, but that he stayed to help. And not merely to supervise. He really pitched in; maybe a little too much so. They hadn't spoken more than a few words all evening, but just his being here was enough to put a spring in her walk. Earlier it was too busy, now it was too crowded to get a personal word in. She drank in his presence, instead.

Maybe she wasn't quite ready to face being alone with him, nor to analyze last weekend's midnight stroll to the dock, but she was more than ready to hear his voice and to see his calm, capable manner with the kids. Especially with Jackie. He seemed to keep one eye on his daughter at all times. And it wasn't that checking-up-on-you kind of look either, it carried more a feeling of support and admiration. As if they were there for each other.

Speaking of crowds, Jake handled the young people's snickers and winking like a pro. Was that why he was keeping his distance? To keep any possible relationship between them out of the limelight? If so, then mission accomplished. Not even she suspected, at the moment.

Would there be time later? Probably not, since they drove downtown in separate cars. He and Jackie would go directly home after the ferry ride, maybe before. No chance to talk about the subject foremost on her mind. Maybe he could be coaxed away from his task for a short while? If she got tongue-tied again, as she did during her phone call, a quick snuggle would be enough to tide her over. Reassure her. Remind her that, while taking things slowly, she was still on his mind. With no emergencies at present they could surely step out on the porch without being missed. She smiled, tapping him on the shoulder.

He looked up, then scanned the room before speaking. "How's the rest of the house coming?"

"Fine." She grinned. "Would you . . ."

"I'm looking for a Ms. James. Ms. Caitlyn James." A man, holding a spiral notebook and wearing a press badge, stood framed in the doorway. Several people were behind him, with cameras and portable lighting equipment.

"I'm with the evening news. We'd like to feature your group in our Sunshine segment." He flashed a smile. "It's a tradition at our station to end the day's doom-and-gloom on an upbeat note, you know. That way viewers will forget the rest and tune again at eleven. Do you mind?"

A chorus of teens answered for her. Several grabbed their purses and rushed off, headed for the small vanity mirror in the hall bath. It was fine by her. A little publicity never hurt any good works project, but how would Jake react? No chance he'd escape the limelight now, based on the wattage that just arrived. She turned to him, biting her lower lip. He was already immersed in reading a release form someone had handed him. Jackie clung excitedly to his arm. Her vision of a private moment vanished as the cameras started to roll. How many more days till Friday?

■ ■ ■

Cait grabbed her briefcase from the passenger seat and swung open the car door. Two days, and still not a personal word from Jake. Hopefully tonight would go well. Her nerves might not be able to handle another setback, in her present frame of mind.

She paused, watching the silhouetted figures mill about behind stained glass windows. Soon the very same women who were serving coffee would be voting on her proposal. She drew a deep breath, tightening her grip on her purse.

Would the council give her plans the go-ahead? She'd have her answer, one way or another, within the next hour.

She hurried inside, hoping to have a private word with the Council Chairwoman, Audra Stockton, before the meeting started. Cait admired Audra. She was a woman of few words, and all of them were pure gold. Her decisions were swift but fair, based on equal input from all sides. Yes, Audra would look at her plan without bias, no matter who got to her first.

The chatting slowed to a murmur as Cait entered the room. One silver head after another turned towards the door. Had the group already heard about the retreat weekend? Formulated an early decision? She lifted her chin and stepped into the room.

"Good, she's here. Our very own celebrity."

"What was it like to be on television?"

"Did the cameras make you nervous?"

Relief ran through Cait. Before she could answer a circle formed around her, posing one question after another. She responded as soon as the noise dimmed. "Believe me, the thanks belong to the teens, not me. It was totally their idea."

Her eyes sought Audra's over the crowd. Was that humor glinting behind her bifocals? Cait smiled in return, then watched as the chairwoman took a leisurely sip of coffee. The questions continued, drawing her attention back.

"They were adorable, weren't they, waving to their parents with those dripping brushes?" The lady on her right mimicked their action. Several women laughed. "Complete with paint on their noses!"

Cait was quick to amend the statement, "And pride on their faces."

Audra's voice broke through the crowd, clear and firm. The circle opened to admit her. "They had a right to be proud. The homeless shelter has never looked so good. Commendable work; an example to us all."

The others agreed. Most of them anyway. One council member, Darlene McPhee, seemed to hold herself apart from the crowd. From the expression on her face, Audra wondered if Darlene's crocheted collar might be too tight. Standing near the silver tea set, she simply sniffed and said nothing.

Audra was glad that Caitlyn was finally getting a few moments of deserved recognition. Compared to the other ladies, she was a newcomer by over a decade. She seemed prepared to take a stand even if it was controversial, and to introduce new ideas. Just what today's kids needed to keep them interested. Audra smiled. A real pistol. That term had been applied to herself, in her younger days.

As Audra expected, complaints regarding the upcoming camping trip had trickled into the Youth Activities office all week. So had rumors of Cait's diplomatic handling of Darlene's longtime quilting partner, Pamela Sydow. Glancing towards the refreshment table, Audra watched Darlene add another lump of sugar to her coffee. Load up, gal, she thought. The sweeter you are during the meeting, the better for us all.

Audra had placed several calls in preparation for tonight's discussion, trying to sort fact from fiction. With each call, she became more curious, especially after seeing the evening news clip with the handsome architect hovering in the background, his own paintbrush in hand. Very curious indeed.

Audra listened as the barrage of remarks continued. Cait was holding her own very well. "How did you draw such a great turnout? That, in itself, was amazing."

Cait nodded in agreement. "Not only did the regulars show up, but three brought along others to help."

"It looked as if you brought a friend along too, dear." The woman who spoke was smiling from beneath her oversized reading glasses. Her tone was uncommonly suggestive, coming from someone with hair that many shades of blue and gray. Several ladies joined in the jesting.

Cait blushed. "Mr. Brandon is the father of one of our newest members. He's also owner of the lodge we hope to use in a few weeks."

Audra hung on each word. So that's it. Explains a lot. Clapping her hands, she called for the meeting to start.

"Let's discuss all of your ideas under new business, along with the others. Ladies, take your seats. Many of you warned me not to run past eight, so let's hop to."

"Why not, for goodness sake?" Darlene followed the others to the round conference table, commandeering her usual chair.

Adjusting her glasses as if to get a closer look, Audra held her gaze. "Tonight's the season finale of Murphy Brown."

Darlene's nose rose a quarter of an inch. Audra ignored her and proceeded with the evening's agenda. She didn't miss a beat. As usual, the meeting ran like clockwork. The first hour passed quickly.

"Then it's decided. Each congregation will host its own Graduating Seniors' Luncheon. Next year's committee members can reconsider the decision, if they choose." The gavel hit home. "Let's move on to summer field trips. We'll go clockwise, starting at my right."

Cait breathed a sigh of relief. Twelve churches represented, and her plan would be one of the last reviewed. Only thirty minutes left. How bad could it be? No matter what the outcome, she could leave quickly. To celebrate or whatever. She collected her thoughts and focused on the current proposal being examined.

"Our outing to the Mariners game will be the last week of June. I've blocked out a group of forty seats right behind first base. If another congregation wants to join us we could double the fun."

"Good idea. A show of hands, then?" The hammer slammed again. "Unanimous. Next, please."

"My group is hoping to rent canoes at the University of Washington and paddle across to Mercer Island." The spokeswoman paused and laughed slightly. "At their parent's request, I've modified the plan. We'll stay closer to shore.

Maybe just paddle around the arboretum, observing the wildlife."

Darlene interrupted, her tone condescending. "Be careful of what kind of wild life you run into."

"Out of order." Audra ruled in warning. "Please continue."

"Never mind, Madame Chairwoman. That's all I have to report."

"All in favor? Good. This just might set an example for other groups to study for their lifesaving certificates. Please remember we need photos for the newsletter. Let us know at the next meeting how it turned out." With a curt nod Audra focused on Darlene. "Now it's your turn."

Darlene straightened and ran a finger around her lace collar. Her words were fast, her tone high pitched. "Seattle First is finalizing plans for their tenth annual picnic, to be held the last Sunday in July. As our special incentive this year, any teenager with perfect attendance can challenge the minister to a game of croquet."

Cait looked quickly around the circle, truly impressed. Eleven carefully guarded faces watched the chairwoman for several seconds, without blinking an eye, without casting a glance in Darlene's direction. Cait was thankful she'd never have to play poker against these women.

Audra broke the silence. "Darlene, don't you think . . ."

"That's all I have to report. Since it's on the church grounds, a vote isn't required. I believe it's Ms. James' turn."

Great lead-in. Cait drew a deep breath, then began. "My group is planning a three-day retreat to the Raging River Lodge, as soon as school is over. Permission slips were passed out last week."

Darlene leaned forward. She removed her eyeglasses and

pointed with the ear piece. "How many parents, may I ask, have agreed to this boondoggle so far?"

"Darlene, please wait until Caitlyn has had her say." Audra furrowed her brow.

Cait paused. Maybe she shouldn't have gotten so carried away with this dream. Well, live and learn. She'd see it through this time. There might not be a 'next' to worry about.

"It's owned by Jake Brandon, a local businessman. He offered us the use of his lodge on Rattlesnake Ridge, in exchange for allowing his teenage daughter to participate. She's new to the East Side area and is trying to meet friends." That much was definitely true, Cait thought. No need to describe the other relationship that was taking shape.

Darlene opened a manila envelope and took out a fistful of letters. "Madame Chair, I brought with me several complaints from the Issaquah congregation, regarding this outing. I recommend that this co-ed overnight be suspended without further ado."

Audra signaled for the letters. Her unflappable composure remained unshaken. "Bring them forward."

"Gladly." Darlene strutted towards the front, reminding Cait of a peacock on parade. One finger fidgeted with her brooch as the other gripped the letters.

Audra reviewed the papers in silence. Finally she lifted her glasses and stared at Darlene. "These letters are all from the same woman."

"Yes, well, Pamela is a close friend of mine. We've quilted together for years."

"To your knowledge, have any of the teenagers' parents complained about this retreat?"

"Frankly, I don't know."

Audra's gaze swung to Cait. "How well do you know the lodge's owner?"

Not as well as I'd like to. She forced her thoughts back to the present. "He's a hardworking man with a reputation for honesty. Jake and his daughter have lived apart for several years. But, whatever he may lack in paternal experience, he makes up for with love and enthusiasm."

Audra heard the tenderness in Cait's voice, as well as the protectiveness. So it's like that, is it? Their eyes met across the room. Well, it's about time.

"I'll conduct the background investigation personally and report back to the council at the next meeting." she said.

"But wait! The camp-out will already be over by then." Darlene stared at the other faces around the table. Their expressions were pained as they tried to hold back smiles.

"Exactly." Audra brought her gavel down again. "Next report, please."

■ ■ ■

Cait peered again at her closet's contents and sighed. How could she have spent so much time and energy thinking about tonight's party, without once considering what to wear? She'd focused on how to get him onto the dance floor if he didn't ask her first, how to introduce him to her co-workers without raising too many eyebrows, and how to suggest they come back here early for a nightcap without making it sounding like a bedroom invitation. Now here she was, totally mystified, looking to Lynn for advice. Lynn, who had made her skepticism over the entire situation perfectly clear from the start.

"How does this look? Will it do?" Cait held an ivory silk blouse and khaki gabardine suit against her. Standing in front of the full length mirror she turned one way, then the other. She smiled, trying to ignore the slight trembling of her hand.

"Better, Mom, but let's keep looking." Lynn took the outfit from her, shaking her head slowly.

The remainder of the week had passed quickly, after the painting party and council meeting. Jake called late last night, after she was in bed. He was quick to offer the purpose of the call, to confirm what time he'd pick her up for the gala. Was Jackie listening in on another line? At the foot of the stairs? After her suggestion that he could call anytime, with or without an agenda, his voice relaxed a bit. Sounded more like himself again.

Tonight Cait hoped his tone would be soft and low, with maybe a little ragged breathing mixed in. She pulled another selection from the closet, a turquoise dress this time, and nodded at her reflection. "This is a definite yes."

Behind her, Lynn shook her head. "Guess again, Mom. I'd say a definite no."

She met her daughter's eyes in the mirror, then tossed the dress on the bed. It joined the other rejects. "I can do this better, and certainly quicker, by myself. Let's bond some other time, okay?" Cait walked back to her closet and stood with her hands on her hips.

Lynn joined her and placed a comforting hand on her mother's shoulder. "Don't let the nervousness get to you. Play it cool. After all, it's just one date. Not a marriage proposal."

"I'm not nervous."

"Face it, Mom, it's not your fault." Lynn took a step forward and ran her hand along the remaining hangers. Her voice was very sympathetic. "Just look what you have to choose from."

"I wear these all the time."

"That's the problem. You've got your power suits for work, wind suits for jogging and, well, those other things are for the grocery store, I guess." Lynn stopped waving at the wardrobe and gave her mother a one armed hug. "What you don't have are date clothes."

Cait matched her serious tone. "Maybe you'd better describe what you mean by 'date' clothes then, because we're obviously thinking of different things."

"You know, the kind of clothes that will make your man beg for a second date."

"My man?" Cait cleared her throat. "I thought that you weren't too overly enamoured with my going out with Jake in the first place. Now you want him begging for more?"

"He's not a bad guy. Much better than the ones that Brooke threatens you with." Lynn shrugged. "I just want, well, whatever, or should I say whoever, makes you happy."

Cait kissed her daughter's forehead. "I'll never know how you grew up so fast."

"Break it up you two, and look at what I've got here." Rose rushed into the room and laid the garment bag on the bed. "We're cookin' now."

"What's going on?"

"I borrowed these from Aunt Brooke. I explained the kind of trouble you were having and she was more than happy to help out." She forced the words out between breaths.

Cait sighed. "I bet she was." It was three against one. She didn't have a chance.

Rose pulled out a jet-black cocktail dress with an off-shoulder beaded neckline. "Oh, Mom, this one would rev his engines for sure!" Her daughter's eyes were as wide as saucers.

"Did I forget to mention that this was business?"

"Business, shmisness. You've just got to . . ."

"No. You got that?"

"But, Mom!"

"What part of no didn't you understand?" Cait snapped. "End of discussion."

A loud honking interrupted their argument. Cait froze and looked over at Lynn. Her elder daughter shrugged her shoulders and walked to the window for a peek. Her advice was very matter-of-fact. "Better decide quickly, Mom. They just drove up."

Cait rushed to the window. Jackie was waving frantically from inside the truck. Jake pulled smoothly into the driveway. Opening the door, he stepped out in one fluid motion. He was tall, dark and elegant in his charcoal suit and burgundy tie.

Her palms grew damp. She wiped them on her robe. He was really here, and soon she would have him all to herself. Sure, the entire office would be joining them, once they got to the hotel. But the ride to and from, he'd be all hers. Would he bring up last Saturday night? If he did, would it be to explain his reluctance to get involved, or to pick up where they left off? Soon, she'd know. Jake glanced at his daughter, then up to the window where Cait stood. He smiled, nodding once in recognition.

Cait quickly stepped away and pulled the collar of her robe closer. "I'm not ready!"

"Then let's get a move on." Lynn grabbed her arm and led her back to the bed.

"I'll let them in." Rose rushed from the room.

Cait breathed a deep sigh, glancing at the garment bag.

"Now, Lynn, let's be sensible. You know Brooke just about as well as I do."

"No harm in taking a look, is there?"

Lynn pulled out an embroidered vest with matching crepe trousers and held it up.

Cait nodded. "Here we go. Something practical." She accepted the hanger from Lynn. "What kind of blouse would I wear with this?"

Lynn slowly shook her head. "No blouse, Mom."

Cait glanced at her daughter for quick confirmation, then sentenced the outfit to the discard pile.

"Next, we have this flaming little number." Lynn raised a lightweight cotton and lycra dress for her inspection.

"Red!" Jackie burst into the room, followed by Rose. "Perfect. My dad just loves red."

The gown had cap sleeves and a keyhole neckline that was revealing but still discrete. The fitted bodice pleated gently into a sweeping, lower calf length skirt. Cait accepted the hanger with reservation. She quickly checked the button that secured the peekaboo opening. "I don't know."

Rose sighed. "It's you, Mom."

"I agree." Lynn swept her hand over the skirt, looking for flaws or wrinkles. "And it's a good length. I think it's a winner."

"Well, maybe I could just try it on."

"My dad just loves red."

"You said that already, and it's not helping." Lynn gave the younger girl a nudge, silencing her. She leaned forward and lowered her voice. "My mom's got the jitters, so lay off. Got it?"

Jackie nodded, then watched as Cait stepped in front of the mirror to check the fit. She whispered back. "That's okay. Dad does, too. They'll be perfect together."

■ ■ ■

"I'm glad they're finally out of here." Rose closed the door, then rested against it.

Lynn nodded, walking into the living room. She perched on the arm of the couch. Picking up a throw pillow from the cushion below, she hugged it to her chest. "Up until the last minute, I thought Mom might change her mind."

"Nah. She couldn't just skip out. It's a work thing, isn't it?"

"I mean about the dress. I thought for sure she'd put that business suit on again."

Rose joined her sister on the sofa. "Wouldn't she have been something? Especially after picking up the can of static remover, instead of her hair spray. Can you imagine if we hadn't caught her in time?"

"That's nothing." Jackie stepped forward. "You guys didn't notice, but my dad just left here wearing one black sock and one brown." She shook her head. "Sad. I didn't have the heart to tell him, not after all he'd been through selecting the perfect tie."

Rose laughed. "Well, he looked pretty good to me, for a man his age."

"What does that crack mean?"

Rose's tone sounded sympathetic. "No offense, but he must be at least forty-something, isn't he?"

"Not quite." Jackie narrowed her gaze and leaned close towards Rose. Their noses were only inches apart. "He's a lot younger than Robert Redford. Women your mom's age still fall for him."

"Do not!"

Lynn tossed the pillow at the pair. "Knock it off, you two. You've missed the most important part."

Both heads turned. "What's that?"

"From what you said earlier, Jake would rather have a root canal than attend a formal event like an office party. Right?"

"Yeah, so what?"

"So then, why is he? Tonight of all times?" Lynn looked at her sister. "And why did Mom suddenly get the urge to replace the pictures on her end table this week?"

"I don't know."

"She suddenly needs to see our smiling mug shots at the end of the day, instead of Dad's? I don't think so."

Rose looked back, wide-eyed. Lynn stood and crossed to the window. She stared out. "Something big is going on here. We have to face the facts. We may end up sisters. Stepsisters, I guess I should say."

Would that be so bad? Visions of shared bathrooms and late night gab sessions raced to Jackie's mind. "You two have each other. I've always wanted a sister."

Rose opened her mouth, then shut it. Lynn broke the silence. "What is it, sis. Out with it."

"I was going to make a wise crack, like 'Here, take mine.' Then I realized it wasn't funny." Tears glistened Rose's eyes. "I would hate to be alone."

Lynn crossed the room and rested her hand on her twin's shoulder. "I feel the same. Even though we don't always get along." She gave her a quick squeeze. "But this could really change things around here. Let's face it."

Jackie swallowed hard, trying to dislodge the knot that had formed. Her mind was now made up. A sister was just what she needed. But she needed to share the bad news, too. It was only fair. "I hate to break it to you guys, but Dad won't give up the lodge. You'd be moving in with us."

"I'm talking about bigger changes than that." Lynn

began to pace. "Think about it. There could be a baby around the house, in no time at all."

Rose and Jackie responded in unison. "A baby?"

Lynn nodded slowly. "My feelings exactly."

Jackie's earlier thoughts of gab sessions were quickly replaced with diapers, bottles and nights alone, babysitting. There'd be another person, sharing some of her own flesh and blood. But then, she'd be sharing her dad too, in a whole new way. She sighed. "I have to think about this."

"Me, too," Rose echoed.

"Well, think fast, because as I said, something big is going on here." Lynn tapped her nail against her bottom lip. Her voice sounded low and reflective. "Very big."

Nine

*L*ifting her head, Caitlyn scanned the dance floor. Did someone dim the lights? Maybe it just seemed that way because her eyes had been closed for so long. The medley that the band was playing reminded her of days past. Her first slow dance, her first ride in a boy's car. Ages ago, when her biggest worry was running out of acne prevention cream or handling post-date kisses.

No need to wonder whether Jake would kiss her tonight. He seemed different somehow, less reserved. She had been pleasantly surprised when he quickly agreed to their daughters' request to stay out late. One A.M., an hour past curfew. She had no intention of staying at the office party that late, surrounded by scores of people. Time alone was what she wanted. Based on the gleam in Jake's eye as he helped her on with her coat, his thoughts were on the same track.

She laid her cheek against his lapel. Thank goodness he was watching for oncoming dancers. She was too busy falling in love to take on that responsibility tonight. His arms tightened, further wrapping her in a warm cocoon of peace and security. Funny that she'd feel that way now, while poised on one of the riskiest brinks of the last seven years. But this was a step she was finally ready to take. He'd be by her side, taking the same risks.

Jake rested his chin on top of her slightly bent head, and felt her breath heat the skin beneath his starched cotton shirt. He really didn't need any more heat at present, not with the blood already pounding through his veins. The seconds ticked by at an infinitely slow pace, and would continue to do so until they were alone.

Cait's OmniCorp associates faded from sight as he closed his eyes and hummed a few bars of the music. He concentrated on the feel of her in his arms, savoring each touch, each movement. So loving, so trusting. Comfortable, too, like a matched puzzle piece. It made his breath unsteady.

He didn't realize that his humming had turned into singing until Cait raised her head. Her smile stopped short of an outright laugh. In retaliation, he slid his free hand slowly down the length of her cocktail dress drawing her tight against his thigh. Her smirking was quickly replaced by a sharp intake of breath.

"Very nice. This fabric feels like a second skin." His fingers stroked in small circular motions over her lower back, sending shivers of anticipation towards her toes. "Burn those starched suits of yours. Replace them with silk."

"You can thank our three little darlings for selecting this. It was part of a last minute SOS package from Brooke."

"I'll thank Brooke, too. Let her know I approve, whole-heartedly." She felt the widening circles he was tracing on her back. "Where is she?"

"Kyle invited friends over for movies and popcorn. When she found out that half of his guest list was female, she decided to stay home."

"Good choice." He laughed, then whispered against her ear. "Can we leave yet?"

Cait shook her head. "There are several people I want you to meet first."

"I'm looking at the only person I'm interested in seeing tonight."

She silenced him by placing her finger against his lips. "There's a keynote address following dinner. We could slip out afterwards, when they serve dessert."

His voice rumbled softly against her touch. "Then prepare yourself for some heavy explaining." He kissed the smooth fingertip, then captured it between his teeth.

She withdrew reluctantly. Her common sense was slipping fast. "I work with these people, remember?"

His gaze focused on her lips. He heard her sigh as he leaned slowly towards her. So tempting. It was increasingly difficult to remember that this was neither the time nor place.

She tilted slightly away. "Just a little longer."

His mouth moved another inch closer.

"I'm serious." Her warning was softened by a smile. She placed a palm against his shoulder and slightly pushed, trying to wedge a respectable distance between them.

"You think I'm not?" He pressed his lower body against hers and held her close. "Think again."

He was right, it was time to go. And it was long past time to put her own needs first, for a change. She smiled up at him. "I'll get my coat."

"Good." He stepped back, then trailed his fingers down her arm. They intertwined with hers. "Remember where we left off."

She squeezed his grip in silent agreement.

Their progress towards the table was agonizingly slow. With each new introduction Jake released his hold on her to shake hands. His smile was warm and genuine, exhibiting much more patience than she was feeling. When the last co-worker turned to go, he nodded again in the direction of their coats. His firm touch on the hollow of her back returned, resting possessively. That one small connection was enough to send chills of excitement through her.

His being here tonight still amazed her. He made no secret of the fact that he usually boycotted events of this sort. It made their togetherness even more significant. She hadn't been part of a couple, a romantic twosome, in years. She tried to keep the blush from her cheeks as she hurried through the crowd, but it was impossible. The rush of adrenaline was too exciting to contain.

A voice boomed over the microphone, interrupting their departure. Disappointment swept over Jake like ice water. He looked at his watch. Thirty minutes tops, that's all he'd spare. The remainder of the evening was his.

From the look on Cait's face, he saw that her reaction was quite different than his. She leaned against him and lowered her voice. "That's Bill Anderson, Vice President of Field Operations. I'd love to introduce you before we leave."

Jake frowned. Her expression seemed overly enthusiastic for having spotted an executive. Her hand tightened within his grasp. Glancing towards the podium, he took in the VP's athletic build and contagious smile. Was this guy something more to Cait than a corporate executive? He no longer needed to force his interest. His curiosity was alive and humming. "Known him long?"

"Forever."

He clenched his jaw as her single word delivered a blow to his gut. Shades of Victoria. She'd used that same tone whenever she described something just beyond her reach. What was it about this guy that caused Cait's voice to turn deep and husky?

Jake was through clock-watching. They were definitely staying.

■　■　■

Bill adjusted the microphone, then signaled for a glass of water. During the interim silence Jake tried to concentrate on Cait's whispered explanation, but it was difficult. His mind already raced ahead, drawing its own conclusion.

"Bill and I first met during my freshman year in college. After graduation we ended up going separate directions. We stayed in contact mainly through Christmas cards and occasional phone calls, until three years ago, when I mentioned that I was looking for something new. Bill surprised me with a recommendation letter, opening the doors here at OmniCorp. He was a marketing rep for them in the Southern Cal area and knew the Seattle office was expanding."

Jake flexed his neck slightly to each side, trying to ease the stiffness. "Then he was also a friend of Todd's?"

"The best, his closest friend. They played basketball together for the University of Missouri."

His eyes met hers and held. "How are you going to introduce me? Just as a customer? A friend?"

She didn't hesitate. Her chin lifted. She returned his

direct stare. "Bill wouldn't believe either fabrication. Not once he sees us together."

The warmth of her response reassured him, relaxing the tendons in his neck and shoulders. "Good. I like him already. Lead on."

They moved closer to the ring of tables edging the risers. His jaw was no longer clenched. He was looking forward to the introductions now. He stood straight, arm wrapped loosely around Caitlyn's waist, eyes focused on center stage.

This evening already had been a big step forward in their relationship. Visions of the future were swimming before his eyes. Amazing how everything was gathering steam so quickly. A bit scary, really, but no more for him than for her. He looked down at Cait, wrapped in the crook of his arm.

His thoughts were interrupted by the sound of applause. Bill was making some sort of announcement. Jake leaned closer to listen.

". . . Geoff Martin will transfer to the Portland office and assume the role of Sales Manager. Effective date, the end of next month."

Geoff bounded up the steps to shake hands with Bill. Jake's eyebrows furrowed into a scowl. Showy dresser, million dollar smile. He'd tangled with flash-and-dash types before, at Victoria's dinner parties.

Cait turned, palms resting against his lapel, eyes sparkling. "This is great. Wait until Brooke hears."

Apprehension prickled the back of his neck. Something was not quite right. "That name's familiar."

"Geoff is the Christmas party ego-monger I told you about earlier. An extremely difficult person to work with, when he wants to be. Unfortunately he wants to be, most of the time. He single-handedly keeps the term 'male chauvinist' alive and flourishing at OmniCorp. It will be a breath of fresh air through the offices, the day Geoff packs his boxes."

Jake tightened his grip at her waist. "You're like a breath of fresh air to me, you know." He suddenly longed to return to the dance floor, to resume the light banter they had shared earlier. The mood of the crowd surrounding him was thick with tension, as if they were expecting more. Instead, Bill stepped away from the microphone, signalling an end to the announcements. Jake could almost feel their groan of disappointment.

Cait glanced upward. "We'll offer our congratulations, then head out." He was staring absently at her. She tugged at his arm and softened her voice to a playful tone. "That is, if you still want to leave."

Her words broke through his stream of thought. He nodded, managing a slight smile. "I do."

"Then follow me." She linked her fingers with his and led him towards the podium.

He was able to assess the two men at close range now. Bill must be in his early forties, based on the amount of gray in his blond hair. Wide shoulders, lean everywhere else. Probably a weekend athlete of some sort. His Armani suit was a classic. Jake could easily imagine him on a championship golf course.

In stark contrast Geoff's hair showed no traces of gray mixed in with the black and his double-breasted navy suit supplied him with all the charm of a used car salesman. As they approached, Bill spotted Cait and waved. He returned Jake's measured appraisal directly. Jake respected that, to him it signified integrity.

When they arrived, Geoff, eyes darting nervously, stepped off the risers and captured Cait in a warmer-than-necessary hug. So he was also the touchy-feely type. He'd hated this part, with Victoria. Memories clenched at his gut again. Mr. Smooth had better keep his distance, and his hands, away from Caitlyn in the future.

She drew back from the forced embrace and stood next to Jake. Her shoulder gently brushed against his jacket front. She felt Jake's hand lightly rest at her waist. "Congratulations and good luck with your new assignment."

"Thanks. Surprised?"

"Delighted is a better word." Her smile was innocent.

Geoff tilted his head towards the man at her side. "Who's the new guy?"

"Jake Brandon."

"From the construction company, of course." The grin slid in Jake's direction. "Issaquah, right? One of our newest accounts. I saw your name on the guest list. Never had the pleasure of meeting you before, always dealt with your partner. Dick, was it?"

"Nick."

"Nick. That's right. Thanks for coming."

Jake watched him silently, keeping all expression from his face.

Geoff continued. "He refers to you as the man-behind-the-scenes, you know. Not the office type. I'm surprised that you permitted Cait to drag you here."

Jake glanced down at her. Nothing would have kept him from her side tonight. "Actually, it was the handcuffs that did it."

Cait couldn't suppress a slight smile, but she changed the subject. Geoff was unpredictable when irritated. Best not to provoke him any further.

"You'll have to excuse us. I want to introduce Bill before the music starts." She saw Bill approaching.

"Cait, good to see you," Bill said.

Jake watched as she was embraced for the second time. This time, she wasn't in a hurry to draw back. Her smile for this man from her past was genuine.

Bill extended his hand to Jake. "Bill Anderson. And you are?"

He accepted the outreached hand. "Jake Brandon, of Brandon and Slater Construction."

"One of our newest customers," Cait said quickly.

Jake looked at her blankly. Oh right, that was admitting a lot. What happened to her plan to recognize their relationship publicly? He drew a deep breath. Maybe he was smarting from her stepping away from his arm when Bill arrived on the scene. Maybe he was expecting too much, too fast. Being unrealistic. Again.

Bill said, "Geoff filled me in on your company, and about the system you licensed from us. It's one of our best."

"We've had excellent support, too." Jake glanced down at the woman still by his side. A blush covered her cheeks as their eyes met. "Many of our employees were novices at computer lingo when the system arrived. Cait made each and every one feel at ease, feel important to the system's overall success."

Bill nodded. "Worker acceptance is key to any new business process. And Cait certainly has that way about her. I'd clone her if I could. She's performed exceptionally from the very start. Makes the marketing department's job much easier, wouldn't you agree, Geoff?"

Jake glanced in the sales rep's direction. Mr. Smiley, still staring down at Cait, had undergone a quick transformation during the course of the discussion.

His jaw appeared to be stiffly set and his gaze narrowed.

His lips resembled a thin, hard line of resentment. He must have finally felt all eyes on him, because he quickly snapped to attention.

When he spoke his voice was as smooth as used motor oil, and twice as unsavory. He looked directly at Jake. "Yes, I've enjoyed working with Cait. For years. Teams with me on all my major accounts. Did she ever to mention that she's my closest partner?"

Jake didn't honor his question with a confirmation or denial.

Geoff nodded, as if to himself. He appeared pleased with his own words. "Quite an enthusiastic worker, if you know what I mean."

Bill shot the man a warning glance.

Jake kept his tone neutral. "Not sure that I do. Care to explain?" He was on to this guy. Cait would never involve herself with someone like Geoff, but it couldn't hurt to listen for a while. Let Geoff tie his own noose in front of management.

"That Cait. Don't know what I'd do without her." His tone oozed again with insinuation. "And now I don't have to."

"Geoff," Bill said sharply.

The remark caught Jake off-guard. Impatience crept into his voice. "Don't have to . . ."

"Be without her." Geoff tilted his head towards his new supervisor. "Bill just approved a proposal, offering Cait the position of Portland Technical Manager. Great idea, huh?"

■ ■ ■

An explosion couldn't have stolen Jake's breath away faster. Childhood memories came racing back, one hauntingly familiar nightmare after another. He was hardly aware that Geoff was still speaking.

"And since she's currently unattached, we're hoping she'll say yes. Right, boss?"

Bill straightened. His voice was chillingly cold. "This is neither the time nor place."

Jake noticed that Bill's eyes were drilling holes directly into the slimeball. A person with any real feelings would have been intimidated by that, but predictably Geoff simply continued his attack.

"It would be a shame if her daughters, or anyone else, pressured her into passing this opportunity by. Not only a promotion, but a chance to keep a few longtime relationships alive and thriving. Nice, don't you agree?" Geoff emphasized his thinly disguised implication by raising one eyebrow.

Jake glanced at Bill. Cait and Mr. Old Family Friend? Her exchange with Bill had been warm and comfortable. In fact, she'd distanced herself from him when Bill arrived.

He straightened, waiting, keeping his fingers flexed instead of balled into fists. That way it would be less enticing to bury one of them into Geoff's chemically-bleached grin.

Cait stared at Bill, her mouth open. She was dumbfounded. A promotion? She had always hoped that one day her efforts would pay off. But not like this. She turned to Bill for confirmation. He nodded once, maintaining glaring eye contact with Geoff.

Then the OmniCorp executive took control of the conversation. "I'd planned to discuss this in a more private setting. Since the word is out, let me at least confirm that it's true. You're my leading candidate. I'd like the chance to discuss the particulars with you while I'm here this weekend.

Maybe over breakfast? We can meet here at the hotel, around ten?"

"Sure," she said slowly. "I don't know what to say."

"There will be plenty of time tomorrow. It's a great opportunity, one you certainly deserve. In the end, despite this mix-up, I hope you'll say yes, after hearing the details." His gaze swung to Geoff. "We need to talk."

"Fine, boss. When?"

"Now. Follow me." Bill nodded curtly to Jake and Cait, and the two men walked off.

Cait stepped closer to Jake. "I can't believe it." She was still lightheaded from the surprise, the anger and the resultant adrenaline. Glancing up, she saw that he was looking through her, rather than at her. She touched his arm to bring him back to the present. "Jake?"

He snapped out of his trance. His voice was flat, his gaze detached, protected, once again, behind a wall of reserve. "Let's go." He ushered her briskly through the crowd. She picked up her purse and they stopped at the coat check. He secured the jacket over her shoulders without letting their bodies come into even the slightest of contact.

Cait followed. They headed in silence towards the front door. When finally out of earshot of the others, she stepped in front of him, blocking the way. "I had no idea this was coming."

"No need to explain."

"What do you mean, no need? I was floored."

"I understand." His voice dripped icicles.

"Well, I don't. Why don't you fill me in?"

"You've been offered a promotion, a golden opportunity. That's all."

"That's it? The end? I haven't even heard the details yet?"

"My business is here, you're on your way up." He

shrugged. His voice was flat. "This is nothing new. I should have seen it coming all along. History repeats itself."

His simple, dismissing movement didn't match the complex emotions she saw clouding his eyes. Cait grabbed his arm, not caring what the gawkers in the lobby might think. "Don't confuse me with anyone else. Especially not with your past!"

Wrenching away from her grip, he opened the front door. "This kind of thing happens. Let's get out of here."

Sure, he was being unreasonable, coldhearted and pigheaded. Hadn't he been called all those names before, plus some? He needed time to think. With luck, the fresh night air would help clear his brain.

He breathed deeply. Cait hadn't caused this, he shouldn't take it out on her. Obviously, she was unaware that the announcement was coming. Still, the situation cut at him.

Cait raced in front of him again and turned, stopping his progress with a firm hand on his chest. "It doesn't just 'happen' to me. Not this fast."

He stared at her in silence. Maybe she was a victim of sorts, too. He didn't know, and frankly at this moment, he didn't care. All that he knew for sure was that it hurt, and he had thought those days were permanently over.

She gripped his lapel harder, crumpling it. "I've waited a lifetime to feel this alive. Don't end our relationship now. Not like this."

"What relationship? I had something you needed and vice versa. Fine. The lodge is still yours for the week. Jackie will still be able to make friends and get settled into her new life. Don't make more out of it than there is." He released her grasp on his jacket, then stepped around her towards the car.

As the locks clicked open, Cait exploded. "You're

running again. That's why you're refusing to discuss this."

"Running?" He walked around to the passenger side and opened her door. "I don't think so."

"I do! From me, from our plans."

"What plans?"

"For later tonight. For . . ." She stopped.

"Maybe we had plans, maybe not. Now I think we'll just call it a night." Jake rounded the front and opened the driver's side. He climbed into the driver's seat, slamming the door. The engine started.

Cait stood in the open doorway. "You have me confused with someone else in your past."

"Maybe." He looked straight ahead, staring out the windshield. His expression was blank.

"You're afraid," she accused softly.

"I need some distance."

"No. Talk to me."

Jake clenched his hands around the steering wheel, then lowered his forehead to rest against them. He ached, everywhere. It hurt down deep, in places that he thought were sealed off for good. He drew a deep breath. "It's more than just the move, Cait. There's something I need to know."

"What."

The cutting edge was gone from his anger. His voice was painfully soft. "I shouldn't ask this, but it's eating me alive. I apologize in advance."

"Ask."

"I'll take you at your word, but you've got to level with me." He slowly lifted his head, raising his eyes to hers. "Are you having an affair with Bill?"

Oh, God. Where had that come from? It wasn't fair, having to deal with both explosive subjects at once.

And what could she say?

Not lately? Anyway, a one night stand shouldn't constitute an affair.

She continued to hold his gaze. "I swear to you that I haven't slept with any man since Todd died." That was the gospel truth. Why did she feel so deceitful uttering those well-chosen words?

Jake continued to search her eyes. There was something else. Something she wasn't saying, but what? He needed to believe her. Without trust there was nothing. Certainly they had more than that.

"All right." He shut off the engine. "I said I'd ask, then drop it." He ran his hands roughly across his eyes then down his jaw. Resting his arm against the back of the passenger seat, he looked over and saw her hesitating. Now what? He waited.

She watched his battle-weary expression and knew she had to finish. Something in his past was driving this reaction; she just didn't know what. Maybe with time, he'd tell her. Right now she'd be the one to share of herself, show him how, before the subject was swept under a rug of deceit. "There's more."

He froze, not wanting to listen, but afraid not to. "How much more?"

"I have two things to say, before I get in the car. After hearing me out you can decide whether this relationship is worth mending or not." She crossed her arms over her chest, the red silk of her dress gleaming under the parking lot lights. "If it's not worth it, fine. Call me a cab and I'll see you around. I can't do it alone and I'm not going to fight my way in."

She paused for several agonizing seconds. "Bill and I were together one night, about ten years ago."

"You've only been a widow for seven."

"I know exactly when my husband died. I don't need to be reminded. It had nothing to do with you or with us. Zip it, until I'm through." Cait paused, realizing that she was about to share her confession with any passer-by who cared to eavesdrop. She began again, her tone softer this time. "You and I have started a relationship that I think is worth working for, but I can only deal with one issue at a time. Tonight's subject is promotions, not personal histories." Her eyes met his with unflinching directness. "Do we take these one at a time, or call it quits without ever knowing what was possible?"

Jake let out the breath he'd been holding. She was angry at him? Infuriating. He should never have let her in, lowered his defenses in the first place. But the plain facts were that she'd wormed her way inside of his life, and his heart. Even his foolish pride wasn't strong enough to loosen the bonds.

She could have kept her secret buried, but hadn't. That meant more to him than words ever could. He still needed time to think, but maybe they could talk awhile first. Aloof was acceptable, confused was understandable, but he refused to be rude. And she was right, he was running again. It was time to stop.

Jake restarted the engine, then looked across the passenger seat. "Get in."

■ ■ ■

They drove in silence to her home in suburbia. Street lights, well-marked intersections. She observed it all, as if for the first time. So different from Jake's lodge on Rattlesnake Ridge. Just one of their many differences, if she assessed things objectively.

She shook her head. Just a short while ago the anticipation of a few uninterrupted hours together curled her toes. Now anger, mixed with apprehension, dug her nails into her palms. A sad ending to such a promising evening.

He pulled abruptly into her driveway and left the engine running. Did he expect her just to jump out? Well, Jake might be willing to part this way, but she wasn't. She turned in her seat, facing him. "Please come in. The girls won't be back for hours. We can finish our discussion in private."

Several agonizing moments passed. He continued to look straight ahead. Dreams of another ending to this evening swirled down the drain. It was better this way, better now than later. Less involved. Then why was he hurting so badly?

When he finally spoke his voice was low and distant. "Maybe in the morning, when I come by to pick up Jackie. We'll talk then." He glanced at her. "I can make it early so you won't miss your breakfast meeting."

The tenseness had fled his muscles during the last half hour, leaving behind a deep-seated exhaustion. He leaned back, exhaling slowly.

She shook her head. "No, now. Together. Before any more assumptions have time to creep in and crystallize. Before middle-of-the-night memories muddy the water any further." Cait laid her hand on his forearm. He didn't draw away.

He watched her reach out to him and exhaled again. Running was easier. Staying meant opening himself up to further pain and disappointment. But how could he possibly hurt more than he did already? He turned off the engine. "Okay."

Cait opened her door and jumped down, not waiting

for Jake to come around for her. When they reached the front door, she fumbled with her key. His hand covered hers, calming her shaking fingers. Together they unlocked the door.

She headed down the hallway towards the kitchen, tossing her purse on the family room sofa. "Should I make coffee?"

"I'd prefer scotch, if you have any."

Cait hesitated for a moment. She'd never seen him drink, not even one of the few beers in the back of his fridge. Quickly scrambling for a suitable substitute, she pulled a chair over to the stove and opened a small cabinet door. What she was looking for was behind the spices. One lone bottle, three quarters full.

"This rum is left over from Christmas. Will that do?" She dampened a rag to dust off the bottle.

"Which Christmas?"

Her hand stilled. When she finally spoke, her words were just a notch above a whisper. "From my last Christmas with Todd. Rum and eggnog around a blazing fire on Christmas Eve was a tradition for us. Since the girls are still too young, and I have no family in the area, the bottle's still around."

She lifted her chin and looked squarely at him. The seconds ticked by. "Never mind. Maybe someday I'll find a great fruitcake recipe."

As she moved to return the bottle to its cubbyhole, he stopped her with a hand on her shoulder. "I'll have some on the rocks, since it's dark rum."

Glancing back, she smiled. "Great. Coming right up."

After fixing his drink and pouring herself a glass of Chardonnay, Cait started the coffee pot. This is for later on, she told herself. It was beginning to sound as if there would be a 'later on.' And if there weren't, then she'd just microwave a cup to go with her morning cereal, reliving what might have been. Warmed over coffee and warmed over dreams.

She carried the glasses into the living room. Jake stood by the fireplace, studying one of several photos lining the mantle. He looked up. He'd taken his jacket and tie off and folded them neatly.

She crossed the room to hand him the drink and glanced at the picture. It had been taken the day she closed on this house. Rose and Lynn posed with her, behind the 'For Sale' sign. A bright red 'Sold' banner was slapped diagonally across it. The bushes in the background were missing several years of growth. Rose wore braces.

"Was this taken before or after Todd died?"

"About six months after."

"Must have been a difficult time for you, making decisions like this all alone."

"Arranging the funeral and packing away memories was difficult. Selecting this house and turning a lifelong dream into a reality? That part was easy." Her smile was bittersweet.

Only easy for a strong, independent woman. One with a clear vision of what she wanted in life and the drive to go after it. He glanced again at the photo. Even though she was smiling, the underlying tension was obvious in her expression. But her fear of the unknown hadn't stopped her from what she wanted. Why couldn't he face life's uncertainties the same way?

He returned the frame to the mantle and began rolling up his sleeves. His forearms were covered with soft, nearly black hair. "Should I start a fire?"

She watched as he rolled. A lot more of him was on display during their afternoon of canoeing, but this small, tantalizing glimpse made her wish he wouldn't stop with just the sleeves. "Ah, no."

He glanced up.

Cait bit her bottom lip to drive the wayward thoughts from her mind. "After spending most of my life in the Midwest, I still like to pretend that summer begins in June. Even in Seattle."

He laughed. "Funny, so do I." He left his sleeves at half-mast.

Sitting on the far end of the couch, she slipped off her heels and folded her legs beneath the flowing silk skirt. She picked up her glass. Jake joined her, leaving ample room between them.

Clearing his throat, he began. "I'm not very good at this, but I'm willing to give it an honest try by going first. I over-reacted. There's a lot of baggage left over from my childhood that I've never been able to put behind me."

"Your father?"

He nodded and crossed one leg over the other. "He died soon after I turned thirteen, but not from old age. My mother's restlessness and ambition killed him."

Cait held her hundreds of questions inside, waiting for him to continue at his own pace.

"They were always fighting about money. We weren't poor; quite the contrary. Dad always seemed to have plenty of cash, but Mother was furious whenever he brought presents home. She'd make him take the gifts back or would lock them away, out of sight."

"Why?"

"I'm sure it was her ego. Must have been jealous of my father's good fortune. Time and time again Dad, my brothers and I paid the price. It was like clockwork. As soon as Dad's new job started paying off, the fights would begin and Mother would start packing." He shook his head and stared into his rum. "She searched relentlessly for the perfect city, the perfect position, constantly moving us. I used to feel guilty for wanting to stay behind. I wanted to let her go, out of our lives. I actually believed it would be better that way." He glanced at Cait. "Dad and I could have managed the little ones just fine. I didn't understand why she had to drag us along. After all, it was her ambition she was chasing, not ours."

"How did your father die?"

"We packed for L.A. when I was thirteen. We stopped overnight in Salt Lake City. Dad called at the prearranged time. They argued as never before." He rested his head against the cushion, cradling his glass in both hands. "The next morning Mother turned the car north and we ended up here in Seattle. Dad was killed days later in an accidental shooting near the airport. We saw it on the news." Jake stared at the ceiling. His words were barely audible. "He was on his way here, to us."

Cait's eyes were bright with unshed tears. She moved closer and covered his clenched fist with her hand.

He lowered his gaze to hers and spoke with bitterness. "Instead of grieving, Mother changed our last name, threatened to ground us if we ever mentioned Dad's name to our friends, then calmly went to work the next day. We didn't even attend his funeral."

Several moments passed before she could respond. Something was missing, like the entire other side of this story. Maybe it was her own maternal instinct that refused to let her accept his story at face value. That, and the fact that Jake's single point of view was so one-sided. It seemed out of character for the loving man that she'd come to know.

Her voice was low, her emotion controlled. "And you

think I'd do the same? You don't know me very well, after all."

"No, there are many differences." He unclenched his fist and laced her fingers with his own. "Your genuine love for your kids; all kids from what I've seen. Your volunteer work with the church. Only a very special person could do all that you do. The only things important to Mother were her career and her independence."

He looked into her eyes. "I know that those same things are also important to you, but somehow, it's not the same. Your hard work and determination are two of the qualities I most admire, because they're based on love. Love of children, love of life. They're what brought us together in the first place."

"But . . ."

He looked down at their interlaced fingers. "From what I've seen and heard of your work, this is a well-deserved promotion. You'd be a fool not to consider it seriously. And I'd be a selfish bastard to stand in your way."

"I haven't even heard the offer yet."

"You will. I'm sure Bill's put together a package that will be hard to resist."

"Just a second." She wrenched her hand away.

"I'm not implying anything, the words just came out wrong. I said I wouldn't question you further, and I meant it." He recaptured her hand and slouched back against the cushion. "It's obvious that he thinks highly of you; would offer only the best." He looked at her and waited until her gaze met his. "You owe it to yourself to listen and to do what's best."

"Where does that leave us then?"

"About a hundred and seventy miles apart."

The grandfather clock in the hallway measured the

passing seconds, then chimed the half hour. Realizing that the girls would be back soon, he pulled Cait into his arms and held her close, her shoulders against his chest. His lips brushed her hair once, then twice, before he settled her head under his chin.

She looked at the empty fireplace and remembered sitting in his living room last weekend. He'd built a roaring fire, but nothing to match the heat that followed. The burning from within nearly consumed them both. What if it had? Would they still be having this same conversation tonight? Probably not. That was why he'd stopped. They weren't ready. They still weren't. He'd said he didn't want to deal with regrets later, on either side. But if they let this relationship go without a fight, wouldn't they regret that too? She knew that she would.

Commitment and trust. The two were intertwined. Unfortunately both were not quite there yet. Not firmly enough to ward off the 'what ifs.' But the seeds were there. They just needed time to take root. "Add stubborn to my list of admirable traits."

"What?"

"If I do take this job, remember that one hundred and seventy miles is merely a three hour drive."

"Only if I speed, the entire way."

"You could fly instead. Or I could. In fact, I could get a private pilot's license if I put my mind to it."

"And your checkbook, too. What about Rose and Lynn? Co-pilots?"

"You're catching on." Cait lifted one of his arms and turned to face him. He held her close against his chest. "Humor me. Take your blinders off and play along."

"All right, let's see. My brother, Drew, would love to have me visit more often."

"That doesn't count because you'd be staying with me. Try again."

Jake laughed, then furrowed his brow as if deep in thought. "Video-conferencing."

"Wrong. Not my idea of reaching out to touch someone. I want the real thing."

He held her tighter. "Three-day work weeks, with four days off for good behavior."

"Hey, you're onto something. Why just visit? Surely there's someone in the Portland area who needs a dream house built."

His smile faded. "Move my business to Portland?"

"You have to admit that it's a possibility."

Gently, but firmly, he moved her aside, then stood. Walking to the window, he stared out.

She jumped to her feet, but didn't join him. "The terrain and climate are practically identical. I'm sure there's a market."

He continued to stare out the window. "Follow you to Portland? Then what? Where else does OmniCorp have offices?"

"Don't draw an analogy with your parent's situation! I was only suggesting possibilities."

"I'm sure that in the early days, Mother 'suggested' ideas too. Before the fighting started."

"Just a minute."

"No, Cait." He unrolled his sleeves and picked up his jacket. "Not now. Our daughters are home."

She glanced at her watch. "This early? There are still so many things we haven't talked about."

He reached for the door, hand gripping the knob. "You and Bill have details to go over first. I'll call you in a few days. After we've both had time to think."

The girls burst in, eyes aglow at finding their parents together. But, before they could remove their jackets, Jake signalled to Jackie that it was time to go.

"Do I have to? I was invited to spend the night."

Jake nodded firmly, propelling her outside. He was lost in his own vanishing dreams. Marching Jackie down the steps, he thought grimly, at one time, sweetheart, so was I.

Ten

"Thanks for meeting me for breakfast, Cait. I can imagine what your Saturdays are usually like." Bill looked around the hotel restaurant, signaling for the waiter.

"No trouble. The girls are old enough to drive. They won't even miss me until their softball game begins. By then, if I'm not in the stands, my name is 'Mud.'"

"Or worse."

Cait raised one eyebrow, then laughed. "Better not be worse."

He smiled at her over the menu, laugh lines near both eyes deepening.

They ordered quickly, then traded parenting stories, bringing each other up-to-date. It was just like old times, when she and Todd made a foursome with Bill and his wife Carol. Their conversation, riddled with humor, flowed easily from one subject to the next. As comfortable as Bill's linen blazer and stonewashed denim shirt.

Their banter reminded her of the late night supper in Jake's kitchen, before passion had entered their relationship, complicating things. That was both good and bad. She and Jake could get through this, she knew they could. But they'd have to remember that things worth having were also worth fighting for.

When it was Bill's turn to spin the next tale, Cait leaned back and observed her longtime friend. He was as striking now as he'd been as a new graduate student, handsome, brilliant and full of life. There were subtle differences though, comparing that former Bill, the basketball jock, to the man she knew a decade-and-a-half later.

The highlights near his temples were more pronounced with each passing year. It was a tribute, a badge of honor. Along with the laugh lines, they were outward symbols of his quick rise into management, despite adhering to an enviable eight-to-six work schedule.

Leaning forward, elbows on table, he wrapped up his narrative on the joys of raising a single son in a houseful of girls. "If he survives his first day of kindergarten without his sisters tossing him off the school bus, then I figure it's all downhill from there."

Cait laughed. "Life would be dull without a little teasing and sibling rivalry now and then, wouldn't it?"

"Oh, come on. Surely your girls don't engage in such nonsense?"

"Of course not." Cait shook her head, a serious expression firmly in place. "Except on rare occasions, like when I'm not looking, or on the phone."

It was his turn to laugh. Cait sipped her juice.

In her estimation, Bill and Carol were luckier than most. They were rescued from the jaws of an early divorce through counseling, and went on to have their three youngest children. She and Todd had the chance to do the same, but after the twins were born he was too busy working his way up the corporate ladder even to consider an expanded family. Since most of the burden of raising the children fell on Cait, she didn't push the subject. Now it was too late.

No regrets, though. Her daughters were a mother's dream come true. Lynn had Todd's serious outlook on life and Rose inherited Cait's own desire to have all things end happily ever after. Good kids. So were the teens in her extended family, her youth group. She loved being surrounded by them, even when they were overly rambunctious.

The waiter reappeared to refill their coffee. Bill used the interruption as a cue to get down to business. "I apologize for the way things were handled last night. Rest assured that was not my plan. If that was an example of Martin's typical performance, then his recommendation was highly overrated."

"Apology accepted. In all fairness, our customers seem to like him." She laughed, then amended her statement. "Well, most of our customers, anyway."

"I met at least one, last night, who is not too enamored of him."

"You're right. Jake's not an admirer."

He nodded. Moving aside his silverware, he made room for his briefcase. He popped it open and retrieved two legal-sized packets. "Here are the details of my offer." He handed her one of the envelopes.

Accepting it, she stared silently at her name neatly

printed on the front. Here it was. What she had worked towards, hoped for. Reality sometimes differed so drastically from dreams. Funny that in finally gaining this she was risking something even more dear to her. If only she had more time to be sure. To see where things would lead.

She listened intently to Bill's summary of the offer. "There's a lot to think about, so I'll set a timetable of one month. Plan a visit to our Portland office to take a look around within the next two weeks or so. Meet the staff, review responsibilities. Stay the weekend so that you'll have time to talk to a realtor."

She drew a deep breath. "I'll be honest. There's a lot to consider."

This time he didn't let the opening pass. "Is one of those 'considerations' six-foot-two, and built like a line-backer?"

She looked up. A question like this would be out of line normally, but theirs was far from a business-only relationship. She smiled, and corrected his statement. "Six-foot-three."

He nodded. "Is it serious?"

Picking up her spoon, she twirled it between her fingers. "For me it is. He feels the same, but he's fighting it. Hard. He ran when Portland was mentioned."

"Lived there before? Bad memories?"

"Lots of bad memories, but not of Oregon. In fact, Jake currently has a brother living west of the city." She absently drew patterns on the crisp, white fabric. "Let's just say that he's committed to staying here."

"Then this will be a tough decision for you, because I think this offer is excellent." He smiled as he tapped the gold envelope. "We'll cover the specifics during your visit. In the meantime you can review the paperwork at your leisure."

"Fine." She tried to inject excitement into her voice. The

resulting sound was forced and unnaturally light. "I'll call with any questions."

"Cait?"

It was all too much, too fast. She needed time to think. Wasn't that exactly what Jake said to her last night? Looking up from the package, she met his gaze. Did she look half as scared as she felt?

"Whatever you decide will be fine with me. You know that, don't you?"

She sighed. This was the real Bill again, not corporate vice president. Just her friend. "Yes, I do."

He switched subjects. First it was golf, his favorite, then on to roller-blading, hers. Their discussion carried them through breakfast, and past several coffee refills. After they finished, they walked together to the hotel lobby. Bill's easy stride slowed to match her small, nervously quick steps. At the elevators, she shook his hand, as she would with any business associate.

"Bring the girls when you come to Portland. Mine would love to see them. So would Carol and I."

"I'll do that. With school out we have plenty of time."

"Great." He turned to punch the 'Up' button on the elevator.

She gripped her purse tighter. "Bill, one more thing. If I don't accept, please don't think . . ."

"Nonsense. Business is business." He rested a hand on her shoulder. "You've earned this promotion and I hope it turns out right for you. But if it doesn't, don't worry. I have several other candidates."

The doors behind him opened. He stepped back, blocking their closure with his foot. "I do have one bit of advice for you, though."

"What?"

"Listen to your head, but follow your heart." He winked at her as the doors began to shut. "That's always worked well for me."

■ ■ ■

Cait pulled into the garage, then hurried inside. Just enough time to change before heading out to the girls' game. She glanced at her watch. Just enough time to check messages and then change, she amended.

Surely Jake would want to get together this evening, to rehash things? Set a new course, work something out? She laid her purse on the kitchen counter and scanned the note pad. As usual, Lynn's handwriting was small, detailed and precise. Rose's was a flowery scrawl and missing some of the more minor details, like the phone number. Luckily, Cait knew the callers.

Her finger moved slowly down the pad, keeping her vision focused on one message at a time. Her reaction was to race ahead, as her pulse was doing, tossing and skipping the ones without Jake's name on top. She forced herself to take it slowly, forestalling any potential disappointment.

When she reached the last note Cait's hand began to shake. Audra had called, indicating it was urgent. Was the retreat in jeopardy again? She dialed the chairwoman's number from memory. More than a half hour passed before she set the receiver back down. Now her hand was curled into a fist.

All her hopes and dreams, headed down the tubes. She'd underestimated Pamela Sydow's connections. Disappointment swept over her. It wasn't that someone was challenging her plans that upset her. If the camp-out was a bad idea, or a risky venture, she'd cancel it herself. It was that the program she'd planned was a good one, and that her kids would benefit from the extended instruction. Being away from their home environment was good, too. It would give the teens the extra focus needed for her message to sink in. And it wasn't as if the weekend had been planned in a vacuum, either. She'd had parental support all the way.

That was it! There was strength in numbers. Either the parents of her youth group were behind her, or they weren't. If they weren't, then the retreat was history. She couldn't do it without their support. There was only one way to know for sure.

Audra said her plans could be salvaged, but she had to move quickly. Pulling open the bottom desk drawer, she rummaged for the folder labeled Church Directory. She began to dial.

■ ■ ■

Rose's mouth hung open. "No."

"Believe it." Lynn nodded curtly, her expression serious.

"No way."

"Mom's calling all the parents right now, scheduling an emergency meeting for tomorrow after the service. Whatever happened, it must be serious."

"Do you think it had anything to do with her date with Jake on Friday night?"

"Your guess is as good as mine. Quit yapping and let's think." Lynn paced their room while Rose sat white-knuckled on one of the twin beds. "When they left here last night Mom was real nervous."

"Yeah, but it was that good kind of nervous. That I'm-glad-I'm-going-anyway kind of feeling."

"Yeah." Lynn tapped her finger against her lower lip.

"But when she came home . . ."

"We didn't see her come home. She and Jake were already here, remember?" Rose jumped up, snapping her fingers. "Maybe, that's it. They wanted to be here alone and we showed up early."

"Then why was Jake frowning and so anxious to leave, bee-brain? Why didn't Jackie still get to spend the night?"

"Oh. I forgot. The big freeze had settled in." Rose picked up Lynn's pacing, circling in the opposite direction.

After a couple of revolutions Rose grabbed Lynn's arm. "I've got it. Maybe they arrived hours earlier, and Mom had to tell him 'no.'"

Lynn looked at her, astounded. "Do you think she'd do that?"

"I don't know. Maybe she wasn't ready."

"'Prepared,' you mean."

"No, I meant . . . well, whatever."

They stared at each other, then simultaneously shrugged.

Rose's expression changed quickly to a scowl. "And because of that he cancelled the retreat?"

"Maybe Mom was the one who called it off."

Rose stepped away, flinging herself face up on the bed. "Whoever did, it's not fair."

Lynn paused in front of the windows, hands on her hips. "You know, I didn't hear the word 'cancelled' exactly. Mom said it was in jeopardy."

"What's that supposed to mean, exactly?"

Lynn shook her head slowly. "Trouble."

"I know what the dictionary says." Rose sat upright. "What do you think Mom meant by it? Is she gonna look for a new place to hold it?"

"I don't know."

"Me neither."

Rose stood, hands on her hips. She joined her sister by the window. "I guess we'll have to wait until tomorrow to find out."

"But it's a Parents' Meeting. We're not parents, so we're not invited. We'll have to wait until they have everything worked out and then decide to fill us in." Lynn frowned. "Translate that to mean, too late."

"But Jake is."

"Jake is what?"

"A parent, sis. We'll get him to tell us."

"Wrong." Lynn shook her head. "I looked at Mom's call list, kind of over her shoulder. His name's not on it."

"I guess it's because he doesn't go to our church." Rose snapped her fingers. "Then let's call Jackie."

Lynn stepped forward, deep in thought. "Yeah. If we're not using the lodge anymore, I'm sure she'd know that by now. If not, she could find out."

"Yeah. She'll figure out something."

"Let's do it." Lynn crossed to the phone. She lifted the receiver and listened. The dial tone buzzed in her ear. "The coast is clear."

"First, take it back." Rose depressed the switch hook.

"What?" She turned. From the tilt of her sister's chin, Lynn knew exactly what. "Oh, the bee-brain remark. Sorry."

"Accepted."

"You know I love you, don't you?" Lynn ruffled Rose's moussed bangs. Her own were too grown out to wear them that way any longer. She had to keep them firmly tucked behind her ear or Mom would trim them short again. She followed the teasing with a hug. "I have to, you look just like me."

"But slightly cuter."

"Not."

They both laughed, then sobered and dialed quickly. Jackie answered on the first ring.

■ ■ ■

The directions to the community church were succinct and easy to follow. Jake adjusted the knot in his necktie for the umpteenth time and mumbled under his breath. What a way to waste a beautiful Sunday morning. Confined within stained glass!

Just the sight of the steeple up ahead was enough to stiffen his spine. His mother, no doubt hoping to save their souls, forced him and his brothers to attend early morning services every weekend. The only time he could remember enjoying it was when he, Patrick and Drew used holy water on their perfectly combed hair to do impromptu Elvis impersonations down the aisle. He couldn't sit without a pillow for days.

Jackie, riding next to him, interrupted his reminiscing. She was wearing a new purple jean skirt and matching jacket which she'd talked him into buying for just such a church appearance. Little did he know that the opportunity would arise so quickly. "Dad, do you think anyone will get mad when we just show up, unannounced and all?"

"You said it was a parents' meeting. That means it's open to parents of all the campers." He squeezed her shoulder. "Since your name's on the list, it should be just fine."

"But it's not like we go to this church. And I really haven't known the other kids for very long. I just don't want to cause any trouble."

"It's a little late for that, isn't it?" Jake watched her play with her cuticles. A worried expression wrinkled her freshly plucked eyebrows. He leaned closer. Was she wearing purple eye shadow? Too bad he hadn't seen her in the daylight before they left home. Although maybe it was better that he hadn't.

His system was still getting used to this full-time parent thing and he had a track record of making rash judgements. He should check with Caitlyn on the latest acceptable standards. No, scratch that idea.

Reaching over, he covered Jackie's fidgeting hands with his. "To tell you the truth, honey, this entire retreat has already been a heck of a lot of trouble. More than I ever bargained for. My weekends are totally shot, phones are ringing, people constantly coming and going, and boxes of stuff are cluttering my rec room."

He didn't mention that not only his solitude had been blown to smithereens, but his heart as well. As hard as he tried, he couldn't believe Cait would cancel the camp-out just because of their fight on Friday night. There had to be some other reason; it was too far out of character for her. He'd just have to shift his imagination out of overdrive, and wait for the reason. And it had better be a damned good one.

He released Jackie's hand to steer into the lot, parking in the nearest space. The church was infinitely more modern than the ones his mother dragged him to. But still there was a feeling of incense and cobwebs that even a good architect couldn't hide. He shook his head and shut off the engine.

Turning, he looked down at Jackie for a soul-searching minute, before drawing her into his arms. "I sounded a bit rough a minute ago, didn't I?"

She nodded against his crisply starched shirt.

"I'd do it all again, no matter how it turns out, just to bring back your smile."

"You would?"

"You bet."

"You're not mad at Cait anymore, either?"

"That's a different story. No, I'm not mad at her, but we do have a few things to work out." He drew back and met his daughter's damp eyes. "Hey, let's not jump the gun. We'll see for ourselves what the reason is."

She sniffled. Jake kissed her forehead. Releasing her, he grabbed his jacket from the rear seat. Time to straighten out this ridiculous mess, whatever it was, and get back on track with their planning. There were only three weeks left.

He wondered how her Saturday morning meeting had gone with Bill. Perfectly, no doubt. He seemed like that kind of guy. Even though curiosity was eating him alive last night, he hadn't called. He thought that giving her time to review the offer would be best. Now he wished he'd ripped the damned thing to pieces. Especially if it was the reason she was cancelling the retreat.

He stepped down from the truck. Hopefully catching Cait off-guard would work to his advantage. Would she really cancel just because she was angry at him? No, that was strictly personal, totally separate from their commitment to the kids. Then what was the reason?

The heavy oak doors swung open noiselessly. He glanced around at the crowd of coffee-drinkers. So far, so good. The service must have just concluded. Jackie spotted someone she knew and left his side, after receiving a nod of approval.

It took just a few subtle inquiries to locate the parents' meeting. It was already in progress in the senior high room downstairs. He re-joined Jackie and briefed her on where he was headed.

"Good luck, Dad. And thanks."

"I haven't done anything yet."

"Yes, you have. You gave up your morning coffee and your paper."

"Let's hope it was worth the sacrifice." He smiled and ruffled her bangs, feeling a surge of parental love. He'd do anything for her, anything in her best interests that is. And from what he'd heard so far of Caitlyn's agenda, albeit from Jackie, this retreat was something he wanted to help make a reality.

Leaning over, he whispered in her ear. "Don't let the coffee warden over there, the one with the blue hair, turn off the brewer before I return. If you succeed, we'll call the whole thing even."

"Dad, she might hear you." Jackie shushed him, still laughing. Then her expression turned serious again. "Remember, don't lose your cool."

"Thanks for your confidence, honey."

"I'm only saying this for your own good."

"Remember those words the next time you're grounded."

"Get real. I'm too old to be grounded."

"Oh, quite the contrary, honey. I'd say you're just the perfect age."

■ ■ ■

Finding the parents' meeting turned out to be simple. Jake only had to follow the sound of raised, irate voices. Even Caitlyn's usually patient demeanor was audibly cracking around the edges.

"That's totally ridiculous, Mrs. Sydow. There is nothing indecent about camping. Everyone, please come in from the hallway and take a seat. I'll run you through our weekend plans step-by-step." Cait moved to the front of the classroom and grabbed a stack of handouts. "Thank you for attending on such short notice. It seems that our upcoming retreat has caused considerable concern among some of our congregation members. Audra Stockton called and informed me that, even though the Youth Council has approved this event, the Regional Office is still concerned. They've received letters, indicating that this event is not backed by the local congregation. My belief is that although there are some dissenters, that's not the majority opinion. That you, the parents of the teenagers involved, do in fact endorse this camp-out."

There were murmurs among the crowd. She raised her voice a notch and continued.

"I could be wrong, and I admit that. All along, I've had the impression that you were behind me on this. Maybe I haven't asked you clearly enough, or often enough. But I am asking now." She twisted the handouts slightly. "If you do agree, please state so on these permission slips today, so I can proceed with the final plans. If you don't, please state that, too. All responses will be forwarded to the regional office this afternoon."

She stepped to the board and pulled the top off of a dry marking pen. "So that you'll have the total picture before deciding, let me recap our plans. We'll leave from the lower church parking lot on Friday night at five sharp. Two drivers have already volunteered, we still need rides for eight more. Anyone wanting to help, believe me, we could use you.

"We'll head out Interstate 90 to North Bend, then stop for hamburgers before traveling up to the lodge." With the marker, she indicated the events on the timetable one by one, with a big red X. "By not cooking out that first night, we'll be able to unpack, and maybe swim before the evening campfire."

Pamela Sydow stood and waved a single finger. "That's the part I'm worried about, Ms. James. The overnight. On behalf of the entire altar guild, I warn you that your plans for a co-ed sleep-over are in extremely poor taste. The elders of this church won't stand for it. Why, when I was running this youth group, we had our outings in the broad daylight."

"Mrs. Sydow, I assure you . . ."

"Keep your assurances to yourself. Ever since you took over, our youth have been doing unheard of things. In my day we painted the walls of the nursery, pulled weeds on the church grounds, and held bake sales. Now you have the youth mingling with the riffraff on the streets of downtown Seattle."

"We were congratulated for working at the women's center on the six o'clock news."

"No matter. And the slave auction you held last fall as a fund raiser! Why I never."

"The teens raised over a thousand dollars by doing odd jobs for our congregation. That will go a long way towards our mission work." Calm down, Cait reminded herself. Sometimes it's hard to accept the changing of the guard.

She began again, her voice softer. It was the same tone she would use to soothe an agitated child. "Certainly no one objected to these healthy kids weeding lawns, washing cars, and baby-sitting children, Mrs. Sydow. After all, no complaints were officially lodged."

"Well, the jobs were respectable enough. But the teenagers selling themselves like that? It was scandalous."

"They had fun, while learning about giving of themselves and their time."

"It was totally unacceptable. And now you're planning to whisk them away for a forty-eight hour pajama party? Well, I'm glad that my letters to the council caused them, and Audra, to rethink their position."

Cait turned to address the parents. "For those of you that don't know, I've submitted an official copy of our plans to the Youth Council. The council chairwoman, Audra Stockton, is conducting a thorough background check, which will also be attached to our trip plans. But, as I said earlier, the key factor in the council's decision is local parent support. It is your voice they are waiting to hear."

She cleared her throat and took a deep breath. "These are your kids. No matter what plans I come up with, and no matter what your teens may propose by way of activities, I would never move forward on something if I didn't have your full agreement. If you don't . . . if you don't support this, I need to know." Her voice broke.

Jake stepped farther into the room, listening attentively. So that was the reason behind the unexpected message left on his recorder, the one from Audra. He hadn't been in a big hurry to return the call. Now he would.

He watched as Cait continued to defend her position. Were the other parents always this quiet? Did she fight all of her battles alone?

"This overnight will be fully chaperoned," Cait continued. "Just try to remember back when your own kids were in their teens . . ."

"Well, I certainly kept a much closer eye on my girls," Mrs. Sydow interrupted. "Their morals were above reproach. Why just the other night, Fred and I were at the cinema. We saw your daughters and a friend of theirs standing in line, unescorted. One of them was wearing skin tight biking shorts, for heaven's sakes."

"The temperature hit ninety degrees that day," Cait said.

"Who knows what they were up to? They were probably planning on sneaking into an R-rated movie. Maybe, if you were still married yourself, you would see matters in a different light. And as for chaperones, Ms. James, who's planning to chaperone you?"

The accusation landed with deadly accuracy, stealing away Cait's breath and composure. Crestfallen, she searched the audience for support. From the expectant faces looking back at her, she felt like the starring role in a daytime soap opera.

Now the old biddy had done it, Jake thought as his hands clenched unconsciously. Attacking Cait's plans was one thing, but this? She hadn't called things off on a whim. She was fighting tooth and nail for this retreat.

It was time for him to butt in. She might resent it, but he was already on the black list. Maybe on several black lists, from the sounds of this meeting. Things could only go up from here.

"I think we've heard enough from you, Mrs. Sydow. Do you have a child signed up for the camp-out?" He stared back at her outraged expression. "No? Then let's hear from those of you who do." His gaze scanned the suddenly silent room.

Cait spun towards the door at the sound of his marginally polite voice. Was it really Jake, lounging against the doorjamb of her Sunday school room? His arms were firmly crossed, his body language gave away no clues of his slipping control. But, to her, the steely determination filling his eyes told the real story.

She felt a shiver of anticipation mixed with alarm. Why was he here? He was practically off the hook. She had to talk him into cooperating in the first place, so why now, after all that had happened between them?

He stepped into the room and scanned the occupants. His cool regard stopped from time to time as he searched the faces in the crowd. "How about the rest of you? Those of you with kids in this group, what do you think?"

No one spoke.

"Are you worried that your kids are going to be doing something during this camp-out that they couldn't do elsewhere? Couldn't do anywhere, if they really set their minds to it?"

Whispered voices and scarlet faces were the only replies, so Jake continued. "Sounds to me like it boils down to two things. Trust and training. Location doesn't really matter. This weekend getaway will give them a chance to discuss some tough subjects. Teach them to make sound decisions." His eyes bore down on Pamela Sydow. "Because sooner or later they'll be too old for chaperones. Then where will they be?"

Mrs. Sydow recovered quickly. "Who are you to barge in here and disrupt things, Mr. . . Mr. . ."

He stopped her interruption flat. "Someone willing to take a stand." His assertiveness commanded everyone's attention. He pivoted to address the parents.

"Correct me if I'm wrong, but hasn't your youth group doubled in size this last year? Ever wonder why? Haven't your kids taken more outings, learned more about their community and given back more of themselves than ever before?"

He put one foot on an empty seat in the front row, directly in front of Pamela. "Have you ever asked them why they hardly ever miss a meeting? Why they would spend a Saturday evening painting a homeless shelter, or teaching disadvantaged children how to play basketball? Why they're not just sleeping in late, instead?" Leaning over, he lowered his voice as he addressed the belligerent widow. "Certainly there's more to it than the chance of seeing the opposite sex sweat in a pair of tight biking shorts."

Muted laughter broke the embarrassed silence. He straightened and challenged the crowd. "Don't take my word for it, ask them. Your kids. The ones who have their hearts set on this weekend. And while you're at it, ask Cait where she finds the time to raise not only her own active teenagers, but to help you raise yours, too."

He turned to Caitlyn. Silence hung between them as his eyes captured hers. When he spoke again, his voice was softer and richly mellow. "One other thing. I suggest that you take advantage of her generosity while you still can. I know I will."

Moving off to the side of the room, he leaned against the wall so that Cait could retake center stage. After all, this was her meeting, her plans, her doing.

Her breath stuck in her throat as muffled questions stirred the audience to life. She stood riveted, unable to think or speak. When had she stopped being just a suburban do-gooder in his eyes? When had he started to respect, instead of tolerate, her ideas? It made a world of difference just to know that he was firmly on her side. The very thought stiffened her spine, and made her heart thump faster.

The noise from the crowd interrupted her thoughts. "Where's that sign-up list? I'd love to drive. My son can't wait to go."

Another voice from the audience spoke up. "Mine, too. I could help with meal planning." Sounds of chairs moving, as people stood, broke through the silence.

"My daughter would probably hang out at the mall, if she didn't have this circle of friends to do things with. Hand me a permission slip."

Cait's eyes remained glued to Jake's as a smile curved her

lips. His confidence in her was contagious. Turning, she tried to wrap things up quickly. She wanted to catch him before he escaped the church. She wanted time alone to thank him.

Parents began standing, heading for the front of the room. Picking up her clipboard and pen, Cait cleared her throat and directed their attention to the sign-up list. "Please add your name next to any activity you can help with. All efforts are greatly appreciated."

As the parents moved forward in the aisles, Jake walked over to where Cait's nemesis sat dumbfounded. He stopped in front of her and responded to her original objection.

"You asked earlier who I was, Mrs. Sydow, and why I was butting in." He narrowed his eyes in warning. "I own the lodge that your teens have been invited to. So you see, I have quite a lot to say."

"Well, I . . ."

"And one more thing. The girl in the biking shorts? She's my daughter."

Eleven

Grabbing the towel from the handlebars, Cait dried her forehead. The odometer was advanced by only twelve miles, yet she was exhausted. And not just physically. The anxiety of waiting for Jake to call was making her temples throb.

Why did he leave after the meeting, without a word?

She thought that she'd hear something for sure, after leaving a 'thank you' and dinner invitation on his recorder Sunday night. But there was nothing. Feet still poised on the pedals, she looked out her bedroom window to the deck below. Rose was reclined on the chaise longue, sketch pad in hand, capturing the first buds of summer.

Soon it would be dusk. She'd grab a couple of jackets, pour two iced teas, and join her daughter for the sunset.

No more moping around, waiting.

Tossing the towel towards the hamper, Cait climbed off her exercise bike and held onto the seat for a moment to steady herself. Ouch. Time to stop skipping aerobics to rush home for nonexistent messages. Starting tomorrow.

She stared at the phone. As if on command, it suddenly rang. Instantly rejuvenated, she bolted to the nightstand, catching it on the second ring. Maybe, just maybe . . . "Hello?"

"Caitlyn, Audra Stockton here."

Her fingers curled tightly into her palm. Oh please, let this be good news, instead of another setback. She swallowed, trying to keep the disappointment from her voice. "Hi. How goes the investigation?"

"Complete. I added my endorsement to the bottom of your request form. It's now signed, sealed and delivered."

Cait released the breath she didn't know she was holding. Closing her eyes, she savored the moment. "How can I ever thank you?"

"Nonsense. I was ready to agree even before the calls started to arrive."

"What calls?" Cait asked sharply.

"Once word got out that this event might be blocked by a petition sent to the regional office, the telephones started ringing."

"A petition?"

"Sponsored by, you guessed it, our very own nay-sayer, Pamela Sydow."

"I can't believe it. Even after Sunday's meeting?"

"Well, rest assured that the parents of your teens support you one hundred percent. The office has never received so much input on a single subject."

Cait smiled and sat on the edge of her bed. She replayed

the scene in which Jake stood before Mrs. Sydow, dismantling her objections one by one. He was brilliant, confident; and, until a week ago, she thought he could be hers.

Her smile faded and her voice turned monotone, as if reciting a memorized to-do list. "I'll mail you the permission slips and pick up the permit. Maps will be sent out to each family, and a packing list too. The committees can begin their planning now. The council will receive a full report, complete with Lessons Learned, at its August meeting."

Audra interrupted. "Is there something wrong?"

"No." Cait tried to stay focused on the positive. The rest would either work out, or not. Dwelling on it wouldn't help. "Everything is fine. This was our last obstacle."

Audra's tone was missing its usual authoritative ring. In its place was concern. "I usually don't pry, but in this case I'm going to make an exception. Is it your young man?"

Cait blushed. "He's not exactly mine."

"Let's not argue. You'd lose, anyway." Audra chuckled. "The story of how he came to your rescue on Sunday, armor gleaming and sword drawn, made the rounds quickly."

"It did?"

"A delightful contrast to the 'every-woman-for-herself' philosophy so abundant these days, wouldn't you say?"

"Yes." A smile curved Cait's lips. She leaned against the headboard. "Unexpected, too."

"Not usually the gallant type?"

"No, not that. Because we were meeting at the church." She cleared her throat. "I probably should have mentioned this earlier, but Jake isn't the every-Sunday type."

"Doesn't surprise me."

"He never goes at all. Bad childhood memories or something."

"That doesn't concern me, either. When he's ready, or when there's a good reason to, he just may come around."

"Like this past weekend?"

"Exactly. Never judge a man by what he says, only by what he does." Audra's voice turned wistful. "Don't make the same mistake I did, my dear."

The comment caught Cait off-guard. Even after years of association, she knew no more about Audra's personal history than on day one. Viewed as a person of firm beliefs and unwavering integrity, Audra was never one to reach out for help. Too self-sufficient for that. Was that assessment wrong? Was she reaching out now? "You, Audra?"

"Yes. I've made mistakes. I've run when I should have stood my ground." She drew a deep breath. "At the time, there appeared to be no other alternatives."

"Well, then . . ."

"I'm not offering excuses. Lives were shaped by my decisions. I take full responsibility. They were mine to make. Mine alone." Her voice started to trail off. "Just make yours carefully, Caitlyn."

She waited, but there was nothing more. "Audra?"

"Oh yes. Where were we?" With a quick clearing of her throat, the older woman shifted gears. Her tone was once again crisp. "That was the past, this is present. If you think your young man is the very special one who will give your life added meaning, then stick with him. Stick by him. Don't run because things get a little difficult." She paused and chuckled. "After all, womankind was made second. The good Lord probably thought there was room for improvement."

Cait laughed aloud for the first time in three days.

"And speaking of difficult times, I have one final note. If there's still room on your list, please add the name Elizabeth.

Her folks live on the north end. They heard about your upcoming retreat and want to be a part of it. They think your idea is outstanding."

"How did they hear about it?"

"It's such a small world, really. Funny how family and friends can pop up at unusual times, and places, when they're least expected." Her tone was smug. Cait heard a second chuckle.

"The subject arose over a family dinner, my dear. Elizabeth is Pamela Sydow's granddaughter."

■　■　■

The late afternoon sun streamed in through the garden window and reflected off the aluminum sink. Cait ignored it. There was nothing worse than wasting a spectacular sunset by moping indoors. She sighed. If it were raining she'd feel less guilty.

"Is there some reason you can't just pick up the phone and call him?" Brooke paused, waving her celery stick in mid-air. "Because if there is, I certainly missed it."

"I already did, Sunday night. To thank him. I'm not about to beg for his attention."

"That was days ago. What if he didn't get the message?"

Cait glared at her and continued pouring the club soda.

"Jackie could have erased it by mistake."

Cait's eyes rolled skyward. Brooke pressed further. "My point is that you should give the guy a second chance."

"What am I going to say?" She yanked open the freezer. With one forceful twist she popped the ice cubes out of their tray and into the container. "I haven't made up my mind about the transfer yet."

"And you won't until you have some facts to go on, other

than salary and start date. Take a few days off, head south. Relax a little. Take the girls with you."

"I can't believe you used that combination of words." Cait slammed the door shut and tossed the empty tray across the kitchen. It landed loudly in the sink. Unconcerned, she pulled out a stool and sat.

Brooke raised her brow and eyed her friend cautiously. "Which words?" She plunged her celery into the dip, then stirred.

"'Relax', and 'take the girls.'"

"So, leave them with me. Take Jake, instead."

Cait coughed. She took a quick sip of her club soda. "That's so outrageous it's funny."

"Why not take him? He's part of this decision, too." Brooke snapped the stick in half and peeled away the loose strings. She popped the smaller of the two pieces in her mouth. "If you still want him to be, that is."

Brooke's pause-and-crunch style of talking, accentuating each point, was getting on Cait's nerves.

"I haven't talked to him since our big blow-up. Sure, he made an appearance at the church, but he was angrier at the crowd than at me." Cait stood. "Now you're suggesting that I invite him on a cozy weekend getaway?"

Brooke watched her friend pace while arguing with herself. To the sink for a sponge, wipe one spot clean. To the drawer for a towel, pat one spot dry. Repeat. On the third pass, Brooke reached out her hand.

"So talk to him. No big deal. Maybe lunch, maybe an evening at the movies with the girls. Spend more time together; then ask him." She patted Cait's hand. "He'll probably suggest it himself. That is, if you can wait that long."

"But how? He hasn't returned any of my calls."

"Call. In the singular. And, as I've already said, he could have missed it." She broke a carrot stick in two and handed Cait a piece. "Listen up. Nick called the office earlier today, said Jake's modem was malfunctioning." She waved her veggie, as if demanding full attention to her newest scheme. "I was planning to drop off a replacement unit for him at three tomorrow. You can run the errand instead."

"How do you know Jake will be there?"

"I don't. In fact, if I was to place a bet, I'd say he won't be." She leaned closer to her friend. "Here's the good part. Are you ready?"

Cait nodded, still leery.

"If I insist that I need to see the cables, too, to do a thorough checkout, then he'll have to make a special trip just to bring them." She raised her eyebrow suggestively. "Won't he?"

Cait covered her face with both hands, elbows resting on the counter top. She shook her head slowly. "Another bait-and-switch."

"Worked the first time, didn't it?" Brooke laughed. She selected a zucchini stick this time.

"Mom, I'm home." Rose swung open the door from the garage. Her bicycle helmet hit the hardwood floor. "Oh. Hi, Aunt Brooke."

"Hi, yourself. Say, when are you going to stop by for dinner again? Kyle's heart is nearly breaking under the strain of your absence."

Rose blushed. "We've been kind of busy these days." She turned to her mother. "By the way Mom, Lynn is dropping Jackie off at her dad's office. Since I rode my bike to the pool, I came directly home." She opened the washer and dropped in her wet suit and towel.

"No time left for Kyle, at all?" Brooke asked.

"Well, he could always call and invite me over or something." Rose averted her eyes and began adding soap. "I'm getting kind of old to be so obvious, you know."

Cait shot a quick glance towards her friend and smiled proudly. Brooke shook her head. "Must run in the family."

Rose left the washer lid ajar. She crossed to the kitchen counter.

Brooke patted the empty stool next to her. "Sit here. Maybe I can help."

"Don't bother listening, honey." Cait reached out and received a quick hug from daughter. "The word 'obvious' isn't in Aunt Brooke's vocabulary."

"I resent that," Brooke said.

"Yuk. What are you guys eating?" Rose peered into the bowl, then wrinkled her nose. "That looks nasty."

Cait peered in, too, although it wasn't necessary. She had been dipping and munching from that very bowl for nearly half an hour. "It's a special recipe, called 'Compromise'. Brooke and I are off the chips, but she can't survive twenty-four hours without hot sauce. Dipping veggies is the best we could come up with."

Rose glanced at Brooke for confirmation. She simply winked. "Life's a pickle, isn't it?"

The door swung open for the second time. "Hey, Mom. Good news. Jake just volunteered to help chaperone on Saturday night."

"He did? You're joking, of course." Cait's voice was sharp.

"For real." Lynn joined the group at the counter, set down the evening newspaper and picked up a carrot stick. She pointed to the bowl of salsa. "Recharging your batteries again, Brooke?"

"Hi, short stuff." Brooke pulled the rubber band from the newspaper and handed it to Lynn. "Pull back your wet hair. I don't want you to dilute your mom's brilliant recipe."

Cait reached across and touched Lynn's arm. She tried unsuccessfully to keep her voice flat, uninterested. "Jake was at the office this afternoon?"

"He was already waiting outside when we pulled up. We were running late." Lynn chose a cucumber slice. "I mentioned that it would be a shame if we had to cancel our outing, due to a shortage of chaperones."

"We're not short."

Lynn shrugged her shoulders then innocently smiled. "I didn't say we were. I just said, if," she said calmly.

Brooke proudly patted the older twin on the back. "That's my girl. You've got real potential."

"Just a minute . . ."

The mutual admiration party continued despite Cait's interruption. "Now your mom has two reasons to see the elusive Mr. Brandon. Good work." Brooke put her arm around Lynn's shoulder and they smiled at each other.

Cait tried again to get their attention. "This could really cause problems. Did you tell him where we're going?"

"He didn't ask." Lynn shrugged. "Obviously, it didn't matter."

"Whither thou goest, I shall follow." Brooke held both hands over her heart and tapped them softly against her sweater.

"Pipe down." Cait's gaze never left her daughter. "Did he say anything else?"

Lynn pulled out a chair and knelt on it. "Yeah. He was mumbling something about everyone having to do his or her own fair share."

Cait shook her head. "I'll have to explain it to him

and give him a chance to back out."

"Then tomorrow at three will be perfect. I'll call and make the arrangements for you to pick up that modem." Brooke stood and gathered her things.

At the door, she turned. "By the way, where is the group off to this time?"

The James family answered in unison. "Roller-blading."

■ ■ ■

"Caitlyn. Well, I'll be darned. It is you." Margaret readjusted her bifocals on the end of her nose. "I haven't seen you around the BASC office for the longest time."

"Hi, Margaret." Cait paused by the older woman's desk and looked past her to the screen. "The system must be treating you pretty well. Your name hasn't been entered on the Help Log lately."

"We're getting along just fine." The older woman patted her monitor. The four plastic picture frames on top jiggled.

Cait leaned close, pointing at the photos. "You might want to find a place on your desk for those. Constricts the air flow, you know. Your unit will eventually overheat."

"I didn't know that," Margaret said. "Thank you so much for the warning."

While the other woman was busy rearranging her personal items, Cait took the opportunity to escape. She walked quickly down the hallway to Jake's office. The door was closed, so she knocked.

"Yeah?"

His abrupt tone was not encouraging. It was too late to leave; she had been seen already by several people. Jake would know that she ran, rather than face him. There was no choice, really.

The door opened. His scowling expression was replaced by a quick flash of confusion, then enlightenment. "I was expecting Brooke. Was this her idea?"

"Bingo. She thought we should talk."

His smile seemed to disappear, his shoulders fall slightly. Drawing a deep breath, Cait amended her statement. "So did I."

He raised his eyebrow, a trace of smile returning. She handed him the box she was carrying. He accepted the new modem and cables, then stepped back. "Please come in."

As she entered the office, she heard the faint click of the door being locked behind her. She took that to mean she could stay awhile and pulled out the nearest chair. Jake remained standing.

"Yesterday I received the go-ahead for our camp-out. You made quite an impression on Audra Stockton." Cait curled one hand into the other and held on tight. She tried not to fidget.

"We talked at length the other night, by phone." His voice was guarded. "She understands my part in this arrangement."

Cait wished she did. She didn't seem to know much of anything these days. Like which way to turn, and if she should call. "Thank you for supporting me on Sunday. The parents' enthusiasm is what turned the tide. I know you didn't have to."

"I wanted to."

Cait sat silently for a moment, meeting his eyes directly. They revealed nothing of what he was feeling. If only there were a way to read him, to know what he was thinking. Well, there was one way. Now or never. She spoke, before the natural impulse to procrastinate caught up with her. "What else do you want?"

His eyebrow raised. "What?"

"What else, Jake? You obviously want this retreat to happen. But since you didn't call back about my dinner invitation, I guessed that . . ."

"I didn't get a message. I just replaced the tape in my machine at home. Jackie wore out the previous one." He smiled. "You could have paged me."

Right, page him for dinner. The very thought brought a smile to her lips. Steadying her voice, she laid her cards down. "What do you want from this relationship? What do you want, from me?"

It was his turn to draw a deep breath. After a moment, he stepped forward and pulled out a chair. Not the leather high-back executive chair behind his desk, but the one right next to hers. He reached forward and unclenched her hands.

"I wish I knew. One instant we're headed for a story book ending, the next an evil sorcerer makes plans to sweep you away." He looked down at her hands, enclosed in his. "I learned at an early age not to believe in fairy tales."

"And I know a white knight when I see one." Cait retrieved one of her hands and laid it on his forearm. His skin was warm beneath the scattering of almost-black hair. "You've slayed a blue-haired dragon for me already. How about if we try fighting on the same side for a while, to make this relationship work?"

"How?" His brow furrowed, and he shook his head slowly. "You have to seriously pursue this opportunity that's been offered."

"But . . ."

"Don't say there will be others. I want you to take this one, and every one. No relationship can be built on a foundation of regrets. I've already been down that road."

"It might not be the right move for me. There's so much I don't know yet."

"You need to find out, quickly. Go to Portland. Do whatever it takes." He stood and pulled her to her feet. "Hell, I'll go with you." His finger rested gently under her chin, lifting her mouth closer to his. "But do it soon, before I lose any more sleep."

She smiled. "You're losing sleep over me?" She watched his lips form a three letter response. It was exactly what she wanted to hear.

He was close to her now, yet still too far away. She leaned forward.

"Is it too late to pursue that dinner invitation?" His hands gripped her waist, pulling her against him. "Or maybe we could pick up where we left off the other evening, on the dance floor?"

"Not tonight." She pulled away slightly, a mischievous smile starting to form. "You need your rest."

"For what?"

"Roller-blading."

"What?"

"That's where the group is headed on Saturday. I heard that you were interested in chaperoning."

"In-line skating? God help me."

"That's the right spirit." She gave him a quick kiss. "After all, it's Christian Music Night."

He shook his head in disbelief, then once again pulled her close, while his muscles were still in working order.

■ ■ ■

It was late, nearly eleven, and every part of her body hurt. Did they really need to skate that last set? Probably not, but it was fun. They didn't need the pizza and pop either, but it was too late for regrets. Plenty of time to pay for their sins in the early morning light.

Cait set her overnight bag down on Jackie's bed and dug for her pajama set. Finding it, she tossed her nightshirt and shorts on to the growing pile of toiletries, cosmetic bag, and slippers. She placed her paperback on the nightstand. Most likely wouldn't get much reading done tonight, but even a paragraph or two would relax her. That, plus the hot bath, next on her agenda.

The lace curtains danced lightly in the night breeze, drawing her gaze. The window behind the love seat was open, just as it had been on that very first night. It seemed like years, rather than just weeks ago.

She flexed her neck and shoulders. Sure, she'd be stiff tomorrow, but not nearly as sore as Jake would be. During the first hour or so, he had spent more time on the floor than he did standing up. But he wasn't a quitter. Thank goodness the skating rink rented knee and elbow pads.

Grabbing her toothbrush and paste, Cait headed towards the bathroom. The lodge was beginning to feel like her second home. Jake's invitation to stay overnight and hike together tomorrow had taken her by surprise. Based on the look on his face, he must have surprised himself, too.

This emotional roller coaster was hard to deal with at times. Their relationship alternated between hot and cold, and would most likely stay that way until her decision was made. Hopefully, that would be soon.

Leaving the door slightly ajar, she set her personal items on the sink and chose a towel from the linen closet. When she bent to turn on the bathtub faucet, her leg muscles reminded her again that she wasn't getting any younger.

Straightening, she sat on the tub's edge. "Ouch." She

gingerly rubbed her hip and positioned the towel under her, before sitting again. The handle marked 'Hot' was cranked up another notch.

Maybe she should have skipped the women's speed skating contest. After all, there was no way to beat Rose, but it was fun trying. Almost as much fun as watching Jake stand for the first time on his in-line skates. What a good sport he was.

A soft knock on the outer door interrupted her thoughts. No way was she going to stand, unless it was a true emergency. "Who is it?"

"Mom, can I come in?" Cait recognized Lynn's voice.

"Sure. I'm hiding behind Door Number Three."

She expected a sarcastic retort, but didn't get one. Oh well, Lynn was probably as tired as she was. Within moments her daughter peeked in and quickly scanned the bathroom. Finding the coast clear, she stepped inside.

Cait glanced around, too. This was silly, of course she was by herself. She shut off the water, noticing Lynn's hesitant movements. "What's up?"

Lynn closed the door quietly, but firmly, behind her. "Not much. What are you doing?"

Cait looked down at the bath bubbles and suppressed a snappy comeback. Something was definitely wrong. She pointed to the empty space next to her. "How about sitting with me for a minute? I'm moving kind of slow tonight." She gingerly stretched one leg. "I'm not as young as I used to be."

"Don't give me that." Lynn sat down. "You still out-skated Jackie and me."

"Now I'm going to soak away all my troubles."

"I heard the shower running earlier. I thought you were already through for the night."

"No. Maybe Jake was showering." She tested the water.

So did Lynn, swirling her hand through the bubbles instead of meeting Cait's eyes. "Oh, then he's already in bed?"

Cait glanced at her daughter's face which was devoid of all expression. What was the point of that last remark? As she continued to watch, Lynn's gaze roamed. First it lingered on the shower curtain, then on the bottle of conditioner. Anywhere but eye-to-eye.

Cait stood and walked over to the sink. Maybe facing away would make things easier. "I don't know if Jake's in bed or not. Didn't you see him downstairs?"

"No."

She fiddled with her toothbrush and tried again. "Then I guess he's out for the count. In fact, I'm surprised the three of you haven't dozed off by now."

"Rose and Jackie are snoozing. I couldn't sleep."

Cait made an inquisitive sound and continued brushing her teeth. Unobserved, she watched her daughter in the mirror.

Lynn chewed her thumbnail for a moment, then continued. "I've been thinking a lot about you lately." She cleared her throat and raised her voice a notch. " . . . you and Jake, I mean."

Their eyes met for a moment in the mirror before Lynn looked away. She reached over and fiddled with the water, turning it from hot down to warm. Cait gave her daughter another wordless prompt, then lowered her head and began to rinse.

"About you and Jake and sex, actually."

Cait's head immediately shot up. Their eyes met again. Bad timing, being caught with her mouth occupied. She raised a single brow.

"Well, we've been talking and . . . we wouldn't be totally shocked, you know, if you and Jake . . . you know." Cait raised her other brow. Lynn forced out the rest. "If you did it."

Cait quickly spit in the sink. Not wanting to waste time on a cup, she swallowed a handful of water. She grabbed the towel nearby, then turned. "Did it?" Amazing how much meaning could be packed into two little words.

"Yeah."

Leaning against the sink, Cait folded her arms across her chest. "That's quite an announcement. You caught me at an unfair disadvantage."

"Yeah." Lynn smiled shyly. "But at least I was able to say it without interruption. It's kind of a touchy subject, you know."

"I know. That's why parents are supposed to be giving their kids 'the talk,' and not the other way around."

"Well, what I meant to say is that it'd be all right if you thought you were in love." Lynn glanced up at her. "Are you in love?"

"I can speak only for myself." Cait looked at her daughter seriously. "I am. But that doesn't mean I know how this will all turn out."

Lynn nodded. "There's a second thing." She picked up the bath oil and began fidgeting with the cap. "You have to be safe. I mean, well, it's been a long time since you were in high school, Mom. I thought you might be due for a refresher course."

"High school!" Cait took the bottle and placed it back on the shelf, then sat down beside her. She coughed in an effort to cover her outburst. Just thinking of her own straight-laced school years, when skirt hems had to touch the floor while kneeling, made her want to laugh. When she finally spoke her voice was calm, gently serious. "Well, darling, it's kind of like riding a bicycle. It's hard to forget how."

"Mom, I'm talking about diseases and protection and stuff like that. Not how to's. I . . . just take these, okay?" In frustration Lynn fumbled in her pocket, then produced a handful of foil packets. She dropped them into her mother's lap. "Here."

Gulping for air, Cait gazed down at the assorted styles and colors. Her eyes widened. "Where did you get these?"

"From Jackie." She shrugged. "They hand them out at our school, too, but only if you ask. In L.A. I think they come with your school books when you register."

They both sat perfectly still, staring at the pile. Lynn was the first to break the silence. "I love you, Mom." Her voice was unsteady. "I want to be able to . . ." A deep breath, "To love you for a long time."

Silence. Amid the steam and stifling heat, Cait was frozen into position.

Lynn stood. "That's all."

Cait's head cleared instantly. Jumping to her feet, sore muscles and condoms forgotten, she pulled her daughter into her arms. She squeezed her tight and rocked slowly back and forth. "I love you too, honey." She stroked her daughter's long blond hair, then kissed her. "You don't have to worry about me, okay? Believe it or not, the same information makes its way to adults, too."

Lynn's voice was beginning to relax. "Really?"

"Really."

Cait drew back until Lynn was arm's length away. Looking into her daughter's eyes, she saw her first smile of the evening. She returned it, then lightened the mood. "Hey, we're going to talk about this same topic during one of our retreat workshops. Do you want to co-teach with me?"

"Heck no." Lynn stepped out of her mother's arms and backed towards the door.

"Maybe pass a few of these around the circle?"

"Mom!"

"Maybe the group has a favorite? We could take a vote."

Lynn reached the door and opened it quickly. "You wouldn't."

"I might."

"I'd die." Lynn stepped into the hall, still shaking her head.

"No you wouldn't. You did fine with me." Cait's voice softened.

Lynn walked away, alone, signalling a time out with her hands. "I'm out of here." She bolted down the steps.

Cait closed the bedroom door, turned, then leaned against it. A smile slowly curved her lips. "Fine, darling."

Twelve

Wet and Wonderful, Power Move, BareBack Rider, Warrior. Cait picked the packets up off the bathroom floor, one by one. She noted each individual marketing slant before tossing them into her cosmetic bag. She shook her head. Thirty-six-years-old and she still thought condoms were supposed to be named after a hollow Greek horse in a classical city.

The downstairs stereo abruptly stopped, plunging the house into silence. Bedtime. She should be exhausted after the uncounted trips around the rink, but instead she was restless. Was it because of these? She looked down at her bag. Hardly. Thoughts of unfulfilled passion had been invading her thoughts ever since their evening stroll to the boat dock. Even earlier, if she dared to be honest. Since their first night together in this very room, when their eyes met over her soup bowl. Piercing eyes that looked into her soul, promising so much.

She held up a satiny blue square with flowery italic script. *An experience in sensitivity.* No, sensitivity would either radiate from the man himself or not be there at all. Someone who would put his own feelings aside for another. Someone who would spend most of his evening backside down on a slate floor so his daughter could skate with friends. Someone like Jake. She dropped the packet into her bag.

The bath water was still hot. She quickly discarded her clothes. Was there time to wash her hair before meeting Jake downstairs? Probably, but did she really want to say good night wrapped in a turban? She nixed the shampoo and simply grabbed her favorite soap from the counter.

Heavy footsteps sounded on the steps outside her door. She stopped. Jake was turning in early. She just assumed that he'd be waiting for her. That he'd want some time alone, to wind down the day together. Instead, she was about to miss him entirely.

Forgetting the bath, Cait scanned the room for her nightshirt. It had fallen to the floor. Picking it up, she noticed several more school samples hidden underneath. She slipped her pajama top on and tucked the packets out of sight in her upper pocket.

The shirt covered her to mid-thigh, but just the thought of being bare underneath made her heart pound. She grabbed the matching shorts and hurried across the bedroom. Hopping first on one leg, then on the next, she pulled the pants on without missing a beat. She yanked open the door with one hand, adjusting the elastic waistband with the other.

Except for the dim light glowing in the entryway below, the hall was dark. So was Jake's expression.

His jaw clenched. He'd hoped to be gone before her bath was over. Better that way. Safer, for both of them. With the kids off to the bunk room and the adrenaline from their outing still pumping through his veins, his body was no longer listening to reason. He was hard from watching her all evening, from wanting her.

The uncertainty of their future made no difference to his hormones tonight. He had to stay as far away as possible, until his common sense returned. And now it was too late.

She was standing in the doorway. The reading lamp behind her softly accentuated her outline. The shirttail was caught in her waistband on one side, revealing her upper thigh. The soft, flimsy material covered a lot of area, but it wasn't doing the job. Nothing was left to the imagination.

Her breathing was labored, like his. He tightened his grip on the glass of scotch. Good thing he'd left the rest of the Chivas Regal bottle downstairs. Temptation like this could drive any man to drink.

Cait took a step closer. "I was coming down to join you."

"I figured that." He swirled the ice cubes around once and took a generous gulp. After lowering the glass, his eyes bored into hers. "That's why I'm calling it a night."

She drew back as if wounded. "You never minded before."

Mind? He'd mind if a fly landed on his nose. He'd mind if the phone woke him at two A.M.

"Bad idea." His gaze raked over her exposed limbs. Wasn't there room in her overnight bag for a full length, velour bathrobe? The kind that zipped to the neck? He'd have to surrender his again, unless she took his hint and disappeared.

She didn't seem to be going anywhere.

"Here, hold this." Handing her his glass, he shrugged off the robe. This was getting to be a habit. He was out of his mind, inviting her to spend the night at the lodge a second time. No, third. His testosterone must have done the asking.

"Interesting."

Was she commenting on him? He glanced at her. She was looking down, examining with skepticism the glass in her hand.

"What is so blasted interesting?" His tone dared her to question him. To lecture him.

She didn't. She simply raised her eyes and waited.

He continued to hold her gaze for five, then ten seconds before it started to slip. Wandering over each exposed inch of flesh. The nape of her neck, where the satin lay cradled against her skin. Her collarbone, exposed by the slight V-neck parting. Her long graceful arms and slender hands, that brought a little bit of heaven with every touch.

"You hardly ever drink."

He glanced upward and scowled. "Nasty habits are hard to break."

Her voice remained soft, not rising to the bait. "You barely touched the rum I poured the other night."

He shrugged.

"The three beers in your fridge are probably flat from age."

"So?"

Her chin lifted a scant degree. "Is it something I said? Did?"

Damn her point-blank questions, delivered with that innocent expression. She knew exactly what the hell was wrong with him tonight: intimate setting, fiery hot emotions, battered resolve.

He watched her, observing the subtle body language. Her tone was gentle but not apologetic. It didn't need to be. The problem was his, not hers. He shoved the robe in her direction. "Put this on."

Her brow wrinkled in confusion.

He retrieved his drink without coming into contact with her fingers. Difficult to do, but necessary. With one swallow the last of the cool amber liquid disappeared, until nothing but naked ice cubes remained. He slammed the glass down on the bannister. She flinched. "That's right. You've finally gotten the message. I'm not safe to be around tonight." Stepping forward, he dressed her in his robe. His movements were abrupt, but his touch was surprisingly tender.

He unfolded the lapels to cover the maximum amount of area. After knotting the belt, his hands remained in position on her waist. He seemed to tower over her.

Looking up, her eyes met his. He took a step backward, towards the staircase. "Leave that on. Sleep in it. I'm going back down for a refill."

She moved forward. He held up a hand, stopping her. "When I walk by here again I want you in your room, with the door closed. And locked."

"But . . ."

"No arguing, Caitlyn. Hell itself couldn't be hotter than the blood running through my veins right now." He stepped closer to his escape route. "We've got to figure this out, and fast. I can't swim in this limbo any longer without drowning."

He left her standing there, alone, with a pocket full of surprises.

■ ■ ■

Jake's deep, rumbling voice drew her down the hall. Cait had heard his shower running earlier, shortly after their encounter in the hallway. Now he was on the phone, his bare shoulders toward her. His empty glass, ice cubes nearly melted, sat next to him on the table.

She hoped to clear the air between them. Didn't he realize that she shared his same frustrations? Obviously not. She'd tell him so tonight. Right now. The answers were not all there yet, but the desire certainly was. And their shared sense of commitment to finding a workable solution, something that would carry them into the future, together.

It was time. No, past time, to do something about the rest of their relationship.

Cait peered through the open door. Jake sat perched on the arm of the reclining chair. His damp bath towel, firmly knotted about his waist, was leaving a telltale ring on the armrest. One well-muscled leg, naked except for the crisp, black curls peppering its surface, showed below the towel's edge.

He must have been dishing out his stern advice for quite some time. Cait felt instant sympathy for the caller. She knew what it was like to be on the receiving end. Making up her mind, she stepped quickly inside the room before her courage fled. The creak of the door was silenced by another one of his outbursts.

"You're wrong, Drew. I told you, she's being promoted up and out of my life. No happily ever after, with the music and lights fading. How can it? You and I both know first hand what happens when someone you love packs their bags every time something better comes along." His voice cracked, forcing him pause.

He was discussing her with his brother? At this hour of night? No longer feeling like an intruder, Cait crossed her arms and listened to his observations. She added them to her mental list of things to clear up immediately.

Jake shook his head slowly in wordless disagreement, then ran his fingers roughly through his damp, uncombed hair. He stood abruptly and paced the length of the fireplace. The scent of ginger alerted him that he was no longer alone. It was her scent.

Turning, his eyes locked with Cait's across the bedroom. Indignation blazed in her expression. Remorse swept over him. He hadn't meant for her to overhear this. His jaw tightened. But even if the tone of his conversation were inappropriate, the content wasn't. One way or another, the words needed to be said.

Looking away, he ended his call. "Gotta go. Unexpected company." He hung up the receiver, but his hand remained tightly in place. "Sorry I woke you. My brother and I have locked horns ever since we were young. He's opinionated and loves to dish out advice."

"Well, at least I know now that your stubbornness is an inherited trait."

The left corner of his mouth lifted slightly as he nodded, accepting her appraisal. The hell of it was, this time Drew was right. He had fallen hard, and there wasn't a thing he could do about it but move on. That was life, and if he was anything, he was a survivor. Somehow, he'd reassemble the pieces of his life, and so would she. "I meant what I said earlier. I refuse to be the reason that you pass this up."

"But there are many kinds of dreams. Don't pack my bags yet."

Her softly spoken words cooled his determination. Yes, he knew about dreams. His nights were filled with her presence, her laughter, and her warmth, long after he was asleep. It made him forget, for a while.

"Listen." He ran his hand roughly over his chin. "Neither of us is thinking clearly right now. It's late and I've swallowed a good share of scotch. That's an explosive combination."

"I can't sleep." She took a step forward. "I heard your pacing; then later, your shower."

"My cold shower. Now, out you go." He pointed towards the door.

Her eyes scanned his skimpy attire and the bulge it failed to hide. He wanted her and was denying it. She had tried fighting his iron control before, head on. This time she'd try bending it with a little subtle persuasion.

"I had no way of knowing the temperature, since you didn't invite me to join you." Another step forward.

Jake saw the playfulness dance in her eyes. He'd have none of it. "You're not staying."

Smiling, she took two steps forward.

His eyes were drawn to his robe. She had loosened and re-belted it. No longer up to her chin, it now framed her slender neck before plunging deep to reveal the smooth skin of her breasts. Was it possible that she'd removed the nightshirt? Sure, it was possible. In fact, probable. He'd take odds that she was naked underneath. She wasn't playing fair.

He paced the length of the mantle, then knelt on one knee before the fireplace. Taking up the tongs, he held on firmly so that his hands wouldn't reach for her, grab for the passion burning beneath the soft flannel, only yards away. He jabbed at the perfectly placed logs, demolishing them into chunks of charcoal. They matched his crumbling resolve.

When he turned to add more wood Cait moved to his

side. Standing close to his bare, raised knee, she brushed the inside of her own against his. A jolt of desire raised gooseflesh on his skin where the two surfaces touched.

Slowly caressing him, she voiced the passion and commitment that she thought she'd never feel again. "I need you, like I need air to breathe. Let's create a new dream together. One of endless possibilities."

Blood thundered through his veins, pounding an erratic tempo in his ears. The edges of the borrowed bathrobe separated with each whisper-like movement across his thigh. He imagined, all too clearly, how soft she would feel beneath the loose flowing material.

His lips longed to kiss her inner leg, which was only a fabric's width away. From there he'd travel upward to where her long, athletic limbs met. Legs that would surround him and hold him firmly to her, if only given the chance. His manhood throbbed painfully in response.

Turning, he stood quickly to break contact. He didn't realize, until a warm rush of air swept against his exposed flesh, that his towel had been left behind on the floor. His startled eyes met her assertive ones. He glanced down. The edge of the towel lay captured beneath her carefully placed foot.

She dropped her gaze and blushed, while still admiring his nakedness. The glow of firelight was the only thing covering him now. It intensified her hunger. She yearned to caress him with more than her eyes.

Raising her gaze, she traced her fingertip across his lower lip. She wanted to encircle his neck and drag his mouth to hers, but didn't. Instead, she waited patiently for his decision, for his surrender. She had come to him, now he must also come to her.

He exhaled. "What about the girls? Have you thought

about what we'll tell them in the morning?" She had to think this all the way through. For him, there was no going back.

"I'm sure the little matchmakers will be overjoyed." Her finger moved lower, to trace her name across his darkly matted chest. "Their tactics have been more and more conspicuous lately."

"Oh, I've noticed. Hard not to."

"I don't know how I'll tell them yet, but I will. One way or another."

"We'll both tell them. When the time is right." He captured her hand. "But just so we have the chance to pick when and where, I'll shut the door."

Cait pulled back in shock, glancing over her shoulder. How could she have forgotten to shut, not to mention lock the door? Smiling, Jake walked gloriously naked across the room, firm muscles rippling beneath taut skin. A small shiver ran through her as she realized that their decision was made. Soon those muscles would be tightening just for her.

When he returned, Cait felt a brief tug at her waistline. The belt was no longer knotted.

■ ■ ■

Jake placed his feet between the two of hers. He drew her firmly into the cradle of his thighs. Heat radiated through the plush robe, scorching his skin. He wanted to move slowly, to make their first time together last forever. But as he encircled her hips with his broad hands and pressed her intimately against his aching lower body, he admitted that self-restraint wouldn't be his long suit tonight.

He kissed her exposed neckline and was rewarded by a low sound. Was it torment, or was it relief? Probably both.

He felt it, too. She leaned back against his hand, granting him freer access. He blazed a hot trail of kisses across her collarbone, then moved downward. Capturing her breast in his palm, he softly stroked. The velvety tip hardened and strained upward. She swayed at the first touch of his tongue.

Feeling the sinking movement, he swept her into his arms. He reached the recliner in two long strides and sat, placing her sideways across his lap. Unable to wait any longer, he brushed apart the edges of the robe. He ran a single forefinger down her right side, sensitizing her skin as he went. When he reached her toes, he gently lifted her ankle towards his mouth, leaning forward for a nibble. Her bent knee moved outward in unconscious cooperation.

The moment the heated air touched her vulnerable softness, Cait realized her mistake. Her pulse rate soared. She was open, fully exposed to his eyes. Blushing furiously, her eyes searched his face for a response.

"This is about to become my favorite chair."

"Jake." She tried to move her knees back together.

"Shhh." He held her in place, kissing her into silence. "Let me see you, touch you . . . love you. Everywhere." Tenderly stroking her inner thigh to where it met the other, he covered her soft curls with his palm.

His mouth covered hers again, then launched a twin assault. Tongue against her lips, hand against her femininity. She let both enter. The searing passion of his touch inflamed her senses, and she strained against him.

Her inner tension mounted and spiralled upward. She had known the simple pleasures between man and woman before, but never was there such explosiveness. Her arms tightened around his neck.

Lightning flashed behind her tightly closed lids. Her heart thundered in reply. Meaningless sounds, whispered against his lips, conveyed her urgency. Involuntary rocking soon created its own, unstoppable rhythm. He played and she danced, to a newly born melody.

Higher and higher she climbed, fueled by his kiss. Their music caressed the stars and frolicked with the moon. When the last note was finally played, its shattering sound echoed throughout her limbs as she hung suspended in air under his hand.

■　■　■

As she regained awareness, Cait felt rather than saw the inflamed condition of his body. His double heartbeat pulsed first against her brow, then against her hip. Jake had sent her on a trip beyond the clouds, but hadn't traveled with her. His selfless patience made her love him all the more.

Uncurling her legs, she rose to straddle him. He tried to upright the chair, but couldn't. From this position, the leverage was all hers.

She eased him back down.

He smiled at their small tug of war. "So you're alive after all."

She nodded. "Stay tuned while I eliminate all remaining doubt."

Bracing her forearms on either side of his head, she settled herself intimately on his lap. His hunger for her stood ready and pulsing between them. He gripped the armrest as her damp curls brushed suggestively against him. Her movements were answered by a quick, low sound.

There was no escape, not that he wanted one. Time for restraint was over. He was hers, for wherever she would take him. Her breasts, poised over him in soft invitation, moved to the new rhythm she set. He captured them in his palms.

She was part spitfire and part centerfold.

Her kisses brushed his forehead, temples and cheekbones as she claimed him for her own. She loved this man, with all his various facets. She already knew that he could growl in anger, now she listened while he purred with pleasure. Her tongue traced a path along his lower lip. His manhood flexed and strained against her still-sensitized skin.

Bracing on one arm, she reached between them. Her fingers surrounded the silken target. He was hot satin stretched over steel. Touching, caressing, and encouraging, she memorized his texture. Her nails enticed his swollen flesh. She savored each and every sound. Finally, when even the slightest syllable became an impossibility, she covered his mouth with hers and drank in his response.

He gripped her waist, urging her forward. Pressing her against him, her movement immediately matched his. It wasn't enough. He needed her closer, as close as two lovers could be. Up and down, the gliding heat of her passion seared his skin, from potent base to blunt tip. Inside. That was the only place that would do. But not yet. She deserved more consideration than that.

Tearing his mouth from hers, he moved her away but a fraction of an inch. It didn't help. Her breathing was as labored as his. Beads of sweat broke out on his forehead. Even without the touch of her skin next to his, his pace continued. He couldn't stop his hips from thrusting slightly. He tried drawing a breath while it was still possible.

"We need protection. The bathroom." Another breath. "In the cabinet."

"No, here." Reaching in the robe's pocket, she held up the prize.

His shock was overshadowed by relief. He wouldn't have to stand or walk. "What? How?"

"Warrior." She turned the package around for him to see the bold lettering, then nodded to confirm her statement. Her smile was playful. "Sorry. There wasn't one called 'Woodsman.' We'll have to make do."

His breathing slowed. He raised an eyebrow. "What ever happened to Trojan?"

She laughed. So his information was centuries old, too. She took comfort in that. "Beats me."

He kissed her, then whispered against her lips. "You have some explaining to do. Later."

Ripping open the packet, she sheathed him with a not-so-playful caress. Laying his head against the cushion, he arched and moved with her every stroke. "No."

She hesitated. "No?"

"I mean yes." An involuntary groan. "But let me help." He completed the task, then lifted her the final inches separating them.

His eyes met hers. "Last chance. Are you sure?" Even this late in the game, he had to know.

"Very." She nodded, leaning forward to kiss him. "But this is a heck of a time for you to ask."

He captured her for a long, slow kiss. With breaths mingling, hearts beating as one, he lowered her carefully down. Their dance picked up again, instantly.

She laid her forehead against his. Her warm, inner recesses were no longer empty. Instead they were filled with life-giving, blood-heating movement. Their closeness and urgency felt completely new to her. His heat burned a pathway to her soul. She pressed reflexively against him, determined to accommodate his full length.

His plan for a slow, tantalizing pace was overruled. The tightness of her muscles answered an unnecessary question. She had waited for the right person, the right time, just as he had. Her teasing, hidden movements eroded his self control. Fast and deep, wet and sleek. Her softness answered his hard need. Holding onto his glistening shoulders, she urged him to take her higher. With him. Their private melody played again.

He trembled as his reticence shattered. They were one now. Body, soul and mind. And with each stroke, there was no turning back.

Hotter and hotter.

Higher and higher.

Their rhythms joined effortlessly until they splintered. The clouds upon which they were dancing gave way beneath their feet. Clinging to each other, as perfectly matched lovers do, they descended back down to earth.

■ ■ ■

It took some doing, but he finally convinced her to abandon the reclining chair for his bed. They slept soundly in each other's arms, until the sunrise bathed the top branches of the Douglas fir with a warm, rich glow. It was the same sight that woke him each morning, but now it seemed fresh and new. He smiled, glancing down at the woman sleeping peacefully by his side. Not so surprising, really, that the world seemed different today.

He stroked the arm encircling his waist. "Caitlyn." No response.

Next he nudged the legs intertwined with his. Out for the count. He ran his hand over her hip. Mmm, nice. Time to get her into the right room before thoughts of another round got the better of him. Before footsteps and children's voices.

He peeled back the covers and got out of bed. No need

to be subtle with his movements. It was time to wake up. He grabbed the robe she had discarded during the midnight hours and several brightly colored packets fell out. His eyes widened as he counted them. Four? Boy, this lady wasn't kidding around. Expectations like this could have a damaging effect on a guy.

He picked them up, then sat on the edge of the bed. "Uh, Cait. Where did you get these?"

"Hmm?"

"Each one's different. Like a sampler. You didn't want to commit to an entire box?" He glanced her way. Her eyes were still closed but there was movement behind the lids.

"You surprised me. Having these in your pocket, and all."

She made a slight sound. Was it laughter?

"Cait?"

"They were a gift."

From whom? His eyes narrowed as he watched her face intently. Soundlessly. He shouldn't have to ask. Surely after a remark like that, she'd volunteer an explanation.

She raised one lid. "From Lynn, in case you were wondering."

He exhaled loudly. Pure relief.

She opened the other eye. "She got them from Jackie."

"What?" Relief flew out the window. He sat motionless.

Cait grabbed the covers, yanking them over her head before Jake could move. Now he was certain that he heard laughter. He tried wrestling the blankets down, but her grip was firm. "It's not funny."

"You should have seen your face."

"She's only fifteen."

"She got them at school. Had no use for them, so she gave them to Lynn."

"Oh." He let go and stood.

No movement, no sound. Cait lowered the comforter and peered out. It was just the break Jake was waiting for. The covering was snatched away with a single sweep. His T-shirt that she'd borrowed was bunched around her waist. She quickly pulled it down.

"Now who's laughing?"

She jumped up and grabbed the robe he held, wrenching it on. "I hope the coffee's ready."

"Aha, so you're not a morning person. These things are very important to get out on the table early."

She swatted him with one end of the belt.

"No coffee, but the sun is up." He wrestled the belt from her grip, then knotted it. Turning her towards the door, he patted her back side. "And any minute now, we could have teenage company."

"I'm moving, I'm moving." She trudged along, one inch at a time. "Ouch. I think I overdid it last night." She heard a chuckle.

Glancing back, she saw Jake grinning. "From roller-blading. Not from anything else."

He swept her up in his arms and kissed her forehead gently. "Of course not."

■ ■ ■

Jake carried her to the guest room. After rumpling the bedcovers for appearances sake, they sat together intertwined on the love seat by the window. The sun slowly rose over Rattlesnake Ridge.

Cait lifted her head from its resting place in the crook of his arm. "Explain something to me. What's the point of my being prudently back in my room, if you're still with me?

Not really hiding much from the girls, are we?"

"Don't think of it as hiding; only choosing the time and place. When we're sure, we'll tell them." He brushed the bangs back from her forehead. "For now, it's enough for me just to hold you. To share the start of a new day."

She peered at him closely, eyes narrowed. "Why Jake, I do believe you're as sentimental as I am."

"Maybe more." Instead of shrugging it off, he smiled and kissed the tip of her nose. "But there is something important that needs to be said. Something I can't ignore any longer." He drew a breath. "I don't want you to get the wrong idea about this, but . . ." His voice drifted off. He glanced away, out the window. "I don't know if I can say it."

The silence hung heavily between them. Anxiety was making its way into Cait's heart with each passing moment. "Tell me." Dampness covered her palms. She rubbed them together.

He looked down at her, cradled in his arms.

She unconsciously braced herself for the impact.

"I love you."

"You . . . what?" She sat upright. "How dare you scare me like that!"

"Scare you?"

"Yes." She sank back into in arms. "I thought you were having second thoughts."

He held her tight. "I was. Still am." He ran his fingertips lightly over the fabric covering her thigh. "And third thoughts, too."

"I meant regrets." She sighed, enjoying his wandering touch. "But don't let my confusion stop you."

He kissed her hair, then modestly repositioned the robe. His tone turned serious. "Actually, it should scare you to death. I know it does me."

She looked up, biting her lip, waiting for him to explain.

"It implies that I know where we're headed. That we can make this work." He caught one of her hands in his and stared down at them. "Frankly, I don't know how we can."

She shook her head, then kissed their intertwined fingers. "It simply means that you want it to. That you'll work with me to find a way. That you want this relationship as much as I do."

A door closed downstairs. Their time was up. Jake stood, carrying her to the bed. "I'll start coffee. Go back to sleep if you like. I should be able to keep three teenagers occupied for at least a few hours."

He laid her on the crisp sheets, then pulled the covers up to her neck, tucking them in. "We'll talk later about our trip to Portland." Leaning forward, he placed a quick kiss on her forehead.

Her arms escaped the blanket and wrapped around his neck. "Not this morning."

"We have to." He drew back and nuzzled the inside of her forearm. "You need to set your interview for as soon as possible. Can't make a decision without the facts."

He released her hold on him, then stepped towards the door. "When I call Drew later, I'll ask him if we can stay at his place."

"We?"

He smiled as he turned the door handle. "Yeah, we."

■　■　■

With a flamboyant sweep and toss, Jake flipped the pancakes one last time, catching them smoothly in the fry pan. He crossed to where the three girls were sitting at the breakfast table. "Who's going to be my first victim?"

The answer resounded in triplicate. "I am."

"Okay. Rose, grab the napkins. Lynn, the forks." He used the spatula to indicate direction. "Jackie, look to see if there's any maple syrup left."

He resumed whistling as the girls scurried off. The hotcakes were scooped from the pan two at a time, then stacked on their plates. "No complaining allowed. Breakfast is my specialty."

Lynn set utensils on each of the five place mats. "You mean it's all downhill from here?"

Jackie laughed. "Yeah. By afternoon Dad can't even heat soup."

"Not fair telling deep, dark, family secrets." He set the last of the plates in front of his daughter. "Save those for the campfire next weekend."

Silence reigned for several moments as the girls dug in. He re-greased the pan, then ladled more batter. The servings were smaller this time, for seconds. He wouldn't start his and Caitlyn's until she appeared at the door.

Caitlyn. A smile slowly curved his lips. Facing away from the table, he let the memory of last night wash over him. Although nothing more was settled between them, he still felt at peace this morning. He'd plan time off for a quick trip next weekend. Nick would cover for him, and not ask questions. Jake could be ambiguous about the reason, but it probably wasn't necessary. He'd lay it out straight. If his and Caitlyn's relationship were to have a chance, they'd have to be clear with everyone about their intent.

That brought to mind the subject of their daughters again. He didn't want to build their hopes too soon. But, until they knew, acting as if things hadn't changed would be hell on earth. Best to keep busy and stop reminiscing. He turned the rear burner to low and concentrated on breakfast.

Jackie could read his thoughts as easily as she was reading the morning paper now. Their secret would be out in no time if he didn't set his mind to something else.

He carried the pan to the table. "Seconds? Dig in. We have a long hike planned for this afternoon."

"One more then, please." Jackie raised her plate towards him.

"Sure. Hold steady now." He flipped the pancake high in the air. It landed smoothly in the center of her plate.

Rose's mouth hung open, impressed. "Wow! Where did you learn to do that? Our dad could hardly toast poptarts without reading the box first. Ouch." She turned towards her sister. "You kicked me."

"Zip it." Lynn glared at her twin. After a moment of heavy silence, she resumed eating.

Jake frowned as he returned to the stove. He didn't want Caitlyn's daughters to think that the topic of their father was off limits. Todd would never be a forbidden subject to him. He hoped the same would hold true the next time Jackie visited her newly married mother, too.

It was important that they know how he felt, so they'd be comfortable around him. He grabbed the coffeepot and rejoined the group. "How about a little Java this morning. Any takers?"

"Don't be silly. We're too young for coffee." Rose waved her fork as if to shoo him away.

Lynn was silent. He moved to stand next to her. His tone was conversational, but pointed. "I'll bet your dad made great coffee."

She glanced up, meeting his eyes. "He did. How did you know?"

"From what I've seen, it's a sure fire way to your mother's heart."

Lynn nodded, continuing to watch him. After a moment she smiled. "You've got her pegged. Without her morning fix, Mom can be a real bear. Wait till you see her."

His smile came easily. He already had, hours ago. Was she really able to fall asleep again, after he left? He didn't dare go up and check. Too tempting.

Grabbing the cup next to the empty place setting, he filled it. "Why don't you run this up to her? Maybe it will smooth out a few of her rough edges before she joins us."

"I thought my edges were already smooth." Caitlyn, leaning against the doorjamb, spoke with a voice as warm as their early morning cuddle. Staring at her, Jake poured hot coffee all over his hand.

"Damn." Racing to the sink, he set down mug and pot, then turned on the cold water. Good thing he'd been standing instead of sitting.

Cait shook her head and smiled. "And you accused me of being a grouch? Maybe you should start sleeping in later."

"I . . ." He stopped as he caught her thinly veiled invitation. He forgot what he was about to say as he appraised her breakfast attire. What was she thinking?

His denim shirt had never looked so good. She wore it over a tank top, rolled up at the sleeves and knotted at the hips. Her slim leggings, peeking out below, caused his body temperature to soar. The throbbing he was feeling, at present, had nothing to do with his burned hand. No, this pounding was much lower.

He tore his gaze away and looked at the girls sitting silently at the table, surrounded by spilled coffee. Good, they were still staring at Caitlyn. He shifted to ease the tightening of his jeans, glad that his adolescent reaction had gone unnoticed by their daughters, at least.

Caitlyn watched him with amusement gleaming in her eyes. She said nothing.

"Great shirt, Mom." Rose was the first to break the silence. "Looks familiar, too, but not quite. Have I ever borrowed that?"

Lynn rolled her eyes in exasperation. "It's familiar, you goofball, because Jake was wearing it last night."

In unison, three pairs of eyes rotated towards him. One accusing, one surprised, one hopeful. No way would their secret survive breakfast now. The pancakes would just have to wait.

"Oh no, the pancakes." He stared at the stove.

Smoke curled from the edges of the last batch as they turned from 'just right' to charcoal. He grabbed the scorched pan and tossed it into the sink. It hissed and sizzled. Shaking his head slowly, he switched on the exhaust fan. Things were quickly going from bad to worse.

Caitlyn's muffled laughter in the background certainly didn't help matters any. He turned, then forced his shoulders to relax. Picking up his coffee cup, he filled it carefully then took a sip. Time to calm down, see what was on her mind.

He rested one hip against the counter. She must know what she was doing. That was enough for him. "Go ahead. Explain."

She was pleased by his reaction to her sudden appearance. He was off-balance. Confused. But trusting, too. Good, because her own world was literally upside down.

She loved him. His gentle attention to her needs, his fierce protectiveness of her and her girls, and his passionate zest for life were what she wanted.

If she could write 'I'm yours' across her chest for the world to see, she would do so. Wearing his shirt from last evening was a highly effective, last minute substitute.

Crossing to the sink, she took the mug from his hand. She rotated it to where his lips touched the porcelain moments before, then raised it to her own. She sipped steadily, her eyes never leaving his.

Last night they shared their bodies, minds and souls. Compared to that, why did this simple sharing seem so intimate, so exciting? Maybe it was because their love, exposed to the public light, stood the test.

She took a second sip as he watched her intently. Her lips curved gently into a smile. "Mine?"

"For as long as you want." Neither was discussing the coffee.

"You said, tell them when I'm sure?"

He nodded, a lump forming in his throat.

"Then breakfast can wait, don't you think?"

Another nod.

Cait turned and faced the three silent teenagers. "We need to talk."

Thirteen

*J*ake stepped over the pile of rebar and joined his partner near the concrete forms. Nick looked up from the blueprints. "Where the driveway begins to slope toward the street, we'd better set the rods no more than twelve inches apart. Up here, the usual foot and a half separation will do."

"My thoughts exactly." Jake tilted his hard hat back from his forehead. He listened to the steady hammering of nails into sheet-rock. "It's coming along fine. My guess is we'll finish at least two weeks ahead of schedule."

"Good. Maybe word will spread." Nick rerolled the building plans and stuffed them into their tube. "I'm headed over to the Kingsley site. Want to ride along?" He idly tapped the cardboard cylinder against the side of his foot.

"Not just yet. The owners are dropping by later with the flooring contractor. There are several things I want to check first."

"Fine. Meet you after lunch." Nick walked over to the company truck and opened the door. After laying the plans on the passenger seat, he began kicking the mud off one boot.

Jake cleared his throat. "I'm planning on leaving town for a few days, maybe later this week. Any problem covering for me?"

"No. Go on. Get lost for awhile." Nick looked in Jake's direction, then squinted. The stress lines edging his partner's eyes were noticeable in the bright sunlight. "From the looks of it, old buddy, I'd say you need a few days by yourself."

Crossing to the vehicle, Jake leaned against the hood. It wasn't necessary to say anything more about the upcoming weekend, but he wanted to. "Actually, I'm taking Caitlyn with me."

"Oh. One of those." He smacked other booted foot against the frame, chuckling slightly to himself. "Why don't you take the whole week off?"

"And the girls."

Nick stopped smiling and straightened. "Plural?"

"Caitlyn has two daughters. Jackie makes three."

"That's no vacation." Nick rested his forearms in the open window frame. Leaning against the truck door, he watched his partner debate with himself.

Jake crossed his arms against his chest, studying the roof line. Despite many years together, the two men rarely shared confidences. For some reason it seemed easier now to open up. It might even round their partnership into a deeper friendship.

"Caitlyn's interviewing for a new job. She's trying to arrange it for this Friday."

"And your role? Tour guide?"

He nodded. "Close. I'll navigate around the city while she house-hunts."

Nick lifted his hard hat and wiped his forehead against his sleeve. "Sounds stressful. Why not take her fly fishing instead?"

"Right." He laughed. Nick definitely had a one track mind. When it wasn't occupied with women, it was on trout and steelhead. He had a rustic single-room cabin in the Methow valley, enabling him to pursue both passions at once. "Yeah, it'll be stressful, especially with the kids along. But it's necessary, too."

Shaking his head, Nick walked over and began picking up scraps of lumber. "You're not exactly setting a new record here as a romantic." He tossed a load into the truck bed. "And if she decides to relocate? Then what?"

Jake drew a deep breath, then slowly released it. "I'll be one step closer to knowing."

"Why help her move away? Convince her to stay, instead."

"I couldn't live with that. I tried it that way before; thought I could convince Victoria to tone down her desire for high living. The only thing that accomplished was to frustrate the hell out of both of us."

He joined Nick out in the yard, but instead of picking up debris, he rested one foot against a bag of concrete. He stared out at the forested hills and at Mount Rainier beyond. Neither brought him the peace of mind they once did. Something was missing. Cait's laughter. "I made myself a promise years ago, never again to live with regrets."

As he continued to scan the skyline, he focused on the

rush of the breeze through the evergreens. He had gotten used to that sound, alone on his deck at the lodge. Most likely he could again. "Whatever she decides, I'll accept and go on."

"Love is hell."

Jake looked quickly at his partner. Except for Jackie, he hadn't said that word aloud for years, until last weekend. And then only to Cait. Was it so obvious?

Nick broke the tension. "Of course, I could be wrong. I don't have any experience with that sort of thing." One corner of his mouth turned up, creating a lopsided smile.

Jake walked over and slapped him on the back. "Someday you will. It happens to the best of us."

Nick's eyes widened in exaggerated horror. "Let's hope it's not soon." He bent to retrieve a few stray nails. "After this weekend, then what?"

"We'll know whether to move forward or to plateau things where they are." He shoved his hands into his back pockets. "At the moment Jackie's expectations are running pretty high. I've got to redirect her if it's not going to happen, before she drives me nuts."

"A long-distance relationship might work." Nick's voice was lukewarm.

"Maybe."

"Then you'd have the best of both worlds, if you know what I mean."

"That's not enough, anymore." Jake drew a deep breath. "I'd better get back to work. Thanks for listening."

"Any time."

"See you at the office around two." He turned to go.

"Wait." Nick pulled off his construction hat and dusted the logo against his jeans. "For what it's worth, I think forcing her decision is the right thing to do. Not knowing has got to be the worst."

"It is." Jake took his hat off and ran his fingers back through his hair. "By next week's camp-out we should know. It could turn out to be a farewell party, of sorts."

"Where will that leave you?" Nick asked.

He kept his voice firm. "Right here. With my daughter, my home and my business. Where I belong." After a moment he broke the mood with a slight smile. "But maybe not." Nodding once, he headed towards the front of the house. "See you."

"Hey, what do you mean by that crack?"

Jake's only response was a wave, over his shoulder.

Nick called after him. "You wouldn't sell your half of the business, would you?"

"What were your words earlier? 'A long-distance relationship might work?'"

"I didn't mean with me." Nick slammed his hat into the truck bed.

The noise made Jake glance back. Nick's normally wavy hair was straightened in front, standing at attention. Above his ears the mop still sported a half-inch dent from one side, around to the other. If Jackie could see him like this she'd call it a classic bad hair day. He laughed and strode away.

Nick shoved both hands in his back pockets, as he stared at Jake's back. "Damn. Now he's got me waiting, too."

His partner calmly disappeared through the frame of an open bay window. A smile softened Nick's worried expression. "If anyone can make this work, he can."

■ ■ ■

Jake gripped the steering wheel tighter and winced at the sound of Jackie pumping her spray bottle yet again. Her newest fragrance, Midnight Magnolia, still made his nose itch and his tear ducts swell. It clashed with Rose's citrus scent and Lynn's musk oil. The girls were engaged in Cosmetic Combat, and he was losing badly. He opened his window in an attempt to clear his sinuses.

"Dad, cool it with the air blast, will you?"

"I am trying to cool it, honey. It was getting stuffy in here."

"How am I going to look good at lunch, if you insist on blowing me out of the back seat?"

He glanced in his rear view mirror. Jackie was protecting her freshly möussed bangs, an outraged expression on her face. Who was she trying to kid? Not him. A trip through the Boeing wind tunnel couldn't put a dent in that do. He'd only allowed it because Rose was wearing the same look today.

Cait patted his knee. He looked over. She pointed to the switch that operated the tail gate window, and silently mouthed the word compromise. He frowned, then reluctantly nodded, rolling the rear window down and his own back up.

The three hour trip to Drew's house dragged on. Most of what was on Jake's mind couldn't be discussed in a crowd, so he didn't contribute much to the conversation. His silence caused an awkwardness that even golden oldies on the car stereo couldn't chase away.

They stopped for burgers at the factory outlet mall in Centralia. While the girls scrounged briefly for bargains, Cait purchased a book-on-tape. The murder mystery not only disguised the silence, but kept their minds occupied the remainder of the trip.

Finally they pulled into Drew's driveway. His A-frame home was situated on one of the many hills overlooking the Clackamas River, on Portland's south side.

Jackie was the first to hop out of the car. "Wow, the view is fantastic. It's been ages since I've been here." She drank in the sunset with an audible sigh.

"Don't faint on us yet." Jake closed his door and stood next to his daughter. He put one arm around her. "Wait until you see the same sight from the loft windows."

"Yeah. You can really see the waterfall from up there." She spun around and pointed to the upper window. "Is that where we get to sleep?"

He nodded.

"Cool."

Rose followed Jackie's gaze as she stepped down from the Range Rover. "This is really great!" She turned towards Jake. "Thanks for letting us come."

"My pleasure."

"Lynn and I thought you'd like to be alone. You know, with Mom." Rose shrugged with a shy smile. She scuffed at some loose bark dust near the side of the driveway. "The invitation kind of caught us by surprise."

"Glad you could still make it, on such short notice." He put his hand on her shoulder. "Since moving is a family event, we thought everyone should be included."

"Yeah, well thanks."

Jackie challenged her friend. "Hey, race you up there?"

"Sure. That okay with you, Mom?"

Cait nodded, closing and locking her door before stretching her legs.

"Then you're on. Coming, sis?"

Lynn poked her head out of the truck, then jumped down. "Yeah, but I don't want to make two trips. Let's get the bags."

Jake popped open the tailgate. Within minutes the girls had their arms loaded with overnight bags and were off.

Jake and Cait followed with their own suitcases.

The teens automatically headed for the main entrance, but Jake rerouted them towards the garage. He raised the lid on a small vertical key pad, mounted on the frame. After punching in a series of numbers, the door rumbled, then lifted. The girls ran on ahead.

"Great, isn't it?" He smiled for the first time since leaving Seattle. "This way we don't need a key."

"Nice not having to look under a rock." She followed him inside. "As long as you don't forget the secret code."

"Impossible." Shifting his suitcase to the other hand, he picked up a bag of charcoal. "Odd, too. Drew and I both installed these encryption devices at approximately the same time. Without knowing it, we both chose the same five digit number."

"You're kidding." Cait held open the inner door, letting Jake go first. "The chance of picking the same sequence is incredible."

"Normally, yes. In our case, we each used the house number of our last permanent residence." Jake paused for a moment. "Our last home with Dad."

He dismissed the thought with a quick shrug. Cait set down her case then touched his arm. "I'm sorry."

"It's not your fault."

She didn't let him brush it off this time. "What I mean is, I have such good memories of my own childhood. It must have been very hard for you."

"It was a long time ago." He looked into her eyes, then bent to brush a kiss across her forehead. "Let's get settled in."

She smiled. "Lead the way."

His gaze held hers a moment longer. His expression turned mischievous. "Did I mention that our bedrooms are adjoining, not counting the bathroom in between?"

"They are?"

He winked at her.

She laughed at his playful expression. "Don't get any ideas."

"Too late." He dropped both bags and pulled her close. "I already have several I'd like to pursue with you later."

They went their separate ways to unpack. Jake finished first. Cait found him with the girls on the back deck, arranging charcoal in the barbecue.

She listened for a moment through the screen door. He and Lynn were engrossed in a deep conversation. The merits of living in a college dormitory versus life off-campus. She shook her head. Not wanting to interrupt, she opted for a self-guided tour. The photos behind the living room sofa immediately caught her eye.

The first was of a Kansas City Royals wanna-be, leaning against a metal bat. His deep-blue baseball cap was pushed back just far enough to show the matching tint of his eyes. A younger Jake, by nearly thirty years, although it was a bit hard to tell through the dust and streak marks.

Directly behind him was a miniature version of himself, with equally dark hair and sparkling eyes. The little fellow was looking at his older brother with undisguised respect. It had to be Drew.

She had been hoping to meet his brother this weekend, but he'd left days before. Sea kayaking on the Oregon Coast. The trip had been planned long before Jake's announcement of their visit. The fact that Drew offered his place without hesitation was evidence of their closeness. Was he the only family member Jake kept in contact with any more?

The next photo was of three youngsters with fishing poles in hand. They were all elementary school age and spaced only a couple of years apart. The two youngest were seated in a flat-bottomed boat. Jake stood next to them in knee-high water. At the end of his line was an hors d'oeuvre-sized fish. Cait hoped that he'd caught more than one.

Holding the boat steady was a man in his early forties. From the jet black hair, there was no doubt that he was related. Jake's father. His admiring smile spoke volumes. His son might as well have landed Moby Dick.

Jake's hand, touching her lower back, startled her. He stood by her silently, studying the old photographs instead of looking at her. His expression said that it had been ages since his last walk down memory lane.

"Do you mind if I look at these? I don't want to pry."

He shook his head and lifted the last picture off the wall. Four people, standing on the steps of an old stone church, dressed in their Sunday best. No one was smiling. The three boys stood in front with their mother behind them, her posture as stiff as the St. Francis statue to her right. It was impossible to tell, but from the grip she had on her eldest's shoulder, maybe her scowl had been warranted.

Cait leaned forward, closely studying the woman's face. The high cheekbones and slim nose looked familiar, but not because they mirrored Jake's. No, there was something about the woman that was hard to pinpoint. Something that nagged at Cait's memory. If the woman hadn't been wearing sunglasses, Cait might have been able to put a finger on what it was. She shrugged.

Jake returned the photo to its hanger and gathered Cait tightly into his arms. They stood there silently for several moments. Finally she drew back and saw that his eyes glistened brightly. She laid a hand on his cheek.

He leaned into it. "I know I can handle it if you leave, but promise you'll always be honest with me."

Cait stroked his skin with her thumb. "Of course."

He pressed her head to his chest. Her wild ginger scent was now so familiar to him. Resting his cheek against the top of her head, he breathed in deeply. "And don't ever stop loving me, no matter what."

■ ■ ■

That particular Saturday was an uncommonly warm day in Portland. The temperature soared towards the one hundred degree mark. Jake maneuvered the Range Rover through the downtown traffic as the girls pointed out the frisbee players and kite flyers crowding the Willamette riverfront park. He heard the words 'hunk' and 'pecs' several times, before Lynn shushed them into silence. Maybe, after dropping off Cait for her interview, they could return to the park for a while. It could be just the distraction the girls needed.

He stopped at a red light. Rhythm and blues drifted through the open window. A lone musician entertained a group of Saturday afternoon sun-worshippers with his guitar, case open by his feet to collect random donations. The scent of espresso and fresh baked goods filled the air.

Jake drew a deep breath. Portland was not so different from Seattle. He could probably be happy here, if he weren't hauling around so much emotional baggage. Maybe he would feel different, living here with a family of his own. But starting over? Again?

Making a sharp left, he pulled the Range Rover into the curved drive in front of the corporate offices. OmniCorp's glass and marble building had been easy to locate along the bustling Willamette waterway. It was the very symbol of corporate America. Men and women, lugging briefcases, rushed through the revolving doors. Stepping out of the truck, Jake came around to open Cait's door.

She looked up in surprise from her page of notes. "Here already?"

She had missed the entire drive? Amazing. What flew by for her was crawling by for him. Difference in their perspectives. He nodded and tried giving her a cheerful smile. "Knock 'em dead."

Returning his smile, she waved goodbye to the girls. "Wish me luck." No response. The sight of tears in Rose's eyes stopped her. "Honey, what is it?"

Reaching into the back seat, she touched her daughter's cheek, then looked at the other two girls. Dry, perhaps, but their expressions were somber. She glanced back at Jake. Hesitation wrinkled her brow.

He laid his palm against her arm. "Don't worry. We'll circle back to the park and watch the sailboats for a while. Maybe grab a snow cone. A few bronzed muscles will stop the pouting party, and I know just the place. Call me on the car phone when you're through."

His hand was strong and possessive as it moved slowly down her forearm, massaging her gently. Its welcoming pressure radiated through her linen blazer. She wished he'd pull her close so that she could feel his warmth.

Now that she thought about it, there were a few not-so-bronzed muscles of his that she'd like to see again. His lily-white backside, to be exact. Why hadn't he come to her room last night? Not safe? She'd missed him curled by her side while she slept.

Maybe it was the photographs that caused him to withdraw, those tangible reminders of betrayal and desertion. Dinner had been awkward after that. When their conversation dwindled away to nothing, Jake had filled the silence with stories of Oregon's rich history. She'd chimed in from time to time, with descriptions of city landmarks, parks and museums from a local magazine. It was so boring that the girls went to bed early.

After rushing through the dishes, she'd filled the tub with warm relaxing water, scented with a hint of bath oil. She'd half-expected him to join her, but the door remained closed. When she was through she'd pulled on her robe and hurried to find him.

She had found him, all right, in his own bed, asleep. Or at least pretending to be. Why did he retreat after pointing out that their bedrooms were connected? She could have pulled the covers back, demanded an explanation and asked to be made love to. That approach certainly worked the first time.

But she wanted him to initiate their next time together, so she retired with the only reading material she could find, an historical guide to the Oregon Trail. Her insomnia instantly disappeared.

Jake urged her out of the vehicle. Time was ticking onward. The sooner this ordeal was over, the better. The girls' silence seemed to take Cait by surprise. What did she expect? Their daughters had been sullen for hours. Was Cait so wrapped up in her interview preparation that she hadn't noticed? Too late for a guilt trip now. "Come on, you'll be late."

"I'm not doing this." She bit her bottom lip.

"Yes, you are." His tone was light, but his message serious. He helped her step down onto the curb. No cancelling, not after the emotional hell he'd been through all morning. They needed to know, and this was an important step. No reneging out of pure and simple maternal guilt.

His free hand cupped her shoulder. "I'll talk to them."

"Thanks." Her voice wobbled slightly. She cleared her throat and fidgeted with her purse strap. "I shouldn't be long. A couple of hours at most." Placing her free hand over his, she drew it into her grasp.

A masculine voice boomed from behind her. "Cait, good to see you again. And right on time, as ever. I'm the one running late. Hello, Rose, Lynn."

The silence in the back seat was broken. "Hi, Mr. Anderson." Rose echoed her sister's greeting.

Cait re-introduced the two men. "Bill, do you remember Jake? He attended the gala with me."

"Of course." He extended his hand. "Bill Anderson. Thanks for accompanying Caitlyn this weekend."

"My pleasure." Jake stared at the outstretched hand, then glanced at his own firmly wrapped in hers. "Sorry. Occupied." He lifted his, revealing their interlocked fingers, then smiled half-heartedly. He was anything but sorry.

He appraised Bill from head to foot. He saw Cait's eyes widen as he did. So he was sizing up the competition, as a teenager would do at a junior high dance. Could she really blame him? How would she react if confronted with someone from his past?

Bill used the awkward silence as an opportunity to leave. "I'll meet you upstairs, Cait. Second floor. Turn right off the elevator. Last door on the left. Good meeting you again, Jake. Bye, girls."

"I'd better run." Jake felt her quick, reassuring squeeze before she released his hand. "I'll call you soon."

His eyes met hers. He had never asked, and never would. It wasn't a trust issue; he was past that. It was just a simple, unattractive streak of jealousy. Just the thought of leaving her with Bill for the afternoon clenched at his gut. The two of them together. What would it be like if she worked here eight hours a day, week after week?

Better get used to it, he warned himself, because that's exactly what she might do. It's all or nothing. Trust doesn't work halfway. He'd focus on their love, and forget the rest. Take one day at a time. Leaning forward, he barely caught himself before giving her a kiss. Too many damned windows. Instead, he stepped back and nodded. "Good luck. Call me."

The emotions crossing his face hadn't escaped her notice. A man of his word, he'd never questioned her again after that night. He had accepted her 'as is,' with no apologies or explanations. And now he was letting her go, so that she could make up her own mind freely.

"You're not getting off the hook that easily." Placing a hand on his shoulder, she raised up on her toes and kissed him. Twice.

The back seat erupted in sounds of approval.

She'd probably tell him about Bill. Not because she had to, but because she wanted to. But not tonight.

No, she had other plans for tonight.

■ ■ ■

Bill was experienced at interviewing management candidates, but rarely did he see someone who was so competent, yet so reluctant to blow her own horn. Today's visit was a mere formality. Cait was perfect for the job. Now, if she would only convince herself it was a good move.

A sharp knock interrupted his thoughts. "Come in."

"Sorry. It took us a little longer than planned."

Bill stood and signaled for her to take a seat. "No problem. How did it go?"

"Great. My meeting with the technical staff overran its

time. They're a great team, full of ideas for improving things."

"Which I hope you'll be joining, very soon." Removing his jacket, he hung it on the back of his chair. He loosened his tie and sat down.

"Okay, let's get started." He picked up his notes. "I've already spoken to the other managers, regarding their meeting with you. Basically they were quite impressed by your technical background and your interpersonal skills. Handling that many questions, for that length of time, couldn't have been easy." He set down the pad and smiled. "Bottom line, you're a hit."

She silently accepted his compliment. Glancing at the organizational chart she was still holding from earlier, she focused on the box highlighted in yellow. It was labeled 'Interview in Process.'

Her throat was suddenly dry. "Bill, if I take this assignment . . ."

"Whoa. Say no more." He leaned forward, elbows on desk. "That was a very big 'if.' Is that the way things are?"

She nodded. "I have to be honest with you. There's a lot to consider. Much more than job responsibilities and salary."

"I know." His tone was serious, but warm.

She lifted her chin slightly. "Jake is a very big consideration. He owns his own business, and a beautiful lodge in the Cascades. But there are other factors, too. My daughters have their friends and school. I'm involved with a local church group which brings me a great deal of satisfaction."

The buzz of the intercom interrupted. Bill glanced at the blinking light. "I normally have my calls held, but we have an emergency brewing at one of our key customer sites. I'll keep it brief."

Cait nodded. Flipping over the papers in her lap, she picked up her pen and began doodling on the reverse side. As Bill listened to the caller he watched her quick movements across the page. That particular habit of hers was very familiar to him.

He had served as a teaching assistant in several of her college programming classes. Frequently her homework contained abstract drawings in the margins. On the day of her engagement to Todd, the border of her paper contained stick figure drawings, bound to one another. When asked about it, she stammered but eventually told him, dismissing it with a simple shrug. They were captive housewives following their husbands, she had explained.

He didn't realize until years later, when both their marriages were in troubled waters, that this was how she expressed her fears and her dreams.

At the moment she was sketching a ranch house, surrounded by trees and lakes. Across the sky was a rainbow with a firmly planted beginning, but with no end. Brandon's lodge. Maybe her mind hadn't decided yet, but her heart certainly had.

He completed his call and cradled the receiver. She saw that he was studying her drawing and quickly put down her pen.

He tilted his head towards her picture. "As you were saying, there's a lot to consider."

"Yes. I'm trying to look at all sides."

"Good." His eyes held hers for a moment. "The best thing for OmniCorp may not be the best thing for you. I realize that."

She nodded.

"But you're perfect for this position. Remember that, too." He smiled as he stood. Together they walked to the door. "I'll call you one week from Monday, to see what you've decided. After that I need to start interviewing other candidates.

"A week should be sufficient." She turned to him and held out her hand. "And thank you."

Bill shook her hand warmly, then released it and pulled open the door. "Be sure to spend some of that time investigating the housing market, both here and in Seattle, before I try talking you into accepting." His eyes were twinkling again.

From their past association, she knew that he'd never pressure her into anything. "Don't place good money on any bets, one way or another."

"I said try, Caitlyn. I can always try."

■ ■ ■

Cait could still hear her daughters gabbing with Jackie, even though they had retired to the loft over an hour ago. Frowning, she turned to Jake. "Are you sure this will work?" She glanced about the bedroom one more time.

The comforter on the guest bed was rumpled and her paperback lay open on the nightstand. Her robe was strategically hanging on a hook by the shower, for easy access.

"Not at all sure." He tugged on her arm. "But the odds are with us. Follow me."

She giggled. It was so unlike either of them that the excitement was overwhelming. When Jake gave her a second nudge she didn't delay any further. They traipsed through their shared bath and into the adjoining room. Once inside, he enfolded her in his arms.

"What if . . ."

"Enough." He silenced her objections with playful bites

across her lower lip. Between nibbles he recounted his plan. "Both bedroom doors are locked. Ditto for the bathroom. If someone knocks, you can grab your robe and scoot on back."

He stepped away and unzipped the jacket of her wind suit. Slipping his arms underneath, he held her close against him. Her muscles were tense beneath the thin cotton T-shirt. "It was a long day, wasn't it?"

"The longest. Especially when we were with the realtor."

"Let me help you relax." He kissed her gently, then with fingertips intertwined he guided her to the master bed. Neither of them believed that forgetfulness was possible, but the pressure of her impending decision could be shoved to the back burner for awhile.

She cleared her thoughts and concentrated on the piece of heaven Jake was offering.

Kneeling, he slipped off her sneakers and socks and massaged her ankles. She stood in front of him, hands on his shoulders, while he slowly rotated one, then the other. "Does that help?"

"Help what?" She sighed. The feeling was pure pleasure. "Help you to seduce me?"

He laughed softly. "You should be so lucky."

"I know. I am." She wove her fingers through his thick, black hair and gently tugged his head backward. Leaning over, she pressed a kiss against his forehead. Her voice was low and inviting. "Come up here and join me."

"Not yet." He applied his soothing magic to her calves, then slowly trailed his fingers upward, along the back of her knees. Her legs nearly buckled. When he reached her thighs he stood and gently cupped her buttocks.

Drawing her forward, he pressed her lower half firmly against his. His arousal throbbed an unmistakable message against her stomach. Her pulse leapt in response.

Her mouth parted and her breathing was uneven. Yes, this is what she'd been waiting for. To experience again the aching sensation that only he could make her feel. She swayed against him.

"That's it. Put everything else out of your mind. Just focus on me, on us."

Reaching past her, he drew back the covers and led her to the crisp, ivory sheets. He sat on the bed next to her, then tugged at the elastic waistline of her running shorts. She obliged by lifting her hips. When the nylon fabric was gone he helped her with the rest. Her T-shirt and bra quickly joined the growing pile of clothing on the floor.

He was motionless, as if drinking in the sight. She wished the lights were out, or at least dimmed. Lying there under his gaze, without anything but her Jockey's covering her, was like nothing she'd ever experienced before.

She didn't object though, as she remembered their first time together. Her stalking him, permitting no escape. The excitement of the chase had made her fingertips tingle. She was tingling again now. Jake must also be remembering. The awareness shone brightly in his eyes. It seemed only fair to let him set the pace this time. Crossing her arms behind her head, she tried not to feel self-conscious and let the experience surround her.

The circle he was tracing on her bare leg slowly widened. With each revolution more skin was taken captive. As he moved upward his touch skimmed the edge of the remaining fabric. She was trembling inside, but made no sound.

He lifted one of her legs. Leaning over, he kissed the bent knee, tasting it with his tongue. His next kiss was inches higher, on her inner thigh.

That was it, all she could stand. She quickly moved her

free leg, up and out to surround him. Captured in an intimate triangle between her unadorned limbs and her cotton panties, surely now he'd move things along.

Smiling, he shook his head at her impatience.

He trailed his fingertip along the lower band of the french-cut briefs, then let his nail trace a path across the center panel without pausing. She curled her fingers into her palm. Later, much later, she'd get even with him for this. It was exquisite torture.

Jake wanted time to stand still. With the camp-out next weekend, and her decision due after that, there was no way to know when there would be another chance.

He would memorize every inch of her lovingly, until he could see her clearly in his dreams. Like a silken image against his closed eyelids, she'd still be with him on those long nights when he slept alone.

His fingertips retraced their earlier path, this time pausing dead center. His palm cupped her intimately, then stopped. He moved forward up her length, placing a kiss against her navel, her ribs, then her breast.

She waited, her heartbeat resounding in her ears. When she could stay still no longer she arched against him to increase the pressure. Unclenching her hands, she gripped his sides, trying to urge him further upward, to where their bodies could move together. He didn't budge. His tongue was hot against her nipple, surrounding it and drawing it into his mouth. The liquid pooling deep within drenched her. Torture. Yes, it was definitely torture he was after. She wanted to laugh, to cry out, to say anything at all. But her jaw was too tightly set. She arched again, against the air this time. It didn't help.

He watched her silent plea and hooked his thumbs beneath the elastic band at her waist. With a little maneuvering, and her willing assistance, he slipped the last barrier off. She was totally exposed to his touch.

She thought for sure he'd kill the lights now, move over her, slip beneath the covers. She blushed deeply as he continued to watch her. Reflexively, she tried to cover herself.

"No." He touched her wrists and moved them back down to her sides. "Let me."

"It's . . . embarrassing." Her voice was unnaturally high, her heart racing.

"For me to look?" He released his hold and intertwined his fingers with hers.

Though she knew it was totally unsophisticated, she couldn't help blushing. Was it possible for a blush to reach all the way down to her thighs? If so, they'd be crimson too. She laughed uncomfortably. "Just . . . don't."

He raised questioning eyes to hers, trying to assess her seriousness.

"The twins, you see, well my body's not like it used to be," she said.

"You're perfect." He leaned forward and brushed a kiss against her abdomen. His breath was warm next to her skin. "Is it something else? You're pulse is pounding."

"The lights. They were always off."

"Always?"

She nodded. "Todd and I followed the straight and narrow, so to speak. We were both virgins and didn't really know, I guess."

"Did you ever want more?"

"Once I considered buying a book, but I didn't want him to think I wasn't happy." She drew an unsteady breath. "Bottom line is that no one's ever looked before."

He brushed another kiss against her skin, inches below

the previous one. "With twins, love, someone must have looked. At least once."

"Yes, but . . ." She cleared her throat and forced her voice to sound very matter-of-fact. "Everyone wore a mask then."

He abruptly stopped, and raised his head. An idea quickly sprang to mind.

"I'll be right back." Swinging his long frame off the bed, he crossed to Drew's dresser and began searching through the top drawer.

She sat up and pulled the sheet over her. "What are you doing?"

"Finding a . . . aha! Here's one." He retrieved a red madras bandana and folded it into a triangular shape.

"Stop that."

"Just what the doctor ordered." His eyes glinting with humor, he reached up and covered the lower half of his face with the fabric, then tied it behind his head. When finished he looked towards the bed and raised his eyebrows. "Will this do?" His voice was muffled.

"Take that off, immediately."

"Never." He put one knee on the bed and whisked aside her covering. She grabbed at the mask, but he subdued her hands overhead. They rolled back and forth, wrestling like kids, until once again she lay under him. He folded up the bottom 'V', freeing his mouth.

"See, it works great." He proved it with a single kiss.

This time, when he began slowly moving down her length, leaving searing kisses in his wake, she didn't consider objecting. Not once.

Fourteen

The crisp manila folder was in stark contrast to the dozen or so dog-eared papers contained within it. Some of the permission slips had traces of soda and chocolate smeared across them. Others had unrelated messages scribbled down the sides. Still, they were the proof Cait needed. Her retreat weekend would soon be a reality.

"Here are the parental forms and medical releases." She waved the folder proudly in mid-air, before placing it on Audra's desk. "All signed and ready to go."

"Great. The only paperwork we have left is the site profile. Did you bring the photos?"

"Right here." Caitlyn tapped her purse.

"Well, then let's get to it." The chairwoman spread the

Field Trip Application Packet before her. "How long do you have for lunch?"

"I left word that I'd return by two. Since I spent most of Saturday at our Portland headquarters, no one cares that I'm taking an extra hour off today."

"Working weekends, too? I don't know how you do it all. Makes me tired just thinking about it." Audra inserted a pencil into the electric sharpener.

Cait waited until the whirling stopped before explaining. "Actually, I was there interviewing. I was offered a promotion, with one major string attached. I'd have to relocate."

Audra was still for a moment. "When would you need to leave?"

"Soon. But don't worry. Summer is usually a slow time for our youth group. After this camp-out, nothing major is planned until the fall." Cait began filling out Jake's name, address and phone number in the heading section, trying to keep her voice free from emotion. It was difficult to imagine someone else taking over her group.

"I was actually thinking of you. What a major change it would be. I had to move my own children several times when they were young. It's difficult, at any age." She shook her head, as if clearing away a bad memory. "For any reason."

"How long did it take for them to settle in?"

"One never did. The other two, well, they weren't quite so mule-headed as my oldest." Audra cleared here throat. "I'll glance at the photos now, my dear. I usually schedule a personal visit to any new site, but, since you've been to the lodge several times, I'll make an exception."

"You'd love it. It's a huge place, more than enough room for the twelve of us." Cait dug in her purse, producing a packet of snapshots. "It's practically brand new. Jake's only lived there a little over a year himself."

"He's new to the Seattle area?"

"No, he's been here several years. Jake moved in when the original owner went bankrupt. At first I thought it was for sentimental reasons, because his construction company built the place. Later I realized it was the lake that lured him to settle there."

"How so?" Audra spread the photos in front of her.

"He loved fishing with his dad, when he was young. See this one?" She pointed to a snapshot of the two Brandons in the yellow canoe. "Definite proof that some traits are hereditary. His daughter, Jackie, is the avid fisherman now."

"Family traditions are important."

Cait nodded. "But I think she's getting sick of trout for dinner. When she's at our house I try to plan chicken or hamburgers instead."

Audra peered closer, noting the strong resemblance. Straight nose, jet-black hair, athletic shoulders. "She's a beautiful young lady. Is she at your place often?"

"Not as often as Lynn and Rose would like. They'd have her over every day if they could. They're filling the summer alternating between tennis, bike riding and swimming." Cait laughed. "Actually, sunbathing would be more accurate than swimming. See all three of them sprawled out on the dock?"

"And not a lick of sunscreen between them, I bet."

"You guessed it."

Audra laid the photo down beside the first and picked up the next. The newly painted bunk beds were drying in the late afternoon sun. The proud artists posed with their brushes in the background. "She's lucky to have made friends so quickly."

"Especially since there are no relatives in the area." Cait turned to page two.

"No one?"

"Only an uncle in Portland. Jake's father died when he was a teenager. He says very little about his mother. I would never pry, but it seems, well, a hard way to live." Cait looked up from the application. "I never let a week go by without talking to my mom by phone. Dad, too, when he's there."

"Sometimes misunderstandings get in the way; force families apart."

"But what could possibly be more important than blood relations? Certainly not pride."

"Never underestimate the power of pigheadedness." Audra quickly flipped through the indoor shots of the TV room, dining area and kitchen. "My husband was addicted to gambling, and never would admit it. He was jovial and carefree, spent money like it was water. I was the family worry-wart, the disciplinarian."

"Kind of a role reversal, from what I've heard of the Fifties."

"Exactly." She shook her head slowly. "But the kids truly loved him, far beyond the lavish gifts he brought home. More often than not, they'd resent me for returning the shiny new bike, the second television or whatever new gizmo he'd found."

Audra arranged the photos on 8½ by 11 inch sheets and began stapling them into place. "That all ended the day he got in over his head. Finally he paid the price with his life."

Cait's head shot up. "I'm so sorry. I had no idea."

"Our family was never the same." Audra's laugh was cynical. "That's a terrible understatement. What I meant was, some things can hurt far worse than a sudden death. Some keep on hurting, day after day." The pressure and speed on the stapler increased. Her fingers moved lightning quick across the page. "My children blamed me. Maybe if I had trusted them with the truth, instead of hiding the real reason for his death, things would be different today. It's hard to say."

"You didn't tell them?"

"Not everything. It would have destroyed the memories they have of their father." She looked up and sadness filled her eyes. "Not a chance. I wasn't willing to trade that for a few Mother's Day cards. You see, I loved him." Tapping the sheets against the desk, she squared the edges, then clipped the pages together. "How is your part coming?"

"Nearly finished." Cait looked down at the paper she'd forgotten about, and quickly finished the last section.

Opening the top drawer of the file cabinet, Audra thumbed through the color coded tabs and extracted an ivory parchment. "Here is your permit, signed by the district. This makes everything above-board. Just make sure it's posted by the front door at all times."

"I will." Cait sat back for a moment and stared down at the document. Audra's change of mood was as quick as her change of subject. She was obviously an expert at stifling this particular pain.

"How soon after the camping trip will you be leaving?"

"Actually, I haven't made a final decision yet." She met Audra's gaze. "I've worked hard for this promotion, but frankly, the shimmer of excitement is gone."

"Why?"

Cait shrugged. "Many reasons."

"Jake?"

"Quite the contrary." She laughed. "He'd write me a reference if he thought I needed one. He's never once mentioned the other alternative. Staying here."

Cait settled further into her chair. Life was so short. The fact that both Audra's husband and hers had died so young was stinging proof of that. Maybe she should come right out and ask Jake, and stop wasting time.

Looking down, she saw that she had rolled the permit into a long tube and was about to twist the middle. She uncurled it and slipped it into her briefcase, flat against the leather side.

"He sends out mixed messages. He won't budge on my considering this job opportunity. But when we're alone, or with the girls, he's loving, attentive and generous. There are no sides taken, no scrambling for authority or turf. It's a close and comfortable feeling." Cait looked up, surprised by her own choice of words. "That's a very unromantic word, isn't it?"

"It does bring to mind bedroom slippers and a pipe."

Cait smiled. "He would be appalled."

"Actually, what you've described is that feeling of family we were just talking about. Sometimes it never happens between two people, no matter how much love is at stake. It's the friendship and togetherness that underlies the flames."

"Because the flames can go out."

Audra nodded. "All it takes is one good rain storm."

"We've never spoken about what the future holds, past next weekend. But I know he thinks about it. I can feel it every time he puts his arms around me." Cait uncrossed her legs and switched their position. "But sometimes an invisible gate slams down, blocking his emotions and pushing me away."

Audra picked up her glasses. She twirled them gently back and forth between her thumb and forefinger. "For protection. Against heartache."

"What should I do? Force the issue?"

The chairwoman shook her head. "Have patience, and use the time to decide what's best for you and the girls. If you and Jake were meant to be, then it will happen, no matter what." She leaned forward, noting Caitlyn's uncertain frown. "Always remember, your family is priority number one."

And so was hers. An idea flashed though Audra's mind. Maybe it was time to stop protecting the past and start guaranteeing the future.

■ ■ ■

The karaoke machine, accompanied by three young voices, blared out the chorus of Whitney Houston's latest love song. No one heard the doorbell until the last note sounded. Since she was the closest, Rose leaped to her feet and bounded down the stairs.

Jake stood on the side lawn. He studied the row of second story windows, hands shoved deep into his back pockets. Jackie loved listening to the Top Ten during their frequent drive from Snoqualmie to Issaquah, so he was very familiar with the song that just ended. But he had never heard it sung with such youthful enthusiasm. He couldn't help but smile.

"Hi." Rose waved from the front steps, still dressed in her swim suit. "You're too early. Mom won't be home for at least an hour."

He knew that. It was the primary reason he had hurried through his final inspection. Last weekend in Portland had been very intense. Confusing, too. With the camp-out just days away, this week was a much needed breather for both of them.

Unfortunately, he couldn't just leave Jackie at the lodge day after day, especially not after she found out that Cait's daughters had ready access to a swimming pool, complete with young male lifeguards.

"I'm just here to pick up Jackie, not to visit. Is she ready to go?"

"No." Rose paused for a moment, biting her lower lip. "We've been busy singing."

He joined her, bracing one foot against the front step. "I heard you."

"You did?"

He nodded. "So did the entire neighborhood."

"Oh." Rose quickly scanned the block.

"Don't worry, it sounded great."

"Hey, thanks." A grin spread across her face. She motioned for him to enter.

He stepped inside, leaving the door open behind him. He didn't want to give anyone the impression that he was staying.

"Have a seat." Rose motioned to the living room. "Were you waiting long?"

He ignored her invitation. "Long enough to consider the old rock-against-the-window trick."

She laughed. "That only works when the windows are closed." Leaning forward, she passed on a coveted secret. "Next time, go around back and stand on the top rung of the swing-set ladder. We'll be sure to see you, if you wave."

"Really?" He raised his eyebrows.

"That's what Lynn's boyfriend does. It works great."

Oh, to be sixteen again. He cleared his throat. "Will you run up and tell Jackie I'm here?" She glanced at her watch, then looked off into space, deep in thought. "Rose?"

"Actually, she's not ready." Now that the words were out

her voice picked up an assertive edge. She met his eyes, hoping to convince him. "Not even close."

"She's not?" Jake spoke slowly, trying to curb his impatience. "Then maybe she could get ready."

"Well, maybe." She nibbled on her thumbnail.

"Dad, are you here?" Jackie leaned over the upstairs railing. Lynn joined her, looking equally disappointed.

Instead of responding to the redundant question, Jake silently counted to three.

"Oh, sorry. I guess you are. But why?"

He forced his voice to stay calm. "I finished earlier than expected. If you hurry, we can still barbecue that trout you caught last night." He paused, having lost his daughter's attention to a series of behind-the-hand whispers with Lynn.

Rose jumped in. "Yes, a cookout. Great idea. You guys could stay until Mom gets home, then we can fix some hamburgers."

"Thanks, but no. Grab your things, Jackie."

"But why not?"

"After a long day at work, your mother would not be pleased to see a house full of uninvited dinner guests."

"But I just invited you."

The look Jake gave her didn't need any further explanation. Jackie leaned back from the rail, frowned at Lynn, then turned to gather her things.

Rose tried again. "Maybe just a glass of iced tea, then. We could sit out on the back deck until Mom arrives, then we could order pizza."

He lowered his voice. "Rose, let it be."

She quickly blinked back unexpected tears. He put a hand on her shoulder. "Stop worrying. We'll figure things out, one way or another."

Lynn slowly descended the steps, her finger drawing

abstract patterns on the bannister. "We couldn't go tonight, anyway, sis. Don't you remember? We're going out shopping later for Mom's birthday present."

Jake abruptly raised his head to glare at Lynn. "Did you say 'birthday?'"

Lynn bent to tie her shoe. She answered lazily, despite the sharpness of his question. "Yeah."

"When's her birthday? Tomorrow?"

"No, on Saturday. I thought we'd stage a surprise party at the campfire." She stood and absently shuffled through the mail on the entryway table. "I'll fill you in later. I wouldn't want to hold you up."

He stared at her for a moment. Sixteen? All three of the girls were schemers, but this one was more polished than most. Lynn one, Jake zero. He gave his victor an admiring smile as he conceded. "Maybe that fish will hold another night."

Jackie shouted from the upstairs hall. "Do you mean it, Dad?"

He nodded. "I'd like to pick out something for your mother, too, and could use a little advice. I'll spring for pizzas when we're through."

"Super!" Jackie exclaimed.

He glanced over to Rose. She was grinning brightly. "Call your mom and ask permission. Tell her we'll be back by eight."

"You got it." She raced off down the hall.

"And, Rose?" She stopped and turned. "Maybe I'll have time for that glass of iced tea, before I leave."

"In the moonlight. Yes." She disappeared around the kitchen corner.

Lynn set down the stack of letters and looked up at him. She smiled. He winked in return.

■ ■ ■

The shopping center was decorated with balloons, tissue paper bells and glitzy streamers in preparation for the weekend bridal fair. Rose gazed at the ceiling, clasping her hands behind her head. She turned a full circle as she took in the sights. "Isn't it just wonderful?"

Jake shook his head in dismay. He had walked right into this one.

Lynn tugged at her sister's arm. "Tone it down, will you? Come on."

They vetoed his idea to shop at the book store and hurried him by the kitchen shop, too. He wandered off while the girls paused near the lingerie windows of Victoria's Secret. They found him across the mall, studying the jewelry displays. Rose and Jackie gave each other a victory sign.

Lynn frowned. "Listen, you two. You're going to blow it. Now come here." The three girls huddled. "Let's tell him we're splitting up and will meet for pizza at seven. That should give him plenty of time."

"But what if he goes back to housewares?"

"Then Mom's better off not marrying him, Rose." Lynn looked at Jackie's indignant expression. She put her arm around the younger girl's shoulder. "No offense intended, you know."

"It's all right." Jackie looked wistfully across at her father and sighed. "He's just romantically-challenged, I guess."

"Yeah." Within moments the twins took off down the mall. Jackie pretended to head towards another wing of the shopping center, but, instead, ducked back into the book store. She purchased an in-bed reading light for Cait and a paperback for herself. Finding a bench right outside, she took up watch within clear sight of the jewelry counter. She was leaving nothing to chance. Before she could finish the first chapter Jake emerged from the store. He had a small but significant package in his hand which he quickly tucked into his coat pocket.

There was no way for him to know, because she was hiding behind a large fern, but father and daughter were both smiling.

■ ■ ■

Kelly dropped a tea bag into a mug of steaming water, then glanced over at the platter stacked with smiley-faced cupcakes. "Did Jackie make these?"

Jake opened the dishwasher and began unloading. "No, Margaret did. She works for me."

"Must be one of those grandma-type personalities." She lifted the plastic wrap and picked one up, peering closer. "They're kind of cute."

"She thinks it's 'kind of cute' for me to have a Sunday school class visiting the lodge this weekend." He shrugged. "I think they'd be a more appropriate dessert for a band of kindergartners, but what the heck. I didn't want to hurt her feelings."

Replacing the cupcake, she scooped an icing drip onto her finger. "Umm. Lots of sugar. That's all the kids will care about." She resealed the platter.

"I'll serve them outside, after dark. No one will know the difference."

Kelly fished the tea bag out of her cup, then took a sip. "So when are they arriving?"

"Soon." Jake opened the silverware drawer. "Cait planned to meet the kids and their parents in North Bend around six. The caravan should be here any minute."

"Twelve kids for a double overnight." She slowly shook her head. "Wow, that would scare me."

"I'm not in charge. Caitlyn is."

"You've really surprised me with this one."

"Why?" He tossed couple of forks in the drawer. "Because I'm usually a selfish bastard?"

"No." It was difficult hearing him over the clanging of the utensils. She walked across to where he was abusing the silverware and shoved the drawer closed. "Because it's making you so nervous. Must be very important to you."

"She is." Jake met her eyes. "And this is important to her. I want everything to go right."

"Then relax." She led him by the shoulders, over to one of the bar stools. "Sit. Now tell me, how can I help? Maybe with the meals?"

"You're already doing enough by being a judge during tomorrow's competition." He accepted the mug of hot water she pushed in his direction, then grabbed a tea bag from the cannister. "Kids this age can take care of themselves. We'll just sit back and supervise."

He paused. Not only was he babbling, but now he was also explaining adolescent behavior to a mother of three. He gave her an apologetic smile. "Sorry."

She perched on the chair next to him. "Something big is up, Brandon, that has you skating near the edge. Is it because Cait is staying here at the lodge again? Too close for comfort, maybe?"

He smiled. "A little late for that." Taking a tentative sip from the side of his cup, he watched her expression soften.

"Well, good for you." She thumped his shoulder. He quickly moved his hand holding the mug, so that the boiling water would splash on the counter instead of his lap. "Do you know what you need, big boy?"

He didn't want to know. Didn't want to be scalded either, so he set the cup down. Time to set the picture straight. "This weekend there are plenty of chaperones. Cait will be staying upstairs in Jackie's room."

"Full circle." She nodded, a look of full comprehension on her face.

Jake frowned. "What the hell is that supposed to mean?"

"In the movies, when the lovers travel back to where they first met, it means that the story line is almost over." She smiled and tilted her head to one side. "You know, happily ever after and all that?"

"Forget it. This is real life." Staring out the window, he willed Cait to arrive. He'd only seen her briefly after the shopping trip with the girls. They'd had no time alone. Sitting out on her deck, with their daughters listening at the upstairs window, didn't count. Giving her more time, and himself too, had been his plan. Now it seemed like a bad one.

"Want to tell me about it?" She placed her hand on his forearm. "I can be a sympathetic listener, if you're interested."

He looked up at her. There was no laughter or judgment lurking in her eyes. How would he even begin? Finally, he drew in a deep breath. "Yeah, I'm interested."

"Then fill me in."

He brought her up to speed on the jumble of activities over the past few weeks. Most of them, anyway. "House hunting was the worst. After the first few stops her daughters didn't even get out of the car."

"Find anything suitable?"

"She didn't say and I didn't ask." He swiveled slightly in his chair, crossing his arms behind his head. "I just kept envisioning her here, sitting on the boat dock with her toes trailing in the water. It's hard for me to imagine her gone."

The silence dragged on for several minutes before he glanced her way. The look in his eyes spurred Kelly into advice mode. "You're a fool, Jake Brandon."

"I know. It would have been easier not to get involved in the first place."

"Hold it, right there. Let me see if I got this straight." She stood. "Even though the two of you are in love, you're encouraging her to leave."

"I want her to follow her dream." He clenched one fist and thumped it against the counter. "What's wrong with that?"

"Why not let her follow her heart, instead?" Kelly asked.

"I think she did that with her first marriage and lived to regret it. What if she regretted being with me in the years to come? I'd rather have her leave now."

"What if she didn't regret it?"

Kelly's habit of answering questions with questions was making his brain hurt. Jake sighed. "We're just too different."

"You're a man and she's a woman. That's good. What else?"

"I like being alone. She thrives on crowds."

"That's why you invited a troop of teens to stay here with you, this weekend."

"I'm not into making long-term commitments anymore."

"Right. That's why Jackie just moved in for the next five to ten years."

He slammed down his fist and stood. "Dammit. You're not listening to me."

"I am. You should try listening to yourself." She leaned closer, hands on hips, unswayed by his scowl. "If you took your blinders off, put away the old self-image for a while, you'd see the new Jake that I see." She lowered her voice as he looked up in surprise. "The Jake that Cait sees."

"Do you think?"

"I think anything's possible." The honking of horns announced the caravan's arrival. Jake froze. Kelly patted his cheek. "Let me qualify that. That is, anything's possible, if you survive this weekend."

He smiled. She linked her arm in his. "Let's go help them unload."

■ ■ ■

The morning workshop was a great success, judging from the animated voices on the back deck. The group moved outdoors as soon as the sun peeked over the ridge. During the first break most of the sweatshirts were peeled off, and a few of the teenagers changed into shorts. With any luck the weather would hold for the Iron Man contest, scheduled for right after lunch.

Jake poured a second cup of coffee. Maybe he'd join them for awhile. His drawings upstairs could wait. Not only would he enjoy watching Caitlyn work with the kids, but he might even learn a thing or two.

He and Jackie communicated well most of the time, but every so often he didn't have a clue as to what she was saying. 'Different wavelengths' his daughter would say, when that confused look crept over his face. Cait often assured him that it would get better with practice. Now was as good a time as any.

He leaned against the door frame and watched her handle the crowd. They were sitting cross-legged in front of her. It was question and answer time. Her tone was encouraging, comforting and not too authoritative. From the number of hands that were raised, there was no doubt she had them interested.

"Yes, Sam, go ahead."

"It's just not fair that we have to deal with condoms, when your generation didn't. It seems like we're paying for problems that we didn't cause. They're messy and no fun. Do you think that's fair?"

Jake choked, but caught himself in time. It was either that or spew coffee all over the crowd.

"Are you okay?" As Caitlyn spoke, a dozen fresh-faced youngsters turned their heads to stare at him. He stared back for a second, then waved. "Just burned my tongue, that's all. I'm fine. Thanks."

She nodded and responded to the question without embarrassment. His own face was flaming. He noticed that two kids were still looking curiously at him. Raising his brow, he grinned at them in exaggeration. "Thank you for being concerned." They quickly turned back towards Cait.

He peered closer to get a good look at the kid who had spoken. My God, the boy couldn't be older than fifteen. Jackie's age. If that child knew what was good for him, he'd stay on his own side of the campfire tonight. Another kid spoke up. This time it was someone with eye shadow the same shade as her shoulder tattoo. "It's cool for guys to carry condoms in their wallets, but what about us? If a girl has one, you know, for 'just in case', then would a guy think she was an easy target?"

"Yeah, and I saw a really cool idea on a TV ad. A condom key chain. Then it's out of sight until . . . well just until."

His eyes met Caitlyn's. These were kids talking. How could she answer them with a straight face? He'd be lecturing, big time. She was looking at him, smiling. No, wait. She wasn't going to ask his advice, was she? He was out of there.

Quickly he made his way to the safe haven of his office. He turned on his computer and immersed himself in his work. Something simple and uncomplicated, like rotating his new design ninety degrees so the owner could sunbathe on the private deck off the master suite in the mid-afternoon.

Maybe not simple, but it was something he understood, at least. He typed briskly to keep his mind focused. Thirty minutes later, when his notes lay crumpled on the floor and his printer stopped, Caitlyn's words floated through his window. He opened it wider. Her voice was now crystal clear. Leaning back in his chair, he stretched his arms overhead, then folded them behind him.

Even from this semi-reclined position he could still see the kids below. It was just like having a balcony seat at the theater, except this was real life and the plot was very scary. Cait's theme for the retreat was 'The Road Less Traveled.'

"Is it easy to say 'No' to drugs?" The heads moved from side-to-side in unison. "All right, then. Tell me what happens. How it makes you feel."

"Kids make fun of you."

"Sometimes even your friends laugh at you."

"Someone tried to scare me into taking some pills once. They threatened to beat me up."

Jake sat upright and narrowed his gaze, trying to identify the last speaker. A girl getting beaten up? My God. What rock had he been hiding under? One more reason to admire Caitlyn. She spoke their language, and they trusted her. The kids probably shared things with her that they'd never dream of talking about to their own parents.

He'd have to try harder, for Jackie's sake.

The discussion below continued. It seemed as if everyone were talking at once. "It hurts when the girls who are laughing are supposed to be my friends."

"And eating lunch alone, or walking home by myself. It's like I'm a freak or something."

"It would be easier to give in. I wonder what would really happen if I did?"

Giving in. Another issue he'd have to face with Jackie over the next few years Dating. Driving. Hell, driving on dates, not to mention dating drivers.

He remembered the first car he'd tried to buy with his college-bound savings. It was a Volkswagon van with thick, dark curtains and plush carpeting instead of rear seats. He'd tried convincing his mother that he would need the space to haul things to and from college. She'd been firm. He'd ended up settling for a VW bug.

Cait joined in and refocused the discussion. "That's why it's important to come up with your own way of saying 'No.' But that's just the first step. The second is to say it often enough, so that it becomes an automatic reflex."

She stood and walked the perimeter of the circle. "Do these temptations go away when you get older?" There went those heads again, shaking in unison. "How about after college graduation? You're right, they don't. In fact, you'll only have more to choose from. Drugs might not be as prevalent in a business office, but drinks after work are certainly common. How about sex?" A series of snickers and chuckling ran through the crowd. Although he was already out of view, Jake slid farther down in his seat. "Okay, so sex remains tempting, despite what we've discussed about AIDS and pregnancy."

Tempting? Was that the word she just used? His eyes

widened as he stared blankly at his PC monitor. He'd always imagined using words like 'responsibility' and 'momentous decision' during any birds and bees discussion. Would Jackie have laughed at him or simply patted his arm, as if the real world were beyond his comprehension?

Now he'd never know. He was obviously years too late.

"What are some other temptations?"

He peeked out the window. There were several upraised hands, Jackie's included.

"Money."

"Yes, stealing. Either by outright robbery or something deceptive, like fraud. Someone else?"

"Power."

"An all time favorite. Back-stabbing and smearing reputations are just a few of the ways to get ahead in the corporate world. Another?"

"Moving."

Jake leaned forward to catch Lynn's words. Did he hear her correctly? He held his breath.

Cait stopped pacing, and faced her daughter across the circle. "How so?"

"For the same reasons you already mentioned. Power, money, peer pressure. That sort of thing."

Cait's voice was steady. "Go on."

"Moving is like running away. You know, avoiding something instead of facing it head on."

Cait simply nodded as if soaking in the words. Jake wanted to butt in from his perch up above. Maintaining the status quo because you're afraid of change, afraid of downstream regrets, was just as bad as running. He knew, because that was his specialty.

He wanted to run down and grab her, selfishly make her decision for her. For them both. If he asked her to stay, she probably would. But, someday, he could end up the bad guy. Instead, he didn't speak. He just sat there silently. This was her show, her group, and ultimately her decision.

"It would depend on why someone was moving, whether it was the right thing or not." Lynn popped an orange slice into her mouth to signal the end of the discussion. "That's all I meant."

Rose looked from her sister to her mother. Her hand shot up. "Could we take a bathroom break?" She cast a quick look over at Jackie.

Jackie stood. "Great idea. I'm long overdue."

The commotion of everyone leaving snapped Cait back to the present. "Take a fifteen minute break, then meet back here. We'll split into small groups for the next hour or so."

Several of the teens huddled around her. "What's next, Mrs. James?"

"You'll be sharing some of your own personal experiences with each other, whatever you feel comfortable with. Then I'd like for you to focus on one situation in-depth, or invent one, and create a short skit for tonight's campfire."

The group groaned in unison.

"Don't give me that. Skit night is a favorite part of any get-together. They can be real or make-believe, serious or funny. Maybe a little of both. Good luck. Lunch is back here at noon sharp."

As the teens wandered off, Lynn hung back to speak to her mother. "I'm sorry if I was out of line."

Not knowing how to respond, Cait silently smoothed her daughter's hair.

"You've always told me to speak my mind, so I did." She glanced up. "I'm not sure at all why we're moving."

"Nothing's been decided yet."

"But you and Jake . . . well it just seems so crazy. Unnecessary."

"There are lots of issues involved, honey. Sometimes I'm not sure what's happening either." She pulled her daughter close and hugged her. Her voice softened as she spoke against Lynn's ponytailed hair. "But you brought out some very good points. I have a lot of soul-searching left to do."

"What if Jake . . ."

"He hasn't." Cait gave her a half-smile, then kissed her on the forehead. Arm in arm, they headed inside.

I haven't, what? He watched the departing figures in disbelief. Obviously mother and daughter could read each other's mind. But, as usual, he didn't have a clue. He had told her he loved her. Were declarations said in the aftermath of passion automatically discounted? Maybe he was too old for this.

Opening the top drawer of his desk, he picked up the brightly trimmed jewelry box. It was small enough to fit into the palm of his hand. Sliding farther into his seat, he abstractly fingered the bow.

Caitlyn's footsteps beat a familiar rhythm on the stairs. He swung his chair around and stood. She paused on the top step. Was she coming up to tell him whatever it was he hadn't done?

He walked towards the closed door and reached for the knob. Her footsteps headed quickly away from him, towards the guest room. Her door clicked shut.

Still holding the box tightly in his fist, he looked down at it. The bow was flattened. The lump in his throat remained throughout the afternoon.

■ ■ ■

A six-person team was assigned to set the table. The noise was deafening. Jackie was surprised that she could still hear the phone over the clattering of plates and silverware.

"Hi, Mom. Wait, let me go to another room." She took the receiver into the TV area and plopped down on the couch. "There, that's better."

"What's going on? Your dad have the baseball game on too loud, as usual?"

"No, my friends are over."

"That's nice, honey. More than one?"

"Yeah, about twelve."

"What?"

"They're really cool, too." Jackie shoved one of the throw pillows under her head. "It's a church group. Dad lent them the lodge for their retreat."

"Do I have the right number?"

Jackie laughed. "You should see him, Mom. He's different."

"How so?"

"There are four kids in the kitchen with him right now, helping cook spaghetti. They've got sauce splattered from one end to the other. Dad said . . ." Jackie lowered her voice an octave, trying to imitate him. "Don't worry, we'll wipe it up later." She laughed again and hooked her legs over the back of the couch. "Can you believe it?"

"Frankly, I don't. Maybe I better speak to him."

"Hang on, I'll get him." She dropped her head over the edge of the cushions and yelled. "Daa . . aaa. . .aad."

"Jackie," Victoria continued when the screeching stopped. "Hold the phone away, before you yell."

"Sorry."

"Before you put Jake on, I want to ask you about school."

"What about it?" Head once again resting on the pillow, she first raised one leg, then the other. She wished she had the ankle weights on. This position worked great.

"William and I will be moving to Baltimore next week, and I'll be researching the junior highs nearby."

"Why would you want to do that?" Jackie snapped her gum.

"Let me finish. Realizing how fast this decision to live with your father was made, I thought it only right that we revisit the subject again."

"Mom, are you trying to say you want me to live out east? No offense intended, but forget it. I love it here."

"Your father is a very busy man."

"He loves having me here, too, I know he does. We're getting along super. He doesn't know much about kids, but he's learning fast. Cait's helping him." Snap, snap.

"Who's Kate?"

"Maybe I shouldn't have mentioned her. Oh well, he'll have to tell you sooner or later." She swung around with her legs still upright, then planted her feet on the coffee table. "She's been a friend of Dad's ever since the car wreck. She's got two daughters, my age. Well, a little older. They drive and everything."

"And they were in a car wreck?"

"No, Cait was. That's how she met Dad. You see, she crashed through his fence, they fell in love and he gave her the lodge. Cool, huh?"

"Jackie, who are you talking to?" Jake wiped his hands on a dish towel.

She scooted up straight. "Mom."

"I see. Why don't you help boil the noodles and let me finish up here?"

"Sure. Bye, Mom. Hey, forget that school thing, okay?

Love you." She handed the phone to Jake, covering one end with her hand. "I told her about Cait."

"I know, I heard you. Now go."

He waited to speak until she rounded the corner. "Tory, you caught us at a bad time."

"Your church group is over? My, my, lots of changes going on."

"Yeah, most are for the better." His tone was polite but impatient as he took Jackie's place on the couch. "How was the wedding? Sorry I wasn't there to give you away."

"Very funny. Seriously, I called to talk over these new living arrangements again. Now that you've had a chance to try it out for a while, I thought you might want to reconsider."

"Stop worrying. She's here, settled in. I love it. We made a good decision."

"But . . ."

"No buts, Victoria. She's staying." He set a magazine on the coffee table, then extended his legs, one booted foot crossing over the other. "All that's left for us to decide is your visiting schedule."

"That sounds so cold."

"I know. It's all I had for six years." His voice softened and he relaxed his grip on the receiver. "She's great. You did a fine job with her."

"She won't be in your way?"

"No." Jake easily read the real question behind her tone of voice. "And just so you won't have to probe any further, I'll tell you the facts straight out." He shifted the receiver to the other hand. "I've finally met someone I see eye-to-eye with. I'm not sure where we're headed because she may move. If her girls and Jackie had their way, we'd be getting married tomorrow." He drew a slow breath. "It's just not that simple, as you know."

"Well, don't over-complicate things. You have a tendency to do that. Look ahead, not back. If you want to spend the rest of your life together, then just ask her."

"Am I paying you by the minute here, or is all this advice free?"

"Free." She laughed. "I only wish you the best. Besides, Jackie can travel out to Boston while you take an extended honeymoon. And I mean extended."

"As in months or years?"

"The longer the better."

He stood and walked towards the ruckus in the kitchen. "Goodbye, Tory. And pass along a 'Good Luck' to William for me."

"Don't you mean, 'Best Wishes?'"

He chuckled. "No, actually I don't."

■ ■ ■

"This next prize is for the tree climbing contest." Cait slowly unfolded the slip of paper. Prolonging the suspense was one of her favorite things to do, second only to hamming it up before a captive audience. "And the winner is . . . Jackie Brandon."

"You're kidding." Jackie covered her cheeks and looked around her circle of new friends, seated on logs before the campfire. They put aside their dripping, marshmallowy treats for a moment to holler, clap and urge her forward. Her father, standing off to the side near the woodpile, was smiling the brightest of all. She felt lightheaded with excitement.

The boy seated next to her propelled her to her feet. She walked as if in a daze. When she reached the center of the circle, Cait presented her with a brightly wrapped box.

"Thanks." Jackie's voice cracked. She took a deep breath before trying again. Tears brimmed and threatened to spill over. "Thank you."

"Don't tell me; tell them." She wrapped one arm about the girl's shoulder, then turned her to face the group.

Jackie swallowed hard. "You're really a neat group."

Rose's eyes began filling with tears. She quickly wiped them away. "We're just glad that somebody finally beat Sam. He's won for two years straight."

Jackie glanced over to where she had been sitting, then smiled shyly. Sam was one of the cutest boys she'd ever met. Earlier in the day he asked her to sit next to him during the evening campfire. He even held her hand for a moment. It was awkward with her dad so close by, though, so she let go.

She opened the box, hoping her embarrassment would be covered up by the flickering of the fire. Smiling, she held up the cleats and read the message aloud. "For the trees in your future and for everything else you set your mind to. May you always climb above the crowd."

Jackie glanced at her father and saw his 'thumbs up' signal. Cait hugged her quickly. She returned to her seat.

The next award went to the winners of the canoe race, Rose and Lynn. They each received tubes of liniment oil. Brooke's son, Kyle, was awarded the overall Iron Man traveling trophy.

"How about a few songs, before we start the skits?"

"Wait. First, we have a little surprise." Lynn jumped up and took over as emcee. Jackie and Rose dashed off to retrieve something.

Within moments the girls emerged with a brightly lit

birthday cake. Thirty-seven candles to be exact. Cait was stunned.

"Oh, no. You didn't."

"We did." Lynn turned to address the group. "Tonight is Mom's birthday. We want everyone to sing real loud."

The traditional song, sung simultaneously in twelve unrelated keys, was one of the most beautiful sounds on earth to Cait.

Glancing to where Jake was standing, she noticed for the first time the red bandana tucked in his denim shirt pocket. Her eyes widened. He smiled and tipped his cowboy hat. Poised with a fire extinguisher in hand, it was obvious that he was in cahoots with the girls on this surprise.

"Make a wish."

"Come on, do it."

Caitlyn smiled, then blew out the candles. Rose and Jackie both caught their parents' lingering exchange. They smiled at each other with undisguised joy.

Lynn shook her head at their silliness and nudged them forward. As they handed Cait the large box, Rose explained the gift. It almost sounded like an apology. "Jake took the three of us shopping for this, Mom. Hope you like it."

She quickly opened it and peered in at the scanty pajama top and tap pants. Her eyes widened as she read the message blazed across the front. *Nighty night, sleep tight and remember, not only bedbugs bite.* Embarrassed, Cait quickly closed the lid.

Rose frowned. "Don't you like it?"

"Well, of course. It's like nothing I've ever owned."

"Dad thought pajamas were a great idea," Jackie said.

"That I did." Jake stepped forward, knowing something was not quite right. He placed his hand on the box. "May I?"

Cait nodded.

Lifting the lid, he picked up the sleep set. He turned and slowly studied each of the three guilty faces. He held up the top, tilting his head towards the risqué lettering. "Looks like I should have asked a few more questions before giving my endorsement." The crowd erupted with snickers and laughter.

Jackie scuffed at the dirt. Rose looked apologetically at Jake, then at her mother. Lynn broke the silence. "We saved the receipt just in case you hated it."

Cait snatched the garments dangling from his hand. When they were safely stuffed away out of sight, she smiled. "Just knowing that the three of you picked this out together makes it very special. I wouldn't think of returning them."

She set the box down and reached for the songbooks, hoping to change the subject. She didn't want to look at Jake. "What should we sing first?"

"Just a minute." Jake's hand on her shoulder stopped her efforts. He reached in his pocket and held out a small package with a crumpled silver bow. "This I did pick out."

She drew in her breath and stared for a moment, unblinking. It was so small, could it be . . . ?

Reaching for the box, she untied the wrapping with shaking fingers. She noticed Rose grab Jackie's hand in a death-grip. She lifted the lid, then paused. It wasn't the ring that for a pulse-stopping instant she believed it might be. It was . . . what? A key chain?

Picking up the heart-shaped item, she saw that there was an inscription. She read it quickly, her eyes clouding with moisture. *Wherever you wander, wherever you roam, always think of this place as home.* Captured within the sturdy golden clasp was a key to the lodge.

Jake clenched his teeth as she stared at the gift,

unmoving. What was she thinking? Did she hate it? Was she expecting something else?

Suddenly she looked up, then mouthed the words 'thank you' through her thin film of tears. Her voice wouldn't come. Raising up on her toes, she kissed him on the cheek. The crowd hooted for more. Cait shook her head.

Lynn leaned forward, examining the gift. A key chain? How strange. She didn't know what it meant, but Mom certainly did. She'd ask later.

Jackie was elated. Her eyes widened at her father's acceptance of this PDS, public display of affection, no matter how small. She rubbed at the quickly forming goosebumps.

Rose grabbed Jackie in a bear hug. She didn't have a clue as to what all this meant, but, if their parents were kissing, it just had to be good.

Fifteen

The Honda braked to a halt in front of the house. Soulful country-western music blared from the car's open window, announcing Brooke's arrival.

Rose lifted her chin above the armful of camping equipment. "Your mom's here." Her voice was loud enough to be heard in the backyard.

Kyle, busy rinsing out the ice chests with the garden hose, yelled in return. "Good, she can help."

"Fat chance." Brooke stepped out and swung the door closed. "You guys made this mess. I'll just watch."

Winking at Rose, she ruffled the younger twin's bangs, then took half her load. Together they walked into the garage. "How did you put up with him for three entire days?"

"I managed."

"Did he try to kiss you?"

Rose blushed and glanced towards the path leading to the back yard.

"Aha. Thought he might, when I saw him packing his breath spray." Brooke set down the box of song books. "Moonlight makes him crazy, you know, but it's not really his fault."

"It's not?" Rose was anxious.

His mother shook her head with mock seriousness. "His father was part werewolf."

"Must be why he always needs a shave." Rose laughed and self-consciously ran a finger along her jaw line.

"I see. Just as I suspected." Straightening, Brooke placed both hands on the small of her back and stretched. "Any other kissing going on? I'm dying of curiosity and I know Cait won't tell."

"Mom won't tell what?" Lynn stepped into the garage, a fistful of veggies in hand. She offered some to the others.

Brooke accepted. Stepping closer, she tugged at the twin's loose braid. "About the ending to the new mystery she lent me. Said I'll have to read it for myself. I'm trading her for the romance I just finished."

"Oh yeah?" Lynn said mildly. "A hot one?"

"Are the other kind worth discussing?"

"Mom doesn't need any new ideas." The older twin shrugged. "I think she's doing fine on her own."

Brooke lowered her voice and gave her young opponent a level look. "This one's worth any time she can invest. There's a half-naked man on the front cover."

Lynn stopped munching. Her own version of Brooke's deadpan tone was firmly in place. "Which half?"

Silence reigned as their eyes met, neither wanting to be

the first to laugh. After a moment Brooke gave in. She wrapped an arm around Lynn's shoulders. "Stay away from my son, okay? He's still an innocent."

Lynn glanced at her sister who was blushing furiously. "It's a deal."

Together the three of them headed to the trunk for a second load. Brooke threw some loose items into a half-filled bag. "So, how did the birthday party turn out? Was your mom surprised?"

"You bet." Reaching in, Rose picked up two sleeping bags. "You should have seen her when she unwrapped the pajamas."

"Based on your description, I can imagine her delight. In public, too. Get into much trouble?"

"Nah. Mom didn't believe for a moment that Jake had anything to do with it."

Lynn grabbed an armful of pillows. "Especially since he had a gift of his own." She smiled and turned calmly towards the door.

"Wait." Brooke hurried after her with a sack of leftover groceries. "This is just getting interesting. What kind of gift?"

"It's, well, personal." Lynn scrunched her nose, tilting her head towards the kitchen. "Maybe you should ask Mom yourself."

Brooke narrowed her gaze for a minute, then took her advice. "Okay, but don't go away. I may have more questions later." Shifting her load to one hand, she opened the door to the kitchen. "Caitlyn?"

"Oh, hi. I was just about to call you."

Brooke set the groceries on the counter. "Forget that. Tell me about Jake's birthday gift, instead."

"The girls are gossiping already?"

"I forced it out of them."

"No doubt." Cait scooted the bag closer and began sorting into two piles, those items that needed refrigeration and those that didn't.

"So?" Brooke's foot tapped against the bare wood floor.

Cait sighed. Neither patience nor subtlety had ever been her friend's long suit. "A key chain."

"And?"

A muffled response came from behind the open fridge door. "And a key."

"Hmm. There's something I'm not catching here." Brooke pulled out a barstool and sat down. "Maybe you could interpret."

There was no 'maybe' about it. She sighed. Crossing to her purse, she rummaged for a moment and produced a velvet box. The name of a popular jewelry store was imprinted on the front.

"Wow. Now we're talking." Brooke held out her hand. She examined the case as if testing that it was for real, before flicking open the lid. "It's beautiful, but . . . ?" She glanced at her friend.

Cait was absorbed with the groceries. No explanation was offered.

Hooking her finger through the loop, Brooke lifted the key ring and studied the inscription on the back. "I assume it's to the lodge?"

Not a word, only a quick, curt nod.

Brooke's gaze held hers. "Does this mean what I think it does?"

She nodded again, her response a near-whisper. "I guess I'm leaving."

"No." Brooke hopped down from the stool. "You don't have to."

"I want to." Her voice was steady. Determination was interlaced throughout the painful explanation. "If only he'd have said the words. Asked me to stay, instead of inviting me to visit." She bit her bottom lip to stop it from quivering.

"Can't you give him just a little longer?"

"I'd hoped he would want me enough to fight for me to stay." She shook her head. "But he won't. Not ever. It's time for me to start over."

Brooke watched her friend struggle a moment longer, then quickly stepped forward. She hugged her, letting Cait give in to tears.

■ ■ ■

The walkway to Audra's front door was lined with rhododendron bushes. Some were heavy with buds not yet in bloom, promising a late summer sweetness. Others were past their prime, already pruned back to await the next cycle.

Caitlyn stopped and picked up a fallen petal, lifting it to smell the fading scent. It reminded her of the days before the weekend retreat, so filled with promise. Now each passing hour slammed home the feeling of time slipping away.

The one week extension offered in Bill's phone message wasn't necessary. She was ready to go today.

There was no doubt that she'd have some kind of a future with Jake. Their girls were very close. Would he become just a friend, too? Her friendship with Bill was proof that it was possible. But in their case her heart hadn't screamed for so much more.

Tucking the petal into her pocket, she climbed the front steps and rang the bell. Audra opened the door immediately. "Thanks for coming on such short notice."

"Your message sounded urgent. Since it couldn't wait

until the next council meeting, I figured I must be in trouble with Mrs. Sydow again."

Audra stared at her blankly.

"That's it, isn't it? Pamela called about the condom discussion at our retreat?" Cait smiled nervously.

"Heavens, no." Instead of returning the smile, Audra glanced outside. Apparently satisfied, she motioned for her guest to enter. "Come in."

Cait followed her into the sitting room. There were several oversized books strewn across the coffee table, illustrating western landmarks. The Gateway to the West, the Colorado Rockies, the Pacific Coast highway. The pictorial guide to old Route 66 caught her eye.

Trying to lighten the seriousness of their meeting, Cait picked up the travelog. "Looks like we've been to many of the same places." Her smile quickly faded as she noticed Audra pacing back and forth before the bay window. Whatever it was, the chairwoman dreaded telling her.

"And talk about coincidences, both of us living in Issaquah. Hard to believe." Cait filled the uncomfortable silence. "If you'd have mentioned that before, Jake and I could have stopped by. You wouldn't have had to conduct his interview by phone."

Audra stopped. "There was no need."

"I know that I gave him a good recommendation, but remember, I'm biased." Cait laughed awkwardly.

Audra didn't smile.

Cait's voice immediately sobered. "He's a good man. You should meet him, keep in contact after I'm gone. He may be interested in lending his lodge again in the future, for other groups."

"There will be plenty of time for that." After a pause she added, as if to herself, "I hope."

She was definitely in big trouble this time. Audra was clearly nervous. Just enough for someone who admired her steel composure to notice. Starting over in a new town was beginning to sound better and better.

Cait swallowed hard. "Whatever I've done, just tell me. Straight out."

"I'm not sure how to begin," Audra said.

"Start anywhere." Cait smiled to ease the tension.

"All right." Audra crossed to the couch. Instead of sitting at the opposite end, she joined the younger woman on the adjoining cushion. "Tell me, are you staying or moving?"

"Moving." She gave a short laugh. "Maybe a good idea, right?"

"What about Jake? You love him, don't you?"

Cait drew back. After a split second, she nodded. "My heart and mind battled that very question a thousand times. Yes, I love him. He says the same. But the commitment seems to stop there. So I'm leaving."

"Why?"

"He's urging me to go. His fear that I'll regret turning the promotion down seems to outweigh any desire to have me nearby." She shrugged slightly. "He's willing to settle for a long-distance relationship, so I'll give it a try. Maybe someday, when the time is right, things might be different."

"But what about this time?" Audra's tone was direct.

"This time?"

"That's all there is, my dear, when you boil it all down. The present. The past can't be changed. The future doesn't come with guarantees."

"But my staying is an option he won't consider. He shuts off any conversation along those lines with words like 'regret' and 'fate.'" Cait tightly interlaced her fingers, then rested them in her lap. "I kept thinking he'd ask me to stay, as we grew closer. I thought wrong."

"Then try again, for heavens sake." Audra covered the white-knuckled hands and shook them. "You've got to fight for what you want. If it's Jake, then go after him. Ask him. Convince him."

"You don't understand. He took me house-hunting." She looked up, her eyes bright with unshed tears. "His feelings couldn't be any clearer than that."

"But . . ."

"I know you want this to end happily ever after. So do our daughters. But it's all quite simple. He let me go."

"That's where you're wrong, Caitlyn. It's not simple."

Cait drew back. Only Jake called her that. Maybe Audra picked it up from her conversation with him.

Audra released the clenched fists and stood. Her voice was sharp. "Mark my words, when love is involved, nothing's simple."

The pacing began again. "I should have stayed once and fought harder. Should have stood my ground. I didn't. I ran, the way you're doing now." Her voice faltered, but she continued, "I convinced myself that it was for the children's sake, but that wasn't totally correct. It was mainly for me. A classic 'change your ways and follow me' game, where the only rules were mine." Her indrawn breath was ragged. "And that's the worst kind of ultimatum."

"But you must have had a good reason."

"I had life and death reasons. But being right doesn't matter, if you lose everything." Audra reached inside her sleeve for a tissue and dabbed at her eyes. "That was twenty years ago. Nothing's been right since."

"You're wrong. Look around you. A beautiful home,

friends who admire and respect you. Something's right, here."

"And you're a survivor, too. Over time, you'll tell yourself that this is enough." Audra indicated the room with wave of her hand, then shook her head sadly. "But it can never be the same, without the other half of yourself."

"Was your husband stubborn, like Jake? Hard to live with, but even harder to live without?"

A curve spread slowly across the older woman's mouth. "There's a very strong resemblance."

Cait absorbed the bittersweet smile. "I don't understand."

The buzzing of the doorbell interrupted their conversation. "You will, my dear. You will." Audra crossed to the entryway and pulled on the handle. She instantly stepped back, to reveal the visitor.

Jake was standing there, framed by the doorway. He stared first at Audra, then at her, before looking back again. "Hello, Mother."

■　■　■

Silence surrounded them. It was as thick as the wall of resentment that had separated mother and son for years.

Jake turned to Cait. She was staring at him in confusion. His anger over Audra's phone call, commanding him here, instantly disappeared. His explanation was eons too late. "I'm sorry. I should have told you sooner."

"You're right. There was no reason to keep this from me."

He nodded. "Lots of excuses, but no good reasons."

Sure, there were plenty of chances. But how did he explain his silence? Cait spoke often of her admiration for

Audra's spirit. How could he say that those very same traits drove him away years ago? She wouldn't have understood. Sometimes he didn't understand it himself.

He extended his hand towards her. "We'll discuss it now."

Cait shook her head, not taking his offering. "Later. You have enough to do, right here. Years worth of explaining." She tilted her head towards his mother, her friend, then tightened her grip on her purse. "If not for yourself, then for her."

Audra stepped forward. "But it's the two of you who need to talk, to clear the air. That's why I wanted you both here, together." She took a deep breath. "Call me interfering. But don't make the same mistake I did."

"Audra . . ."

"There's so much between you, that neither of you realize. It shows in everything you say and do. Don't walk away from it."

Reaching out, Cait touched Audra's arm. "If it was meant to be, it will keep. But you and Jake need to work things out, before he and I can move forward."

Releasing Audra, Cait reached for the door. Jake covered her hand with his. "Wait for me."

"I have been waiting." She drew a slow breath, signalling her fatigue. "I love you, so I'll wait. But not much longer, and not tonight."

"Don't leave."

She shook her head. "This is for you to work out alone."

"I love you." He drew her fingers away from the knob and caught them in his. He kissed them gently. "I've tried showing you in so many ways."

"I know you do. But it just might not be enough." She squeezed his hand, then let go. Seeing two of the people she cared for so much, still standing miles apart, filled her eyes with moisture. "Good luck." Quietly, Cait excused herself and shut the door behind her.

The mechanism clicked into place. The sound was soft, but still Jake flinched. Mother and son were now alone, for the first time since he was eighteen.

He shifted position, then stared at Audra. She stood motionless near the couch. "You always did like games. Mysteries. So go ahead." This was her show, and he wasn't privy to the script. Unlike the years of his rebellious childhood, he dutifully awaited his turn.

Audra walked calmly into the small living room. Jake hesitated. She glanced back. "Sit down."

Her tone took him back years, to school books and lost friends. It infuriated him. "Tell me, what the hell is going on here?"

"Something we should have discussed years ago." She faced him. "Watch your language and sit. I'm still your mother, no matter how hard you've tried to forget that fact."

He chose the chair nearest the door.

"No, here." Audra indicated a spot on the sofa. "Then I won't have to drag this across the room." She indicated a packing box partially hidden behind the arm of the couch. Moving company stickers, brittle with age, still sealed the top.

Stepping over the coffee table, he took a seat. "All right, I'm listening."

"Good." Audra picked up a letter opener from the mantle and slit open the crate. After wiping the dust away, she lifted the lid. "These are your father's things."

He leaned forward, eyes widened. She had his complete attention. "From California?"

She nodded. "And from Wichita, St. Louis, you name it. From all the dozens of places we moved, trying to escape his past."

"Escape his memory, you mean." His gaze narrowed. "Why are you showing me this now?"

"Because it's time." Her voice was firm. "And because you're about to follow in the Brandon family footsteps and make the biggest mistake of your life."

He glared at her but kept his mouth shut, wanting to listen more than he wanted to argue. Sliding closer to Audra, he was careful not to touch even the hem of her cotton skirt.

He peered inside. A .38 special was the first thing he saw. The second was their old family portrait. Across the youthful, spic-and-span faces was a crudely drawn note. A death threat.

"Your father was a compulsive gambler."

He stared, but kept his eyes lowered, avoiding hers.

"I scrimped and saved, trying to pay off his debts. Each time, as soon as the slate was clean, we'd move. Then he'd dive in again, over his head. It became a vicious cycle." Audra's fists were tightly clenched by her side. "Each time he swore it'd be different. But it never was."

Jake nodded, indicating he'd heard each and every word. Moving aside the gun, he picked up the photograph. Beneath it were loose-leaf papers of various size and condition. Alphabet letters, hastily clipped from a magazine, were glued together to form words. The messages were all similar. It was like a low budget gangster movie, except this was real. Very real.

"When we stopped overnight in Salt Lake, on our way to Los Angeles, I realized the last page of directions was missing. I looked for them in his suitcase, thinking he might have placed them there, instead of in mine. During my search, I found this." She handed him a small portfolio. He opened it.

Inside were tight, handwritten lines of dates, names and locations. Next to each was the amount still owed.

"I always refused to leave before settling the debts. My purpose was to start over, not to run away." Her voice was flat. "But he kept a second list."

Jake stared at the yellowed pages, fingering the familiar scrawl. The hair on his neck stood at attention.

"I had scratched only the surface, clearing the credit cards and overdrafts. He was in serious financial trouble, and so were we."

"Did you confront him with this?"

She nodded. "It didn't faze him. He was an eternal optimist. Told me that in a city the size of L.A. we could easily slip into obscurity. Start over."

Audra stood and walked to the window, leaning against the wall for support. "I felt betrayed. When he called that night, announcing the fancy new house he'd lucked into, I knew it would never end."

Jake finished for her. "We headed north the next morning."

Audra's confirmation was unnecessary. He'd never forget that day, or the curt way in which his mother brushed aside his questions. Since he was the navigator, their new direction couldn't be covered up.

"You changed our name. Wrote him off."

"Only after your father was tracked down and killed. I was afraid for all of us."

"But why Stockton? Why not your maiden name?"

"Too easy to trace. By then I was desperate, not thinking clearly." Audra gave a short laugh. "We stopped for the night, just past the Idaho border. I went in to sign the guest registry. Next to it was a menu taped to the counter."

She looked away from the window. "French Onion soup was that night's special. The last good bowl I had was in Stockton, Colorado."

He smiled. "To think that we might have been called Minestrone."

"No, that never would have worked. We don't look Italian at all." She covered her mouth, suppressing a laugh.

It wasn't right to add humor to such a serious conversation, but somehow it felt good to him. Brought him back to his early childhood, back to the days when he and his mother laughed frequently. How could he have forgotten those times and only remembered the bad?

Audra stared at him for several seconds, also lost in the past. She shook her head, forcing the rest of the story out. "I was too afraid to attend his funeral. But you, you taunted fate and moved to L.A."

She rubbed her hands briskly over her arms, trying to ward off a chill. "As if that wasn't enough for you, you spit in its face by changing your name back to Brandon. I was so scared." She crossed and sat next to him on the couch. "I was wrong not to tell you, then."

"You didn't know where I was. No one did, for several years."

"Drew let it slip once. I was stunned, couldn't speak. He thought that I didn't hear him and let it ride."

"I didn't want to be found, didn't want to be interfered with." He swallowed hard. "I wouldn't have listened."

Her eyes remained fixed on him, her voice was low and hesitant. "Thank God nothing ever happened to you."

Reaching over him, into the box, she retrieved a khaki fishing vest and laid it across his knees. Next she lifted a faded grey-green shirt. The flannel was still soft. "So many years." She pressed the checkered garment against her face and inhaled its scent. "I want you to share this with Jackie."

He nodded. The vest was the same one in the photo at Drew's place. It still had several hooks attached. He would never forget those early morning adventures on any lake or river that was near. "He must have loved us, despite all this."

"Yes."

Jake touched one of the sharp barbs, pricking his finger. A small dot of red quickly formed. He stared at the glistening spot. "How could he let it happen? Cause it to happen?"

"He could never forget his first love. Poker." Audra's voice was unsteady. But if she stopped there might never be another chance. "By the time I found out where you were living the damage was already done. And you were an adult. All I could do was pray."

Jake didn't like being the focus of anyone's prayers, but didn't want to show disrespect. He busied himself by pulling a handkerchief from his pocket and applying pressure to his fingertip.

Clearing her throat, Audra pulled several sets of rubber-banded envelopes from the box. "Here are the bills from St. Louis. These are from Denver. They're all marked 'paid.'"

She stacked them on the coffee table. "This is proof that what I'm saying is true. At first I saved them in case someone ever came after us. Later, I saved them for you, so that you'd believe me."

He placed his hand over hers, trying to stop the anxious movements. She brushed it away and continued stacking. "Mother, stop."

"No, look at them. You made it very clear that no explanation would ever be good enough. Look at every one."

"I'm sorry." He reached for her again. "Please, no more."

Audra raised her head. Jake met her eyes. "And thank you. You were right, you know. What you said earlier."

She looked at him, questions crowding her tired features.

"You shouldn't have to explain yourself to me. I appreciate it that you did."

Audra simply nodded.

Turning her palm over, Jake linked his fingers with hers. She stared at the contrast. Her slender bones and age-marked skin were cradled in his broad callused grip. The days of her comforting him were long gone. Now he comforted her.

He cleared his throat. "After all this time, why now?"

"Not to ask forgiveness. It was my life and my choice. I did what I thought was best. You may never agree with my methods, but realize that it was my responsibility as a parent to protect my family." She squeezed his hand before releasing it. "My biggest mistake was in not telling you sooner."

She stood and began reloading the box. "I'm telling you because you're about to make an even bigger mistake than I did, if you let Caitlyn walk out of your life. Especially if it's because you're afraid."

"I'm not afraid to love."

"No, I think you're afraid to be hurt." She grabbed the lid and plunged the contents into darkness again, both the good and the bad. "You fear that someday she'll desert you, just as I left your father, so you're pushing her away. Before she has the chance to leave."

He got to his feet. "That's not true."

Audra smiled. "Then don't convince me, convince her."

"I will." Reaching into his pocket, he retrieved his car keys and headed for the door.

■ ■ ■

Jake. Audra's son. Cait silently wished them both luck as she drove along the gravel road to Rattlesnake Ridge. There were vast amounts of bitterness to bury before either could move forward. Audra's determination was pitted squarely against Jake's stubbornness. What an eventful pairing off. Too bad she had no right to stay, yesterday.

She had asked him for an evening to think and he'd nodded his agreement. Her phone was silent all evening. And now, after a long sleepless night, she wanted this over with. Decided.

Cait glanced at her daughters hunched silently in the back seat. They'd overheard her discussing the soon-to-be vacant position of youth director with the Sunday School co-ordinator, and hadn't spoken to her since. Once Mrs. Sydow caught wind of it, word had spread like wildfire through the coffee hour. Her cup grew cold as she accepted the well-meaning congratulations from friends and acquaintances. It took forever to escape.

Amazing that, after so many years, none of her church family really knew her. Not one person probed beneath the surface. It was taken at face value that she was moving for business reasons. They thought it made logical sense.

But they were wrong. Jake had never asked her to stay.

For weeks Rose had been hinting at wedding bells, a new younger sister, and changing names. Her happily-ever-after theme song had started playing shortly after the canoeing incident.

Lynn, on the other hand, discussed their destiny from a purely practical viewpoint: attending a different school, here in Snoqualmie, resigning from her part-time job because it was too far to travel after classes were through. Somewhere she probably had tucked away a new morning shower schedule, ready for negotiations with Rose and Jackie.

But he'd never asked her to stay.

Was it 'no' he was afraid of hearing, or 'yes?' He didn't want to stand in the way of her dream. Too bad he didn't realize that, either way, she lost. Because loving Jake, and having her love returned, was her most fanciful dream of all.

He'd made up his mind, and her mind by default.

She'd created her home with a mix of one part sweat and three parts love. Could she replace it overnight by browsing a multiple-listings catalog? She gripped the wheel tighter, smoothly executing a turn.

No doubt someone could take over the youth group and lead them into the future, but could she ever replace those kids in her heart?

He'd never asked her to stay.

She straightened, pulling at the shoulder belt. Time to heed Audra's advice. Time to yell from the treetops the anger and frustration she was feeling. She'd fight for what was hers, for what she believed was meant to be. "We're staying put, girls. Right here."

Rose looked around, brushing at the tears still lingering on her cheeks. "What do you mean?"

"We're not moving."

"Do you mean it?"

"Yes, I do."

Lynn had been eyeing her mother thoughtfully. She broke into the discussion. "But what about the big promotion?"

"Bill has a long list of candidates. He'll select someone else."

Lynn got right to the point. "What about Jake?"

"He doesn't have the same choice that Bill does. Jake's stuck with me."

"I meant . . ."

"He'll get used to the idea." Cait caught a glimpse of Lynn's worried expression in the rear view mirror. "Like it or not, with him or without him, this is our home. Where our hearts are. And we're staying."

Rose leaned forward and gave Cait a big squeeze. "Yes. Way to go."

Lynn gave her mom a 'thumb's up.'

"Loosen up on me, honey." Cait patted Rose's hands. They were gripping her shoulders too tightly. "I'm still driving."

As the car rounded the final corner, they instantly spied a hand-drawn 'For Sale' sign nailed to a tree. How odd. It wasn't here before. Didn't this acreage belong to Jake? A similar sign was posted by his driveway. What was going on?

"Look at that, Mom."

"I see it." Cait slowed the car to a crawl.

"Was it there last weekend?"

"No." She steered her Toyota down the narrow lane. His truck was parked by the front porch. She pulled alongside it. When did all this transpire? Jake must have posted the signs, but why? He loved this place. Was this another of his solo decisions?

It was too painful for her to imagine that she'd never be here again. Never relive their memories by the lake, or make new ones. Was he cutting off this part of his life because, in his mind, their relationship was over?

This place was a part of them both. She wouldn't let him take the easy way out.

"Mom, do you think . . . "

"I don't know anything, but I'm about to find out."

Shutting off the engine, she stepped out. The door slammed behind her. "Wait here."

■ ■ ■

Twelve hours after leaving his mother's condo, Jake was still pacing. Sure, he took a sleep break. He also cooked, ate and showered. But, even when his feet weren't moving, his mind continued to pace.

After Cait had left yesterday, his normally coolheaded mother really let him have it. Right between his pride and his prejudice. He shook his head. On top of all her worries about the bills, the threats, and the death of their father, she had to deal with him, too. And he had delivered her the worst blow of all, because his lasted twenty years. Thankfully, he was too old to spank.

There was no way for him to rewind the clock. His teen years had been spent being critical instead of supportive, eroding away his trust in people. His cynical twenties distanced him from anyone trying to get close. The result was a divorce and a teenage daughter he was only now getting to know. His thirties? Detachment and defense were his current specialities. But that was over.

Damned if he would waste one more day on a past that was already written. The future. It held untold potential.

He picked up the phone and placed a three-way call. When both his partner and brother were on the line, he spilled his new proposal.

"Nick, you've been after me for years to take more risks, to expand our operation. Drew had an excellent proposition just the other night."

"Oh, yeah?"

"How familiar are you with the Willamette Valley area,

south of Portland? The housing market is strong there, so is road construction. I think it's time to set up a second BASC office."

Ideas were tossed back and forth. Adrenaline built up and spilled over the top. Jake paced the length of his kitchen, then moved out into the hallway and rec room, thankful he had a portable phone. The call ended with each man being assigned several action items.

As he hung up from his call, the front door crashed back against the wall. He set his notes down on the counter. The coffee mugs hanging overhead rattled. Wolfie, who had wandered in earlier offering a little canine company, woke from his noontime nap.

"Where are you? How dare you plan to move without telling me."

He'd recognize that tone of voice anywhere. She'd used it last weekend when someone started the evening campfire early. With gasoline.

"I'm here, Caitlyn. In the kitchen."

Her heels rapped sharply against the wood floors. She was swearing under her breath with each step. How did she expect to continue teaching Sunday school with language like that?

He wouldn't have to wait long to find out what his latest mistake was. Leaning against the counter, he folded his arms across his bare chest and waited for the fireworks. They were about to begin.

Cait barrelled through the kitchen door. "I saw the signs. Planning to run again? You're nothing but a coward. A predictable coward at that."

She paced back and forth, hands on hips. "Furthermore, I won't be bullied into moving because it's the right thing to do. First you make my decisions for me then you . . ."

Finally catching sight of Jake, her breath stuck in her throat. He wore loosely-tied sweat pants and a bath towel which was casually draped around his neck. Nothing else was on but the radio.

Her voice stuck in her throat.

"Then, I what? Take a shower? Posting all those 'For Sale' signs worked up a sweat. I wanted to be fresh when I asked you to marry me."

"What?"

"I'm following you to Portland. Nick and I agreed to accelerate our business plan by a few years. Drew's going to help open our new branch office."

Cait stared at him in disbelief.

"It will be risky." He took a step towards her. "But letting you walk out of my life is a risk I won't take."

"I don't know what to say."

"Then say yes." He drew her into the circle of his arms. "I love you. My place is with you."

"But your lodge. How can you give it up?"

"Nothing is more important than my being with you, wherever that might be." He placed soft kisses on her forehead and across her temples. "I can build other lodges, other homes for us to dream in. You just choose the place."

"Then I choose here. Raging River Lodge. There are too many memories for me to consider giving it up." She drew back as a new idea sprang to mind. "Maybe we could reopen the lodge someday. After all, there are so many teens who could . . ."

Jake heard the new scheme forming and quickly interrupted, "Is that a 'yes?'" He pulled her arms about his neck.

"No." She met his eyes, then smiled and snuggled closer. "But this is." Her lips met his and sealed their future.

Moments later a trio of excited voices exploded from the doorway. Cait turned to see Jackie, Lynn and Rose. Woofie sat hunched by their feet.

"About time, Dad."

"Finally, Mom."

"I knew it." Rose hugged her sister and sister-to-be. "Yes, I just knew it!"

Jake opened his arms, inviting the girls to join them. Over their heads, his eyes met Cait's. "This time, anything is possible. As long as we dream it together."

About the Author

Mary Sharon Plowman has lived in Issaquah, Washington with her husband, David, and their three children since 1986. She has been an avid reader of romance since her Nancy Drew days, when she secretly longed for Ned to kiss Nancy. The idea for *This Time,* her first novel, grew from her own search for a mountain lodge to house a women's retreat. In addition to her passion for writing, and working for Boeing Computer Services, she still allows time for reading three to four novels a week. Her current writing project is a romantic suspense, tentatively titled *White Powder.* Look for it in the spring of 1995.

Introducing

HEDGE
of
THORNS

by
SALLY ASH

The summer heat held the Sydney suburbs in its grip. The sultry temperatures of the day dropped only slightly with the setting sun. Even the breezes off the waters failed to make sleeping comfortable. Because there were screens across the windows to keep flying insects out, Leigh Pendleton was able to leave the bedroom door ajar in an effort to create at least a pretense of draught.

Her small son, Peter, slept wearing a skimpy pair of

cotton briefs. Leigh chose the most lightweight of her nightshirts and abandoned as much as a sheet. Even so she slept only fitfully. Perhaps it was some night creature going about its lawful business in the gum trees which woke both her and her son almost simultaneously. Whatever it was, Peter said dopily and a little peevishly, "Mommy, I'm thirsty."

"I'll get you some water, Punkin."

The living room was cut into diagonal halves by the slanting moonlight; one half silver and soft gray, the other deeply shadowed and purple. She padded silently on bare feet, the polished wood feeling cool to her soles. A movement, followed immediately by a burst of sudden light from the kitchen area, arrested her progress.

"Oh!"

The light came from the opened door of the refrigerator. Ben was squatting on his haunches before it, delving into the back spaces of the cabinet. He turned, still on his hunkers, at her indrawn breath.

She advanced a couple of paces into the room. Ben, she saw, was wearing no more than a towel, wrapped round his lower half and tucked in upon itself. The light from the open cabinet played on his shoulders and upper arms, on the expanse of his tanned chest, on his ruffled, blond hair. He looked like a young hero from some Greek epic.

She ran her tongue over lips which were suddenly dry. The night air had been hot before. Now her skin prickled as internal heat sought the surface.

Ben straightened himself slowly, holding a can of pop in his hand. Suddenly the atmosphere was charged with the sort of breath-holding excitement engendered by a ticking bomb. He knew he must defuse things. He cast about in his mind for something, anything, which would act as a dampener. "Caught in the act," he said, like a kid found with his hand in the cookie jar. "I was hoping to catch the little green man napping."

Leigh repeated, "The little green man?"

The silence stretched like a coiled spring.

Ben cleared his throat, but his voice remained husky. "This isn't neutral territory, you know. You're beyond the demarcation line."

"I . . . Peter wants a drink."

But neither of them seemed capable of motion. Tension, like electricity, sizzled along taut wires.

"Leigh, if you stay there I might forget about being the prince. I've got a mortal side too, you know."

Still unable to move, as if her feet had put down roots, Leigh repeated, "The prince? What prince?"

"The one in doublet and hose. Velvet hat and ostrich feather."

Again she had to pass her tongue across her lips before she could speak. "You've lost me."

"It doesn't matter." Ben let his gaze linger on the shadowed shape of the young woman whose existence had rearranged the course and meaning of his life. Only four steps away, only four easy strides separated them. Under the towel which he'd casually knotted about him to cover his customary lack of night attire, his body responded to her presence in the expected manner.

She was wearing one of those T-shirt nighties again, the ones he found so very enchanting. Far more sexy than any black nylon and lace. This one was so skimpy and see-through that her every curve was silhouetted against the silver sky. He could even see in outline the V at the top of her legs. The sharp moonbeams created hollows of darkness at her throat and shoulder.

Just four steps away. And she still hadn't bolted, hadn't moved one muscle.

The words they said were unimportant. Their bodies exchanged conversation in a manner more primitive and far louder than shouting.

Ben thought, "We could do it now. I could pick her up and carry her back to my room. She would let me . . . " His virility screamed with approval at the very idea. He could anticipate how it would be, this sating of his overwhelming thirst for her. And he'd behaved bloody well, hadn't he? Didn't he deserve some reward? And by not bolting, even after his warnings, wasn't she giving tacit permission?

But then what would happen tomorrow, after his moment of heaven? Would she be demanding to be put on the first plane back to Seattle? Would she accuse him of shattering her trust? That fragile trust which he'd worked so hard to achieve. And what, in the long run, was more important?

The message of his body was plain to read, but Ben knew that he wanted more. He wanted the sort of commitment which went well beyond the immediate satisfactions of the flesh. He wanted a 'silver hairs amongst the gold' sort of commitment, a lifetime promise. And in the end that was far, far more important.

He cleared his throat, silently ordering his unruly part to remember who was boss hereabouts. "You said Peter asked for a drink? What does he want?"

Somehow she'd forgotten all about her Punkin. Somehow she'd become so caught up in the startling things which were happening inside her that his request had slipped from mind. "Water."

She couldn't remember ever before having experienced a feeling like this, not even in the happy days when she and

Pete were dating; before their marriage and the hideous slide into despair. This feeling was like stepping outside her skin, a sensation of being drawn to another body by sheer magnetism. It made some inner core glow like radium in a darkened crucible. It made her come alive again.

"And you, Leigh. What about you?"

"Me?" Why was Ben talking at all, when he should have been taking her in his arms and kissing her and . . ?

"Yes, you. Do you want a drink?"

"No. Thank you."

Ben took some bottled water from the refrigerator, poured a splash into a tumbler, handed it to her. His voice when he spoke again was the other Ben's. Not the young Greek god, nor the Nordic warrior, but Father Ben, Ben the good friend. Ben whom she trusted.

"Bloody hot, isn't it? I gather we've all had trouble sleeping."

"Yes. It's bloody hot."

He took her shoulders as he kissed her goodnight. But, although her breasts brushed against his chest through the cotton nightshirt and he could smell the sweetness of her, although in her stillness she was shouting at him, the moment had passed. The passion was under control.

"See you in the morning, then. I hope you get back to sleep without too much difficulty."

Goodfellow Press/ *This Time*
7710 196th Ave NE, Redmond, WA 98053-4710

1. How would you rate the following features? Please circle:

	readable			excellent	
Overall opinion of book	1	2	3	4	5
Character development	1	2	3	4	5
Conclusion/Ending	1	2	3	4	5
Plot/Story Line	1	2	3	4	5
Writing Style	1	2	3	4	5
Setting/Location	1	2	3	4	5
Appeal of Front Cover	1	2	3	4	5
Appeal of Back Cover	1	2	3	4	5
Print Size/Design	1	2	3	4	5

2. Approximately how many novels do you buy each month? _____

   How many do you read per month? _____

3. What is your education?
   - ❏ High school or less
   - ❏ Some College
   - ❏ College Graduate
   - ❏ Post Graduate

4. What is your age group?
   - ❏ Under 25
   - ❏ 26-35
   - ❏ 36-45
   - ❏ 46-55
   - ❏ Over 55

5. What types of fiction do you usually buy? (check all that apply)
   - ❏ Historical
   - ❏ Science Fiction
   - ❏ Romantic Suspense
   - ❏ Mystery
   - ❏ Western
   - ❏ Action/Adventure
   - ❏ General Fiction
   - ❏ Time Travel/Paranormal

6. Why did you buy this book? (check all that apply)
   - ❏ Front cover
   - ❏ Back cover
   - ❏ Like the setting
   - ❏ Know the author
   - ❏ Like the ending
   - ❏ Purchased at an autographing event
   - ❏ Liked the characters
   - ❏ Heard of the publisher

For current Goodfellow Press updates:

Name: _____

Street: _____

City/State/Zip: _____

We would like to hear from you. Please write us with your comments.